PI

ALSO BY HP MALLORY:

Standalone Contemporary Romances:
Bronco
The Handbook
Mountain Man

Paranormal Romance and Fantasy Series:

THE JOLIE WILKINS SERIES:
Fire Burn and Cauldron Bubble
Toil and Trouble
Be Witched (Novella)
Witchful Thinking
The Witch Is Back
Something Witchy This Way Comes

THE BRYN AND SINJIN SERIES:
Sinjin
The Scent
The Gentleman

THE DULCIE O'NEIL SERIES:
To Kill A Warlock
A Tale Of Two Goblins
Great Hexpectations
Wuthering Frights
Malice In Wonderland
For Whom The Spell Tolls
Eleven Snipers Sniping (Short Story)
A Midsummer Night's Scream
Grave New World
Pride and Poltergeists

THE LILY HARPER SERIES:
Better Off Dead
The Underground City
To Hell And Back
Persephone

THE PEYTON CLARK SERIES:
Ghouls Rush In
Once Haunted, Twice Shy
Brown Eyed Ghoul

Co-Authored Series:

The Ice Wolf Series (Co-Authored with JR Rain):
Ice Wolf
She Wolf

PRIDE AND POLTERGEISTS

Book 9 of the Dulcie O'Neil series

HP MALLORY

PRIDE AND POLTERGEISTS

by

H.P. Mallory

Copyright © 2018 by H.P. Mallory

All rights reserved. Without limiting the rights under copyright reserved above, no part of this publication may be reproduced, stored in or introduced into a retrieval system, or transmitted, in any form, or by any means (electronic, mechanical, photocopying, recording, or otherwise) without the prior written permission of both the copyright owner and the above publisher of this book.

This is a work of fiction. Names, characters, places, brands, media, and incidents are either the product of the author's imagination or are used fictitiously. The author acknowledges the trademarked status and trademark owners of various products referenced in this work of fiction, which have been used without permission. The publication/use of these trademarks is not authorized, associated with, or sponsored by the trademark owners.

For Finn

Acknowledgements:

For my son, Finn, who makes this world magical.

For Len, thank you for always believing in me and for your encouragement. I love you.

To my editor, Teri, at www.editingfairy.com: Thank you for a job well done, as always.

To Crystallee Hopkins: Thank you for coming up with the amazing title!

PROLOGUE
Casey James, Special Agent
Human

I stood at the head of the room, listening to everyone breathe. Their inhales and their exhales, their rattling lungs, their coughing, their sighing, and their muttering. It was the only sound in the world, soft as a whisper and cold as death, because they all knew why we were here. People didn't come into the Situation Room for tea parties. They came to make war. Occasionally, they even came to prevent it.

The door opened and closed. The muttering stopped and every head turned. President Odyssey took a seat at the head of the table, flanked by her chief of staff and the secretary of state. The first was a short, spindly, little man named Simon Richmond. I didn't care much for Richmond. The other was a woman with stark, white hair and burning, blue eyes called Hana. She was beautiful, flawless as a porcelain doll, and just as disturbing.

Hana was the only magical creature in the room. The only monster in this human administration, and she walked like she knew it—with a certain confidence and bravado. She was a Valkyrie—a spirit guide to the brave and reckless, and also an empath, capable of reading the intentions of everyone in the room. Something which made her invaluable as secretary of state and was likely the only reason she was allowed to have a job in the human government. In general, humans were suspicious of anything that didn't resemble them. I couldn't say I disagreed with that generality. In my position, I'd encountered numerous Netherworld creatures that were anything less than law-abiding.

"Madam President," I said in greeting.

President Leandra Odyssey inclined her head, squinting, wearing the magma-and-hot-water look I'd only ever seen when she was about to declare war. She didn't say hello.

"What's this about?" asked Richmond, already writhing in his customary confusion. Balding, with a ring of white hair surrounding his head like a crown, grey eyes, and a nose that never seemed to stop twitching, he reminded me of a mole. The chief of staff wasn't accustomed to being out of the loop. Not that anyone else in the room knew much more either.

"You'll know soon enough," I said, trying but failing to keep the bitterness from my voice.

Richmond's face turned pink with what little rage he could muster at two o'clock in the morning. Hana was standing behind him, a silver shadow with her arms crossed, the barest hint of a smile on her lips, too sharp to be genuine and too dull to be hate. Hana's liquid, blue eyes landed on Richmond only for a second. She didn't move, or even blink, but I knew what she was doing.

A second later, Richmond was calm. He took a deep breath and settled into his chair like he hadn't spoken at all, courtesy of Hana's power and her magic ability to put the chief of staff back in his place.

I swallowed hard. Hana wasn't supposed to do that. There were, in theory, clauses that prevented her from using her powers on coworkers—but if it meant Richmond would shut the fuck up, I wasn't about to call her out. I had to wonder if Richmond was even aware that Hana had magicked him, but I quickly dismissed the thought because it wasn't important. The most important issue was: what the hell was going on with the Association of Netherworld Creatures, the ANC?

President Odyssey cleared her throat. It was two o'clock in the morning on a Saturday, and the look in her eyes told me this had better be damn good.

"There's been a breach in the ANC," I said.

The entire room sucked in a collective breath. The Association of Netherworld Creatures, the organization responsible for keeping the peace among creatures of magical and other uncanny origin, weren't exactly doing their job. And that was bad news.

President Odyssey's fingers curled into a loose fist, but she said nothing. Hana looked at each of the generals, admirals, cybersecurity personnel, and secret service in turn with a strange look on her face, one of haughtiness maybe. Whatever it was, I had trouble identifying it, and that realization left me nervous.

Hana's eyes settled on me and a chill shook my bones, an iciness that meant she was probing me for intention. Clearly, she didn't know that I had enough experience with those who are magically inclined to realize when one is trying to use her powers on me. I did my best to ignore it, and her, reaching into my pocket and wrapping my fingers around a small, green-grey stone.

"Garrison Hart was one of our assets, tasked with monitoring the Brokenview ANC and its portals," I said, doing my best to thwart Hana's abilities. Even though I was human, I had some of my own tricks up my sleeve.

But back to Garrison Hart … There was at least one human agent in every ANC branch in the world, most of them American, Canadian, and British. All were FBI, carefully selected and trained at sites more secretive than the CIA's farm. Their job was to make sure the Regulators at the ANC were doing their job and keeping their kind on the straight and narrow, or risk mass deportation. These human agents were assassins, thieves, and liars by trade, and they were damn good at what they did—never making mistakes. "According to Marcus Ream—Garrison Hart's manager—there was a disparity between his last two reports."

"Disparity?" said Richmond, but I could see President Odyssey lingering on the word "last."

I nodded and palmed the tablet on the table in front of me. In response, the other tablets scattered around the table suddenly lit up, displaying two scanned FBI documents side-by-side.

"These are Hart's final two debriefings," I said. "The first is routine stuff, mostly active ANC case files and lists of people caught stealing office supplies or sleeping together. Nothing too substantial." Most ANC reports looked like that. The Regulators were good at their jobs, and the surveillance was nothing more than a precaution. *Usually.*

"And the second?" asked Richmond.

I sighed. That was where the problems started. "The second briefing we received three days ago. Same brand of intel, same lists, mostly the same people, but written in an entirely different voice."

"A different voice?" asked Hana, eyeing me narrowly. Her words were soft, barely more than a whisper, but everyone heard and they went silent, completely still. She continued to almost glare at me while I returned the intensity of her stare. I wasn't someone who backed down easily.

I faced President Odyssey. "If I may?" I asked as I nodded at my tablet.

President Odyssey motioned with her hand that I should start reading. So I did.

"Nothing more to say about the boys in custody. Their Feisty," I started as I glanced up at everyone in the room. "Spelled t-h-e-i-r." Then I returned to my reading. "Keep chewing at the bars like animals. Thomas Harley keeps visiting T.P." I glanced up at everyone. "I believe the initials stand for Tootsie Pop, who happens to be an attractive blond that sits down the aisle from Garrison." I took a breath. "Or I suppose he could be talking about toilet paper." Everyone snickered, except for Hana. I glanced down and continued reading. "I think he and T.P. are banging. Nothing going on here much. Mostly should be reported that this coffee sucks.'" I cleared my throat and adjusted my glasses as I faced everyone in the room.

"So he's not so good at spelling," Richmond started. "So what?"

I turned to face him. "So Garrison Hart earned his undergraduate degree at Yale and his graduate degree at Harvard," I retorted, my eyebrows meeting in the center of my forehead. "When was the last time you met a Yale or Harvard graduate who didn't know the difference between t-h-e-i-r and t-h-e-y-'-r-e?" Richmond didn't respond, so I continued, this time giving all of my attention to President Odyssey. "In the remainder of the report, the words 'gross' and 'reeking' are used to describe the creatures in custody, the coffee is continuously denigrated and, coincidentally, also spelled incorrectly three out of five times that it's referenced. Hart makes multiple inappropriate comments about his female coworkers, giving them nicknames he's never used in previous reports. He continually goes off on unrelated, unnecessary tangents and keeps referring to the werewolves in custody as 'wolves,' while he previously referred to them always as 'weres.'"

General Tate wrapped his large hands around his tablet, mulling over the information I'd just provided and squinting at the words in question as he nodded slowly. His brow furrowed the longer he looked at it, clearly trying to solve the meaning of the shift. He was an impossibly large man with a square face, a set jaw, and a long, white scar running the length of his nose. He had the cold eyes of a wolf, and he spoke only marginally more often than Hana. His voice was gravelly and deep, on the rare occasions I ever heard it.

President Odyssey examined the documents, drumming her fingers against the table. Short, auburn hair framed a pale face lined with shallow wrinkles. She looked up at me with solemn, silver eyes, her lips pressed together in a thin, red line. I guessed one couldn't smile often with a job like this.

"Last?" she said slowly as she looked up at me. "You said this was Garrison Hart's last briefing?"

I nodded once. "His body was discovered by hikers less than two hours ago. In Virginia."

"Virginia? How the hell did he get there?" asked Richmond.

"We think it's likely that he was discovered by Netherworldian creatures, killed, and transported via portal, wormhole, or dematerialization," I answered.

"Discovered?" Richmond asked incredulously. "The ANC is well aware of our presence in their agency. They always have been. So what do you mean by *discovered*?"

Maybe if you'd give me ten seconds to finish a sentence, you'd know by now, I thought as I took a deep breath. "I believe there has been a breach in the ANC," I said, my patience shattering like glass. I faced President Odyssey. "We've received no communications from anyone in the agency, and the head of the branch has yet to contact us regarding Hart's death—or his disappearance." I faced Richmond with a brief nod. "You're correct, ANC officers knew Hart was there and they've never had a problem with his presence before." I let that sit in the air for a minute. "So if we agree that ANC officials knew Hart was there, we can also concur that they know he's gone, and yet, they haven't uttered a word about it."

"Then you think the ANC officials are in on it?" President Odyssey asked me pointedly.

I shrugged. "Whether they were a party to Hart's death or not remains to be seen." I reached for a glass of water on the table before me and downed it. My throat was well beyond dry. "Madam President, what I can tell you is that the Brokenview ANC office is no longer under our control."

Odyssey didn't look surprised.

"Is this an uprising?" asked General Tate. "If there's been no communication …"

I shrugged. "We don't know," I said. "The ANC appears to be functioning properly from the outside. They may be staging an uprising, yes, or they may be operating under duress, unable to call for help." If the ANC were rebelling, they would have murdered an acting human emissary and a federal employee, and that would mean war and deportations, and then protests and riots on both sides. "God willing, it's a coup, and one that we can stop."

"Any word from Special Agent Vander?" asked Odyssey.

Knightley Vander was a highly reputable Regulator for the ANC and their chief contact in Human-Preternatural Affairs. I led the human surveillance of the ANC on my end, and he was in charge of his. I shook my head. "I tried contacting Vander as soon as our team discovered Hart's body, but have received no reply." That was more than a little disconcerting. While Vander and I didn't always get along, we had a good working relationship. I could count the times on one hand when I'd called and Vander didn't call back. I couldn't help but wonder if this protracted silence meant Vander's ANC in Splendor, California, was compromised as well.

"How do we know Hart wasn't killed out of context?" asked Richmond, irritating me to no end. "Maybe he was helping the Regulators with a case that got out of hand. Maybe they don't even know Hart's dead yet. Hell, they might not even know he's gone;

they might just think he went out for a drink or something."

It wasn't the craziest theory. The human agents stationed at the various ANC offices often lent themselves to ANC investigations, if only to the break the monotony of their own, less thrilling surveillance jobs. And if Hart had only been dead for a few hours, or even a few days, I might have believed it …

"Because seven hours ago, we received another report in Hart's name," I said. "One that was very similar in voice and spelling mistakes to the second brief."

"So?" asked Richmond. "Hart might have sent it before he died."

"He didn't," I answered. "Hart has been dead for three weeks."

Richmond's mouth popped open. President Odyssey inclined her head, clicking her nails against the table. Hana took a single step out of the shadows. Her pupils dilated as she examined me, tasting the chemicals seeping out of my skin that would tell her what I was currently feeling. I felt strangely violated.

"What else?" Hana asked in her deep voice. "What else do you know?"

I swallowed, hellishly uncomfortable. Hana had a way about her that made you shrivel in her gaze.

"Several months ago, every registered ANC portal went offline all at once, and every ANC office in California went dark. And they *stayed* dark for several weeks. When they came back on, the acting head of the ANC, Caressa Brandenburg, told us it was a mass malfunction caused by a weather anomaly in the Netherworld. She also informed us that the former head of the Netherworld, Melchior O'Neil, had died in a car accident." I took a deep breath. "No one at the CIA bought it, of course, and, interestingly, right around the same time, all of our assets in the Netherworld became compromised—as in captured or killed just before the fighting started."

"Fighting?" repeated Tate.

I nodded. "The acting director of the CIA sent in Rowena Gem. Rowena is ex-KGB, absolutely insane, and the only person we were certain could insert herself into Brandenburg's pecking order totally unnoticed. Rowena discovered there *had* been a coup, and the portals had been shut down by the former head of the ANC, Melchior O'Neil, before his death. We believe this was done in an effort to control travel to and from the Netherworld and to prevent his insurgents from getting through. The coup was executed by the heads of the ANC in Splendor, Moon, and Estuary, California, as well as several of O'Neil's people. They brought an unsanctioned army through a temporary portal and decimated the existing Netherworldian government. Melchior O'Neil was killed in his home."

"So this is a coup," repeated Richmond. "They've deposed their own ... what did they call him?"

"Head of the Netherworld, colloquially," I answered, "but I believe the official term is Magister."

"Bit pompous," said Richmond, crossing his arms, and for once, he wasn't entirely wrong.

"Perhaps," I answered. "But there's more. The brunt of Melchior's power apparently came from some less than reputable organizations. Potion smugglers, creature traffickers, money launderers, mercenaries. It was less of a coup and more like a revolution, according to Rowena."

"Who are her sources?" asked Richmond, growing grouchier by the second.

I suppressed a sigh. "I realize it's two o'clock in the morning, but *surely,* you know I can't tell you that?" I replied. "Rowena knows what she's doing. If you don't trust her intel, perhaps you'd like to go and collect your own?"

Richmond made a face and sat back, resigning himself to be tired and bored. I turned back to the president. "It is my belief, as well as Rowena's, that this was a necessary power shift. Apparently, popular opinion had been against Melchior for some time."

"He was a dictator," a new voice announced from behind us.

The door slammed shut before a lithe, Arabic woman with stark, black hair appeared. She was dressed in a green penny coat, a white blouse, and blue slacks. She pulled her gloves off slowly and strode to the front of the room to stand beside me, grinning at us all with the half of her face that hadn't been burned into oblivion—she hid the red, webbed scars under an ivory half-mask with a single black garnet where her eye should have been.

"Rowena," I said with a smile as I turned to face the rest of the room. "May I present Special Agent Rowena Gem."

Rowena was human, but barely—the magic that scarred her was still stuck in her skin, and now ... she could do dangerous things. Now, her blind eye could see things no one else could.

"Agent Gem," said President Odyssey, nodding in deference. "Good of you to join us."

Rowena greeted her in turn and faced each person in the room. Everyone was deathly silent. "I don't believe the Brokenview ANC has fallen out of contact of its own volition," she said, her voice heavily accented. Rowena had a magnetism about her, an allure that demanded attention with its enticing subtlety. Or maybe it was only because she was pretty. "Melchior maintained power through fear. He bred terrible beasts to patrol the Netherworld skies and terrorize the population. The original electoral system has been out of play for more than fifty years, and nearly everyone in his administration was linked in some way to the potion rings. Many of his personnel were being blackmailed, including a member of his inner circle that later joined the resistance. The administration that replaced him following the coup has linked him officially to the deaths of more than twenty ANC Regulators, including three of our own operatives."

"Potion rings?" asked Tate.

"Magic drug lords," Richmond answered, crossing his arms.

Rowena cleared her throat. "Over the last three months, Caressa Brandenburg's administration has been struggling to maintain power. Melchior's forces had originally scattered, but the major potion rings and crime lords are now banding together under another banner, an unidentified magical creature that calls itself the Darkness. Whoever and whatever it is, it or they are very powerful, as well as the rings they are pulling together. The Darkness vastly outnumbers the ANC, and it is gaining ground. I find it extremely likely that the Brokenview ANC is no longer under ANC control, and now a stronghold for this Darkness character." Rowena gave me a rather pointed glance. "The last thing the ANC has time to care about right now is government oversight. They are at war, and losing it, badly."

"Well, just hijack my presentation, why don't you?" I muttered, but I was smiling.

Rowena grinned back at me before turning to face President Odyssey. "Madam President, Brokenview may not be the only compromised branch. And if it *has* been taken by the Darkness, then every civilian in Brokenview is also at risk, as well as everywhere else the ANC has influence. This ANC conflict is spilling out of the Netherworld and it's putting our own people in danger."

President Odyssey cocked her head, linking her fingers together. "And what, exactly, are you proposing I do, Special Agent James?" Odyssey asked as she faced me.

Rowena looked at me too. She had the same clearance I did, but a hell of a lot more experience. The only difference was that my badge said "Special Agent" and hers didn't, so it was my call.

"Send in a task force to identify the power players and take them out," I said. "If they're organized well enough to overtake an ANC office in a major city without anyone noticing, they're more dangerous than Melchior ever could have been on his own."

"You want to run a black op over the ANC's head?" Hana asked softly, her tone and words revealing doubt, verging on anger, almost. "You want to assassinate the ringleaders before they can do anymore damage?"

I felt my jaw clench, but I said nothing. Rowena laid a hand on my arm as she turned toward Hana and shot daggers at her. The secretary of state bowed her head and stepped backwards, indicating that she wouldn't try to second guess me again.

President Odyssey nodded. "Very well. Special Agent James, select your team."

"Marcus Ream," I said immediately. Marcus was CIA. "Judy Collins and Kent Jacoby." Judy was ex-MI6. And Kent? Kent was just insane. "And, of course, Rowena," I answered.

"Done," said Odyssey. "Where do you intend to start?"

"With the person at the center of the conflict," answered Rowena, her lips tightening. "The woman who is truly responsible for killing Melchior O'Neil. His daughter, Dulcie O'Neil."

CHAPTER ONE
Dulcie

I was only dimly aware of the gun.

When my finger closed around the trigger, my wrist screamed with the recoil, and then all I could see was fire. The blaze disappeared quickly, along with the shadows it cast. My maker, my mother, stared down at them, speaking slowly, offering her blood to the silhouette sprawled on the ground. The other—the tall one, a lanky creature vibrating with an old kind of fury—lurched forward. I pulled the trigger again, bracing myself this time. Yes, that was better. The recoil shot up my arm, but the second time, it made it all the way to my shoulder, dispersing the impact into the rest of my bones.

The tall, lanky silhouette fell without a sound. My mother turned to me, smiling, her fangs protruding from beneath her lips. Cabernet red.

"Well done," she said, and I swelled with pride.

My mother's servants carted the still shadows away. She went with them, trailing black hair, leaving perfect red footprints in her wake. I wondered where they were going, and if they intended to come back. If the silhouettes were still alive, then Mother was in danger, and I couldn't allow that.

Antoine will protect her, I thought, and the words relieved my worry. Antoine was nearly as old as Mother—his power wasn't quite so grand, but he was formidable in his own right, and staunchly loyal. Brave, too, and brutal in ways I could only aspire to be.

I sat on the bed and rang a bell to call Sebastian. The butler appeared a moment later in a rush of cold wind and blue light, smiling amicably.

"Madam Dulcie," he said, bowing, before he handed me a steaming cup of tea. I smiled as I drank it, observing Sebastian with undisguised admiration.

"How is it you already know me so well?" I asked, confused as to why many of Mother's servants seemed so familiar with me and yet I didn't know any of them. Green tea, a touch of sugar, and an obscene amount of honey. All in perfect sync.

Sebastian smiled. He looked like Mother when he did that, sly, coarse, and wildly intelligent. Although Sebastian was centuries old, he didn't appear ancient at all. He was a vampire and not much younger than Antoine. As a result, he had a spectacular power swimming inside him. I could sense it moving through his frozen blood, tendrils of raw starstuff, desperate to warp the fabric of space and time. The electric cold of it was palpable, even from here, and I found it … well, electrifying.

"We have watched you a long while," he said, pushing a shock of lily-blond hair out of his face with a hand gloved in white. There were pink stains on his fingertips, bloodstains that defied the power of bleach.

"I pride myself on knowing you," Sebastian said, and I realized the long period of silence where I'd been unabashedly staring at him. I smiled.

Then my smile fell. "Who were they?" I asked, gesturing to the blackening pools of blood by the door. I opened my mouth to taste the iron drifting languidly through the air. The chemical vapor tasted tangy on my tongue, sweet even.

"Intruders," said Sebastian, his voice dark with scorn. "Men foolish enough to believe they could steal you away from us."

I laughed at the notion that anyone thought they could steal anything from underneath Mother's nose. She was all-powerful. "Did they have names?"

Sebastian shrugged. "Most likely. I believe your mother knew one of them, or she seemed to." He leaned closer and said, "I don't believe theirs was a pleasant kinship."

"Hmm, doesn't look like it would have been," I said with a laugh. "Considering she wanted me to kill them both." I took a long drink of my tea. Few of Mother's relationships were cordial. The water scalded the back of my throat and I sighed happily, relishing the popping vibrations as the skin knitted itself back together and the pain vanished. "What were their names?" I finished.

"Bram and Knightley," Sebastian answered before he faced me expectantly, as though he thought I should recognize the names. I didn't. I shrugged to tell him as much, and he beamed broadly. "Is there anything else I might do for you?" asked Sebastian. He was the only one in the house not dressed in bizarre regalia, the only one in an honest-to-Hades black and white suit. Perhaps that was why he stood out to me.

I looked him up and down, taking in the curving pectorals and the swells of his biceps that were barely concealed beneath his clothes. "Maybe later," I said, wiping a drop of tea from my mouth with my thumb.

Sebastian grinned. "Ring if you need me." He stepped back and disappeared into nothing with a sound almost like a scream.

"Showoff!" I said with a laugh. I had to bite my tongue and cross my legs to keep myself from going after him.

With a deep breath, I forced the fire—which had quickly become a ravenous inferno—away, sighing until the urgent sting in the pit of my belly disappeared. It was quite the endeavor, not helped by my mind's insistence on picturing what I kept trying to ignore… for now, anyway.

Standing, I walked onto the terrace, toward the great, white French doors, which were open wide to the impossible night. A vast, black forest blanketed the earth, its thick shadows full of curious noises and hidden monsters. My wings, paper-thin flaps of gossamer green, flowed back and forth languidly at my back, tasting the frigid air. Clouds and smoke obscured the sky, but through the gloom I could see the barest trace of the moon. It was a thousand times closer here, bigger and bolder, tearing the seas to pieces with its incessant gravitational pull. I felt a kinship with the sea that I didn't expect, but the feeling that we were the same somehow continued to intrigue me.

Somewhere below, I heard the snapping of a forest beast, a chimera or a burish ferret's crackling breath. Suddenly, a purple flash of fire appeared between the trees, overlapped by a surprised squeak, and seconds later came the sound of breaking bones. I sipped my tea and listened, closing my eyes to focus on the sound of long, ivory tusks tearing through skin, the starving snarls of a beast half-crazed with hunger and the fading heartbeat of its unfortunate snack.

The door behind me made no sound, but I could feel it when it opened—a subtle vibration in the floor, and the slightest shift in temperature as the warmer air from the body of the house swept into the room. I turned and beamed at the entrant, wrapping my fingers around the warm mug in my hands.

Mother strode through the doorway with blood on her hands and a broad smile on her face. Rivulets of red flowed from her mouth down her chin, staining the white of her blouse. She seemed at ease, but there was a severity in her eyes I couldn't fathom.

"Are they dead?" I asked. Antoine had not returned with her, so I assumed he was disposing of the bodies. I hoped he was enjoying himself.

"Yes, princess," said Mother, removing her black blazer. "Thank you, my darling. The danger is gone." She put her hand to my cheek. "You were very brave."

I sighed my relief. "Sebastian says you knew one of them?"

Mother's smile softened, and she laughed. It was a harsh noise. She moved to the edge of the balcony, laying her hands flat on the alabaster banister. "Yes, I did. Long ago."

I wondered how long "long ago" meant for someone as old as she. I moved next to her, entranced by the way the moonlight made her skin glow. She was the most beautiful creature I had ever beheld. "How long ago? Sebastian said your relationship with him was unpleasant." For Mother, that could mean any number of things. An ex-lover, perhaps, or someone she tried but failed to kill.

That thought gave me pause. There were not many creatures capable of besting Mother.

She scoffed. "Unpleasant. That's one word for it." Her face fell, and the expression she offered me next was grave. "He is the man who killed your father."

I stiffened, nearly crushing the ceramic mug between my fingers. Yes, I remembered the man now, standing over Father's body, dragging the blood from Father's limp form. A vampire like Mother, but younger, and very arrogant.

She laid her hand on my shoulder, comforting and cold as ice, and I felt myself relax. "I know you hurt," she said softly, sitting on the bed beside me. "I know, princess. Don't worry. He will pay dearly for it."

"Will?" I said, my throat tightening. "He isn't dead yet?"

"He is," Mother said, squeezing my hand. "And this time, he will stay that way."

I nodded and leaned into her. "I love you, Mother," I said, and I meant the words with everything inside me. I didn't know where I would be if not for this beautiful creature.

I felt her smile. She rested her chin on my head and stroked my hair.

"I love you, Dulcie," she replied. She pulled back and brushed away a strand of my hair, tucking it gently behind one of my pointed ears. Her smile was the most captivating thing I had ever seen. I could only smile dumbly up at her.

"Dulcie," she said. "Sweet, sweet Dulcie. You want to protect me, don't you?"

I was appalled that she could even ask me such a thing when the answer should have been obvious already. "Of course!"

Mother smiled again, and I relaxed.

"Good," she said. She took her revolver from the holster at her hip and flicked open the cartridge, examining the shining steel bullets within. They glittered like stars, like blood in sunlight. "Because there is something I need you to do for me."

CHAPTER TWO
Sam

The ANC was a scene of absolute disaster.

The holding cells were in pieces. Rebar and concrete had pierced through every wall, breaking windows and smashing cars parked too close to the door. The pixie and the two werewolves we had in custody were in the ICU with twenty broken bones between them, and the pixie was threatening to sue. Yellow caution tape was strung up around the crater the wormhole had formed, with half the building and most of the side lot folding in on itself. The hole was a hundred feet deep and half as wide, swarming with witches testing the air and the earth, trying to figure out where the wormhole came from—and where it let out.

Okay, let me explain.

My name is Samantha White. I'm a witch in the employ of the Association of Netherworld Creatures, and for the last week, I've been conducting a massive investigation into the disappearance of Dulcie O'Neil.

Two weeks and three days ago, the head of our ANC, Knightley Vander, brought in a prisoner. High profile, extremely dangerous, disgustingly slick. His name was Jax—if he had a last name, no one told me. Jax was here for less than a day before he broke the entire fucking building.

Jax turned himself in, telling Knight that he wanted out of the game, that he was ready to confess and share intelligence, blah blah blah. According to Jax's story, every potions smuggler and their grandmother had it in for him, so Knight needed to get him somewhere safe ASAP. That's why Knight brought Jax here—to the ANC headquarters in Splendor, California—hoping that, since this was a lesser base, nobody from the Netherworld would think to look for him here.

Big mistake.

Apparently, this was Jax's plan from the beginning—his mission, actually. He had orders from somewhere way up the ladder to get to Splendor, kidnap Dulcie by acting as the anchor for a wormhole (one of the most volatile methods of travel in existence), and take her … somewhere.

Later, Knight found out that Bram, a vampire who'd spent his life riding the line between good and bad, was responsible. Bram oversaw the criminal rings, second only to somebody called the Darkness. Under the leadership of the Darkness, the potions rings were banding together to overtake the ANC. Apparently, Bram was caught up in all of it but wanted Dulcie's help to thwart the Darkness, insisting that his plan was to dissemble the evil organizations from the beginning. In Bram's words, "it was in the best interest of the Netherworld to maintain the balance." That probably meant Bram was losing influence and needed an escape because Bram was only out for Bram and nobody else.

Now Dulcie was missing, the Brokenview ANC was a base of operations for the Darkness, and both Bram and Knight had gone radio silent.

Just another Monday, I thought, cracking my knuckles while reminding myself that it was now one o'clock in the morning on Tuesday. *I'm losing my fucking mind.* My joints popped hard, and I winced as I began the steep descent into the crater.

The dirt had been burnt by the wind until it was hard as concrete, and the sheer suction of the wormhole compressed everything within a hundred-yard radius into stone. A week later, the ground was still smoking, and whatever was left of the magic that brought the wormhole here was now seeping out of the calcified earth. Cracks deep enough to be ravines radiated from the center of the bowl, flooded with rainwater. And every now and then, the earth around it would shake. Violently. None of which boded well for the people who went through it, but I was trying to be optimistic.

"Anything?" I called out.

The witch closest to me, a small woman with red hair and freckles, looked up from her clipboard. She pushed her glasses up her long nose and sighed, shaking her head. "Whoever brought it here, they covered their tracks. There's no ephemeral residue, no spiritual fingerprints, no alchemical signatures, nothing. It's like it was never even here."

That meant there was no way to tell who sent the wormhole, how long it was here, and, more importantly, where the other anchor was. They'd been telling me this for days, and every time I heard it, I lost a little more patience. "Thanks, Gelvie," I said, suppressing the rising urge to curse and scream and set something on fire—which, if I didn't get a lid on my anger, might have happened on its own.

There must have been fifty witches or more, brought in from Moon and Estuary and every city that could spare them. Each one carried a wand or an enchanted metal tablet in their hands—finding materials that can contain the spell-equivalent of an entire lab is tricky. Most of the tablets and the wands were glowing blue, which, unfortunately, meant they had nothing.

Not that I was surprised. At this point, I was seriously entertaining the idea of getting a mug with *Nothing new?* printed on the side of it. I imagined myself taking passive-aggressive sips out of it while my employees debriefed me. But maybe that wasn't such a great idea; Hades knew I was already drinking more than enough coffee as it was.

Gelvie gave me an apologetic shrug and assured me that I would be the first to know when they found something. I nodded curtly, my fingers curling into fists at my sides.

Gelvasra Henthres was the head of the Magical Anomaly Detection Committee—the crime scene investigators in the employ of the ANC. Witches, mostly, with the occasional empath or Valkyrie skulking around, looked for ghosts, spell echoes, and "emotional insurgencies," whatever the heck that meant. Maybe they were hoping the person anchoring the wormhole on the other side was angry enough to leave a footprint.

Not that it mattered now. Wherever the hole took them, Dulcie and Jax weren't there anymore. They'd gone from some forest in the middle of nowhere to one of Bram's numerous mansions and later to the overturned ANC in Brokenview, where a witch had recognized Dulcie and sent word to me.

Oh, did I forget to mention? The Netherworld had control of, like, half our ANC bases, and I could only imagine that number rapidly growing.

So, that's about how my week was going. I walked around the hole for a little while longer, hoping that lightning would strike somebody and we'd suddenly know where Dulcie, Bram, Knight, and Jax were. I was trying desperately not to think of them as missing persons, but as time passed, that conclusion was getting harder and harder not to draw. It had been—what? Three days since Knight and Bram went looking for Dulcie? And they hadn't radioed in. Nobody had, but that was mostly owing to the political upheaval currently going down in the recently usurped

Netherworld. Caressa was probably even more stressed out than I was.

I went back to my office—what was left of it, anyway. Three of the four walls remained, striped in beige where the wormhole had violently ripped my pictures and certificates away, even dragging the paint off with them. The carpet was soaked through with rain and mud and coffee. Everything smelled like gas and wet dirt.

I ambled over to the Mr. Coffee plugged in to the only remaining outlet this side of the building. The machine gurgled and spat, then a thin, black line poured into a green mug with an angry face stamped into the side, proudly declaring its aversion to Mondays. There was creamer somewhere, but it was one o'clock in the freaking morning, which meant I didn't possess the wherewithal to even try to find it. Instead, I downed the bitter, black liquid like bad medicine, screwing up my lips at the virulent taste. I was half-tempted to get some mandrake out of the confiscated potions vault—mandrake being a potent, highly addictive, Adderall-like substance mostly used by college students during desperate cram sessions and deadlines.

But I knew I wouldn't do that. As an officer of the law, I decided not to drink the evidence. So black coffee would have to do.

Please let Dulcie be okay, I thought. *Let them all be okay.*

Something fluffy brushed against my leg and I smiled, looking down. A half-grown golden retriever sat on the carpet, its tail wagging and tongue flopping: Dulcie's dog, Blue. He was a gift from our old boss (who also happened to be on a long list of people Melchior O'Neil was blackmailing into working for him, but that's another story). She'd brought him to work with her the day the wormhole sucked her and Jax into the ether.

"Come here, boy," I said, and Blue jumped onto my lap, whining and licking my face. His collar shone in the low light, iron meshed with Celtic braiding that winked when it caught the light around his throat. It was enchanted, every braid painstakingly imbued with physical and magical wards, replicating a bracelet I'd given Dulcie to protect herself when she was neck-deep in the potion game. Hades only knew if it *worked*, but at this point, I had to take any reassurance I could get.

I wrapped my arms around Blue and gave him a good squeeze, burying my face in his soft fur. For ten seconds, the feeling like I was about to explode vanished. Maybe everything was going to be all right. Maybe they'd lost their phones or had no reception. Maybe Knight had finally found Dulcie and they were fucking each other into the next life. The idea made me feel a little better. If they had each other, that was a thousand times better, regardless of where they were.

The phone rang, and I nearly jumped out of my skin.

"*Hello?*" I muttered.

"Samantha?" said the caller.

I nearly spat out my coffee. "Caressa!" I leapt out of my office chair, hard enough to send it skidding back into the wall. Blue tumbled to the ground and looked up at me in confusion. "Have you heard from Knight?"

There was a split second of silence and a soft clicking sound: Caressa clucking her tongue. I swear I could *feel* her grimacing through the phone. Caressa was one of Knight's oldest friends—and an old flame, too, if the rumors held water—so a grimace and a clucking tongue probably meant she had about as much information for me as everyone else on my team. Zip. Zilch. Nada.

"I'm guessing that's a no," I said, sitting back and forgetting my chair wasn't there to catch me. I sat hard on the wet ground and didn't bother getting up, letting the icy rainwater soak through my skirt and freeze my ass.

Caressa sighed and I heard a thunk! It sounded like an elbow on a table, followed by a rattling, like pens in a cup. It might have also been bullets, but I was trying not to think about that. "Yeah. Sorry."

I sighed too, running my free hand through my hair. "Don't worry about it," I said.

"Anything on your end?"

I couldn't suppress a snort. "What do you think?"

"They're doing their best, Sam," Caressa replied, almost sounding defensive.

"I know," I said, "but it's been like this for *days*. I mean, who knows where they are by now?" With the Brokenview ANC portals at their beck and call, they could literally be anywhere on the planet. Hell, they might have even been in the Netherworld, as slim a chance as that might be. For Dulcie's sake, I hoped she was here. Her magic wouldn't work in the Netherworld. And on the other side, her wings manifested. Big, translucent fairy wings that she had no clue how to control. Knight assured me it was hilarious, but they were no advantage to her when she was trying to escape.

"You still there?" Caressa asked.

I snapped myself back to the present and coughed. "I'm here. Sorry."

"… and Dia hasn't found anything?" she continued hesitantly.

Dia Robinson was the head of the ANC in Moon, California. Most of the witches on staff were hers, but I hadn't heard anything from her in days. "MADC said there was nothing to find." *Nothing but a giant hole in the ground.* My throat tightened and I felt my eyes watering. "*Nothing*," I said quietly.

"It's gonna be okay," Caressa said, her voice much softer now. "I promise."

I laughed bitterly and tried to smile, even though she couldn't see. Blue came up and started gingerly licking my cheek, his big, black eyes awash with concern. I scratched his head and felt the hot tears flowing soundlessly down my face. Blue kissed them away.

I took a deep breath and sighed. "I know," I said, even though I didn't. "Caressa, I'm not getting paid enough to worry this much."

Caressa laughed. "Me neither, sweetheart, believe me. Listen, I've got to call General Maxwell and see if we can't get his garrison out of the mountains."

Now it was my turn to laugh. General Maxwell was a dark elf, a Netherworldian Army man of significant repute. He was as bull-headed as they come, and absolutely *convinced* that Melchior was still alive. He feared Caressa was trying to lure him out of Fort Blaster in the mountains to kill him and all of his force. "Good luck with that."

"Thanks, I'm gonna need it. Listen, if you need anything—"

There was a beep, and then silence. I looked at my phone and saw it was roaming; all the bars had vanished. "Caressa?" I said, but she was already gone.

"Shit," I grumbled, throwing the phone across the room. It hit the wall and the back broke open. Blue cocked his head and pounded his tail against the carpet, letting out a low whine. My stomach was tying itself in knots again, sheer panic rising from the pit of my stomach. *That's what you get,* I thought, remembering the eight other cups of black coffee I'd drunk in the last forty-eight hours. Too much caffeine, if there were such a thing.

Not when you're at war, I thought. Which wasn't entirely true, not anymore, but it sure felt like it. This war was colder, though, looming like mountains in the dark. The Netherworld was gathering under the Darkness, sure, and Dulcie was missing, that was a given, but it felt like I was overlooking something. If I'd been anybody else, I would have written the feeling off as nerves. But I'm a witch, and that means my hunches are rarely unfounded.

I ran my hands over my face and pushed myself roughly onto my feet. My desk was scattered with papers and reports, most of them utterly useless in our search. No one at any ANC from here to Dubai had heard a word about the Darkness, and no one could seem to locate *any* of the big names in the potion world. Larx Manthrey from Crossbones, Henrick Torgiono from Mayhem, to name a few of the older players, and *Jax.* Hades only knew where he was. Dead, if we were lucky, or dying, and hopefully, very slowly.

"Why does everything have to be so damn complicated?" I muttered, sifting through the papers without reading them. I'd been through them already a thousand times, all the collective information we had about every bad guy in the business, and there was nothing there I could use. Of course, it was *extremely* likely that a hundred or more reports had been redacted or destroyed when the Brokenview ANC went down.

The lamp by the wall flickered and went out. There was a sound like a trombone being thrown down a flight of stone stairs, then the lamp came back on again—the backup generators kicking in.

I frowned and walked out to the hallway, peering left and right. Nigel, an air spirit, came floating down, transparent, ghostly, and ravenously handsome. I'd sent him to do recon on the power outage—mainly to find out where it began and where it ended, along with anything else he could tell me.

Then I had a thought. Wormholes are typically generated by extremely powerful magical entities—extremely powerful, meaning: nothing short of a very angry demigod. They *could*, in theory, also be created by inducing extreme electrical surges in a place with highly magical concentrations in the air or water. Places like nymph lakes and ancient, giant fortresses in the mountains, where they first mined the magic ores used in mood rings. If that were the case, the resulting power surge would have been enormous and bright enough to see from space, causing a blackout the size of Texas. Maybe we could track them that way.

"*Miss Samantha?*" Nigel's mouth didn't move, and he spoke in a stage whisper.

"Sorry," I said, shaking my head. "Out of it. What's up with the power?"

"*Citywide blackout,*" he said.

"Citywide?" That didn't sound good. "What caused it?"

The apparition shrugged. "*They're looking into it. Seems to be a total grid failure.*"

"Grid failure? What does that mean?"

"*Mass malfunction,*" he breathed. "*Enough lights go out, the whole system flips.*"

"Uh huh." I nodded, biting my lip, and Nigel drifted away.

I turned back to my office, kneading my temples with my knuckles. I had to sleep. The ground wasn't exactly comfortable, but it was flat and, thankfully, not on fire, so I lay down on my back and closed my eyes. Everything shut down immediately, my whole consciousness going luxuriously black.

When I opened my eyes, the sky was still black, and all the stars were present and accounted for. I sat up and rubbed my head, groaning, feeling less like I'd slept and more like I'd just been roundhouse-kicked by a Titan.

I looked at my watch; fifteen minutes had passed. Probably as much of a reprieve as I would get for a while, at least until the twenty gallons of coffee drained out of my system.

"All right," I said, craning my torso to the left to pop my shoulder. "Back to work, I guess."

I stood, brushing my fingers through my short, brown hair and trying to look at least a little bit awake.

Everybody was tired, and ready to punt a small goblin through a wall, but I was in charge. If anybody needed to pretend they were unfazed, it was me. Even if I were falling apart.

I stood up, cracked my neck, and popped my knuckles. Then I noticed Blue standing by the missing wall, his hair standing on end, growling into the dark.

"Blue?" I said. He didn't respond, standing stock-still, hackles raised, throat rumbling.

"What's the matter, boy?" I knelt beside him and tried to pet him, but the growling got louder. He crouched and bared his teeth at nothing.

Three seconds later, I felt it too. A sharp energy wafted in the air, a smell like burning grass and a subsequent tingling that gave me goose bumps.

I grabbed Blue and dove under the desk just as the explosion rocked the building.

Yellow-black shadows were cast by the billowing fire, and I felt the walls and floor crumbling with the force of it. The sound was muted at first, then it shifted into a high ring, and I realized I'd whacked my head on the table when it first went off. I reached up to touch my throbbing skull, and my hand came away red with blood.

"Shit," I muttered, barely hearing myself. The hair on Blue's neck was still standing on end, and he hadn't stopped growling.

For ten painful seconds, there was nothing to observe but silence and smoke. The smell was acrid, strong enough to burn the back of my throat. I heard sirens, the human fire department rushing to our aid, and I had the fleeting thought that we needed to call them off.

Then I was dimly aware of a rush that sounded like water, then shouting and a sound like hail—bullets, I realized—followed by the crimson and gold flashes of defensive and offensive magic.

I crawled out from under the table and tried to stand. The whole room turned upside-down, and a second later, I was face-down on the ground. I felt Blue nudging my shoulder with his nose, whining and growling, even barking now too, but I couldn't see at what.

Get up! I thought furiously, and I did, hauling my body onto my feet, bracing myself against the table and taking deep, slow breaths until the world re-stabilized. The walls were gone, all of them, reduced to piles of grey-white rubble. The sky was awash with all the wrong colors, green lightning and the blue tinge of a witch's hellfire. White flashes like grenades, along with yellow bursts in the barrels of countless automatic weapons seemed to be everywhere. I could see the parking lot now, swarming with rescue personnel and witches, half running for their lives, half returning fire on a massive group of gun-wielding silhouettes that could only be here for one reason.

The ringing stopped, and suddenly, that was all I could hear—the incessant chittering of machine guns firing four hundred rounds a minute, only marginally covered by a very loud scream.

"Come on!" I shouted to Blue, drawing my pistol from my belt—an Op 7, the magical equivalent of a Glock, loaded with bullets spiked with highly toxic dragon's blood. I pressed myself against the wall next to the Mr. Coffee, which now lay on its side on the carpet. My Monday-hating coffee cup was in pieces too, scattered at the base of the desk. The angry face stared up at me accusingly.

I closed my eyes and tried to focus, if only to get my frazzled brain to locate the site of the explosion. Sniffing the air, I could identify the burning asphalt and melting rubber, as well as a stench, like wet feathers and water boiled dry.

"*Shit!*" I ran—*ran* being a very loose term, since it was more of an urgent waddle—into the hall and toward the front of the building. I headed toward the lot and the cars and the wormhole as well as nearly half of my employees.

The closer I got, the louder the screams were. And the sound was changing. It started as fear, but now it was more urgent, like a desperate battle cry, the shrieking of someone on their last magazine. Some part of me thought *power outage,* and I realized this should have been obvious. Of course the outage wasn't a natural malfunction. But I didn't have time for that now.

Suddenly, Blue grabbed my skirt between his teeth and dragged me to one side, behind one of three walls left standing in the whole structure. A hot flash of fire and force drove me to my knees, kicking up a cloud of black dust.

I got back to my feet, panting, looking over my shoulder at the black scorch mark on the ground where I'd been standing only seconds before. "Thanks, buddy."

Blue obviously didn't reply, but kept looking behind me at the smoke cloud that was rising up like an angry wave. He started growling, taking very slow steps backwards, and I realized he saw someone or something inside it. A silhouette began to take shape as I watched and stumbled across the ruined floor, coughing.

I started to level my gun at the shadow. But a different kind of shadow coursed through me, a lead-heavy sense of fear and dread, and I pressed myself against the wall. Blue did the same, hunkering down at my heels. He sniffed the air and released a low whine. I looked down and saw his tail start wagging. He scratched at my foot, his mouth open, and tongue lolling out over his teeth.

"What?" I whispered. "What is it?" Maybe the shadow belonged to Gelvie or one of the other witches; or maybe it was Elsie the secretary.

Rocks and dust shifted around the corner, and the silhouette loomed into view. It was too short to be

Gelvie and too thin to be Elsie. The shadow in the smoke was encased in fire from head-to-toe, wearing the flames like a mantle and its shadows like a crown. The face was obscured, but I saw a long, black dress and bare feet. Her skin was red with the heat of her own magic, and blood streamed down from a gash in her chest that she barely seemed to notice. She flicked her wrist, and a small, white ball of hellfire flung itself into the ground twenty yards away, exploding on impact. I closed my eyes at the pervasive light, violent and hot, bright as burning magnesium. When it faded, a plume of silvery smoke hung in the air, three stories tall, slowly settling over the ruins. There was a gaping, black hole at its base with a table on its edge, half of it completely vaporized.

The shadow stepped forward, and then she had a face.

I sucked in a breath. "Dulcie?"

CHAPTER THREE
Sam

Dulcie stood in the ruins of the ANC, blood all over her face and hands, ash sticking to her sweaty skin. She was something out of a story, Hades's mistress, pale as paper and dressed in the colors of death.

What is wrong with her? I thought. *Fucking Icarus, what the hell is she doing?*

I heard footsteps, and a horde of gunmen ran past her, trolls and ogres, along with a hodge-podge of other unsavory creatures armed to the teeth. Several nodded their deference to her as they bounded past, saluting or stopping to bow, while some even shouted, "For Dulcie!" before they unloaded their steel magazines into the empty air. My heart fell into my heels as Dulcie beckoned them on, watching passively while they ignited what remained of the offices and storage rooms into a blazing fire.

One of them stopped. He was bigger and taller than the rest, with a single red stripe sewn into his bulletproof vest, maybe a sign of his station. He said something to Dulcie that I couldn't hear, and she gave him a broad smile.

"Make it hurt," she said, and the man ran off.

I must have gasped, or tripped, or maybe she could hear my pounding heart, but whatever happened, Dulcie turned her head to the right and found me. Her eyes, green as summer meadows and glowing with excitement, narrowed. I didn't have time to move.

The way she looked at me seemed like she couldn't see me. Of course she could, but *she couldn't see me*. She couldn't see who I was, what I meant to her, or how much we'd been through together. She was looking at me like I was no different than any other unfortunate asshole who happened across her path.

The wall burst apart and I was flung forward with Blue, my gun flying out of my hand. We landed hard on the cracked, stony ground and rolled before slamming to a halt on a mound of broken bricks and floor tiles. I pushed myself up on all fours, swallowing hard against a stabbing pain in my side. My hands were covered in soot and deeply scratched, already starting to sting.

Dulcie laughed behind me. I turned my head and watched her through bleary eyes as she strode forward, elegant and terrible, her dress sweeping through the ash that was still settling onto the floor. The fire that wreathed her was silver now, throwing embers white as stars into the sky. She blinked slowly at me, totally without recognition.

"Dulcie?" I started, hoping she would recognize me, and in doing so, snap out of whatever the hell was holding her mind and memory captive.

She flicked her wrist, and I went flying. When I hit the ground, a searing pain ripped through my side—breaking a rib. It punctured something, maybe a lung—yes, definitely a lung. I inhaled and coughed, tasting salt and iron. The pain was unbearably hot and almost indescribable, but my difficulty breathing was what concerned me the most.

"Did you think we'd forgotten you?" she said as her eyes narrowed on mine. Her voice sounded wrong; it was much deeper and broader than it should have been. *"Did you think we would forgive you?"*

Forgive me? We? What the hell was she talking about? "Dulcie," I croaked, but it wasn't much of a word—more like a strangled squeak. "Please … it's me …"

Then Dulcie approached me, the heat of her silver fire beating down on me. She touched my sleeve and it instantly caught fire. Her expression turned dark, more vicious. Vengeful. I fumbled for my gun and saw it across the room, stuck under a slab of rubble from the foundation wreckage. *Shit.*

In the lot, where the wormhole crater was, came a wave of gunfire, a scream, and then silence. Someone laughed with a deep, bellowing sound. My blood turned to ice.

Dulcie leaned down and grabbed my face as she turned me back toward her, and hatred swam in her eyes. I glimpsed a hatred I had no clue she could have possessed.

"This is for my mother," she whispered. *"This is for the old way."*

Dulcie's mother is dead, I thought, but I dared not say it aloud. Her fingers wrapped around my throat and squeezed, burning my skin like branding irons. I pulled at her hand, trying to scream, but her grip was an iron vise. Her teeth shone against her fire, glittering like jagged gemstones. There was blood in them, dried between her gums, but it wasn't hers; it couldn't have been. This blood was red, and fairies bleed gold.

"Dul … cie … it's … Sam …" I grabbed her wrist and thought of arctic winds and glaciers, as well as every other cold thing in the world before a frozen wind began to sweep through me. Dulcie's white skin turned blue around my fingers, cracking and splintering, but she didn't flinch. A black fog crept into the edges of my vision, and my lungs screamed for air.

She was just so strong. So damned strong.

And then Dulcie was gone. Her nails raked against my throat before she was torn away by a tall, black shadow, plunging its hands through the fire and grabbing her by the shoulders. It flung her away with all its strength, and I couldn't see the rest. I was on my side, coughing up blood and gasping for air, my broken body doing what it could to survive. My head was throbbing, and every time I moved, it got harder to breathe.

A wet, black nose pushed itself into my face, and Blue started licking my cheek, whining softly. Walls of fire exploded around me, and I saw Dulcie on the ground, hoisting herself onto her feet with a murderous look in her eyes. The shadow that tore her away was running toward me, shouting something I couldn't hear.

Then he got closer, and his words took a shape. "Let's go!" he yelled, grabbing me by my arm and heaving me up. I screamed as my ribs rubbed together, the searing pain completely engulfing me.

"Sorry," he said, but he didn't sound very sincere. He lifted me in his arms like a small child and turned away from the flaming Dulcie, running headlong through a gap in the fiery, white walls. Blue followed at his heels, barking like mad.

I looked over the man's shoulders. Dulcie was on her feet now, lifting her hand and muttering under her breath—a spoken spell. Whatever it was would be a hundred times more powerful than the explosions she'd been conjuring on a whim. There was anger behind her intentions now, and her rage would only make her that much more powerful.

I muttered an incantation, forcing myself to concentrate, trying to ignore the thrumming pain emanating from my broken rib and pierced lung. I imagined shadows and water, wind whistling through cracks in stone walls, rivers unimpeded by rock. The man and Blue and I felt it all at once: a vibration that started in our feet and went all the way to our throats when the magic took hold. Dematerialization was a touchy spell, and ideally, not one to use in a pinch, but I was out of options. Shadows swam in from nowhere, glittering like black ribbons full of stars, wrapping themselves around us and turning us into ethereal darkness.

In the last second before we disappeared, the spell died in Dulcie's hands, and I swear she mouthed, "Sam?"

CHAPTER FOUR
Knight

I woke up. That alone was weird, because the last thing I remembered was getting shot in the heart. I tried to sit up, which, predictably, was a mistake. Bolts of pain jolted through me, hot as branding irons, a violent sting I could feel all the way down in my bones. I opened my mouth to scream, only managing to whimper a faint whine. I closed my eyes in exhaustion as I attempted to drum up any residual strength I could muster. Which wasn't much.

I spent a moment breathing, letting the pain fade into a dull throb. When I opened my eyes this time, I looked around before I tried to speak again.

I was lying on the cold, hard floor inside a room that was small, quaint, cozy, even. Striped, beige wallpaper, plain molding, a full bed, a chair, and a table by a window. It was crosshatched with fire wards that would vaporize me if I got too close. I could smell it from here, a vague, burning haze hanging around the edges of the room, imbued into the walls, the floor, and even the fucking ceiling—as though I intended to punch my way out of here! Or try to shimmy my very large self through the heating vents.

Here, I thought. It took me a second to remember where that was.

The pain returned with shallow waves as I strove to remember everything in frustratingly blurry detail. I'd found Bram, prostrate and dying ... Together, we located Dulcie in the Netherworld, secreted inside a mansion in the middle of who-the-fuck-knows-where? Someone was with her ... I shut my eyes, twisting sideways, and a boiling shock ran the length of my body, my mind rejecting the memory with everything it had.

The Darkness, I thought, *Dulcie was taken by the Darkness. By Jax ...*

Then it all came back. The memories the witch in Brokenview had filched from Dulcie's mind suddenly replayed for me. The blood and bruises, Jax's fists hammering into her skull, his eyes on her bare body, stripping her down to her soul. Bram, blood-starved, catatonic, drinking from her until everything went black.

Rage began to instantly overtake me, and with it came resolve, as well as strength. I had to get the hell out of here so I could get Dulcie and steal her away from the Darkness. More memories suddenly invaded my already overrun mind.

A mansion. Bram's mansion. The silhouette of a massive house, wreathed in trees and darkness. A broken window and stairs. It had been way too easy to break in; something was wrong ...

Dulcie, I thought, digging my nails into my arms, *I saw Dulcie.* I felt like I was going to be sick. *Dulcie in a black dress ... Dulcie with a gun.*

Sweat beaded on my forehead. I opened my eyes, not even realizing I'd closed them. Now I was panting. "Oh, what the *fuck?*" I muttered, reaching up to move the matted hair from my eyes. My chest rose and fell with deep, heaving breaths. *Dulcie shot me,* I thought. She shot me, and she was even smiling when she did it.

But, no, I shook my head. *That makes no damned sense! Dulcie wouldn't shoot me! Dulcie ...*

But I knew the truth in my own words. She had shot me, and she'd intended to kill me.

I rolled to one side, pushing myself up with one arm. The pain was nothing less than excruciating. It might have been a better idea to just lie down and stay there until my body stopped telling me to go fuck myself. At this point, I was just being spiteful. I pushed myself up with a roar—more of a girlish squeal, actually—and felt something in my chest tear open. A half-open wound appeared like a seam that was ripping itself apart. Something warm and wet flowed down my chest: blood. Lots of it.

Well, fuck, I thought as I looked down.

I discovered two things at that moment. First, I was shirtless, and, as I mentioned before, glistening with sweat. The room was ripe with a smell like sickness, rotting flesh, and bile, which I realized was me. Sweat, sure, but the smell was coming from my blood—which, for whatever reason, wasn't red. That was the second thing. It was orange, almost yellow, and flowing too thick, almost like syrup. The smell took a seat on the back of my tongue and I feared I would vomit. I collapsed against the wall, breathing heavily, but couldn't get any air.

Whatever was in that bullet, I wasn't handling it well.

Then another thought altogether. I actually *felt* the dragon's blood entering me, the thickness of a poison your body knows shouldn't be inside your veins. I shouldn't have felt sick if it were draconic, I shouldn't have felt *anything*. Dragon's blood is toxic in the extreme to any Netherworldian creature it comes in contact with, but not humans. Any creatures with touches of magic were especially susceptible to it. Creatures like me, a hellfire-forged guardian from the realms of Hades. But for all my abilities, I was still susceptible to dragon's blood, so it naturally followed that since I'd been shot with a bullet soaked in dragon's blood, I should have been dead right now.

Maybe … my head throbbed as I groped for the memory. A white-hot stab of pain in my chest, darkness, fire … a silhouette standing over me. The taste of something hot and sour in my mouth, flooding me with all the wrong kinds of energy.

Blood. Vampire blood. Bram's, probably, but even that seemed a bit farfetched. Bram's blood could bring someone back from the brink of a lot of things, but *firenza draconia* poisoning wasn't one of them. Maybe Dulcie had a change of heart in the aftermath and used her almighty fairy dust to fix me. If she had, however, I wouldn't still have a wound to bleed from. Even Dulcie couldn't fix *everything,* despite whatever she might tell you. Assuming she tried at all …

Then I saw her standing before me, smiling pleasantly, a gun in her hand, her wings dutifully pinned at her back. I didn't understand because I hadn't heard or seen her come in. It was as if the air just spat her out.

Dulcie, what the hell happened to you? I thought because I still couldn't speak. My stomach roiled and I curled up like an embryo, feeling lost and small.

"What have you done to yourself now?"

I blinked, failing to recognize her voice. When I looked up, Dulcie was gone. Standing in her place was a woman with her arms crossed. Tall, lithe, extremely pale. Eyes red as roses and hair black as pitch, framing a face that might have been smiling.

I'm not doing well, I thought to myself as I shook my head. *How could I have thought this awful woman was Dulcie?* Clearly, I was hallucinating and confused.

"You," I said as I glanced up at her again, just to make sure she was really there. Unfortunately, she was. I recognized her now. I knew who she was. Meg, Bram's maker and Dulcie's captor. And now, apparently, she was my captor too, or so I guessed.

"Me," she said, closing the door. She waved her hand and the wards clicked into place around the locks; the liquid latticework threading itself through the wood and metal, ready to incinerate anyone if they tried to leave.

"What do you want?" I asked, practically growling. I had to clench my eyes shut against the pain caused by speaking. I wasn't sure how my voice was even coming out, but it was, all the same.

Meg raised her brow. She lifted her wrist to her mouth and bit down, hard. "Drink," she said, holding the open wound out to me.

I scoffed and looked away, shaking my head. There was no way in hell I would drink whatever flowed through her veins. I'd rather be dead. I briefly considered attacking her, but just the thought of moving sent a feverish shiver through me. I was way too weak. I could barely manage to flinch.

"Hard pass," I said shakily.

Meg pulled up her spine, attaining her full, considerable height. Her eyes darkened. "I'm trying to help you!" she snapped as she glared at me. I tried to hoist my knees up so I could achieve more of a sitting position, but my legs wouldn't comply.

"I don't need your help," I seethed, even though my body was screaming at me that I did.

Meg leaned down and ran her hand across my chest. I didn't have the strength to move away. Her palm came away all orange and sticky. She tasted the corrupted blood and made a face.

"I beg to differ," she said. When I didn't move, she groaned and stood back, crossing her arms.

"You have questions," she said. "Drink, and I'll answer them."

"My questions aren't worth whatever filth you're trying to feed me."

She smirked, turning up her chin. "Allow me to remind you that all of this," she waved at me and then to herself, "is merely an act. You are nowhere near as powerful as I am, therefore, if I want you to drink from me, you shall."

I laughed. Loudly. The sound that came out of me was more of a snorting *squawk* that sent another burst of blood streaming from me. I kept laughing even though it hurt. It was my way of defying her despite her speaking the truth.

"I am a patient woman so we can continue with this back and forth," Meg said as she smiled at me knowingly. "At least for a good while longer."

I looked down at the wound—wider now, and spilling pus—and the laughter cut itself short.

"Are you finished with your silly games?" Meg asked as she dropped to her knees beside me, and I just faced her blankly.

I wasn't going to win this one and I knew it. Truthfully, I wasn't ready to die yet. Not when I still had Dulcie to save and Meg to destroy. I did the only thing that I could.

I drank. Albeit reluctantly, and with a lot of gagging. The taste was, as always, like stomach acid and freezer burn. I forced myself to swallow it and struggled hard not to immediately retch it back up again.

Meg's blood started to work only seconds after passing my lips. My body began to knit itself together, open muscle scabbing over and painting itself with new skin. A wash of cold air went through me, driving out what was left of the dragon's blood, or whichever toxin remained in my system, and replacing it with the cold blood of a master vampire. I was swimming with an electricity I had no clue how to receive.

"Okay," I said, sitting back, wiping the blood from my mouth. I felt stronger and much more like myself. I glanced up at Meg and leaned against the bed. I still wasn't strong enough to get onto my feet. That would take a bit longer. "Where the fuck is Dulcie?"

Meg tutted. "So brusque. Try again, only nicely this time."

"Where *the fuck* is Dulcie?" I repeated. My muscles pulsed, absorbing Meg's blood, practically begging me to pounce on her and tear out her stationary heart. But even I could tell, although tired and borderline hysterical, that she was formidable. To say the very least. There was something in the way she stood, and the tilt of her head, and the casual slyness in her smile that reminded me of Bram; no, something worse than Bram, something much more powerful than Bram.

Meg was the fabric of nightmares. A creature that had walked the Earth for a very long time, and who was very accustomed to getting whatever she wanted. Attacking her would be ballsy at best, fatal at worst, but either way, stupid. And it probably wouldn't go well—being Bram's maker indicated she was many centuries old, an impossibly long time for something to be alive, even a vampire. Her age and race endowed her with a spectacular strength.

She inclined her head and offered me that shark-toothed smile, her fangs glinting in the dull light. "Dulcie is ... shall we say ... elsewhere?" she replied, and her response seemed to amuse her. Probably because it wasn't technically a lie.

I scowled. "And where exactly is *elsewhere*?"

"Somewhere away from here," Meg replied, looking like she was trying not to laugh. Her eyes flashed with a bad light, yellow and unseemly, the decaying remains of her humanity and her sense of humor.

"Oh, for *fuck's* sake," I said, my temper flaring the second I found the energy for it. "If you're not going to give me a straight fucking answer, why are you even here?" Most likely, to screw with me. Bram enjoyed his asinine little games, so it stood to reason his maker did as well.

"Dulcie is tending to her other duties," Meg said, pushing her hair back over her shoulders. There were strands of silver in it, practically glowing, braided thinly beneath the black so she virtually glittered whenever she moved. I wondered if the discoloration came from the near-death experience she suffered at Bram's hands. If only he'd double-checked his handiwork.

"What the fuck does that mean?" I demanded.

"It means, she is taking care of the business in which I have instructed her. She has a purpose to fulfill, and she is seeing to it."

"Her duty," I repeated blandly. *That doesn't sound good.* "What did you do to her?"

"I reminded her of who she is. And *what* she is." Her lips puckered, full and red. I blinked at them, and for a second, I couldn't look away. "I simply allowed her to become everything that she was meant to be."

I swallowed. The blood wasn't sitting well. "And what is she meant to be, exactly?"

Meg giggled. The sound struck the walls and fell flat, like a broken bell—but when it stopped, there was one terrifying second where I wanted nothing more than to hear it again. I didn't understand why. Maybe she was glamouring me. As a Loki, I shouldn't have been susceptible to being glamoured, but stranger things had happened, I supposed. Now it would be in my best interest to try to fight whatever power she was raining down on me.

"More," said Meg. Her tongue snaked across her frightening teeth.

"More than what?" I said. My words came slowly.

Meg made a show of considering it. "More than she was," she said at last. "More than anyone has ever been before."

Power, I thought. Power and a glamour strong enough to force Dulcie completely out of her own mind. *Doing her duty* ... I didn't want to think what that might mean, but I suspected it involved violence.

"More than you?" I asked.

Meg snorted. "Yes. More than me ... and more than her father." She looked at her hand, turning it over as though she could see Melchior in the fine, white shadows of her knuckles. She offered her hand a disdainful smile and shook her head almost sadly.

Turning away then, she walked to the window to peer out into the colorless slab of night. She looked back to face me and smiled, and for half a second, she almost seemed happy.

It was gone an instant later, if it were there at all. "Dulcie has ..." Meg drew her hand across the windowsill, letting her nails drag over the glass, "acquired her destiny."

"Acquired?" I repeated. I couldn't take my eyes off her hand. Long, slender white fingers, nails just long enough to break skin. They moved like a spider, swift and agile, strangely enthralling.

I swallowed and realized I was gaping. "Acquired her destiny?" I sounded hoarse so I cleared my throat. "What the hell does that mean?"

Meg stopped and shrugged. "Perhaps one day I'll tell you."

"One day?" I said. So she intended to keep me alive. But what the hell for? "And you're not killing me now because …?"

Meg turned to me and walked across the room slowly, leaning in close enough that I could feel the chill of her breath on my throat. She drew her nail down the side of my face, leaving a warm, red line in its wake. The blood raced down my cheek. I refused to move, balling up my fists at my sides, staring her in the face. I wouldn't blink; I refused to let her cow me.

I know, I know. Stupid Knight, looking the vampire in the eyes. I never said I was a smart man. Defiant, yes. Stubborn, yes. Angry, yes. Smart? Well, not at that moment.

But her eyes didn't change. They stayed the same burnished orange they'd been since she walked in. They didn't shrink or grow either, or pulse with the unwashed magic of the places where dead things walked. She just looked at me. Not with tenderness, but something very close to it. Something almost like pride. It was weird, and I began to wonder if maybe I was hallucinating again—imagining this whole exchange.

"I'll leave you to recuperate," Meg said softly, and she stepped back. As she pulled away, I became aware of her smell, rotting roses and wet dirt, a cloying sweetness strong enough to choke me. She bit her lip with her fangs, drawing blood. It dripped down her chin, the brightest red I have ever seen. I followed it down her face, her throat, into the dip of her collar, over her breasts.

I pried my eyes away, head pounding, and by the time I managed it, she was already at the door. She waved her hand, pulling back the magic strings before opening it wide. The wards around the frame twitched and sizzled as she held them back by sheer force of will.

"Oh," she said, halting, "I almost forgot. Antoine?"

Her servant didn't enter the room, but I heard a scraping noise in the hallway. Shoes scuffing against the polished floors, the muted thumping of a lost fight, the distant whimpering of someone begging for his life.

For a second, I thought it was Bram. But Bram didn't beg; he insulted or threatened. And I seriously doubted she would want us in the same room, braiding each other's hair and plotting our escape.

Meg stepped aside, and a man was rudely thrust into the room.

I blinked at him, stunned. His hair, long and brownish gold, was slick with sweat. Scratches and punctures from, I assumed, his encounter with Antoine. A wild panic shone in his eyes. He looked at me and paled.

"You," I said, suddenly feeling a rush of health warming me. My strength seemed as if it doubled as I slowly got to my feet, my hands curling into fists. Renewed rage was brewing inside me, rage that was fueling my strength.

"Him," Meg agreed.

Jax.

My humanity instantly shattered. Hades's fire came flaring to life inside me, the ancient power that gave me sway over everything corporeal. It reached across the room, silent, invisible, searing the air as it went—probing him, examining his mortality, looking for the edge of his soul, or whatever remained of it. I was searching for some leverage I could use to drag it off his bones.

Jax was a Loki, too, and he could feel the fire when it invaded him, recoiling from it. The authority that once comprised his life's blood was now toxic to him. He strayed from his purpose. He pissed on his divine ordinance, and I could taste it in his soul—Hades's derision, his anguish, his *wrath.*

Meanwhile, in my own blood, I felt his blessing. His sanction. The green light to destroy the man who violated Dulcie—and to do it however I damn well pleased. Jax didn't belong to the old fires anymore. He was no longer a Loki in my mind. Much less anything to care about.

"Vander," he squeaked, casting a desperate look back at Meg, while realizing this was a death sentence. Hades had abandoned him long ago, but even now, with his magic decades cold, he could sense the blaze inside me. The divine furnace, hungry and betrayed. Eager, almost desperate, to unmake him. It scalded his essence, and he nearly screamed.

Meg graced us with her smile, an impossibly white line of perfect, yet ominous, teeth. She could feel it too, she must have. She lifted her hand and her fingers curled in the air, wrapping around the invisible, orange ribbons stretching between us.

"All yours," she said to me. "Consider it a gift."

She left and closed the door. The wards clicked back into place.

And then it was just Jax and me.

CHAPTER FIVE
Sam

I woke up. Eventually.

Hades only knew how much time had passed. It was dark and I felt groggy, heavy, like I'd been out for more than the three hours we had to wait until sunrise. The sky was starless and the room was black, suffocatingly dark—

Wait, hang on … my eyes were still closed.

I opened them. Slowly, agonizingly, wrenching myself from sleep. The sky was cobalt-grey above me, clouds and smoke and straggling stars. The sun was poking up from behind the horizon somewhere to my left. The wind was cold, but after the blazing fire, I welcomed it.

I could still smell smoke and hear sirens, so we couldn't have gone too far. Not that I'd intended to. Dematerializing *yourself* any distance is a taxing exercise, let alone moving two people and a dog, and trying to accomplish all of it with a punctured lung.

The muted sirens were distant, and the burning smells grew fainter. I felt grass underneath my back. My guess was that I'd gotten us as far as the park on Seventh Street. We were several blocks away, and probably a good twenty stone buildings lay between us and them, and by now, I hoped, the National Guard too. Groaning inwardly, I knew this would bring the human government oversight down on us fast. Once they learned Caressa had deliberately kept the extent of the insurgency from them …

Suffice to say, it wouldn't be pleasant.

A man loomed over me, derailing my train of thought. I squinted up at him. The light was dim, but I could make out most of his features. Sharply focused eyes, dark hair, square glasses, and a rather disarming grimace. He wore suit pants and an ash-coated, blue dress shirt with the sleeves rolled up to his elbows. He was a little ruffled, a little lanky, and not much taller than me … Frankly, he seemed a little nerdy, but in a sexy way. He had the kind of face that could look in or out of place at the back of a library. Pretty ripped, too, from what I could see. His shirt was slick with sweat, plastered against a well-toned body.

But that observation wasn't important at the moment.

"You're awake," he said, sounding surprised.

"Yeah," I answered as I started to sit up.

He put his hand on my chest and gently pushed me back down, cradling my head as he did so. "Don't even think about it," he said, gesturing to my side. I looked down and saw a swathe of white bandages wrapped around my exposed midsection, which was stained cranberry red around my ribs. I moved myself left and right experimentally and didn't feel anything poking at my lungs anymore. Things were looking up.

"Oh," I said, unable to think of anything else appropriate.

"Oh," the man echoed, sitting back in the grass as he smiled at me. We were behind a cluster of dwarf holly bushes, in the shade of several sparsely leaved trees. He leaned against the trunk of one of the closest trees, looking like he'd been kicked by a manticore. Cuts and bruises covered his face, black soot stains on his shirt … and what appeared to be gloves of liquid red were crusted into the skin of his hands …

And yet, yeah, this guy was still pretty cute. Even with the nerdy glasses and all the dirt. Then I remembered my bandaged body. "How'd you know how to do that?" I asked as I indicated my ribs.

He shrugged like it was no big deal. "I'm a field surgeon." Then he glanced at my bandages. "That's an extremely temporary fix, so try not to move too much."

Even as he said it, I could feel the broken bone grinding against its sisters, held together by paper-thin strands of desperation—mortal magic, or what little they could muster as a race. I felt my eyes narrowing in confusion, but failed to find the wherewithal to ask about it. Besides, I lacked the strength—the blood supply, specifically—to examine the strands more thoroughly and get the answer on my own. Either he was the lamest warlock in the history of magic, or a human with far more power than he should have possessed—which, granted, wasn't much, but it still gave me cause for pause.

"Um … thanks," I said. "Thank you." Shoddy work, but whatever he'd done would have to hold until

I could get home and fix myself properly. That is, assuming I *could* go home. I feared my neighborhood was swarming with Darkness employees.

"What the hell happened back there?" the good doctor asked, snapping me out of my daze.

"I don't know," I answered honestly. "The power went out right before an explosion …" It all came swimming back, the fire, the screaming, and Dulcie … Then, a small, rational part of my brain kicked back on, and I added, "I have to call Caressa."

The man pressed his lips together, and I could tell he was fighting the urge to look away. He fastened his eyes on mine and said, "I already tried to contact Splendor ANC in the Netherworld."

I swallowed. "Tried?" That sounded more than just bad.

The man nodded. "I called Brandenburg's direct line, and Caressa wasn't the one who answered. I was told she had taken administrative leave …" He frowned at me. "I'm guessing that isn't true."

I shook my head, feeling like I'd been sucker-punched. All the breath went out of me and I squeezed my eyes shut, struggling to resist the rising urge to hyperventilate. The world swam in a circle around me and I closed my eyes. Blood leached out of me into the bandages, and the accompanying dizziness sent me spinning.

"What?" I could barely get my voice to work. I swallowed, cleared my throat, and forced the vocal cords to vibrate. "What about?" *Hell,* every word I said trailed away into gasp. "Dia?" I was way too weak to try to heal myself, another bitch of a realization. What I wouldn't have done for a proper witch and a few shots of vodka right then ...

"The Moon ANC experienced a breach much like this one," he replied, "although they did not include your flaming friend."

My *flaming friend,* my numb mind parroted. I sat up, despite his protests, and backed myself into another tree. By the time I was still again, my vision had gone all fuzzy and I was panting.

"Be careful," he said with a note of concern in his voice.

I grimaced, but not at him. I was suddenly extremely aware of the soreness in my side; the muscles were protesting their stitches and whatever he'd used to support the displaced rib. The bone itself felt sore, throbbing all the way down to the marrow. I squeezed my eyes shut and took a deep, long breath until the pain finally subsided.

All at once, my eyes shot open. "Blue," I said, panicked, "where ... where's Blue?"

"Blue?" he asked before his confusion cleared. "Oh, the dog's keeping watch." He jerked his thumb to the left, and I saw a fluffy golden tail poking out from behind a nearby tree, thumping languidly. I breathed a sigh of relief and almost started crying.

"Blue, come here," I said, my voice small and tight. My eyes watered as Blue stood up and came padding over to me, licking my face and nuzzling my shoulder. I winced, but didn't even try to stop him, wrapping my arms around him and burying my face in his soft fur. For a second, I was back inside my office, worrying about Dulcie, and the ANC wasn't in shambles.

My shoulders started shaking, and I let the tears fall. Too much, this was all just way too much. I couldn't do it anymore; this was never supposed to be my job. I was never supposed to be the one to save the world! What the hell was Knight thinking by leaving me in charge? And now everyone else was gone, *everyone* was gone, and I was *it*. Just me and Blue and this guy with the glasses and dirty smudges all over his face. That was all that remained of the ANC.

Panic sank its teeth into my shivering skin, and for a solid minute, I forgot to breathe.

Dulcie ... I couldn't even form a question to go with my thought. I was just confused and angry but, more than anything else, scared. My eyes stung with tears, streaming soundlessly down my cheeks.

I should have known, I thought. *I should have known the power outage wasn't any accident, and I should have been worried when Caressa's call dropped, but I was so tired and ... And none of this is my job! Still, I should have known, I should have sensed something before it happened, a surge when* *they used a portal, a disturbance when full-metal Dulcie arrived, I should have known, **I should have known** ...*

I felt a hand on my shoulder and looked up to see a pair of warm, brown eyes very close to mine. I didn't realize I'd been saying all of that out loud until I stopped talking.

"My name is Special Agent Casey James," said a soft man's voice, reaching down and squeezing my hand. "I'm with the FBI, Preternatural Division. I'm here to help."

Special Agent. Human Special Agent. Government agent, government help. Government reprimand, too, but there'd be plenty of time for that later. I nodded slowly. Something in his eyes drove the panic out of me. Damn, this man was pretty even if he were human. Then I remembered that whole shoddy magic bit. "Are you ..." I whispered.

"Human?" he finished. "Yes, I am."

I nodded. I didn't want him to look away, although he didn't seem like he wanted to either. Or maybe that was just my imagination.

"What are you?" He sounded so calm, like we were just having a normal conversation at a coffee shop.

"Wiccan," I answered. He nodded as if he weren't the least bit surprised.

"A witch," he said. "A spellcaster?"

"Sometimes." Potions were easier than spells, but occasionally you did whatever you had to do. Like the dematerialization thing. *Probably why I was unconscious for so long*, I thought, *and didn't wake up when he was performing impromptu surgery.* I was suddenly very grateful for that.

"What's your name?" he asked.

I reached up to dry my eyes on my sleeve, only to find that the bottom part of my sleeve was burned away. "Sam," I replied, wiping my tears with the heel of my hand instead. "Sam White."

"Short for Samantha?"

I nodded.

"All right, Sam. We're going to figure this out, okay?" He gave my shoulder a light squeeze.

"Okay," I said. My breathing slowed and my voice returned.

"I'm looking for a fairy named Dulcie O'Neil," he continued. "Do you know where she is?"

The tears threatened to spurt again, and I had to look away to catch my breath. "She was …" I sniffed. "She was the one throwing around all the hellfire." The one *way* more powerful than she should have been, even on her best day. Dulcie was many things, but a Netherworldian war machine was never one of them. Casting that much hellfire, and that *kind* of hellfire, should have knocked her out cold, but seeing how *strong* it was … Normally, hellfire was little more than a fancy flamethrower, blue in passing, green when the caster knew what she was doing. I'd never known anyone to cast white fire or use it like a fucking *grenade.*

Casey's face fell. "Ah," he said.

I swallowed. "Yeah." I shook my head. "Something's not *right*. Dulcie would never *do* something like that. She was a Regulator for the ANC," I continued as I glanced up at him, wanting him to understand that whatever he'd observed from her wasn't really my best friend. "She was the best at what she did." I realized I was shaking and squeezed Blue a little harder. He wriggled out of my arms and turned to start licking me in the face. I smiled and ruffled the fur on his back.

"So I've heard," he answered, but he didn't sound convinced, which, of course, made sense, given what he'd just seen.

I sighed. "What was the reason you were looking for her?"

Casey started petting Blue too. "To ask her some questions about her father."

"Why? He's dead."

Casey nodded. "That he is, but his network is still very much alive. We hoped Dulcie might tell us something about his colleagues, since she was briefly on the inside."

"Um … with all due respect, Special Agent," I started slowly, "Netherworldian crime lords are the sole responsibility of the ANC. Aren't they?" They were unless the American government just decided to up its game in light of our recent failures, which I couldn't blame them for.

"When they are contained to the Netherworld, yes," he answered. "But now, your ANCs belong to dangerous creatures, and they're putting Earthly civilians at risk. That's when it becomes my job." He looked like he expected me to start yelling at him or something, but I just nodded. We'd been defeated, I already knew that. Our ANCs were mostly, if not all, now under the power of the Darkness. Knight and Bram were missing, and I was three blocks from a building Dulcie O'Neil had razed to the ground with powers she never had before. We were clean out of our league and then some.

Casey got a look in his eyes then, a sense of cold, hard determination, the likes of which I'd only ever seen before in Knight. "Sam, we could be just a two-person army here. None of our agents in any ANCs located on the western seaboard have reported back in weeks, some have not for months, and half of your lower administration is dead. If we're lucky, Caressa's ANC is still standing, but I sincerely doubt that. This ANC was a final blow somehow. It was big, it was loud, and it was flashy. Your people won't be able to help us. I'm all you've got right now, and you're all I've got, so we'll have to work together."

The word *alone* hammered itself through the empty space in my skull. I nodded before asking shakily, "What do we do now?"

Casey looked confused and pushed his glasses up higher on his nose as he frowned at me. "Really?"

"What do you mean 'really'?" I answered with a shrug and a frown.

"Sorry," he said with a lopsided grin that made him look all of twelve years old. "I just … I was expecting a little opposition. Our departments typically don't get along particularly well."

I smiled sadly at him. "I think it's a little late in the 'Darkness Takes Over the World' game for a pissing contest."

He chuckled. "Yeah, I guess you're right."

"Tell me what you already know," I said, barely managing to keep my voice steady.

Casey sighed, running his hand over his face. He looked like he hadn't slept in a while, which was probably the truth and then some. "The Brokenview ANC has been compromised," he said, "taken down from the inside by the insurgents Caressa was fighting for the last few months. Agent Knightley Vander isn't taking my calls, and more than half of our agents in the ANC have gone dark, suggesting to me that every American-run ANC is no longer under our control." He paused. "I can't comment on our foreign ANCs at this time."

Well, shit! "Knight isn't answering your calls because Dulcie was kidnapped by the Darkness more than a week ago," I said. "I haven't heard from him either."

Casey frowned, but he looked anything but surprised. "Why didn't he call that in?"

"He abandoned his post to go looking for her himself," I answered. "He probably didn't want that on the record. And we didn't know the Darkness was responsible for Dulcie's disappearance until after Knight located Bram, and by then …" I grimaced. "By then, there was no force in hell that could have persuaded Knight and Bram to turn around." I prayed their recklessness hadn't cost both of them their lives. "They're both stubborn, to say the least."

Casey shook his head, grimacing. "Vander always has to be the hero." He sighed. "So, Dulcie—she was the one throwing … hellfire?"

"Drawing on the original inferno in the Netherworld," I said. "Supposedly. It's just a name for the spell."

He nodded, but only looked more confused. "Do we have any idea what the Darkness wants with Dulcie? Does Dulcie have any information they would find valuable?"

"Well, she was Melchior's daughter, but that's her only connection. And it's not like her father played much of a role in her life. So basically, no, she wouldn't have known anything." I sighed, long and hard. "If all the ANCs are gone ..." *Fuck, that hurt to say.* I swallowed. "Then the Darkness wouldn't have needed her to secure the portals. Maybe they think they can use her somehow to unite her father's people? I don't know." I frowned. "But ..."

"What?" Casey asked.

I bit my lip and shook my head. I hadn't and still couldn't make sense of this next part. "She, Dulcie said she was doing all of this for her mother, but her mother has been dead for more than a decade. And she mentioned something about the 'old way.' I don't ..." My head started throbbing and I cut myself off, groaning. "None of it makes any sense, to be honest."

"It appeared she was working directly for the Darkness," Casey said flatly.

"I know," I answered as I shook my head. "But she isn't with the Darkness, I *know* she isn't. She would never do that." The silent argument that she *had* done exactly that throbbed between us.

"She's worked with their kind before," he said.

"Strictly under duress," I replied, trying to obliterate any further doubt, but I couldn't muster the anger it required. All I could think about was Dulcie, wreathed in silver fire with her hand around my throat. "I don't understand, she, she would *never* ..."

"I know," he said slowly, looking pained, "I know. Sam, Vander's told me a lot about Dulcie, and if there's one thing I believe for certain, it's that she does catastrophically stupid things to protect the people she loves." He sighed. "So, yeah, this doesn't exactly fit the bill."

I nodded, trying to keep my growing panic at bay. "After six years of working with her, I'd say I know her pretty well. Not only that, but she's also my best friend." Or she was.

"Do you think maybe Vander went rogue and Dulcie is protecting him?" Casey asked as I immediately shook my head.

"Knight wouldn't go rogue. He's as dedicated to his position as Dulcie is. And even if I agreed with you for the sake of this argument, Dulcie tried to *kill* me. Protecting Knight, if he did go rogue, and trying to kill me just don't add up. So, no, I don't believe she's protecting Knight and, no, I don't believe he's gone rogue either."

"Okay, argument made and won."

"She had this look in her eyes like … like she didn't even know who I was. Like she was …" *possessed* was what I wanted to say, but the word stayed lodged in my throat.

Casey nodded slowly. "Any idea what might have caused that?"

I sighed shakily. "A hundred things. Arsonflower overdose, prolonged exposure to *belisdra ordum* or any of its sister flower spores, pseudo-physical magical influx, a bad reaction to a different creature's blood in her system … But any of those would just inhibit her memory; they don't explain how the *fire* …" I trailed off, reserving my comment that she looked like something straight out of *Poltergeist* to myself.

"What do you mean?" Casey asked, leaning forward.

"Hellfire is supposed to be blue," I responded, "and sometimes green if you're dealing with an extremely capable wizard. Dulcie's was *white*, which means her magic was strong enough to burn away all the color, and the only creatures powerful enough to do that are either in permanent hibernation or *dead*. Dulcie couldn't be that powerful. She's a fairy, not a freaking goddess. She isn't capable of *any* of the things she just did; it just isn't possible." Then I swallowed. Hard. "Unless …" It almost didn't deserve my consideration, but after everything Dulcie had ever done to protect us … Dammit! Maybe it wasn't so farfetched. If Knight were still missing, and Dulcie was here setting Splendor on fire …

"Unless?" prodded Casey.

I swallowed. "Unless she's done something catastrophically stupid," I said. Like giving herself over to the power of an endo-ethereal demon from the original inferno. Or fusing with another equally powerful creature. Or even by drinking diluted ichor from one of a hundred goddess pools in the wild, things that would *definitely* kill you if you didn't have some extremely powerful help. "The Darkness must have made her do something," I said, and I felt my throat closing up. "I, I don't know what, but if this is what she can do, it's really bad. Like, nuclear meltdown bad."

"That sounds really bad."

I almost laughed, but the gurgle that came out of me was full of panicked bitterness. I could feel myself teetering on the edge of total hysteria as I took a deep, long breath, digging my fingers into the loose dirt beside me. "It is," I said, drawing out each word, forcing myself to be calm.

"Are you okay?"

Oops, apparently that wasn't working. I opened my eyes and found Casey's fascinatingly warm brown eyes fixed on me, brimming with concern. I noticed his five o'clock shadow which I hadn't realized before. I imagined him with a full-fledged beard and couldn't stop myself from laughing when the image I conjured looked like a lumberjack flip-calendar.

"That's a no," he said, and I realized I was cackling like, well, like a witch. I couldn't seem to get hold of myself, even long enough to tell him I was fine (which I wasn't).

Great, I thought, *now I'm going insane.* I guess stress, sleep deprivation, too much caffeine, and nearly being murdered by your best friend will do that to you. Who knew?

"Do you think you can walk?" he asked. I realized the sirens were getting closer, and, on further inspection, so was the fire. I felt a cold jolt of electricity creeping up my spine that meant somebody was using an unanchored—and therefore hilariously unstable—portal.

"No," I said, "but we need to get moving." I started to push myself up, digging my nails into the bark of the tree. My side screamed in agony and I felt a fresh supply of blood soaking the underside of my bandages. I collapsed back into the grass. "*Fuck*," I muttered, sucking in the air through my teeth.

Casey was on his feet a second later, looping my arm around his neck. "Come on." He stood up slowly. My muscles stretched and groaned, but the nerves around my ribs seemed content to bitch about it more quietly.

"You good?" he asked.

"Fan-fucking-tastic, let's move," I said, and Blue followed right behind us. He rolled his eyes and we started walking—shuffling like drunken disco dancers, actually, but that's not the point. No, the point was the rush of unnamable energy that struck me from nowhere, and the sharp pulse that followed.

It slammed us both to the ground. A wind overwhelmed us like a tsunami with unmitigated power streaming out in all directions. I heard glass shattering, stone breaking, and something piercing my side, digging through the bandages like a dagger. I felt the stiches splitting, and saw my blood flowing onto the ground, staining it black. The buildings around us trembled and cracked, while the bark of hundred-year-old trees split down their centers. From everywhere came the sounds of metallic screeching of cars that were swerving and braking to avoid the irregular shafts of concrete thrusting up toward the sky.

Trying desperately to ignore the pain, I propped myself up on an elbow. Only after I was sure that Casey and Blue were both accounted for and alive, did I dare to look over my shoulder. A grey cloud full of liquid fire billowed up from the ANC, flattening itself beneath the underside of the sky. Colorful flashes like lightning illuminated its insides, and the reds and yellows and cobalt blues of highly flammable potions went up in smoke.

My stomach twisted in on itself. If the building hadn't been gone before, it sure as hell was now. *Power surge,* I thought, but for a moment, I couldn't connect it to anything. It just stuck in my brain like a painful thorn, shouting something through a bullhorn I couldn't understand. *Power surge,* I thought again, and then, *wormhole.* Power surge, wormhole. Maybe … I couldn't concentrate long enough to start the thought, so I had to forget about finishing it.

"Oh what the *hell*," said Casey. He was on his knees, looking around at the fresh carnage and up at the steadily rising black smoke. For a long time, the only sound was that of the breaking earth and car alarms, along with rushing water that streamed from all of the demolished hydrants and hissing steam from the ruptured pipes.

"What was that?" he asked, but the way he said it made me think he didn't really expect me to answer. It was a question to the universe, a general *what-the-flying-fuck-is-going-on?* addressed to no one in particular.

For whatever it was worth, I knew what was happening. The spell was called Singularity, and it did exactly what it sounds like it might do—compress massive amounts of energy into a fine point, and release that energy in an unmitigated expulsion of force and fury.

We limped away. Blood streamed down my forehead and face, coloring everything I saw in a sticky, watery, cherry color. I stared at the ground, watching the cracks in the road, the ravines swimming in sewage and grass and stone, the shadows of metal and rubber and smoking steel, the stench of burning skin coupled with the broken voices that continued screaming without any intelligible words.

I didn't lose consciousness, not completely. I kept moving, and my mind became an objective observer. I saw everything without being there, all the darkness our world had inflicted here imbued me with a hollowness I'd never experienced before. A deep, yawning blackness in the pit of my stomach wound its way like smoke and felt like acid ink when it climbed up the back of my throat.

I scoffed when I realized what it was. The acceptance of defeat. The realization that we underestimated the enemy, that our mistake has cost everyone we know their lives. Your body is ready to finally clock in for the end of the world. I felt like Atlas, struggling to support the whole world's incompetency, which was now settling on my shoulders. Of course I couldn't do this. If Caressa and Knight and Christina and Dia and Dulcie *fucking* O'Neil couldn't do it, then of course, neither could I.

Gelvie's dead, I thought. Along with everyone else, but hers was the face that haunted me in my head. I didn't know why.

CHAPTER SIX
Dulcie

Standing in the ruins of the ANC, I savored the smell of burning skin still hanging in the air. An officer in a red uniform, a fireman, and several of his crimson compatriots ran past me with hoses and water buckets and axes. Fire blazed around them, broad walls of liquid red reaching for the stars. Between the shattered glass and busted stone of collapsed buildings, people ran and screamed, but their yelling was fainter now than it had been before. Most of the people making the noise were now dead, leaving Splendor in a state of sublime silence.

The last sounds that remained were the ones that only I could hear: the labored breathing of men dying under slabs of concrete set to the misty haze of busted fire hydrants. I spotted the quivering excess of the scar the wormhole left in space and time. I could see, if I squinted, a transparent white line strung across the sky. I could have opened it, if I wanted to, and let the emptiness swallow whatever remained.

My fingers twitched at the idea, but I resisted the urge. Mother said to wait, so wait I would. There would be plenty of time for more carnage when all of this was over and done.

A line of blue and white cars pulled up to the curb—the police, detectives, and other crime scene personnel had apparently survived the collapse of their station. I watched them exit their cars with obvious disinterest, illuminated by the fire and the blinking red and blue lights. They pulled things out from their bags and car trunks: guns and clipboards and equipment, but what they thought that could learn from the flattened earth around me, I had no idea. They all knew there was magic, and would have been interested in little else.

Fine. Let them wave their toys in the air, let them confirm what they already suspected. Maybe it would speed things along. I intertwined my fingers together and let my arms hang limp as I observed the scene.

The whole world was a rather unseemly grey, as though a storm cloud had fallen from the sky and imbued its color on everything it touched. Smoke was everywhere, the thin, dispersed fog of a thousand different fires burning across the city. Bodies littered the broken concrete, the only other color in the whole world. Among them was a woman, a slight creature with a clipboard clasped tightly in her crumpled fingers and the look of petrified shock on her face. Red hair fanned out on the ground behind her, singed at the edges. Her skin was charred, her clothing burnt away to nearly nothing. I tilted my head and knelt before her, touching her freezing skin—which was almost warm, compared to mine. The stillness in her veins filled the air around her, turning it cold. It was a rather curious quirk of witches' blood that I've never fully understood.

The poor creature had a name tag. The only legible word on it, however, was *Moon.* A transfer, a call-in, perhaps to examine the air around the wormhole Jax used to save me. Though I could not explain it, something in my heart suddenly shattered. Then, the name Gelvie began to drum between my ears incessantly.

G*elvie,* I thought, although I couldn't place her name nor where I might have met her before, much less why I should have cared that she was dead.

I closed her eyes, troubled by my inability to explain the feelings coursing through me and nearly threatening to choke me with their intensity. "You weren't supposed to be here," I said, hoping she'd escaped my last command—but the burns at her throat and the long red lines in her legs told me she hadn't. I could feel the remnants of her pain, and I heard the echo of her scream, both of them slicing across my spine like dull razors.

I shook the sounds away. *No matter*.

The officers ran past me, ignorant of my presence. I watched them putting out the fires and carting the bodies away, consoling the small number of surviving souls with blankets and whispers, and I waited. I wasn't concerned that any of these humans would bother with me. Why? Because they couldn't see me. I decided to use an invisibility shield to avoid the numerous questions that would no doubt follow as soon as anyone saw me walking amidst the rubble completely unscathed. Who knew? Maybe some of them would realize I was the one responsible for all the carnage in the first place.

Where are the rest of them? I thought. And then, as if responding to my inquiry, they arrived.

A long line of black vans, seven to be exact, and each filled to bursting with agents in suits and ties and sunglasses, all of them armed to the teeth. They leapt from the caravan with practiced ease, the polished veneer of a long career, instilling a calm they didn't feel. Several hulking figures walked among the state officers, snapping orders and asking questions, flaunting warrants that gave them complete sway over the case.

Finally, I thought. With luck, they'd discover us and we'd make the morning paper—in a town that still had one, of course.

I closed my eyes and muttered a spell, splitting the world before me. Splendor undid itself in a swirl of blue and blistering red, twisting into nothing as the portal wove itself through numerous dimensions.

"Home," I said, and that's precisely where it took me.

###

We lay in bed in the room where the two men died, Bram and Knightley, I think their names were.

Sebastian's hands gripped my waist, his glassy eyes plastered to the ceiling. I could *not* figure out what I was supposed to do with my own eyes. Closing them felt too impersonal, but I couldn't connect my eyes with Sebastian's. I wasn't sure why. All I could do was to stare at the black headboard. I rocked back and forth, twisting myself around his erect friend, trying to find my own G-spot—which, as it turns out, was damn near impossible.

At least Sebastian was having fun.

I felt my legs trembling with exhaustion and, as I dropped myself down, Sebastian erupted into a spasm—whatever I'd done, he apparently liked it and then some. Vampires don't have any sperm to speak of, but I could feel his body going through the motions of the expulsion, pulsing and throbbing before becoming stiff when he realized he had nothing to give. The glassiness faded from his eyes and he blinked, gasping for unnecessary breath he didn't need.

He looked at me. "That," he said, "was brilliant."

He had the good sense not to ask if it was good for me, too. I wasn't in the mood to lie. I rolled away from him, my expression flat. I was previously debating and subsequently refusing to mimic his breath, if only to *pretend* he'd done something moderately useful in the last two minutes.

More like a minute and a half, the jaded part of me thought. It was better than nothing, I supposed.

"Perhaps you'd like some refreshment?" he asked.

I'd like some decent sex, I thought bitterly, but I ignored that thought and smiled up at him instead. "That sounds great."

"Tea, princess?"

"Scotch," I answered. At the very least, I intended to get drunk tonight.

Sebastian rose from the bed, clothing himself to the best of his weary ability, and bent the world around him until he disappeared. When he was gone, I groaned and flopped back on the pillows, bemoaning Sebastian's pitiful state of affairs. *So much buildup for so little payout.* He was well endowed, to be sure, but the size of the sword was not nearly as important as the man who wielded it—and Sebastian was a very poor swordsman. It was most likely because Sebastian was merely out of practice. Mother seemed to fancy the other breeds of night creatures more for the last decade or so, leaving poor Antoine and Sebastian to practice on their own accord—not something they often found the time to do in the house of a fallen magister. So maybe he'd been gifted once, and merely rusted from disuse in the absence of a proper partner. No wonder he was so excited about me.

I sighed, resigning myself to give him another chance—another series of chances, actually. Sebastian was, bar none, the most beautiful man I'd ever laid eyes upon, and dammit, he was going to learn to fuck me properly if it killed us both.

We should be so lucky, I thought.

I frowned as soon as the thought left my head because I didn't understand what it meant right away. Lucky to die? Lucky to kill, maybe, but never to die. The sudden thought of leaving Mother on her own nearly turned my insides over.

Lucky to be dead, the voice in my mind persisted, only this time with more vigor.

I shook my head, and the thought fell away, buried beneath a sudden, ravenous hunger. My stomach gurgled and my blood turned hot, prickling the underside of my skin. I could call Antoine and request something, but after Sebastian's pitiful performance, I wanted nothing more than to be alone.

Somewhere in the woods, I heard the dismayed yawning of a chimera, casually patrolling the fence. I stood away from the bed, stretching, scanning the floor for my clothes. My black tights were fine, but the dress was in tatters—Sebastian made a poor lover, but his foreplay was pretty commendable. I walked to the vast black wardrobe at the wall. Inside were dresses of vermillion and mauve, deep burgundy and stark black—each one hand selected by Mother just for me. I ran my fingers across each of them, some soft silk, others plush velvet, and stopped at something long and green, a floor-length halter dress with a slit up one side, all the way to my hip. I smiled as I pulled the gown out, remembering Mother's words.

You must always remember the simple power you have as a beautiful woman. That power alone is enough to persuade men to do your bidding.

I dressed and left my room. The hall outside was predictably empty—although several nameless servants piddled about, carrying cleaning agents and bloody rags, but they made no sound. The silence gave the house a vast, cavernous feeling, like a secret mansion hiding deep underground.

I walked the stairs with bare feet, absorbing the cold from the stone. My hand curled around the spinning banister, feeling every crack in the veneer. My teeth were sharper, my skin colder, but I still lacked the night vision that Mother's kind possessed. Focusing intensely on small details, supposedly, would help me with that skill. I knew where the stain was splitting, and where the wood had been hammered flat, and where a bump existed where there once was a splinter …

Here was a shadow I didn't know. And a voice to go with it.

Three of them were sifting through the vents with shadows in the den to escort them. One voice belonged to Mother—the other two were distinctly masculine, and one of them whispered with the hint of sibilance.

Right, I'd forgotten. Mother's compatriots were dining with us tonight. *How rude of me*, I thought as I entered the living room, folding my hands, and offering the shadows a demure smile. Standing by the fire was a werewolf in a lavender suit. He was smoking a pipe and grinning lasciviously at Mother; while a draconian male in the flowing, red robes and yellow sash of an alchemical merchant stood nearby. They heard me enter and directed their smiles at me.

"Ah, and this must be our little Dulcie," said the wolf, flashing his sharp teeth and cold eyes. The fire was making him sweat. He extended his hand. "Desmond Vosh. At your service."

I shook his hand and he bowed deeply with a flourish, his eyes immediately landing on my breasts as soon as he observed my deeply plunging neckline.

"It's a pleasure," I said as I turned to address the scaled monstrosity beside him. He straightened his sash and his face twitched into what I could only assume was a grin.

"Sess vakal do'rim," he said. "Lehl Sigurnd Thramn." *Greetings from the burning places. I am Sigurnd Thramn.* I couldn't understand how I managed to understand his tongue, but I also didn't consider the topic for very long.

I heard myself reply, "Sesh vakan la'kin. Vogahn Thas vidamn." *Greetings from the green places. House Vogahn welcomes you.*

Sigurnd's grin widened, exposing two polished fangs, the red cords of his occupation burned into their enamel. He spoke to Mother, never taking his eyes off me. "What wasss that about blooming late?"

I felt Mother scowling behind me, and the air around her was turning hot. I looked back and she was smiling, her hands clasped together, her eyes burning with irritation. "She is ... coming along."

The drake clicked his tongue and took a moment to examine me, his eyes conspicuously lingering slightly too long on my shoulders—an odd place to covet, but Mother had already told me that was what the drake valued. Something about narrow feminine frames being rather hard to come by.

"I'd ssssay," he said. "Ssskin's cold, eyesss changed ... ssshe hasssn't much further to go, I'll wager."

"On the contrary," said Mother, her voice cold as steel, "she has barely begun. Perhaps you gentlemen might like a drink?"

The pair of them nodded, and Mother dematerialized into a puff of black, glittering smoke—an unnecessary gesture, but sometimes, she just couldn't help herself. Especially in front of such important guests.

"Ssso," said the draconian, "Lady Vogahn." A reptilic tongue shot out of his mouth, lapping at the hazy air.

"Lord Thramn," I said. "It is an honor to host you in our home. And you as well," I said, turning to the werewolf. He was of a lesser house, a bannerman of sorts, the captain of a ship he didn't own—powerful, but hardly in his own right. The werewolves as a race were always subject to one rebellious faction or another, and always far too disorganized as a society to be autonomous without hurting themselves. They smelled putrid, even this cultivated specimen, despite being draped in colognes and scented fabrics.

I smiled at him, trying to keep my criticism at bay.

"You're a pretty little thing," said Vosh, with a deferential nod to show he meant it honorably. "Spitting image, wouldn't you say?"

"Indeed," said Thramn with a thoughtful hiss. "Ssstriking resemblance. Uncanny."

"Forgive me, but I must disagree. I look nothing like Mother," I said.

Thank Hades, thought the voice.

Quiet! I thought back. I felt my smile twitching as I wondered where this voice was coming from and why it had only cropped up most recently. It spoke in my own voice but the words sounded alien to me, so I had to wonder if they came from my own mind. Perhaps a Grenoo sprite had somehow managed to crawl into my ear and was now vexing me from inside my head?

"We aren't referring to your mother, my dear, but to your father," said Vosh. "The hair, the eyes … the ghost of Melchior lives in you, I swear it."

The fucking hell he does!

Shush! I resisted the urge to shake my head again, contenting myself with tilting it slightly and letting my smile appear nostalgic. As soon as I was alone, I would burn that fucking sprite right out of my head! "But if I'd known him better," I started wistfully.

You did. You put a bullet in his fucking stomach.

"Now," said the draconian, leaning closer, wrapping a cold, scaled hand around my shoulder. "I don't want to excssite you, darling, but it would appear that your mother hasss made a match for you."

"A match?" I repeated incredulously. It was a bit early to be forming familial alliances—as we'd only just begun our attack on the human establishment. I frowned openly. "Whatever for?"

"Oh, a reward, I sssuppose," said Thramn, waving a hand dismissively. "It won't be until long after we've sssettled all thisss." He gestured vaguely toward the room, and, I guessed, to the Netherworld in general.

"Whose reward?" Hades willing, they'd be better in the sack than Sebastian, poor fool.

Thramn's words came slowly. "The ... draconiansss ..." His tongue escaped his mouth again in an excited tic, "... have been ... *mossst* loyal, wouldn't you agree, my lady?"

The draconians were, bar none, our most powerful ally, but it seemed impolite to say so in front of Vosh. "You have," I replied carefully.

Thramn pulled back his arm, musing. "Dragonsss," he hissed, "vampire, and fae ...would make sssuch *powerful* children." He traced the line of my shoulder with a single long claw, and I wondered not for the first time how draconian anatomy compared to humans. "The iron handsss of the next world."

I tried to smile at Thramn, but there was something inside me that was rebelling against every word that emerged from his mouth. I couldn't explain the feelings, but they plagued me all the same. "Our legacy?" I asked.

Thramn smiled. "Perhapsss ... but we ssshall sssee."

Antoine entered then, carrying a platter of wine glasses filled with lemons and ancient sangria. I thought it a touch casual for such honored guests—we'd have been better off with old bourbon and scotch—but Thramn and Vosh seemed delighted. Maybe they just didn't know any better.

Nobody cares about your fucking wine etiquette.

"Hush!" I whispered, my heart starting to pound inside my chest as my palms grew clammy. *Damn that sprite to the fires of Hades!*

"Pardon?" said Vosh, swirling the dark wine in his glass.

"Ah, nothing," I responded, perhaps a little too quickly. The world tilted and lurched, but I managed to keep my footing.

Thramn cocked his head and squinted at me. "Are you well, my lady? You look a bit ... piqued."

"No, I'm fine," I said. "A little hungry, I suppose."

Thramn nodded. "If your fangsss are mature, I offer you my blood gladly—although I must confesssss I've been told it is rather coarsssse."

"Maybe later," I said. My fangs weren't sharp enough to puncture skin yet, let alone scales—and I certainly didn't need Thramn having an orgasm he wasn't ready for and falling into the fireplace. But that may have been why he offered in the first place.

Thramn nodded, downed his wine, and looked toward the door. There was a soft creak, a gust of cold wind, and the soft *pop* of impolite magic. "Ah! the disss-asss-ter himself!" Thramn said, walking across the room. "Maessstro, my friend, how have you been?"

I looked at Vosh, who shrugged, and turned to Thramn. The disaster in question was a man, a vampire, judging by his gait and pallor, frozen somewhere in his forties. The *pop* must have been him materializing. Good looking, as they all were, and conspicuously well endowed in his suit pants, he had dark hair, silver eyes, and a gentleman's grin. He kept his hands in his pockets and his laughter in check, while his smile seemed to be a circumscribed thing stretching no farther than the width of his nose. Thramn clapped him on the shoulder with a massive, scaly hand—and the maestro didn't seem to appreciate it, although he didn't shrug him off.

"Welcome," I said cautiously, hoping he came here invited.

The gentleman extracted himself from Thramn's increasingly slurred conversation—draconians are comic lightweights—and came to me.

He held out his hand. "Ezra Sheen," he said, leaning down. He was a rather tall specimen, and lanky, like a fit man who's just past his prime. "It is a pleasure." I took his hand and instantly felt a rush of something. Energy. Power. But there was more to it than that—something that spoke of his kinship with me, and with Mother.

He kissed my knuckles, his eyes never once leaving mine. "You are a vision."

I smiled at Ezra, suddenly wishing I could have been betrothed to him instead. Thramn wasn't exactly what I would have labeled a ladies' man. "Thank you, sir."

Ezra stayed where he was, my hand in his, his eyes delving into mine as those bizarre feelings of closeness continued to flow between us. "Hmmm," he said, running a thumb over his lip, clearly thinking about something. Then his expression made a microscopic shift, his eyebrows lifted, and his irises relaxed, as though he'd found the answer to a riddle.

His smile expanded and he stood upright, dropping my hand. "Tell me," he said slowly in a soft tone. "Where is Meg?"

"Mother is …" The sentence trailed away on its own. I blinked and swallowed, feeling confused. Ezra raised his brow, his fingers curling into each other.

"Mother?" he said, then his voice turned cold. "Ah. Yes. How could I have forgotten?" he drew his finger down the side of my face, tracing my cheekbone, my chin, my throat. "Little Dulcie."

His stare was becoming unnerving.

He inclined his head slowly to me. "Dulcie," he said, drawing the name out slowly and deliberately.

He looked toward the fire, drinking in its colors, and my wits returned to me in a rush. I cleared my throat—horribly rude, but I couldn't seem to breathe. "If you gentlemen don't mind, I, I think …" *Stop stuttering,* "I think I'll go see what's become of Mother."

Vosh and Thramn nodded politely. "Very well," said Vosh before he turned to Thramn, launching himself into a critique of his drink—which he seemed quite taken with. He was saying something about strawberries and a bitterness like winter. Ezra watched me when I left, his eyes boring into my back as he pretended to listen to Vosh.

I made it down the hall and around the corner before I allowed myself to relax. I slumped against the wall beside one of a hundred portraits of Mother, trying to breathe slower, my heart pounding. The dizziness was still overcoming me, and the whole world was swinging like a pendulum before me.

Just hungry, I thought. *I haven't eaten in a while, so that's all it is. Just eat something. Anything.*

I pushed myself off the wall with the full intention of killing someone in the kitchen, but a strange sight at the right end of the hallway stopped me. Mother, closing a door behind her, cut off a garbled moaning and the humming of some machine.

"Mother?" I said, approaching her. "They're looking for you. In the den." They weren't, but it would have been impolite for her to be gone very much longer. They were, after all, *her* guests, not mine.

She smiled when she saw me. "Dulcie, my beautiful princess," she said, opening her arms. "I meant to ask. How was your little excursion?"

The ANC. "Successful," I replied, approaching her. She pocketed something, a key, and set her back against the door. The mechanical thrum was louder now, and overlaid by the clicking of gears. "Unless they're completely incompetent, they'll know us by dawn."

"And they are all …?" she asked, tilting her head at me.

"Dead," I said, perhaps a little too quickly. *No,* I thought, *there was one, the girl, who got away.* But as soon as that thought entered my mind, something repressed it, obscuring it until I couldn't remember it anymore.

Mother nodded. "Good." Her smile widened, but it seemed a bit stiff. "I hear you and Sebastian have become … better acquainted?"

"We have," I said, but she already knew that. Why ask me now? "Though …"

"He lacks proper technique," said Mother, clucking her tongue. "I'm aware of that. Don't worry, he learns quickly."

I didn't doubt that, but something about the way she said it made me pause. Her posture was a bit stilted, and her eyes had a distracted look in them. The dim light of lamps suspended from the walls struck her face hard, drawing harsh shadows on her cheeks and jaw, carving lines of old anger into her skin. Whatever lay beyond the door was old and important, some ancient grudge that reeked of secrecy.

"Mother," I said slowly, "what …" I looked toward the door, then at her, and thought better of my question.

But Mother knew what it was anyway. Her face shifted into an expression I couldn't read, something between vacancy and irritation. It might have conveyed anything. Then she relaxed and smiled at me. "Would you like to see?"

Mother wasn't one to share her secrets, but I nodded. She withdrew the key from her pocket and unlocked the door.

"I warn you," she said, "this is an unpleasant thing."

I refrained from saying I wouldn't have expected anything less.

The scene within was … almost archaic. The walls and floor were dark, a shining black that wasn't black, glittering with early morning sunlight, that spilled through the slits of a tall window. They seemed to concentrate on the far wall, where a man was slumped against the floor, shackled in onyx and silver, the consecrated metals that even Mother would have been crazy to touch. They burned and chafed his skin, turning it red and black and purple wherever it touched him. His skin was red and blistered wherever the sun kissed it, and steaming, and it really reeked of smoke. Like the flesh of an unfortunate animal cooking on a spit. His breath came in long, rattling drags. Glassy eyes, white as milk, stared at a spot of refracted light on the floor—the eyes of a vampire just beyond the brink.

"This …" I started slowly.

Mother nodded. "The vampire who killed your father."

How strange. He didn't seem particularly powerful. Certainly not potent enough to do in my father, not without significant help. His skin was pale, even for a vampire, papery white and dry as sand. He looked for all the world like a single touch would have broken him into a hundred thousand pieces. A papier mâché figure, brittle as sandstone. He moaned, vibrating with every breath, his body half convinced of its own mortality. He looked like he might have been handsome once, dark, chiseled, and irritatingly suave.

"Does he have a name?" I asked. I'm not sure why I wanted to know what it was.

Mother frowned and laid her hand on my shoulder. "He did," she said. "Once, long ago. But it doesn't belong to him anymore."

"Who does it belong to?"

Mother took a deep breath. Her nails dug into my shoulder, drawing blood. I didn't mind.

"*Me*," she said. Her eyes burned—she'd been after his name for a very long time.

I didn't know what possessed me to say what I asked next. "Did you love him?"

I felt Mother go stiff at my side. She slowly turned her head toward me, her eyes ablaze, dragging her nails down my arm with a systematic kind of rage. I blinked at her in confusion.

"I'm sorry," I said. "Have I upset you?" Some part of me—a deep, distant, carnal bit of my brain—was thrilled by the idea. I quashed it down the moment I realized it, horrified, trying my best to replace it with the fear I *should* have been feeling. Mother could tear me in half if she really wanted to, and I couldn't imagine that as being a pleasant experience.

*Tear **her** in half,* I thought. *Rip her in two and see how **she** likes it.*

I recoiled from the voice. It was dark, angry, and feminine, but there was no way it was mine. I would never, *ever* hurt Mother. Yes, as soon as I was alone, I would banish that dreadful sprite from my head and tear it into pieces.

"It … is all right," said Mother, releasing her hold on my shoulder. She wiped my blood away with the hem of her sleeve, and a few moments later, the wounds had closed themselves.

A muffled, deep voice came shivering down the hall. *"Meg!"*

"What was that?" I asked, startled.

Mother sighed. "An ungrateful houseguest," she said. "I'll take care of it …" She blinked, and smiled. "Actually … Dulcie. Come with me."

She took me by the hand and led me down the hallway, toward a door laced with wards of fire. The cry of "Meg!" sounded again and again from within, only louder this time, and much more distraught. Beneath it was laughter. Antoine fell in with us from nowhere, matching Mother's gait step-for-step.

Mother stopped outside the warded door, positioning me to the left of the frame. "Stay right here," she said, "and be quiet until I call. All right?"

I nodded. *I'm not a fucking child*, I thought but shook the rude words right out of my head, afraid for mother's reaction if I'd actually said them. Suddenly, I had to physically resist the urge to strike her.

No, no, be nice, be good to Mother, be respectful, I thought, shaking my head. *Enough of this.*

Fuck you.

Mother waved her hand, the wards snaked back, and she entered the room.

CHAPTER SEVEN
Sam

Splendor took the Singularity hard. Buildings that could withstand eight-point earthquakes were in a thousand pieces and damn near everything was still on fire. Governor Vance declared a state of emergency, and now the streets were swarming with rescue personnel—and even from here, inside my sanctum of wards and guards and spellworks, my impossible web of protections, I could taste the burnt-iron and blood of bad magic. Magic strong enough to cling like static to the people responsible for it. The streets swarmed with creatures carrying black clouds, choking auras as thick as ash, dark enough to sting anyone with the right kind of eyes from more than a hundred yards away. I could feel them even when I wasn't looking. The overpowering heat combined with a bone-chilling cold, ice, and thunder, and the ropey tendrils of demons bound to lesser souls.

In layman's terms, it meant the Darkness's people—*Dulcie's people*, I thought, although I was desperately trying not to—and they were everywhere. Had I been a judge of preternatural auras, I would have suspected they were looking for something. Probably me, but I was trying to be optimistic.

We went back to my house. It was probably a stupid thing to do—okay, it was *definitely* a stupid thing to do—but I was desperate for someplace familiar. And when I suggested it, Casey didn't argue, although he looked dubious.

We approached the quaint, little, suburban dream with our hackles raised, Casey with his gun in hand, and me with a large stick I found in the yard. I held it up as best I could, trying to look huge and imposing, but the muscles around the stiches had cramped until they were hard as stone and would only move so far—which is to say, not at all. I got my elbow just about to my shoulder before I almost screamed.

Not that it mattered, since there was nobody there. I ran a cursory spellcheck on the house and its thousand wards (and I do mean thousand)—I've made a habit of compounding my spells after Dulcie's initial run in with Melchior. I discovered not one of them had been breached. After opening the door with a key I'd hidden inside a false rock, I slowly shuffled inside, Blue darting past me to check for demons and any small animals.

Casey gave me a very strange look once the door was closed. "Oh, hell!"

"What?' I replied. Then I felt the blood running down my side and I looked down. My shirt and skirt were stained red. The spirit strings were barely holding, but the skin seemed to find another way around them to mend itself. "Oh." Now that I was looking at it, *really* looking at it, I could feel the stinging and burning of my nerve endings as they began to reactivate, desperately trying to kick my bones back into place. My body cried out for avocado oil, owl feathers, and sage, but when my head began pounding, I started to see stars. *Damn! How long have I been bleeding?*

Casey's face twisted. "God, I'm so sorry."

"Don't be, I'm not dead," I said. "I just need …" I blinked. What did I need? "Oil."

"Oil?" he asked incredulously.

"Potion," I said. "To set the bone and … close the …" The world spun, and I barely caught myself on the wall, jarring my displaced rib. I gasped as a shock of pain ran the length of my body, making my bones vibrate. I was definitely in no shape to be working on myself.

"Where's your bathroom?" Casey asked.

I stiffened. "What?"

"Bathroom," Casey repeated like I was dumb. "You know, bathtub, running water, toilet, et cetera."

I stared at him blankly and he gestured vaguely to my wound, maybe not looking quite nauseous, but something very close to it.

"We need to clean this, disinfect it, and rebandage it," he said. "And you need some sleep."

"Oh. Um, that way," I said, and I pointed toward the hall.

He helped me out of my shirt. By that, I mean he cut my shirt away with his pocketknife, dragging the blade through my blood-soaked blouse and throwing the strips in the sink. His fingers grazed my skin, sending cold shocks of electricity, absent of magic. He smiled at me when I caught his eye, trying to look as reassuring as he could manage. His thumb caught the skin under my arm, prodding a freshly-formed bruise, and I winced.

"Sorry, sorry," he said, slowly pulling away the last bit of my sleeve. I was just wearing my bra now, a simple white thing that was stained all the wrong shades of red. For three-tenths of a second, I was wildly uncomfortable, furious that I lacked the pitiful strength it required to cross my arms. But when I looked at him, he was staring at my face and smiling. Not grinning, not laughing, just the smile of a doctor trying to put his patient at ease.

"It's okay," he said without looking down once. He just stared at me with those alabaster eyes, all cool and collected and cute as hell.

My nerves melted into a puddle and I smiled back.

"Do you mind if I take a look at it?" he asked.

"Oh. Um, yeah," I said. "Go ahead."

Casey knelt in front of me, pulling down the side of my pants just enough to expose the point of my hip bone, where the long red line ended. I was caked in blood all the way down to my knees, with still more seeping languidly from the half-open cut. Dulcie's magic, the silver-green shadow of whatever she'd become, clung to the open skin, preventing it from scabbing over. He gently pressed his thumb into the base of the incision. I winced again and my rib strained against his primitive magic.

"How's it feel?" Casey asked, sounding wary of the answer.

I took stock. The blood was flowing again, but slower. His cosmic threads were frayed, hastily strung out from nothing and hammered into reality with Stone Age charm and raw fury. A child's work, the tested waters of a witch or a warlock on the ass end of third grade—but still more than he should have been capable of if he were only human.

"Not bad," I said. Not good either, but I probably wouldn't bleed out.

He scoffed. "That's sweet, but come on. I know I suck at this."

I grimaced. "Uh … not great. The threads are tearing and the bone's starting to feel heavy." Then I asked him the question I'd been meaning to for a while now. "How did you learn how to do this?" I cleared my throat. "How is it you're human but you seem to possess magic too?"

"That's a long story," he answered with a quick smile. "And one I'll tell you over coffee someday when the world isn't blowing up around us." He stood slowly, keeping his hand on my hip. "You mind if I go through your medicine cabinet?"

"Go ahead," I said, and he opened the mirror. I wondered why he avoided getting into all the hows and whys of his primitive magic, but he didn't want to so I had to temporarily shelve my fact-finding mission for the moment.

"You have bandages around here somewhere?" he asked.

"Yeah. Top left. The white ones are non-adhesive."

He took the bandages down and weighed them in his hand as he examined my bare stomach. My skin prickled under his gaze. "God, that … that looks like it hurts."

"It's fine," I lied. "Really."

He knelt in front of me again, squinting at the line, gently pulling his thumb through the sheets of blood. "We need to clean this." He looked from me to the porcelain tub. "Do you think you can manage it yourself or …"

I swallowed. *Or do you want to be bathed by a total stranger?*

Yes! Although it was hilariously awkward and weird, I couldn't exactly refuse him. I didn't think I had it in me to clean the blood away myself, not with so much bad magic still pouring out of it like a waterfall, and he was right. If we just let the blood congeal, it could easily flare up, get infected, and maybe poison me, which wouldn't help anybody.

And I was already half-naked anyway.

"I think …" I shook my head, uncertain of how to say it. "I can't really move, so … You know." I shrugged.

He nodded, and his face didn't change. "All right. Come here, then." He looped my arm around his head and together we limp-waddled to the bathtub. I sat on the edge, my bones creaking like clanking metal as we moved.

"Do you want to leave that on?" he asked, indicating my skirt. From anybody else that would have been an invitation, albeit a poorly constructed one, but the way he said it made it seem utterly normal.

"Um … no," I said. It would have been impossible to get off once it was wet, and I didn't relish the idea of bathing in a dirty skirt. "Can you, um …" *Don't you dare blush, Sam, don't you blush!*

I blushed.

Casey had the manners and good grace not to mention it. "Of course."

It was already unbuttoned. I stood and let him gradually work it down over my thighs. His hands moved slowly, pulling one side down lightly, then the other, shimmying it over my skin, taking great care to leave my underwear exactly where it was. The fabric slid over my bruises and bleeding abrasions, which I hadn't noticed before. Clenching my teeth, I wrapped my fingers tightly around the rim of the tub.

"It's okay," Casey said softly, and I nodded, swallowing a whine.

He got the skirt over my ravaged thighs and it fell to the floor, burnt and blackened, in filthy contrast on the white veneer. I sighed, throbbing.

Casey lifted his hand to my thigh, placing it gently on the skin below a particularly nasty red. It wasn't so much of a scrape but an entire layer of skin that was sheared off, a burning, crimson splotch the size of my hand. Casey frowned at it, his thumb moving back and forth.

"Can you sit down?" he asked.

I nodded and sat slowly. His hand stayed where it was.

"It doesn't look that bad," he said. "The bleeding's almost stopped." He dipped his hand in the water, which was steaming now, and its thick haze settled over the room like fog. "I'm going to touch it, and you have to tell me if it stings, okay?"

"Okay," I said, bracing myself.

He gently touched his thumb at the center of the wound. I flinched out of reflex, but it didn't sting too badly.

"Does it sting?"

"A little bit," I said. "Um …" I put my hand to my head, suddenly dizzy. The room shrank and grew and I had to remind myself to breathe.

"Easy," said Casey. I didn't realize I was starting to lose my balance until he caught me.

"Oh," I said stupidly. "Um. Thanks."

"Does that feel okay?"

I nodded, closing my eyes, inhaling the steam, and letting the moist heat fill my lungs and cloud my head. The dizziness abated, replaced by a vague nausea.

"You have a cup somewhere?" said Casey. "Or maybe a washrag?"

"There," I said, pointing to the cabinets. He pushed himself onto his feet to retrieve one, opening the cabinet and whistling.

"Lotsa towels," he said, grabbing one at random.

"Yeah," I agreed.

Casey sat on the ground, soaking the towel.

"So, um ..." I said, searching for a source of conversation, but there was only one that kept prodding my mind. "So you're really not going to tell me how you know how to do this?" I gestured vaguely to the fraying magic.

He grimaced like the question itself hurt him, squeezing the rag over my shoulder. "I ... work in the Preternatural Division," he answered simply.

The air went cold. "So?"

"So," he said, "it's protocol."

"Protocol ... what? To know magic?" Something about that rang false.

He hesitated. His hand hovered over the water and he bit the inside of his cheek, ostensibly thinking. "Do you know what a siphon is?"

I swallowed hard. *Siphons.* Human excess and pure shadow, dragon blood and batshit crazy experimentation gone miraculously right or horribly wrong, depending on whom you asked.

Okay, story time.

Once upon a time, a little more than a decade ago, supernatural creatures like witches and vampires and supersonic bunnies with laser eyes made themselves known to the general public en masse. Behold the creepiest things you've ever heard of coming to life, working in your office buildings and living on your street, even going to school with your kids, and *teaching* your kids. People didn't like that. It scared them, and honestly, it probably should have. The year after the initial "Hey, look, magic!" came all the violence and hate that sequestered those with magical leanings to places like Splendor and Estuary. Subsequently, demonic fires, nymphs calling the agitated forests to demolish entire suburbs, and *lots* of murder occurred.

Naturally, more people were scared. They demanded more security, something they could use to fight back against all the monsters that ate their bullets for breakfast. So their beloved government endowed them with an exorbitant amount of money to hire a group of insane chemists, genealogists, and molecular biologists. After five years of grotesque monstrosities, they made the siphons—humans that were capable of manipulating magic. Dragging the unholy energy out of warlocks, dryads, and angels, they created primitive, unschooled magic, brittle as obsidian. They lacked the control of a three-year-old, but it was enough to stay the world's terrified hand. And enough to convince them that we couldn't totally eradicate all of them if it took our fancy to try.

I almost laughed. Siphons were the monsters' monsters. They were a nightmare's nightmare, the shadows in the alley of a pitch-black world. And I was sitting half-naked in front of one, tired and angry, totally exposed. *Do I know what a fucking siphon is?*

"Yeah," I answered.

Casey laid his hand on my shoulder, hot with steam, and I flinched.

"I'm not going to hurt you," he said.

Gee, why did that feel like a veiled threat?

"Really." He squeezed me lightly and softly. Perhaps begging me to believe him.

I looked at him and he tried to smile, but his face refused to let him, his eyes going iron hard with regret and worry as well as something else I couldn't identify. The cold steel of a man resigned to his fate, I guess, but that didn't seem to cover it.

Here's the thing. Siphons weren't really dangerous. They weren't supposed to hurt anybody. Their whole purpose was to pretend they had enough magical capability to defeat a magical mob in a fight. Honestly, there wasn't a whole lot Casey could have done to hurt me, nothing that I couldn't return tenfold on him. Well, that is, if I were healthy anyway.

Casey swallowed, making a visible effort not to look away. "You've ..." he laughed. "You've seen what I can do with this … ability of mine. It's kind of pathetic."

I began to smile. "More than kind of," I said.

His smile broadened, and he laughed again. "I'm … I'm actually a doctor. If you can believe it. Probably could have fixed this a little better if I had the right tools, but … yeah." he sighed. "I'm sorry, Sam."

Something thrilled me when he said my name—my heart seemed to hammer, pleading for him to say it again. "Don't be," I said. "I'm just happy you knew how to set it at all." That was actually a rather disturbing thought—if anybody else had tried, they might have shattered the bone into a million bite-size pieces, or turned my blood into salt. It could have been quite harrowing.

But thanks to Dr. McDreamy, all I had to complain about were the insignificant details of his technique. I admit I was always one to look at the positive side. Yep, I'm a half-full cup, not a half-empty one kind of girl.

Casey smiled at me, softly, his amusement playing tricks with his eyes. "Guess that's something," he said. "Can you lift your arm?"

I did, and he squeezed a rag of hot water over the wound. Blood sloughed off into the tub, turning it pink. It burned like hell, but it was a good heat, like the tingle in frozen fingers when you thaw them by a fire.

"Easy," he whispered, and I realized I was cowering.

"I'm okay," I said.

We sat in silence as he slowly rinsed all the dirt and ash and broken glitter of bad magic off my skin. I stared at the rippling grey of his reflection in the water, and at the wall, as well as the fogging mirrors. Eventually, I looked at him. I watched him ministering to me, and felt him slowly rubbing all the red stains off me. He only looked up once, and it was at me. Not at my half-bared breasts, or my legs. Just at me. Staring, smiling. There was something impossibly reassuring about that smile. It was small and soft, almost casual, like nothing about this was strange.

"I think," he said softly, "we're good."

I blinked. "Um. Oh. Okay."

"How do you feel now?"

"Good," I said, nodding. "I'm … good."

Casey pulled the plug on the tub and the water started gurgling away. "Can you stand up?"

"Maybe." I put my arms on either side of the tub and pushed myself up. Or I tried to. My left arm buckled under my weight and I slipped back into the water too hard, nearly slamming my head against the back of it. Casey caught me just in time, sparing my head from falling only inches onto the glass.

"Okay, okay," he said, easing me back down into the water. "Are you all right?"

"Yeah," I said, struggling to breathe. Casey's arms uncoiled from around me and all three images of him sat on the rim of the tub, their warped faces spinning like a kaleidoscope. Clearly, I wasn't okay.

"We'll let the water drain," he said, "and I'll carry you. All right?" He put the back of his hand on my forehead. "Just relax."

"Uh-huh," I said, barely hearing him, my forehead pulsating. *Deep breaths, deep breaths, come on, deep breaths.* I forced myself to inhale. For a while, the only sound I could hear was the automatic fan, desperately inhaling the steam. *Relax.*

After a few minutes, the bathroom was clear, and I started to feel cold.

The last of the water wound down the drain with exaggerated bubbling. Casey looped his arms under me, placing one behind my back, and one under my legs before he lifted me out of the tub.

"It's okay," he whispered as he carried me into my bedroom. "I've got you."

I murmured wordlessly into his shirt, drinking in his unique smell—aftershave, dried sweat, dirt, and the faded scorch of Dulcie's fire. My cheek pressed against his chest, and he held me a little tighter.

Placing me gently on the bed, he whispered, "Wait just a second," like he was soothing a baby to sleep before he disappeared. When he came back, he had the white bandages and a towel in his hands. My vision swept in and out of focus. It was almost too hard to blink.

"I …" The word came out as little more than a gasp. I took a deep breath and pushed myself up, slowly, agonizingly, into a sitting position.

"Are you okay?" asked Casey, his face strained with worry.

I nodded. "Yeah. Fine." I swallowed against my writhing stomach. "I'm …"

Casey uncoiled the bandages and started to wrap them around my middle—one hand holding my stomach, pressing his palm firmly against my skin. I sat stock-still as he wound it around me, going up and up and up until my whole torso was swathed in white. A thin, red line formed against the underside of the gauze, but it didn't spread, a good sign.

"You shouldn't sleep in wet clothes," he said. "Okay?"

I nodded numbly. "Okay."

"I'm going to shower, and then I'll go out and sleep on the couch, if that's okay." He cleared his throat. "And I'll probably have to wash my clothes unless you've got some spare clothes in a men's size large lying around here?" The way he asked the question was cute, but I could tell he was probing, wanting to know if I had a boyfriend.

"No, I'm afraid I don't. Just a woman's size medium, but I doubt those will fit you."

He chuckled and I yawned, long and loud, stretching my mouth as wide as the unhinged jaw of a snake. How long had it been since I'd slept? *Four days,* my beleaguered brain answered, *going on five. Go the fuck to sleep.* "Mmm-hmm," I said to myself, dragging my weary eyes up to Casey. "Thank you." I couldn't think of anything to add so I just smiled at him.

He smirked and put his hand on my cheek—then seemed to realize what he was doing and pulled away, clearing his throat. "You're welcome."

"Hey, could you, um …" *Hades, why isn't my mouth working?* "On my dresser … could you, um, grab me some, uh …"

He nodded and went to the dresser I indicated, a curving, black wooden thing with veins of blue painted across it to look like corrupted turquoise. "Which drawer?"

It didn't even occur to me to be embarrassed. "Top."

He walked back over to me with panties, bra, and a short, black sleeveless sleeping shift. "Do you think you can …?"

"I'll be fine," I answered, taking the articles from him. Weirdly enough, he managed to pick out a matching set. "Thanks. Really. For, um … you know. Saving my life."

"No problem," he said. "Now, let's get some sleep. We can figure this all out in the morning, okay?" he added.

"Okay." I nodded as he made for the door, his footsteps muffled by the thick, beige carpet. Blue stuck his nose into the room to meet him, whining softly.

"Hey, there's dog food somewhere in the kitchen. Could you—"

"Sure," Casey answered, scratching Blue on the head. "Come on, boy, let's get something to eat, eh? Sleep well," he said before he shut the door.

CHAPTER EIGHT
Sam

When I awoke next, I was staring at the ceiling with heavy covers draped over me. The light outside my windows had dimmed into the satin-black and silver of twilight. I dragged myself from the bed, my side throbbing like an aching tooth, moving as slowly as I could manage. The room was large, mostly occupied by a queen-sized bed, a black vanity with makeup and hair-care supplies strewn across it, and a chalk-blue wardrobe. A tall window overlooked my backyard, a long stretch of green, ringed by the silhouettes of trees with sharp leaves.

Now was as good a time as any to get up, but my body wasn't complying with the whole "waking up" thing. My bones creaked and groaned like the boards on an old ship, grinding against each other whenever I moved. "Okay," I said. "Okay." *Come on, we can do this.*

I pushed myself off the bed, warily testing my balance. I didn't immediately pitch over, which I considered a good sign. The dizziness was gone, along with the headache, and I was reasonably awake. I lifted my shift to look at the bandages, which were soaked through with red, but now in a narrow rectangle rather than a vague, amoebic stain. So, better, but still wanting. However, I would deal with that in a minute.

I dressed as quickly as I could, which, with my body on strike, meant painfully slow. I slid on yoga pants and a long-sleeved, purple shirt, tennis shoes, things that wouldn't snag.

Things that'll be easy to run in, I thought. That was a pleasant picture, running from full-metal Dulcie and the other Darkness creatures with a broken rib and whatever the hell else was wrong with me.

But I had to reserve my thoughts about my impending doom, my possessed best friend, and my missing boss for later. Right now, my rib hurt and I was hangry. I went to the kitchen with the full intention of bleeding into a silver bowl to make one of a hundred different concoctions, one that might better repair my bones—*noxi idrocal* for the pain, *theris validranum* to speed the mending on the molecular level—but I changed my mind when I smelled cookies. Cookies and a burnt-charcoal haze that smelled suspiciously like fireworks.

Casey, I thought. When I heard someone humming, however, it didn't sound like him.

I couldn't think of any explosive agents that might have smelled like melted chocolate, but I was still moving slowly as I rounded the corner into my living room. The lights were on above the counters and oven, and a single lamp illuminated the pastel couches and the dark dining room table. A woman with long, blond hair and shadow-grey eyes sat with a cup of steaming green tea, drinking from one of my numerous mugs while reading something on her phone. White, sleeveless, athletic shirt, stretch-black shorts, and pristine, white tennis shoes. She had a gun at her hip, and a smaller pistol strapped to her ankle, which was casually slung over the arm of her chair.

She looked up as I came in. I stiffened, and she smiled.

"Sam, right?" she asked, standing and pocketing her phone. "I'm Judy."

"Um," I started, wondering if thieves nowadays broke in and baked cookies before they took off with your televisions and iPads.

"It's okay, we're with Casey." She extended her hand.

I blinked at her and gave her hand a cautious shake. She had a firm grip. "Judy," I repeated, my heart pounding. How the hell had she gotten in? "And where is …"

"Bathroom," she said. At that exact moment, the door to the guest bath opened up and Casey came sauntering out.

"Sam!" he said, beaming when he saw me. "How are you feeling now?"

"Better," I said. His hair was slick from his recent shower, and he smelled like strawberry shampoo. Oh, and one more thing … he wasn't wearing a shirt. He was only covered by my white towel which he wrapped around his middle. His skin glistened (yes, glistened) with hot water, steam curling off his arms.

He smiled at me with shining, white teeth. Prying my eyes away from his chest was almost painful.

"Good, good. Oh, this is Judy," said Casey. "She's with us." Then he headed for my laundry room where he was, presumably, in the middle of washing or drying his clothes.

"Judy and I just met," I said with a little smile at them both.

She laughed and looked me up and down. "Hi to you, too," she said, squeezing my arm. We were matched in height, but she was smaller, nothing but muscle stretched tautly over bone.

Which reminded me, I had a mortal wound to take care of.

"Nice to meet you," I said, my wits finally returning. "I'm sorry, I need to do something in the kitchen."

"Kent's a little busy in there," said Judy. "What do you need?"

"Kent?" I asked.

"Demo guy," she said absently. "So what do you need?"

"Um …" I tucked my hair behind my ear, feeling a little bad for what I said next. "I need to set a bone."

Judy snorted. "Yeah, Casey told me about his temporary patch job," she said, throwing a dubious look in Casey's direction. He held up his hands and shrugged. "How's it holding up?"

About as well as a paper airplane in a hurricane, but it hasn't hit the water yet. I smiled and said, "Not bad, but I think I can do better." Casey grinned at me from where he was pulling his clothes out of the dryer. I wasn't sure why, but I liked the image of him in my house, tending to such boring chores.

Judy laughed and walked over to the kitchen.

Casey carried his clothes from the laundry room and walked right up to me, the strawberry smell increasing tenfold. "So, how are you? Really?"

I took a deep breath, feeling fire on my skin, and tasting ash in the back of my throat. My legs started shaking. "I'm … okay. Not really, but I'm … I'm okay." I wasn't sure what that meant, but Casey nodded.

"Yeah," he said. "That, uh … sounds about right. I'm sorry."

"Don't be—"

"No, I mean, for all of this. I'm sorry it happened." He put his hand on my arm.

I sighed. "Thanks," I said. "I … yeah. Thanks." I smiled weakly, fervently ignoring the dead witches and burning buildings that were still wedged in my brain. *Don't cry, don't cry, don't you fucking cry!*

Casey squeezed my arm, leaning down to look at me. His eyes were soft and calm. "It's okay," he said. "I mean … I mean, it's not okay but … it'll be okay. We're gonna figure this out."

The images swiftly faded and I felt steady again. *Inhale, exhale.* "Yeah. Okay."

"Okay," he said as he straightened up, smiling. "I don't know about you, but I am *starving*. And I think," he added, heading for the kitchen, "that someone made cookies."

I followed him before I noticed three more people for the first time.

The first was tall and lean, a burning cigar between strong fingers stained with motor oil and ink. Aged maybe in his forties with brown hair, a tweed jacket, and brown dress shoes that seemed to have been hammered into an off-grey after thousands of hours pounding the pavement. There was a woman sitting at the island in front of him, drinking coffee and staring at nothing. She was Arabian with dark skin, black hair, and wearing a white half-mask to cover savage magical burns. The bright red scars, crimson and black webs of burns caused by all the wrong kinds of divine intervention, were still very visible. Old magic simmered inside her, a muted brightness like beams of sunlight through fog. I could feel the ethereal residue even from here, thick and sour, like stagnant water.

And the third was a short man with shaggy, reddish-brown hair—Kent the demo man, if I had to guess—piddling around the kitchen wearing a plaid shirt with rolled up sleeves and my *Kiss Me, I'm Wiccan* apron, his hands coated in flour. Every appliance in the room was doing something. My dishes were done, my counters were clean, my hand towels, of all things, had been neatly folded. And the chocolate-and-fireworks smell, warm and divine, was deliciously radiating from the half-open oven.

"Ah!" Kent said when he saw me in the thickest Scottish accent I'd ever heard. "Perfect timin'." He opened the oven the rest of the way with his foot and pulled out a tray of chocolate chip cookies. Until ten minutes ago, the mere thought of food would have sent me reeling, but now, the aroma was enough to make me salivate. He scraped one off the tin and folded the crumbled, melting mess onto a plate, handing me a fork along with it.

"Thanks," I said, practicing my self-restraint. It was all I could do not to shovel the entire plate into my face.

Kent flourished an oven-mitted bow and grinned at me with slightly crooked teeth. "We heard ye've add ah roof day," he said, and his smile turned sweet.

"Rough day" didn't even *begin* to cover it. "Thanks," I said, trying not to think about it.

"Dinnae worry, Ah'll clean all o' this oop." He gestured to the extremely clean counter. The only mess I could spot was a bag of chocolate kisses that spilled onto the granite, and even that was very small. I quirked a brow at Kent and he offered me an apologetic shrug.

"Meet my team," said Casey, gesturing to the motley group. He pointed at them in turn. "This is Marcus,"—the one with the cigar—"Rowena,"—the one radiating wild magic—"and Kent"—the one baking cookies. Marcus nodded at me, and Kent beamed over the tray. Rowena looked up and smiled with half her mouth.

"Evening," said Marcus, nodding to me.

"It's a pleasure," Rowena offered. There was a deep sadness in her smile, the fixed expression of someone who'd seen too much tragedy. I tried to smile back and she looked down at her coffee, grimacing before she returned to her private thoughts.

"This is Sam," Casey told his team. They all nodded grimly. Kent patted my arm, looking like he felt sorry for me.

"Sorry 'bout your friend, love," he said. I stiffened, and suddenly, I could sense their pity as acutely as an icy wind. I felt like a lost child in a room full of adults, scrambling to figure out where she belonged. It was a peculiar sensation, and they weren't doing anything in particular to instigate it—but it was there all the same. I couldn't help feeling impossibly small.

"You're all FBI?" I asked, stuffing my mouth full of hot dough and chocolate. They were clearly government overseers, but that division spanned half a hundred organizations, official and otherwise. Rowena and Marcus seemed the type, but Kent was the antithesis of a government agent, the kind of man with a thousand unsanctioned secrets. Not to mention the whole baking thing. That didn't really fit the FBI mold …

"Rowena and I are," said Casey. "Marcus is on loan from the CIA." He didn't say anything about the other two, and I didn't ask, although Kent had a mad glint in his eye. A long, painful silence followed in which everyone looked at each other, no one quite sure what to say next.

Judy eventually shattered it with a single loud clap. "What exactly did you need for bone-fixing, sweetheart?" she asked, pushing Kent out of the way and flinging open the cabinets.

I swallowed my mouthful of cookie and pushed myself back from the island, standing. I was starting to shake, although I couldn't say why. Nerves? Shock? Maybe hunger, it had been quite a while since I'd eaten. I tried to remember the last time I'd put anything in my stomach besides coffee—and now, an obscene number of cookies. But I couldn't remember the last time. *Damn, it's been days, hasn't it?*

"Sam?" Judy asked, pulling me from my reverie.

"Right," I replied. The spirit-stitches Casey had woven through me were fraying like the ropes of an abandoned ship, drawing tautly against a material break they were rapidly losing hold of. I moved slowly around the island and opened a lower cabinet to reach the onyx and silver salad bowl I used for my more volatile potions.

"There's a couple of blue canisters in the pantry labeled VS," I said, "and there's a Tupperware container in the fridge of portabello mushrooms and freeze-dried glow worms."

Judy nodded and disappeared into the walk-in pantry. Marcus raised his brow when I listed off the ingredients, but said nothing as he took a long drag of his cigar. The smoke smelled like sweetgrass and spice.

I set the bowl on the counter and Judy laid out the materials before me. I rolled up my sleeve and tested the veins in my arm. I was still a little dizzy, but I could manage to lose a quarter cup or two without passing out. Probably.

"Whatcha got there?" Kent loomed out of nowhere, casting a long shadow over the stone. He clasped his still oven-mitted hands under his chin and grinned at me with unabashed curiosity.

I smiled at him and turned up the bowl so he could see the inside. A spiral of jagged grooves was carved into it, sloping gently towards the center to carry blood and spit and plasma.

"Well, that's somethin', then, in't it?" he muttered, craning his neck to get a better look. "What's it fer?"

I opened a drawer in the island, exposing a neat array of thin knives and scalpels. Silver and ironwood and oak, gold and river stone, glass and steel, all reflecting the dull kitchen lights. I ran my hands over them, selecting a needle-thin blade of glass and jade—transparency and truth, the material elements to color my blood and name the potion's purpose.

"Pretty," said Kent. "What's it do?"

I held the blade up, turning it between my fingers and watching it refract the light. "It cuts things open," I said, drawing it across the underside of my forearm. A thin, red line formed in its wake.

Kent nodded, pursing his lips. "So it does."

I turned my arm sideways and bled into the bowl. The red struck the stone with a hissing whisper, and the echoes of old power washed through me like liquid sunlight. The blood rode the spiral to the center and a thousand eyes, stemming from the first Wicca, lent me their wisdom before a cold lethargy overcame me. My confidence returned in full force and I grinned down at the congealing concoction, resisting the ever-present urge to snicker like a mad scientist. This was my element. This is where I could do my good, *this* was my job. And I was really good at it.

Kent watched in fascination as I crumbled up a horde of colorful ingredients and added them to the bowl, oohing and aahing while asking every third second what this powder did and where that claw came from, and if I had to use hawk feathers or any old red feathers would work. I didn't mind. I answered his questions, letting my years of study and full repertoire of knowledge flow out of me as I ground and mixed and pounded. For the first time in weeks, I didn't feel helpless. And it also wasn't lost on me that Casey just stood there, leaning against the counter on the opposite side of the kitchen, watching me with a placid expression on his face.

The resulting potion was a thick, green paste that most closely resembled a sturdy custard, an occasional blue pocket of air bubbling up and popping with a spectacular splash. Kent leaned in and sniffed it, prodding it with his finger.

"What's it do?" he asked. He stuck his finger in his mouth and made a face. "Tastes like lemon."

"It fixes broken ribs," I answered, laughing before wincing because laughing hurt.

Okay, now the hard part.

Telling myself I wouldn't be shy, I pulled off my shirt and set it on the counter. Kent sucked in a breath, which didn't surprise me—I could feel the hot wetness in the gauze sticking to my skin.

"Here," said Casey, stepping forward. He found the edge of the bandage and slowly started to peel it away, holding his other hand against my stomach to steady me. I looked at the wall as he undid it, moving his hands around me in circles, some part of him always touching me. I swallowed. Kent coughed.

"There." Casey stepped back, a wad of reddish-black fabric between his fingers.

Judy whistled. "Wow. That's ... damn!"

I looked down. Now the magic was waning, and I could see the wound coming apart at the seam. The skin around it was the color of a rotten apple, the blue and sandy yellow of a fresh bruise. The broken rib bulged against my skin, tugging plaintively at its restraints.

"I'm—" Casey started.

"It's okay," I said, with a reassuring smile—or I tried to as a wave of nauseous pain rippled through me. I wasn't sure how my face looked just then, but it was enough to make everyone around me appear more concerned.

"I'm fine," I said, even though it wasn't true, and I got to work.

Lathering the wound with the paste as gently as I could, even the slightest pressure was nearly enough to make me vomit, so it was slow going. The more I massaged it in, the faster it would work, but fucking *hell,* it hurt. Kent nibbled on a cookie, watching the tonic disappear into my skin, bubbling slightly and turning hot. For a moment, it stung, but thirty seconds later, it had absorbed all the way to the bone, and I could feel it shifting my skeleton, knitting everything back together.

There was a loud *pop* and I gasped as the rib was wrenched unceremoniously back into place.

"*Shit*," said Judy, covering her mouth at the sound. "You okay, hon?"

I leaned on the island and nodded, pressing my lips together. The sharpest pain was gone. All that remained was a vague throbbing, like the pulsation in your gums after pulling a tooth.

"Okay," I breathed after a moment. "Okay." I stood and gave my body an experimental twist. My muscles twinged, and I could feel a cold ache running like ice water through the center of the bone, but at least now, I could move. I took my shirt from the chair and shouldered it back on, buttoning it as I spoke.

"All right," I said, breathing deeply. "That wasn't fun." I looked around at Casey's team. They stared at me with calm expressions, examining me carefully. Marcus looked particularly ponderous. I couldn't place the expression on his face, but it seemed to be heavily veiled with interest. The look of a man curious to see how I'd fare.

I swallowed and glanced at Casey, my fingers shaking. I was having trouble keeping myself upright. "What now?"

"Now," said Judy, cracking her knuckles, "we start killing bad guys."

Kent giggled and muttered, "Boom!" under his breath. Marcus rolled his eyes and inhaled his cigar.

"Bad guys," I repeated, electric clouds of fear bubbling up from nowhere under my skin. "Right. And … just how are we going to do that?"

Rowena and Casey exchanged a look. "We hoped you could tell us," she said. The energy she gave off brightened when she spoke. I wondered if she knew she had the capacity to cast spells, and whether she would use them if she did. I doubted it—whatever caused the scars in the first place had likely soured her taste for the arcane.

"Wait, what?" I asked, dragging my attention from her aura to the topic at hand. "Me? Why? I don't know anything," I said, adding hastily, "not *anything*, but I don't know much. I'm a witch, I do forensics, and paperwork, I …"

Realization suddenly dawned on me, cold as iron, the liquid bitterness of dread. If they were asking me what we should do next, it meant there was no one else left to ask! It also meant there was so much more to this puzzle that I didn't know.

"What happened?" I asked quietly. *A breach much like this one,* Casey said. Fire and bullets and brimstone, the full wrath of the dark collective coming down on our heads. My vision blurred. *Oh, Hades, Caressa … Dia …*

Casey opened his mouth, hesitated, and closed it again, his face turning slightly pink. His muted energy, the barest scrapings of magic I'd missed in him before, shone with the telltale yellow of fear, the purple of regret, or maybe pity.

"What. Happened?" I said through my teeth. Casey went stiff and said nothing.

"The ANCs that were not under the control of the Darkness as of yesterday morning were … dealt with,"

Rowena told her coffee. She looked up at me, piercing me with her single dark eye. "Same as yours."

Yep, I thought. I nodded slowly. "And the ones that weren't?"

"Have gone into total lockdown," Rowena said, "citing a mass security breach."

"These ANCs, half o' them are in highly populated areas," Kent continued. "We cannae afford ta risk the lives oove our own people."

"We also can't afford to risk a black operation which could become an inter-parallel incident in which we find ourselves going to war with your people either," said Rowena. She turned to me. "And that's why we're here. To dismantle it all from the inside before it comes to that."

"Shit," I whispered, feeling faint. The first and last lines of magical defense were gone. Eaten away by monsters playing the long game into nothing. Every last hero we had was now dead or lost or locked away.

Leaving me, myself, and a small army of five to save the whole world from an impossible evil, hell-bent on burning the whole planet to the ground. *Wonderful.* My optimism—whatever was left of it—abandoned me, shriveling up like a feather in a fire. What replaced it was something cold, hard, and really angry.

"How long do we have?" I asked. My voice took on a gravelly quality all its own.

Casey shrugged. "President Odyssey told us a month, but now …" He scratched his neck and shook his head. "Now that month might be reduced to no more than days. She'll be feeling a lot of pressure to retake the ANCs by force."

"Lots of superstitious weirdos in the White House," said Kent.

"Lots of *weirdos* in the White House," Judy amended quietly, throwing a dubious side-glance to Kent.

I needed a drink. Not coffee or tea, either. I went to a cabinet and pulled out a tall amber bottle, filling a short glass. It was a wildly expensive scotch Bram had given me once when we were … involved. I'd never been a drinker, not even recreationally, and after we broke up, I didn't even want to look at the damn thing, so it was still full. I resisted the strangely powerful urge to just bottoms-up the whole bottle into my mouth. Instead, I took a long swig from my glass. It burned my throat and scalded my stomach, which felt fan-fucking-tastic.

"What day is it?" I asked, staring at my drink.

"Still Tuesday," said Casey.

I nodded. "Well, to hell with Tuesdays," I said as I looked around. "What's the plan?"

They looked between each other.

"Right," I said, making a face. "That's right. Me. I'm the plan."

"Sorry," Judy said, shrugging. "Dulcie was plan A, I promise."

Which made me the contingency plan. I took a deep breath and sighed loudly, biting into another cookie. "What exactly do you think I can do?"

"You're the last line of reliable contacts in the ANC," Casey said, and then I understood. No ANC, no database, no intel. The organization they were here to dismantle now had total control over the archives, which meant that any information they'd been given already was totally worthless.

All that's left, I thought.

"Start from the beginning," said Marcus, putting out his cigar on a saucer and flicking it lazily into the trash. "Tell us everything you know about the Darkness and those who follow him or it or them, whatever the hell this thing is that we're dealing with."

I sighed. Better start from the beginning, the *real* beginning. "Okay, so … it wasn't a power outage when all the portals went dark." I wondered what the penalty was for lying to the government about a rebellion/war that *you* started. Not that it would matter if Caressa were dead …

Judy snorted. "Yeah, we know."

"Wait … you do?" I couldn't keep the surprise from my voice.

Judy shrugged. "'Course we do. Did you think we wouldn't notice? I mean, it took us a bit to figure it out, but …"

"When we reconnected with our agents in the Netherworld, they told us what happened," Casey explained.

Okay, that about ended all the secrets. Casey had his arms crossed now, and looked every bit the scolding parent. But it didn't seem like any of them were going to give me the "Why didn't you tell us? We could have helped you" speech, so that was good. There would be plenty of time to play the blame game later.

"So …" I cleared my throat and tucked my hair behind my ear. "We, um … deposed Melchior O'Neil." *Deposed.* The word felt so archaic.

Casey nodded.

"Caressa was second in command," I said, "on the professional side. I don't know who Melchior's second was on the potions side of things. And um …" Suddenly, it felt like I knew nothing about the whole ordeal, like I'd skimmed a history book and could barely recall the names of the players, let alone what they did. "We thought we were doing okay. Melchior's people outnumbered us, but they were disorganized." I almost laughed, shaking my head. "Until the Darkness appeared. Whoever the hell that is."

"So you don't know who the Darkness is?" Judy asked, eyeing me narrowly.

"Your guess is as good as mine," I answered honestly. I shot back the rest of the glass and swallowed it hard. I wasn't normally a scotch girl—

Dulcie would have been proud. "Back to what I do know," I started. "Knight brought in this guy, Jax something. I forget his last name. Actually, I'm not even sure I ever knew it. Anyway, Jax's presence at the ANC in Splendor was supposed to be temporary, just long enough to find somewhere more secure to hold him. Turns out, coming to Splendor was Jax's plan all along." I shook my head, still furious with myself as I replayed the particulars. "I should have felt it! I should have been able to *tell* something was there."

"What something?" asked Marcus, shaking his head. "What are you talking about?"

"The anchor," I answered. "Jax had an anchor with him, or maybe he *was* the anchor, I don't know. But that kind of spellbinding glows like fire and messes up the air around it, I should have been able to *see or sense* …"

Casey laid a hand on my shoulder. I cut myself off and shrugged him away, sighing. "Sorry," I said. "The whole point is that Jax served as the anchor for a wormhole. It's what devastated our ANC so bad."

"An' here Ah thought that was all Dulcie," Kent said, and Judy elbowed him in the ribs. He flinched and glared at her.

"Not all of it," I answered. "Half the building got torn away when the wormhole opened up. It left a giant crater in our front yard. I had …" I swallowed as my throat closed and poured myself another shot.

Downing it chased the tangled cobwebs from my chest. I let out a quick breath. "I had witches on site, running tests, trying to find out where the wormhole was going. They're ..." *They're all dead*, I thought. But that didn't matter now.

I cleared my throat. "Knight found Bram—um, a vampire we know."

"Bram?" Casey repeated.

"Yeah, he's a friend of sorts, I guess. A friend of Dulcie's anyway. He's not exactly on the straight and narrow, but Dulcie always relied on him for leads on the bigger, badder guys. Anyway, it turned out Bram had kidnapped Dulcie, but he did so in order to *protect her*." I tried not to spit out the words, but they came out smoking anyway.

"Protect her from what?" Rowena asked.

"From the Darkness, I guess," I answered with a shrug. "Bram, as usual, was trying to play both sides so he could 'maintain the balance' or something like that between the ANC and the potions rings. I don't fucking know." I refilled the glass to the brim and drank. Heavily. "Then something ... *happened*. I don't know what. Bram got discovered, maybe by Jax, maybe the Darkness found out on his own." I shrugged. "The point is that Bram lost control of his people. Jax tried to... drain Bram, I guess, and beat Dulcie within an inch of her life."

I shuddered. The witch from Brokenview hadn't just sent me word that Dulcie was there, she also sent memories. Dulcie's memories and her point-of-view were played in cinematography, filched from Dulcie's mind in the two seconds they had physical contact. It was ugly, to say the very least. Brutal. Unforgiving, which is exactly what Knight would be when he found Jax. Some morbid, angry part of me wanted to watch.

Casey looked like he was about to ask for details, which I had absolutely no intention of giving him. Dulcie was hurt, and that was all he needed to know. I felt vile for telling him even that much. "Jax left Bram with a troll or a goblin or some underling and took Dulcie … somewhere. Brokenview first, but those portals can lead literally anywhere."

"And Jax is working with the Darkness?" asked Marcus.

I nodded. "Yeah. We don't know why the Darkness wants Dulcie, but apparently, he wants her alive. And it isn't for ransom either; it's been too long."

"How long?" asked Judy.

"A little over a week," I said.

"Brokenview?" Casey asked, pulling himself out of a grimace. "That base isn't under our control, any information they gave you—"

"Is perfectly sound," I interrupted. "I knew the witch in high school, and the message came in a daydream—totally secure, extremely difficult to cast. If she weren't worried about being overheard, she'd have *called* me on the phone." I realized I was close to shouting and took a long breath. "Their ANC has been overturned, but they're not with the Darkness." At least, *she* wasn't, but I wasn't about to plant unnecessary doubt. "I mean, they weren't when she reached out to me."

Marcus was nodding, Judy was scowling, and Casey was pushing his glasses up onto his nose. Kent was just standing there. None of them said anything, but they all seemed to be thinking intently.

"Most of the ANCs don't even know they've been overtaken," I said. "And the ones that do are fighting back, just quietly." The burning blue cloud from the ANC filled my vision, and I blinked it away. Half the taken ANCs—which I guess now meant *all* of them—were in the middle of huge cities, some of them close to suburban areas. An internal insurgence, even in service of retaking the base, could have nightmarish consequences.

"Could we contact this witch again?" Judy asked as she faced everyone in the room. She leaned against the counter, twirling a set of keys on her finger. "Maybe she could tell us where Jax and Dulcie went. Or what their superiors have been up to, if they're Darkness cronies."

I shook my head. "I could try, but I don't know that it would matter. Bram said nobody knows *anything* about the Darkness, not even within his own ranks. And Jax and Dulcie probably portal-hopped for hours, so who knows where they are now?"

Judy nodded and hopped up on the counter. "Okay, so, no Brokenview. No witches, no archives, no Darkness. And no way to know where Jax and Dulcie went."

"We're off ta ah great start," muttered Kent.

"Hey, I'm *trying*," I snapped. Kent jumped. Nobody said anything as I got hold of myself.

Breathe, I thought, *just breathe.* Not that I *wasn't*, but a reminder seemed in order. I touched my throat, massaging the skin at my collarbone, and winced as I stretched the long red burns Dulcie had given me.

Then something sparked. "But …" My nerves were frazzled, every single receptor in my body went on high alert, bracing for an attack that wasn't coming. I was touchy, bitchy, but there was also a peculiar clarity that came with it.

"But?" said Casey.

"But there's only a handful of creatures that could have given Dulcie powers like this," I answered.

"Given?" Marcus asked.

"Yeah. She, uh … she can't normally … do … *that*." I couldn't find better words, so I just let them hang stupidly in the air.

"Would they be registered?" Judy asked.

I shook my head. "I wish. The only ones on record are dead gods and demons older than dirt, most of whom are in prison." However, if the ANC really had gone to shit, it stood to reason that *nobody* was in prison anymore. I did a mental tally of everyone

Dulcie and I had put in jail over our illustrious careers and felt sick to my stomach. "If we can find someone who *knows* those circles ..." The demons with fire and sand in their hearts, the monsters with iron eyes and silver claws and memories of a time when the world was empty. The gods of the old world, the ego of the cosmos, manifested. They'd be impartial, and above our petty, mortal conflicts. And if we could find one who was willing to help us ...

I touched the burns on my body, which were steadily scabbing over, turning grey with scar tissue. They were radiating magic, something holy and unclean all at once. The energy of a creature too strong for its own good, a kind of magic that shouldn't exist. It was faint, the heartbeat of a dying animal, too weak to use as a fetish—but enough for someone else.

"They could track Dulcie," I said, dropping my hand. The thought of a demon, even a goddess or an angel, getting close enough to touch me made me sick, but we were out of options. Rowena cocked her head at me, examining the burns with her single dark eye, and she seemed to understand.

"What do ye mean by circles?" said Kent. "What kind o' monsters are we talkin' aboot here?"

I answered simply. "Old gods. Angels too, as well as demons." The deep, apathetic roots of the spirit tree. Powerful, and notoriously full of themselves—likely the result of thousands of years of mortal reverence and fear. Being worshipped will do that to you, I guessed.

"Demons?" said Kent, grimacing. "That's … ambitious."

It's crazy, is what it is, I thought. And it wasn't going to be easy. Demons were less than accommodating, old gods always wanted *something*—sacrifices, virgins, firstborns, et cetera—and angels were nearly impossible to find, if they bothered to walk the Earth at all. The places demons lived were hot, desolate, and inhospitable, while the gods kept to whatever remained of their altars. Angels walked the thin line between life and death, a place that even advanced witchcraft had no hope of breaching, not to mention how taxing it was to try and talk to *any* of these creatures. Gods and demons loved riddles, and angels only spoke to those they deemed "worthy." I could guarantee that none of us qualified.

"It's what we've got," I said as I shook my head against the realization that the only demon I knew was one I'd rather not even consider for the job. "If we can find one willing to … *examine* … this,"—I gestured vaguely to my burns—"it'll be a matter of seconds before we know where Dulcie went."

"And if we find Dulcie," Casey started, warming to the idea.

I nodded. "We find the Darkness, and we end this."

"Provided we can also find an amicable demon, angel, or god willing to talk to us," Judy added.

I winced. "Yeah." That was the part that didn't sit well with me.

Casey shrugged. "Sounds good to me," he said. "Any idea where to start?"

I opened my mouth, ready to say no. "Yeah, actually I do," I said, my surprise obvious in my tone. I felt my face twisting into something like a grimace and I looked sideways at Casey. "But you're not gonna like it."

CHAPTER NINE
Knight

I watched Jax who was trying *really* hard not to look at me.

He was in bad shape. One black eye, a hundred lacerations across his chest and arms, blood fucking everywhere ... he was fully primed to die. Sweaty, sad, and already fading. But it wasn't good enough. Not after what he'd done to Dulcie. Not after the torture he'd put her through, not to mention the humiliation. And now he would pay for it.

He swallowed audibly, his eyes going wide as soon as they met mine. When he finally found his voice, he started to ramble. "I'm sorry," he blurted out, blood and spit spilling out of his mouth. "I, I didn't mean, I don't know what happened to me I just, it just got out of hand—"

I was on him in a second, grabbing him by his shirt and slamming him against the wall, hard enough for his head to leave a shallow crater in the painted plaster.

"Didn't *mean* to?" I seethed, my mouth right next to his ear, His throat pulsated under my hand, his thrumming heart practically *daring* me to tear it out. I squeezed until his face turned red, then purple, then black, and he scrabbled at me helplessly, his fingers tearing the skin of my knuckles, breaking it open in spots, but I didn't care. Red seeped out from beneath my nails, turning my hands pink.

Jax's mouth opened and I felt his throat vibrate, but no sound came out. His mouth moved, so maybe he was speaking, but I didn't hear a goddamn word. I dragged him forward and threw him with all my strength at the window—the glass shattered, caving in on itself, but it held long enough for Jax to be grazed by the iron-hot security strands. He hit the floor hard, screaming. The smell of burning flesh filled the room, and steam rose from his arms as the thin, red lacerations appeared on his face.

"What's the matter, Jax?" I asked, stepping forward. I kicked him hard in the face and heard his nose snap. As he clutched it, wailing pitifully, blood gushed onto the floor. I knelt down and grabbed his hair, pulling his head back until he was staring at the ceiling.

"Are you *scared*?" I whispered. "Scared like Dulcie must have been?"

Jax whined, his shoulders shaking with tears I didn't know he possessed. *No,* I thought, *Dulcie was stronger than him.* For half a second, all I felt was pity. This hulk of a man, this monster, crying at my feet, a natural disaster pleading for his life. It was pathetic.

Then he finally said something I could hear. "She …" he coughed, spitting blood into my face, "she *deserved it.*"

With my fist tightening on his hair, my other hand moved of its own accord, darting up from my side like a snake and punching him right in the side of his skull. Jax screamed as he fell backwards, his head smacking against the wall. He moaned a desperate, wordless, inhuman cry of anguish, and all he could manage to say was, "Please, please, please, please …"

"Please?" I asked incredulously. "*Please*? Are you fucking kidding?"

I threw him aside and sat back, panting. He curled into the wall, hugging his knees. I scoffed and kicked him in the back, hard enough to push him into the opposite wall. He curled up tighter, and as he dropped, I saw a big, red splotch under the window. I grabbed him by the hair and slammed his face into the floor, making his skull rattle. His shoulders shook and his breath rasped. There was blood in his throat, turning his words to a gravelly croak. "You don't *get* to beg, do you fucking understand me?"

Apparently, he didn't. "Please …" he moaned, "Please … just … please …" His words were tight and soft, brimming with fear.

And something stopped me. Some line in my body went taut like a leash, pulling me backwards. *No,* I thought, staring at Jax's bloody body. Imagining his hands on Dulcie, tearing her clothes away, dropping her, broken, in front of a blood-starved Bram … *No!*

I couldn't understand it. *I should kill him*, I thought, *I should blind him and rip out his tongue, I should gut him with his own fucking teeth.*

No.

The word resounded through my brain like a struck bell, deep and brassy, heavy, halfway muffled. It lingered there a moment, then faded like an echo, leaving behind a feeling of profound weariness. I was confused enough to be silent and still for three seconds.

At the fourth second, the word came again. This time, it had friends.

No, it said, *you ... should ... not.*

"I ..." I stretched my fingers and clenched my fist, exhaling sharply. A feeling overcame me, a casual coldness, a lethargy that made my hands feel numb. I shook it away and glanced over at Jax when I realized what was going on.

It was telling that he was using Loki telepathy to communicate, but I supposed it made sense when I took in his jaw, which was shattered, the bones pressing against the underside of his skin in all the wrong places. I stood, cracking my knuckles, looming over him like a giant, a mountain, a dragon, and still seething. *Just lie down and fucking die!*

Not ...

"Shut up," I said, driving my heel into his back.

Jax. Not ...

I stopped. *Not Jax.*

The voice lumbered out of the darkness, a weathered presence trying desperately to stay awake. It smacked its lips and yawned at me. *So if you aren't Jax, who the fuck **are** you?* I thought in reply. It was still nothing but a shadow in the corner of the room, a moving shadow, stretching and pulling back again, taking the shape of something.

Meg? I wondered.

The voice chuckled. The laugh sounded amused, like I was so far off—not even in the same zip code far off.

Who are you? I thought. Jax was trying to get on his hands and knees. At first, I assumed he wanted to put up a fight after all, but when he finally did it, all he could do was vomit and fall back down again. My pity came rushing back in.

Fucking pathetic, I thought.

Yes ... he ... is ... isn't he?

And yet I shouldn't kill him? I argued with the shadow's voice.

The presence murmured to itself, and I imagined it shrugging. It was taking a more definitive shape now, the dull reverberations hardening into a recognizable register—a masculine voice, deep, thunderous, and ancient. *Perhaps ... you should*, he said. *But ... not ... now.*

Jax moaned and coughed, broken, and for one sick moment, all I had for him was empathy. *Stop it!* I thought, *stop making me feel that!*

The feeling vanished, leaving me just as hot and hollow as before. The voice sighed mournfully. *My ... **justice** ... is not ... yours ... to ... dispense. The Loki's ... hour ... will ... come.*

I frowned. *Your justice?*

The voice took a deep breath. *Mine.*

Yours? And who the fuck are you?

He chuckled. *An ... old friend ... old, very ... very old ...*

I don't know you, I said, glaring at the shadow as it meandered this way and that. I had to wonder if I were losing my mind and seeing things that weren't actually there.

You ... don't know ... your own ... maker?

My blood ran cold before confusion overtook me. *My own maker? I didn't have a maker. Unless ...*

No, that was impossible, that was *fucking* impossible. *Hades doesn't exist,* I thought back to whatever creature was trying to impersonate a god. *Hades is just a legend.*

Is that so? the voice demanded, angry and offended. *Explain ... yourself ... then. Your ... world ...*

You don't exist, I thought more fervently. Hades was a dream, a heroic story, the fire and brimstone of a civilization long ago. *You're not real.* Far more likely, he was a hallucination, courtesy of Meg, and caused by my lack of sleep, lack of food, and the fact that I died and came back to life. *Get out of my head!*

This ... is what ... she wants. Kill ... him ... and you ... play ... right ... into ... her ... hands.

Jax was staring at me now, confused by my silence. He dared to look hopeful—or maybe he was sneering, it was hard to tell through all the blood on his ugly face. I took a step toward him and he cowered again, shaking like a fucking leaf.

Let ... him ... go, the shadow said. *His ... end ... will ... be ... appropriate ... to ... his ... deeds. But it is ...* he took a deep breath, *not ... your ... responsibility ... to bring ... about.*

Across the room, Jax laughed weakly. "What's the matter?" he smirked through red-streaked teeth. "Getting squeamish?"

Jax didn't have to be bleeding. It was enough to look at him to make me squeamish. I opened my mouth to tell him so, but my tongue turned to lead, dropping like a dead weight in the center of my mouth. I couldn't speak. Or even make a sound.

You've got to be fucking kidding me, I thought, turning away from Jax and back toward the shadow that purported to be my maker.

Leave him ... be.

You don't get to fucking decide this, I replied mentally, storming back toward Jax, imagining his ribs splintering and digging into his organs. Jax flinched and glared up at me.

"Make up your fucking mind," he said.

The voice sighed. ***I will not tell you again!*** It railed at me with the fury of one who had no patience or appreciation for being disobeyed. Well, he picked the wrong Loki to order around. As much as he disliked insubordination, I'd never been one to follow anyone's rules.

I didn't even feel myself move, but in the next second, I had Jax pinned against the wall, my hand at his throat, my fingers digging into his flesh, tracing the outline of his esophagus. "This is for Dulcie," I seethed, pulling him forward and slamming him back into the wall so hard that the plaster broke and the security wards beneath it pressed into his back, scarring him with a steaming, crosshatched brand. HIs face turned blue. My knuckles went white, and my bones nearly broke through the skin before I let go.

He dropped like a sack of flour, coughing red blood into his hands. "Always … knew you were … weak."

"Shut up," I said, resisting the urge to kick him again. Instead, I turned around, clenching my fists, trying to keep myself from pulling out my own hair. *Stuck between a rock and something with really sharp teeth and laser eyes. Fuck!*

I let the anger leach out of me as I gasped. "Meg!" I shouted. Striding to the door, I pounded on it, and the heat of the wards made the wood tremble. "*Meg, get your ass in here!*"

Ten seconds passed before I heard footsteps and whispering. The door opened without a sound, and suddenly, Meg's slight, white figure was standing before me, smiling. One hand was against the wall, the other resting softly on her hip, a carefully calculated pose. Antoine stood behind her, frowning passively in his pointed slippers.

"Finished already?" she asked, raising a brow. Her smile curdled.

"Just get him out of here," I said, half wondering if my delirious mind would start up again, proclaiming it was Hades, himself.

Meg gave me a once-over, observing the thin sheen of blood on my skin, along with the dark purple splotches on my clothes. "Did you at least have fun?"

"Fuck you."

She seemed amused by that. "Antoine," she said, while staring at me, "if you would."

Her manservant pushed past me, hefting the choking Jax into his arms. For a moment, I thought I'd crushed his windpipe—but as he was carried past me, he had enough breath to tell me to *go fuck myself.*

Meg made a show of waiting until Antoine was well out of earshot. "I must admit, I'm rather confused." She pricked her lip with a fang and put her finger to the blood, rubbing it between her thumb and forefinger. "I thought you'd ... enjoy his company." She glanced at the blood stains in the corner of the room. "I thought you'd make more of it than you actually did."

"Not in the mood," I seethed, standing stock-still in the center of the room and staring at her lips and the blood now smeared across her chin. It looked like a wine stain against her flawless porcelain skin …

"Oh?" Meg replied, crossing her arms and leaning against the doorframe, a cheeky grin on her face. Like she was daring me to try and get past her. "I wasn't aware vengeance needed a particular mood to express it."

I felt my eyes drifting to the blood again and looked at the wall instead. "Yeah, well. You learn something new every day."

"Hmm." She kicked herself off the frame and sauntered towards me with long, deliberate steps. Her hips swayed, encased in her tight, black pants, guiding me to her stomach, the slightest suggestion of her breasts beneath her billowing blouse … I shook my head, getting angry with myself that I was even aware of her body. I shouldn't have been. It made no sense that I was. Not after all the hatred I harbored for her.

"What's the matter?" she asked. She was right in front of me now, staring at me with eyes of liquid black, like the night, distilled into nefarious shadows. I stared right back at her, at those deep pools of black ink.

"Um …" I answered stupidly. She smelled like cinnamon, rust, fire, and motor oil.

"I have another gift for you," she said, running a finger down my chest, lingering in spots of Jax's blood and drawing circles in it. "I hope you like this one better." Spreading her hand flat against me, she turned back to the door, softly calling, "Dulcie."

My heart stopped, and she heard it, grinning. For another moment, the door was empty, and I stared blankly out at the cold hallway. I briefly thought Meg was fucking with me.

And then …

Dulcie. She was standing tall even though she was small. At first, she was hesitant, and her eyes were downcast as she entered the room.

"Yes, Mother?" she asked as she faced Meg.

I felt like I'd been sucker-punched in the gut. *Mother? Fucking hell, what did she do to you?* Everything about her was wrong. Her hair was curled, her eyes were the wrong shade of green, her wings weren't out of her control, and she wasn't telling anyone to go fuck themselves … She also wasn't staring at Meg, or at me, in the face, or demanding to know what was going on. She was quiet, polite, docile. *Broken.* I stared at her, the long, blond hair, the lithe, pale frame in that stupid, fucking dress …

"Dulcie," said Meg. "You remember Knight, don't you, Princess?"

"Knight," Dulcie echoed, with an unchanged expression as she glanced up at me. "I do." Her eyes narrowed. "He murdered Father. Didn't he?"

Meg allowed her smile to turn somber. "Yes, my darling. He did." She turned back to me, toying with my shirt. Dragging her nail down the sleeves, she ripped them off, casually shredding it to ribbons until I was shirtless. My chest was still coated in sweat and blood.

Why aren't I stopping her? I thought to myself, panic overtaking me. *Why aren't I pushing her away, or even trying to fight her?*

My hand moved on its own, landing on her shoulder and squeezing the frozen flesh beneath. She touched it gently.

"Sebastian, do you enjoy him?" Meg asked Dulcie from over her shoulder. Meg's eyes never left mine, and that odd smile continued to dance over her mouth.

Dulcie nodded, but she appeared confused. "I guess." Turning to the side, she suddenly whispered something angrily. "*Stop it! Stop it! Stop!*"

"What was that?" Meg asked as she frowned and moved her gaze back to Dulcie. Now was my chance to throw her eyes away from me, but I didn't. I just continued to stand there, immobilized. As if I were suddenly paralyzed.

"What does he lack, my dear?" Meg turned back and looked at me directly, as if in heated anticipation for Dulcie's response.

"Technique," Dulcie answered, and I felt a twinge of raw jealousy combined with doleful pain that nearly splintered me.

Meg nodded. "We can remedy that." She turned to look at me, but my eyes were fastened on Dulcie. I was seeking the slightest glimmer of hope, some trace that could prove the real Dulcie was still inside there somewhere, and that this witch hadn't completely conquered her soul.

Meg gripped me by the head and stared straight into my eyes. Her irises shifted, turning gold, grey, and silver until they finally faded back to abysmal black. And I just melted. Immediately, I felt my bones turning to fire and my lungs frosting over, every part of me was instantly and ravenously hungry for …

For her. With a hazy realization, the barest scrapings of consciousness in a bad dream, I tried to step back, but my body refused to move. My feet weren't obeying me, they couldn't run and I couldn't scream or do *anything* that might have gotten me away from her before …

Meg pressed her lips onto my throat. A hot stream of blood spurted between her teeth as she nipped my skin, tasting it, testing me. I reached up to touch the blood, grabbing her by the hair and wrenching her head back, using everything I had to drag her off me—

But I released my hand a second or so later. She was so soft, so shiny, so perfectly black … I caressed her. I ran my fingers through her hair, I smelled it. I kissed the top of her head, and I dragged her up to kiss her cheek, her lips, and her throat.

What the fuck am I doing! I railed at myself. But I couldn't stop. I wasn't directing my own body and there was nothing I could do to resist Meg's obscene glamour—it was a power I'd never witnessed in another creature before.

Meg pulled back, gasping. "Take notes, darling," she said to Dulcie. "Sebastian is going to need them."

"N ... no!" I protested, barely loud enough for me to hear. Meg looked at me, biting her lip, and blinking slowly. She ran her nails down the side of my face, drawing more blood, and leaned in to lap it up like a fucking dog.

Don't let her do this, I thought, but that part of me was quickly morphing into another voice, a different person, someone who couldn't possibly understand how *good* this actually felt ...

Dulcie's head tilted left and she squinted, almost like she was trying to close her eyes but couldn't quite do it. Tears streamed down her cheeks, but her expression couldn't explain them. Her face was curious, but her eyes were broken and empty, if that were possible.

"I won't be your fucking puppet," I spat out at Meg in a scathing tone. While trying to drag myself away from her influence, I could barely manage a whisper. More like a whine, the numbed moanings of a ghost: wordless and desperate.

Meg laughed as she pushed me onto the bed, in a long and haunting sound. "You already *are*."

CHAPTER TEN
Sam

For the record, I didn't like relying on a demon either.

"His name is Dagan, and you'll probably want to shoot him," I said. "I can't stress enough how important it is that you *don't*." Demons didn't like being shot, especially by humans.

"Okay," Casey said slowly. "What exactly are we in for?"

We stood in the back parking lot of a squat, black building with a single neon red sign over its door that read: *Pain*. The "Painful Pleasure Park," as its owner liked to call it, was sandwiched between an empty lot full of thrumming cicadas and another empty lot covered in busted concrete.

"A sadistic, narcissistic, and outrageously unhelpful demon with an ego the size of Texas," I said. Dagan made Bram look like a *saint*. "Tread carefully. He *really* likes hurting people. It's … kind of his thing."

"He hurts you and he's dead," Casey said with authority as he stared at me, his expression warning me not to argue with him. Not that I intended to. Not at all! My heart was in the midst of releasing butterflies and rainbows and I struggled to keep the smile off my lips. There was something about a protective man.

"He won't hurt me," I said, although I didn't fully believe my own words. "Dulcie and I have worked with Dagan a few times in the past. He knows it's best to keep on my good side so I don't bust his ass for whatever goes on behind those closed doors."

"He's not stupid. He must realize the ANC is in trouble," Casey pointed out.

Yeah, good point, but I reserved comment and just shrugged. I faced the bigger problem. "The other thing is that I should … probably go in alone."

"Alone?" Casey barked at me. "There's no way!" His expression told me he thought it was a stupid idea, end of story.

"It's going to be hard enough to get Dagan to talk to me," I started. "But if I've got a crew of human agents with me, he's going to laugh in all of our faces." Not pretty, but it was the truth. "I'm less than convinced that he'll be willing to help me as it is." Demons weren't exactly forthcoming in general as a species. And this one, in particular, *loved* beating around the bush and speaking in riddles.

I thought there might be an innuendo in there somewhere, but decided it was probably best not to worry about it.

"I don't want you going in alone," Casey insisted.

"I'll go with you." Rowena stepped forward, her arms crossed, the magic in her skin making her restless. She was fighting the urge to tap her foot, drumming her fingers against her arm. Still as stone, tidal waves of energy were pulsing inside of her, begging her to be reckless.

"Okay," I said. She could handle herself. Yeah, Dagan was a demon, but Rowena was a hell of a lot scarier. Whatever she was.

"Be careful," said Casey, frowning at both of us, but looking relieved that I wasn't going in alone. "Don't be a hero."

I snorted. It was a bit late to try to be anything else. Casey scowled at me and I waved him off.

"We'll be careful," I said. "Promise."

Rowena and I stepped up to the illustrious side door, an average-looking thing of red metal with a neon sign blinking benignly above it. I focused on its incessant buzz, inhaling until my lungs began to hurt. I was a hundred yards out of my element. Interrogation was always Dulcie's game, never mine. My time in the field was limited, almost nonexistent. My work involved books, spell theory and arcana craft, magic and chemistry. Not this. Not guns and demons and sex clubs in the middle of the freaking night.

But Dulcie wasn't here and I was. And like it or not, I had to interview a demon.

This is going to go sideways fast, I thought as I shouldered the door open.

Pain wasn't a very pretty place. Plush black carpet, which must have been new because it lacked the stains of the trade, and there were brand new leather benches in front of every door. Two on either side were ready for a busy night, when Dagan's patrons would patiently have to wait their turn. The walls were a deep, unsettling red, the kind that turns orange if you blink too much, and adorned with detailed charcoal renderings of naked people doing some Grade-A nasties. All of them were women, arching their backs, eyes half-closed, mouths gaping open, bleeding from one wound or other, bruised and squished and bitten. One of them had sharp, metal clamps attached to her nipples and her, um …

Four black marble doors, two on either side of the hallway, led to various "pleasure chambers" that were well supplied with unpleasant toys. Moans and raucous laughter escaped from beneath them, muffled and clear all at once, not to mention the screaming, so much *screaming*. But I guessed that was the point of this torture palace.

Dagan's office was located at the end of the hallway, a door just as black and unforgiving as the rest of them—but this one was slightly ajar. The sounds coming from within were more than a little disturbing. Moans, sure, but so *many* of them, a hive mind with a thousand mouths groaning. And a metallic clinking, something that sounded like chains. And *definitely* turned out to be chains.

Rowena and I looked at each other and I shrugged. She stepped forward and pushed open the door with one hand, peering inside. She didn't appear nervous, not in the least. I wished I could say the same for myself.

Then she stiffened. "Oh," she said. "That's interesting." She looked back at me with a dubious expression. "After you?"

She pushed the door all the way open and we stepped inside. I nearly collapsed, my face turning into a grimace as I examined the shadows writhing on the ground. "Interesting" wasn't the word I would have chosen for what was going on in front of us.

What did we have here? Dagan, naked, in a pile of other people, who were also all naked. Stiff dicks and flopping boobs and lots of blood and gags as well as a plethora of other unnamable toys, the room fairly vibrated with their moans. They made the ground, as well as each other, tremble, like the building itself were achieving an orgasm.

"Um …" I cleared my throat, still trying to comprehend that I was standing there, in Dagan's club, and watching him have sex with a lot of people at once. "Dagan?"

Dagan's head appeared from under the legs of a dark-skinned shapeshifter. His tongue lolling, he was smiling with the drunken euphoria of an addict savoring his last fix. The woman glared at me.

"Samantha," he said, visibly surprised but not exactly displeased to see me. "I hadn't thought I'd see you again."

Dagan had dark hair and his skin was pale as the dead. He was ripped to high hell, fire and brimstone flowing through his veins like hot water, along with an excess of whatever chemical makes you insatiably horny. He was a direct source of the crooked, dealing mostly in pain and sex. None of his actions were inherently illegal, but his establishment attracted a less than reputable crowd. Bad guys came through here all the time seeking angry, cathartic sex. When Dagan felt charitable, he told us where they were, and what they were up to, and which dominatrixes they preferred. His smile was disarming in a rather sociopathic, I-promise-I'm-not-going-to-kill-you sort of way. He had the look of a man who always kept a gun in his pocket and a dick as hard as frozen lead. He was a piece of work, to say the very least, but also useful. Sometimes.

However, he was utterly incapable of controlling himself. "Care to join us?" he asked, his tongue snaking out over his lips. I wanted to bend over and hurl right there.

"Absolutely not," I said, my mouth dropping open with disgust at the very thought.

"Pity," he said with little interest. "What about your friend?"

Rowena didn't dignify him with a response. The air turned thin as the magic in her skin crackled and burnt. Maybe her body was requesting permission to turn Dagan into a pile of smoking bones. She took a deep breath and grew calm a moment later.

"We need your help," I said to Dagan, trying to sound wearily irritable. Dulcie always said that's what worked best with him—being as bitchy as possible, especially if you were asking for a favor. My voice trembled under my tongue, which I hoped to hell sounded like thinly veiled rage.

"Ah," Dagan said, gyrating against the backside of a young elf. "This is about your demolished workplace, I assume?"

Well, yeah. I guessed it was probably all over the news by now, but it still unnerved me that he knew. "It's mostly about Dulcie," I managed, looking at the wall. Red wooden panels were hung with pictures and permits, along with Dagan's favorite "marital aids": iron clamps, vibrators, ball gags, and *knives*, some of which still had the last victims' blood on them…

"Dulcie? Very well," Dagan responded, sinking his teeth into the shapeshifter's leg. "Though I'm not sure how you think I can help you. I may be many things, but a necromancer isn't one of them." Dagan dragged his tongue across the shapeshifter's wound, lapping up the blood like a thirsty dog—and in a manner of speaking, he was. I tried not to gag.

"Dulcie isn't dead," I said.

Blood leaked out around Dagan's lips, pouring down onto the woman's skin in thick, black tendrils. She moaned. So did everybody else, but presumably for different reasons. Hopefully, they hadn't melded their minds for this—a shared consciousness would increase their ... ugh, *ecstasy*, for lack of a less disgusting word, tenfold, but it would also entangle their memories. The longer they stayed under, the harder it would become to disentangle themselves. Physically and mentally, but mostly physically, they tied themselves together with chains and ropes as well as something that looked like strawberry licorice. The ligations were at their ankles, their wrists, their throats, and their *testicles* ...

"Sam," Rowena whispered, and I realized I was gawking before I swallowed and coughed.

"Dulcie is missing and I need you to help me find her," I announced.

"How would I manage that?" he demanded, a smile appearing out of nowhere. "And, moreover, why the hell would I want to? Dulcie going missing makes my life infinitely easier. What a breath of fresh air it would be not to have her poking her little nose in here whenever she damn well pleases."

It took a solid ten seconds for me to suppress the urge to set him on fire. When it passed, I pushed my hair back, exposing the silvery-red burns. The magic they radiated was dull, like the glow of a candle through tempered glass, but Dagan could sense it. He quirked an eyebrow at it and for a moment said nothing before he thrust his tongue into someone I couldn't see.

"This is the answer to how you're going to find her?" I snapped. "As to your reasons why you don't want to—please spare me; I'm not interested."

He frowned. "Not Dulcie's typical fingerprint, is it?" He pulled back from his partner, or was it a victim? I didn't know what to call her, but he pulled back just long enough to look at me with visible derision. Someone draped her legs over his neck and tried to drag him under the twisting mass of flesh and sweat again. He bit hard into her calf and she withdrew.

"No. Dulcie is currently under the management of someone or something else," I said, unsure of how much I could admit to Dagan. Maybe I'd already told him too much. "Regardless, I need to find her."

"And why would you want to do that? I was under the impression she was trying to kill you."

"How did you know that?" I demanded, eyeing him warily.

He chuckled at me. "How would I not know that, Sam?" he demanded. "The whole city seems to be on fire, and Dulcie is rather well known around here. You know what they say about bad news."

"It travels fast," Rowena responded, just in case I didn't know what they said about bad news.

"Madam White?" Dagan asked, pulling my attention back to him, albeit uncomfortably.

"What?" I replied before I realized Dagan was addressing my boobs. I crossed my arms and snapped my fingers, and a shock of blue lightning struck him from behind. It traveled straight through him and into his naked friends before they all moaned in chorus.

"Ooh," he said, eyes narrowing. "Do that again!"

Can't say I wasn't tempted, but we didn't have time for fun. "Dagan, I need your help," I insisted. "Help me find Dulcie."

Dagan's mouth curved up. His friends looked at me, reaching toward me with hands and claws and pincers. "If you would just come a *touch* closer …" He raked me up and down with eyes of molten red, rubies glowing with unmasked desire. My skin tingled and turned warm, the vague sensation of an unholy creature offering a suspicious bargain.

Unfortunately, I had to do Dagan's bidding. The only way he would be able to locate Dulcie was by touching the magical print she left on me—the red scars that still burned my skin. I took a step toward him and he touched me, but not where he was supposed to—not on Dulcie's mark. Instead, he touched the inside of my wrist and I was suddenly overcome with a bolt of lightning that ricocheted through me, leaving a streak of blistering pain in its wake.

I pulled away from him instantly, gnashing my teeth as I caught his smug smirk, which only fueled my anger all the more.

No more Ms. Nice Witch.

I didn't even have to move. I just looked at him and commanded my power. In response, Dagan erupted into brilliant blue flames, colder than a glacier, obscuring his chest and face, drawing the stone-black blood of his kind. His naked friends scattered and moaned, half of them rolling away, the other half dragging themselves closer to the burning Dagan. Some were begging to share his fire, shrieking with pleasure as their skin melted, blackened and froze. Rowena took a cautious step back, but she didn't seem especially perturbed.

I let the combustion die after twenty full seconds of blood-curdling screams. It was the most satisfying sound I'd ever heard. A part of me was worried by that. The other part was having a lot of fun setting Dagan on fire.

The blaze died, the smoke cleared, and Dagan sat before me, a smoldering wreck. His skin had gone grey, fire-forged muscles tightened with burning ice. The cold surrounded him, pressing against him like a strangling hand, squeezing, and slowly letting go. His breath frosted in the air.

There was a long, tense silence. The only sound was Dagan's breathing, ragged and, of all things, terrified, but still, he hesitated.

"The ANC is gone," I said as I crossed my arms against my chest and tapped my toes. "Dulcie is missing. And I *don't. Have. Time. For. This.*"

"No ANC?" Dagan whistled before he smiled broadly. "What on earth will become of me, then, when I refuse to help you?"

"I'll cut your dick off and fry the pleasure centers in your brain," I threatened. I didn't realize how brilliant my response was until I saw the blood drain from Dagan's face.

All right, castration it is, I thought.

Dagan smiled, trying his damnedest not to look concerned. I narrowed my eyes and imagined his little friend bulging, pulsating, before starting to burn. He twitched under my gaze, fighting the urge to writhe—part of him was enjoying it, but another part of his carnal brain knew the pain meant I had him where I wanted him. I could have given him the clap if I really wanted to, using only a lock of his hair and a drop of his blood. And there were plenty of both in this godforsaken place.

"Find Dulcie," I said. "*Now.*"

"Of course." Dagan stood slowly, deliberately, fondling his friends as he stood up just to act like my threats didn't concern him *that* much. But I knew better.

"Be quick," I said, and he nodded. He was shaking. I'd never seen him so scared before. It was deliciously satisfying on some primitive, angry level, but mostly just weird. I almost felt like telling him that's what he got when he messed with witches who were out of time.

He laid his hand on a patch of my scarred skin and closed his eyes. My skin turned cold, then hot, then cold again as he siphoned the last of the magic out of me, filling his eyes with it, and casting out his awareness into the world like a lure. I saw everything he did—the light and silver shadows that bound the world together, the webs of dimensions that linked the Netherworld to the Earth like a baby to its mother. The footprints of powerful magic pressed into the ground.

He didn't have to say anything. When he found her, I knew.

Dagan pulled his hand back slowly, running his fingers through my hair as he did. If he were anyone else, the gesture might have been tender—but it was Dagan, so it just felt dirty.

"Satisfied?" he asked.

I couldn't help myself. "With you? Never."

Dagan twitched at hearing that, but his sleazy grin didn't falter. "We'll be here for a while," he said softly. "If you decide to return."

"When hell freezes over," I answered.

I made some disgusted noise in the back of my throat and stalked out the door. Rowena followed, closing the door behind us. I could already hear the grunts and moans and shrieks of the resuming orgy, daring to be as loud and obnoxious as possible.

"You sure you don't want to kill him?" Rowena asked with a little shrug.

I stopped walking. She said it with all the calm of a friend asking where I'd like to go for breakfast, or what my favorite color was. I shot her a "what the hell is wrong with you?" look, and she just blinked at me, totally chill with the idea of an impromptu, why-the-fuck-not? murder.

"You ... you're *in* the FBI, aren't you?" I asked slowly. Not that I was entertaining the idea of killing Dagan (no more than I usually did).

Rowena shrugged. "Sometimes." The magic in her skin trembled, condensed, and coalesced into a glowing, green sheen in the back of her eye. Her expression didn't change, but something inside her pulled back, her shields dropping to expose what lay beneath—the burning heart of chaotic good, the lawmaker with a hundred broken bones, maybe a little too willing to cross the line. In the twisting fires, I could almost see the creature that burnt her, a towering skeleton of ivory and black, bleeding from everywhere. It was a rather disturbing sight.

"We've got time," she said, shrugging.

"Um ... I think I'm okay," I said, all the while wondering what the hell she was. "Maybe later."

Rowena's magic dulled and her gates closed as the visions abated before she nodded as though nothing had happened. "Okay. Just let me know if you change your mind. The world would be a better place with one less demon in it."

"Uh-huh," I answered, swallowing hard.

###

Casey and company were waiting for us in the lot, leaning against the hood of Casey's stark black SUV and doing their best to appear impatient. They were the pinnacle of ragtag spies, half-lit by Dagan's cheap neon sign. The only thing to break the illusion was Kent, sitting cross-legged on top of the car, carving a tiny stick into a spear with a switchblade. The car was what really cemented the cliché, but I didn't care to point that out.

"What happened in there?" Casey asked, walking up to me as soon as he saw us. There was a twitchy energy about him, like he was a coffee cup away from bursting into flames. Poor guy was pale as snow. I figured he must've heard the screaming.

"An orgy," I said. "It's over now."

Casey looked me up and down, grimacing, color flooding his cheeks. "Oh. Um … did you—"

I made a vague, revolted grunt, cutting him off. "No!" I said, the mere thought of it making me gag. "I can't believe you would even ask me that!"

Kent giggled from his perch on the car. "So, ah. How'd it go?"

Marcus blew smoke and smiled. "The interrogation or the orgy?"

"The interrogation," Kent answered in his thick, Scottish brogue. "Ah can guess how the orgy went." He chuckled.

Casey groaned, pinching his nose. "What happened?" he asked me.

Rowena shrugged. "Well, no one's dead." Maybe it was my imagination, but she almost sounded disappointed.

"Dagan found Dulcie," I said. "She's in the Netherworld." That sucked because it meant my magic—along with Rowena's and Casey's, now that I thought about it—wouldn't work when we met the big, bad Darkness. It also meant Dulcie couldn't blast us into fiery oblivion, so, you know, pros and cons to every situation.

Marcus quirked his brow, taking a long drag from a fresh cigar. "Netherworld. Unpleasant place," he said, as though I didn't already know.

"Yeah," I responded, thinking of all the unfriendly monsters Melchior bred to convince the Netherworldians they needed his protection—monsters that were most likely enjoying an absurd amount of freedom with the fall of the ANC. My stomach twisted. Hades, it probably looked like a war zone over there. "No kidding."

"Okaaay," Judy said, crossing her arms. She was wearing yoga pants and a blue tank top, and for a fraction of a second, looking a hell of a lot like Dulcie. "So, how we planning on getting there?"

"We could dig our way," Kent offered, squinting at his stick.

"Or," Judy said, "we could go the old-fashioned way."

"Are you perhaps referring to one of the many ANC portals that no longer exist?" Marcus asked, smirking in his own shadows.

"Well, no," said Judy as she grinned.

Casey frowned. "Judy, *no*."

"I know, it's the *worst* plan, but—"

"Absolutely fucking *not*," Casey said.

"I'm sorry, Casey, but do you have a better idea?"

"Judy …"

"Come on, all we have to do is ask *nicely*. You can do that, can't you?"

I stepped between them, confused as to what the hell was going on. "What are we talking about, exactly?"

"*Not* something we're going to do," Casey said, looking over me at Judy.

Judy looked past me, smiling smugly at Casey. She crossed her arms. "I'm calling her."

"No, you're *not*."

Judy pulled out her phone. "Watch me." She dialed and put it to her ear.

I turned to Casey. "Who's she calling?"

Casey pushed his lips together and closed his eyes, exhaling long and loud through his nose.

Someone answered Judy with a high-pitched hello.

"Margaret? Hi!" Judy said, barely keeping her laughter to herself. "It's Judy! I know, it's been a while. Listen, can you do us a *huge* favor?"

"Casey?" I asked as I turned to the person in question, wondering what the hell was going on. "Who's Margaret?"

He opened his eyes and groaned. "My mother."

CHAPTER ELEVEN
Dulcie

Don't look, the voice inside my head insisted. The source of the voice wasn't a wayward sprite who'd crawled into my ear either. After multiple magical attempts to clear the sprite from my mind, I had to face the fact that the voice wasn't anything palpable that I could forcibly remove. I had no explanation for why it was there or who it belonged to. It just was. And at this moment, witnessing Mother having sex with the man who killed Father, the voice inside my head was terrified. *Don't you **fucking** look!*

But I had to. I couldn't look anywhere else or pry my eyes away from them. Mother was on top of him, moving back and forth, her body rippling. His clothing was in shreds on the floor, torn and soaked in fresh blood. His hands scrabbled over her slick, cold body, a drunken rock climber trying to find purchase on the face of a sheer, marble cliff. The bed held fast beneath them, metal and wood straining against Mother's desperate energy. The man looked up and sideways, then at the ceiling, or the covers, or the wall, or the window, anywhere but at her. He trembled and tensed with her movement, begging her to continue, but his eyes were hollow, deep pools of liquid black.

They shouldn't be black! the voice railed. *They're blue, Knight's eyes are blue! What the hell is she doing to him?*

Having sex, I thought irritably, now fully aware that I had a stubborn tenant inside my head who wouldn't move out and, apparently, there was nothing I could do about it.

As I watched them, a sinking feeling rose within my stomach, making me feel as if I might retch up my last meal right there on the floor. But I didn't. Instead, I pondered what Mother had been talking about when she said this idiot could teach Sebastian a thing or two. As far as I could tell, this man was fighting Mother at every turn. She seemed to be enjoying it, but it appeared so chaotic to me. He pushed himself into her with a petrified look on his face, like rigor mortis, the expression of an animal dead from fear. Even Mother had more urgency to her movements than he did.

Stop them!

"Shut up," I whispered as I clenched my eyes shut and shook my head.

"Are you watching, Dulcie?" Mother demanded, her voice hoarse and thick with desire.

"Yes, Mother," I said, blinking my eyes back open. The words came out as croaks. I cleared my throat and said louder, "Yes. I'm watching." I cleared my throat again. "I don't understand what you think this man could teach Sebastian."

"It is all about passion," she answered. "Tell Sebastian to be more deliberate. Like this." She pulled herself back and slowly drew herself across the man, moaning, arching her back violently.

"Ah," I said. "All right." I couldn't imagine Sebastian doing that correctly, but it was worth a shot.

The hell it is! the voice yelled back at me, nearly in tears. *Stop him! Stop her! Fucking **kill her**!*

No!

*You fucking **bitch**, don't you remember anything? Don't you remember who you are? Or who Knight is?*

My head pulsated and throbbed as an image materialized in my mind: me and this man, this murderous stranger, tangled up together between stark white sheets.

*Remember **that**?*

I fell back a step, horrified. Why would I have ever had sex with *him*, the man who *killed* Melchior?

Melchior. No, not Melchior, my *father*.

Knight didn't kill him, the voice replied. *Knight wasn't even in the fucking **room**!*

Shut up, shut up and pay attention, I thought, squeezing my eyes shut, opening them when I started to see spots behind my eyelids. *Mother wants you to watch this and you better not dare upset her.*

Fuck her! Make them stop!

Mother's hands were on the wall now, lacing it with long, deep gouges, ripping away the paint with reckless abandon. The bed creaked and moaned beneath them, straining with their excessive momentum. The man, Knight, the black eyes that should have been blue, moved with the robotic jolts of a man half-asleep. He was bleeding from a hundred different places, desperately enjoying every tenth second of it. Mother's moans came faster, faster, faster. Knight began to grunt, scream, and growl, making an eerie, primal noise that might've been anything, but it sounded mostly like pain.

No! the voice cried, panicked. *Knight, what are you doing, what are you **doing?*** Her voice rose to a fever pitch, growing panicked, no, terrified. *No, no! No! Knight, please don't do this, please!* Now she was sobbing, screaming, throwing herself at invisible walls and making my forehead pulsate. I felt her tears in my eyes, bubbling down onto my face, landing on my throat. My entire body ached with a pain I'd never felt before.

And then it was over. The room exploded with screams of ecstasy and Mother burst violently backwards, her mouth open, staring at the ceiling. They both stiffened, and Mother fell away, breathing evenly, while Knight lay in the bed, panting, twitching as though he couldn't control his own body.

He can't, the voice said, but I wasn't listening. I was staring at Mother, now all cool and collected, unimpressed by her own raucous display. She slowly put on her pants, blouse, and jacket, buttoning it up as she said to me, "There. Try *that* on Sebastian sometime." She smiled acidly and threw a look over her shoulder at the writhing Knight. He managed to turn himself over and was now staring at the wall, digging his own nails into his arms.

Mother straightened her blouse, checked her reflection in the window and strode out, stopping at the door. When she passed me, she smiled and petted my head like I was her loyal lapdog.

I hate her, I thought, and this time, I wasn't sure if it were my own voice speaking to me.

She stepped out and closed the door. The wards wove themselves back together, a glittering lattice of burning red. The room went quiet and I was suddenly very aware of the blood. I turned to face the bed. The man, Knight, was on his back now, with his eyes shut tightly. Tears streamed down his cheeks.

He grabbed his hair and shrank into himself. For a moment, I thought he might scream.

I heard myself saying, "Are you all right?"

*What the **fuck** do you **think**?* the voice growled.

Knight dropped his hands and turned around to face me. His eyes were no longer black, but the most beautiful shade of blue I'd ever seen. He lifted his eyes to mine for a split second before he dropped them again, looking helpless and angry. He pushed himself up, his eyes milky, distant, and horrified. I couldn't help but notice that he was remarkably well endowed—he put Sebastian to shame and then some. It seemed almost excessive.

"I … I couldn't …" Knight balled up his fist and slammed it into the wall, breaking the plaster and burning his knuckles on the wards. "I *didn't* … I didn't fucking stop her! What the *fuck!?*" When he turned to face me, he shook his head after releasing a drawn-out breath. "And you saw the whole fucking thing."

"Mother wanted to teach me something," I responded simply.

With a growl, he was suddenly right in front of me. His eyes were angry and his hands formed fists around each of my upper arms. "Goddamit, Dulcie, that creature isn't your fucking mother!" He shook me slightly, tears burning his eyes until he furiously blinked and they rolled down his face. "I know you're stronger than this," he said in a softer voice. He dropped his hands from my arms but continued to hold me hostage with his eyes. "I know you can break whatever fucking spell she has you under."

His eyes were awash with something I might have called concern in someone else. He looked a bit like Sebastian, dark hair and tall, but where Sebastian was thin and elegant, this man was carved from stone. Muscles taut with tension, a perfectly defined jaw, and eyes like ice. He emanated raw power.

"I'm not under any spell," I responded coolly. It occurred to me then that I should probably turn around and leave, but I didn't do anything. It was bizarre, but it felt like my feet wouldn't budge.

He smiled sadly at me as he shook his head. "Maybe it's better this way," he said finally. "Maybe you'll never be the same again." He said the words as if he wanted to believe them, but there was something in his face that rejected the thought. "If this is who you are now, I'd rather you not know the truth about what just happened," he continued.

The other woman inside me burned me with her anger. "I do know the truth," I heard the words leave my mouth. "And I'll never forget it."

The man jerked his attention away from his hands and back to my face. "Dulcie?" he said softly. "I'm so sorry. I … I don't know what happened, I just couldn't … my body, it wouldn't, nothing was working, I couldn't stop it." He took a deep breath. "I'm so sorry, I'm so fucking sorry …"

"Sorry," I repeated, growing confused as I shook my head. "You did as Mother bid you," I answered frankly. I wasn't sure why, but this man's sorrow was unsettling to me. He needed to understand that there was nothing he could have done to stop her. What Mother wanted, Mother got. "Mother's power far exceeds your own." He immediately began nodding, as if he couldn't argue that. "There is nothing you could have done to stop her, so there is no point in continuing to lambaste yourself."

He didn't say anything right away but just stood there looking at me. It was like he was searching my eyes for something behind them. Or someone.

"Dulcie?" he said my name, and it caused a soft breeze to awaken within me, something that brought a wave of tranquility with it. "Do you know me? At all?"

You killed my father, I thought, but I couldn't bring myself to say it aloud.

Of course you know him! the voice yelled at me. *You love him and he loves you!*

"*That's ludicrous!*" I said out loud, affronted. The man's expression fell immediately. I supposed he figured I was speaking to him. Not that it mattered.

"Where's Bram?" he demanded, his voice souring.

Bram. Bram. I knew the name, but from where? Another life, another world. A relic from the time before Mother. Whoever this Bram was, he couldn't have been important. "I don't know any Bram," I said.

"Yes," the man insisted, walking towards me again. "Yes, you *do*." He grabbed my arm, digging his fingers into my skin. "You know him and you know *me*."

I looked down at his hand. His touch was warm and soft. I could *feel* the pleading in his eyes, a palpable need for something he couldn't bring himself to ask for. He seemed on the verge of tears. Heavy, fat tears, the kind you shed when you've lost something very dear to you. I couldn't imagine what that might have been.

"You know me," he said, his voice growing more quiet, less than a whisper, and trembling.

I stepped back. "No," I said. "I don't." But my heart was pounding and I couldn't deny the truth I glimpsed in his eyes.

Yes, you do, the voice whispered. I could feel her rage building, throwing herself against my skull until my head was throbbing.

Stop it, I thought, trying to force her back, but she wouldn't relent.

You know him, she said, *you know him!*

"No," I said.

The man stepped forward. "Dulcie?"

You love him, you stupid idiot! the incessant voice ground out.

"No!" I shouted, placing my hands at my ears, trying to drown her out. I screamed, a wordless vibration, and fell back into the wall. The fiery wards burned my skin, but I didn't move; I couldn't. I curled into myself, squeezing my eyes shut until I saw stars. *Mother wouldn't lie to me,* I thought back at that horrible, awful voice that continued to vex me. *Mother never lies. This man is evil! He killed my father! If Mother says he's evil, he must be!*

You killed your father, the voice responded in an unconcerned, almost bored tone. *Knight had nothing to do with it. You know Knight isn't evil! He's the only man you've ever truly loved.*

I refuse to believe anymore lies! I railed back at her. *You will not convince me that I know this man or that he is anything but a murderer!*

A vision filled my head then. Sharp and disjointed, the panicked recall of someone out of their mind. Sheets and sweat and hands against walls, moans and trembling limbs, corded muscles pressed against me. This man, this monster, was going in and out of me with long, deliberate strokes. Staring at me, practically unblinking, drinking in my features as though he'd never see me again.

Suddenly needing air, I threw myself from the room. I could hear the man calling after me, but I didn't respond. I slammed the door shut behind me and leaned against the wall outside, panting. The wards did a nice job of burning me, but they must have recognized me all the same because they released me. As I glanced down at my burned flesh, the wounds immediately began healing themselves until there was nothing left but porcelain, flawless skin.

I felt a hand on my shoulder and nearly jumped with alarm. I looked up to find Antoine, smiling down at me, offering me a cup of tea. "My apologies," he said, "I should have announced my approach." He took a few seconds to study me. "Are you unwell?"

I took the tea from him and drank deeply. "No. I'm fine." *Why am I lying to him?* I opened my mouth to correct myself, but nothing came out.

Antoine nodded. "Very good. Shall I tell your mother you will not return to the gathering? You seem a bit … flustered."

"Yes, please tell Mother I'm not feeling very well," I said and smiled at him with gratitude. He patted me on the back and walked away, whistling.

When he was gone, I dropped the cup and ran. It shattered behind me, a sound I felt all the way to my bones, freezing my marrow. I wanted to get to my room, to dead bolt myself inside and scream until my throat was raw. I wanted to tear out my hair and set something on fire.

I ran straight into a tall silhouette, standing coolly in the center of the hallway. "Ah," he said. "Where are you off to, little one?"

"I ... I ..." Ezra was staring at me with those curious iron eyes, one brow quirked by the question he wasn't asking. "I don't know." The tears were flowing harder now, blurring my vision, but I refused to let them fall in front of him. I felt foolish showing any weakness in front of a creature who certainly wouldn't respect it. But I couldn't help myself.

Ezra took my hand and squeezed it. "Perhaps, Dulcie, I may be of some assistance?" he gave me a look pregnant with meaning, but I couldn't parse it out. He was smiling, not leering, but he *wanted* something; what was it?

"Please excuse me," I stammered, darting past him, fighting the urge to dematerialize to the comfort and seclusion of my bedroom. Instead, I ran the length of the hallway until I reached my door. When I opened it, Sebastian was inside, sitting on my bed, waiting for me.

I burst in and threw myself into his arms, now sobbing uncontrollably. I gasped and heaved and choked, my lips stretching, my heart tearing, and my stomach eating away at itself. I dug my nails into his arm and into mine, more than longing to die at that moment.

"Sweet princess," he said. "What on earth happened to you?" He stroked my hair and held me close, shushing me.

I shook my head, burying my face in his shirt. "I don't know!" My mouth opened in a silent scream.

"Shhh," Sebastian soothed me. "You're safe now, Princess."

The other woman inside me laughed. *The only person who will keep you safe is Knight.*

Shut your fucking mouth! I thought back at her furiously.

"Darling," said Sebastian. "Look at me." He kissed me. I kissed him, and then … We were naked and hiding, trying not to think. I let him bury himself inside me again and again and again, grabbing me, squeezing and pulling like a child until I was bruised, but the voice wouldn't go away. It tore my mind to pieces, filling me with memories I couldn't bear to watch. Beds and sheets and blood, a dark dungeon and strong arms grasping my shoulders, night clubs and dark hair, blue eyes that always kept their promises.

"Mother?" I said, trying to scream, but my voice wouldn't work. A dog, a woman, a witch, a friend. A building with white walls and a motorcycle, a blanket on a cliff, hands on my wrists, holding me down, delighting me with orgasm after orgasm ... "*Mother.*"

Stop calling her that. Your mother is dead!

An army, a portal. A library. A gun in my hand. Smiling at the vampire on the brink, victorious. A bullet buried in Melchior's body. A sting in my back when my father rose, just enough breath in him to pull the trigger and kill me.

CHAPTER TWELVE
Knight

I stood there for a long time, staring at nothing, alone in my fucking prison, naked and burnt and cold. Bleeding from the pricks in my neck, my stomach, and my arms, I felt numb from the inside out.

What the fuck just happened? I thought. Over and over and over again, I was unable to think of anything else. *How could I do what I'd just done? And in front of ...*

I couldn't finish the thought. The image of it ran through my mind again, set on permanent replay, an infinite loop of fire and ecstasy laced with the lightning jolt of fear. Cold skin and dark hair and ... and *Dulcie* ... just standing there. Watching passively.

And then I wasn't alone anymore.

"What the fuck do you want?" I spat at the shadow I spotted in the corner of the room. The air in front of me turned hazy white, and the foggy silhouette of a man began to form. He appeared to be in his fifties, judging by the grey in his hair, eyebrows, and beard. Although he was older, he appeared quite fierce—as powerful and strong as any representation of Neptune or Zeus. His presence was large and imposing. He was built exactly as I.

That was quite a display, his voice quivered, sounding as if he were underwater.

"*Display?*" I swallowed the urge to scream and pounce on him. Not that it would have done any good—he was transparent, merely a spirit. "Why didn't you *stop* me?"

It was not a conflict that concerned me.

"You've got to be fucking kidding me."

I never kid. He waved his hand, and there was a hiss in the walls like something breathing.

"What was that?" I asked.

The wards are gone, the spirit responded. *You are free to go now.*

"You couldn't have done that ten fucking minutes ago?" I asked, forcing my voice to remain at a stage whisper.

No, he answered, but he started explaining once my brows rose in question. *Meg would have noticed you were missing and raised the alarm. She is not alone in this house—and clearly, you are no match for her, let alone her companions.* Even as he was speaking, his form continued solidifying, his words coming faster. It was gradual, but the fog of his being was still condensing into something that almost looked real.

"Whatever," I said. "Thanks for nothing." I started heading for the door.

Stop! he commanded.

And I stopped. Frozen like stone, I couldn't move for the better part of ten seconds. Not paralyzed, exactly, but *compelled.* As though whatever he was about to say was the most important thing I could possibly hear.

I summon you by your honor and your charge, by the fires that bore you and the darkness that fed you, by your ancestors and the sacred duty they upheld—

"What the hell are you talking about?" I spat out at him, still motionless. "*Summon* me?"

I am formally calling you to fulfill your purpose.

"My *purpose* is to get the hell out of here and save Dulcie," I responded icily.

No, it is not.

"Yes, it *is*," I insisted.

He shook his head. *No.* Lifting his hand, his fingers slowly curled into a fist. Clearly, he wasn't used to being defied.

"What are you?" and then I felt it. A searing heat in a hollow behind my heart, burning fingers wrapping themselves around my bones, scalding my organs, calling on its sister powers that still lived inside me. I swallowed hard, blinking, my mind filled with visions of magma and black water as a large, square hand reached out through the murkiness to pull me from the kiln ...

Creation, the ghostly voice ricocheted through the room, or maybe it was only in my head. *The Loki, the legion created in my image to defend the Netherworld.*

No, that can't be real, I thought. *You're nothing more than a hallucination. I've lost too much blood, and been through too much.*

Listen! He was growing more delineated, more concrete, as the seconds sped on—becoming less transparent and more opaque until it was difficult to see through him. *What you witnessed is the original, the very first Loki. Your ancestor.*

I immediately shook my head but none of it made any sense. Or rang true. *It can't be.*

Yes, the spirit insisted. *It is all true.*

I gazed in awe as the images of the first Loki being born from the fires of Hades continued to rampage in my head. The *first Loki*—born generations before me, my historic and ancient relative by many times over, my oldest grandfather. Hewn from hard steel and liquid starlight, fire flowed through his veins, and boiling magma occupied the mere shadow of his heart. A warrior of the oldest order, one of hundreds, forged in the fires of …

I blinked at the apparition. Runes of fire scarred his face and arms, curling into the backs of his eyes, spiraling off into deep, dark nothing.

"Hades?" I whispered, dumbfounded.

Took you long enough, he said, totally unimpressed.

"You …" I shook my head, feeling dizzy. "You … aren't real."

On the contrary.

"You're *not*. You *can't* be." Hades was a legend, a myth the ancients used to explain the existence of all the planets, as well as the Earth and the Netherworld, a god to whom they could assign all the stories that clarified why the two worlds were separated. He wasn't a *deity*, not anymore, barely more now than a character in a children's story—no more real than Santa Claus or the boogeyman. He seemed so trite and out of style, having lost most of his clout during the thousand years of war and famine and death, occurrences that he hadn't bothered to show up for.

In short, he was either a pathetic excuse for a fairy tale, or a totally apathetic god. The latter was definitely the worse.

"You can't be real," I said again. *Not after everything you've allowed to happen. Or the way you **chose** to leave the world.*

Hades sighed dramatically and appeared perturbed but didn't say anything.

"You're no more now than a fucking *story*." Hades chuckled but didn't say anything. "No. No, I'm hallucinating or dreaming." Maybe it was a side effect from Meg's glamour, or maybe I was going into shock. Fuck, I'd been through a hell of a lot. "This isn't happening."

I assure you, it is.

I laughed—a long, bitter sound. I wondered if hysteria could cause hallucinations as well. "You *assuring* me." *Hades, Hades,* I thought. Lord of the Netherworld, my *maker,* for fuck's sake. How the hell could I just sit down and swallow that whopper?

Hades rolled his eyes, like he was dealing with an indignant child on behalf of someone else and had no obligation to be nice. *I'll be brief. You know Meg, the self-appointed queen of this twisted coalition?*

"Yeah," I said, crossing my arms. I even *felt* like an indignant child. "And?"

You must stop her.

I scoffed. "That's been the plan from the beginning. Since long before you got here."

The red runes on his face gleamed brighter, and when he spoke, his voice sounded harsher. *No. Your plan is to kill her. You must dismantle her network. Demolish and destroy **everyone** who still stands beside her.*

"And where the fuck were you when Meg *started* this?" I demanded. "If you're Hades, the almighty god of the Netherworld, why don't you do it yourself?"

Hades shrugged, but acted like he was expecting that question. *I am not in my true form,* he answered.

"What the fuck does that mean?"

It means that I am simply a projection of myself. My true self lies buried in a canyon deep within the bosom of this planet. It is surrounded by impenetrable magma and lava rock. I am sleeping the thousand-year sleep.

"Then how did you manage to appear here right now?" I inquired.

You called to me and my subconscious mind replied.

"What do you mean, I called to you?" I asked, eyeing him narrowly. "I have no recollection of praying to Hades for help or guidance."

No, your subconscious mind alerted me. And my subconscious mind is that which you see and hear now.

"I don't know what to make of all of this," I said honestly.

Hades sighed, sounding almost sad before he held out his hand. The ghostly skin began fading, exposing a black skeleton beneath. A light formed in his palm, a reddish-orange bulb that glowed like a wick of fire.

Accept this, he said. *It will heal you and restore your strength.*

The bulb drifted up and toward me, entering my chest with a flare of white fire, while a shock like lightning and cold mercury struck me. Boiling tar and lava filled my veins until I was burning right down to my soul—Hades's unconditional blessing, his green light, his patronage. His power flowed inside me now.

Then the apparition vanished. I took a deep breath as I crept silently into the hallway.

The lights were dim and the floor was cold—beige marble veined in pink and gold. On the paneled walls of dark wood hung a series of small seascapes and portraits, as well as lanterns that twinkled like stars. And in case you missed it, I still didn't have any clothes to replace the shirt and pants Meg shredded to pieces with her teeth. So I was very naked and cold.

Actually, I was fucking *freezing*.

Interesting, said Hades, appearing again in a silent swirl of smoke beside me—either he was incapable of actually walking, or he just liked to show off. Dematerialization was not an idle spell, even for creatures that inherently possessed magic.

What? I growled in thought, trying not to draw attention to my effort at escaping.

I didn't know that.

Know what?

That it shrinks when it gets cold. Fascinating ...

Shut up, I replied mentally as I paused outside the first closed door I came across. Putting my ear up to it, I listened for any sounds on the other side.

What are you doing? Hades inquired.

I'm trying to locate Dulcie.

That woman is not your concern.

Yes. She is, I said, my temper flaring. *As a matter of fact, she's my number one concern.*

I should be your only concern, he started.

Well, you're not. Neither you nor your fucking crusade, I finished after searching for the right word. *I'm not leaving without her.*

Yes, you are.

The hell I am! I protested furiously. *You are not my god. Do you understand that? You allowed Meg to ... and Dulcie to ...* I made a disgusted noise in the back of my throat. *You are nothing! I feel zero obligation to help you.*

Hades chuckled, like he hadn't even heard me. *You're naked, unarmed, and hilariously outnumbered. What exactly is your plan?* He paused for a moment. *And shall I remind you that as soon as this woman, Dulcie, sees you outside of your prison, she will simply alert the others? She is not in her right frame of mind.*

My plan is to kill Meg, I answered loudly. If Meg put Dulcie under some kind of trance, killing Meg would surely break it to pieces. Of course, that kind of instantaneous unraveling wouldn't be exactly kind to Dulcie's mind, but she'd already survived much worse.

Your plan is foolhardy, Hades answered. *It is ill-conceived. In your current state, you are incapable of destroying Meg. All you will manage to do is get captured, yet again, and become her prisoner.*

I'm not leaving without ...

You will have your chance, Hades interrupted, nearly spitting his reply at me. *You will have the opportunity to save your lover and destroy her keeper. But now is not the time.*

Hades took a deep breath—his shoulders rose and fell to the sound of an inhale. He performed it with perfect mimicry of the action, even though he had no lungs. *Now you must serve a very different errand.*

What errand would that be?

You must go to the Mountain in the Deep, he said, *to the Shadow Places. From there, you will call your brethren together and feast on the bounty located in the heart of the mountain. Prepare yourselves for war with the Abyss—*

I don't take my orders from you, I said, turning on him and getting right in his face. Hades didn't flinch. *I don't care what you are or what you think you're here for, my job is to save Dulcie. Yours is to stay out of my way.*

Hades inclined his head and sighed. *I grow weary now and must return to my body. I will revisit you when you have escaped ... that is, assuming you survive your brief detour.*

Just fucking go then, I spat, and he disappeared in a flash of black smoke.

Good fucking riddance, I thought, turning my ears to the swirl of sounds now coming from downstairs. Distant rumbling, clinking, and the slither-and-slink of dryad roots and draconian tails—they indicated a substantial crowd.

Fine. I ran the gauntlet through fiercer fires for Dulcie before.

I sighed, taking a step forward, and the air went cold. It seemed to be trembling with energy, like tangible static.

Shit.

Maybe I stepped on something. Or maybe they heard me cursing. Hell, maybe they could *smell* me; but half a second later, I knew I wasn't alone. Two vampires emerged from the shadows on the walls, manic grins on both of their faces. They were males, and hysterically thin and old, radiating unholy power. Dark suits and bald heads with rubies for eyes. Emaciated, as though their skin was stretched tautly over sharp bones, I realized they were not vampires, but thralls. Those were half-souls, indentured for their lives to menial tasks like guard duty. Inhuman, sociopathic, and very unfriendly.

The thralls exchanged excited looks, crouching before they pounced.

I didn't know what I was even expecting them to do. Thralls, generally speaking, are tall, lanky, skeletal creatures that reeked of death. Their odor followed them like a smoky halo, and imbued them with a general sense of foreboding. They possessed a little power that was usually confined to liquified shadows and, occasionally, a small bout of fire. It depended largely on the experience of the necromancer conjuring them. In short, they were about as threatening to me as angry finger puppets.

So I wasn't prepared when they suddenly exploded.

They left the ground snarling, their long arms outstretched, and were airborne. The first split himself open from throat to groin, splattering me with congealed blood and black muck. It made a blood-curdling shriek before it slammed hard into the floor, its paper-brittle bones shattering on impact.

The second one's ruby eyes went wide, and suddenly, it also split in two pieces—a torso and two legs, and each chunk began flying in the opposite direction. The legs hit me full force, while the torso sailed over my head. It collided violently with a lamp suspended from the wall. Broken glass rained down on me and I shoved the pair of legs away, scuttling backwards, panting and staring in disbelief.

The thralls were no more than smoking heaps now, blood-smeared black suits, crumpled up on the floor, and the spell binding them here was rapidly leaking into the atmosphere. Then I saw a shadow standing above them. Tall, and remarkably nonplussed, he was clapping all the dust from his hands and wiping the blood from his fingers. He sighed as he shook his head.

Ah, shit. Probably a security guard, summoned when the thralls were destroyed. Meg was, no doubt, on her way, and I couldn't see how to get around this guy, not if he was that fast.

He stepped over the thralls' piles of dust and smiled at me, his mouth stretching just enough to expose two sharp canines. *Great.*

"Hello," he said, adjusting a pair of silver cufflinks that needed no adjustment. "Knight, I presume?"

"How do you know my name?" I demanded.

"I see you are quite underdressed for the occasion," he answered, completely ignoring my question. Steel grey eyes roved over me, along with the suits and the floor. He looked down to a red door at the hall's end and pressed his lips together as he sighed.

"How do you know me?" I insisted.

"If it's all the same to you, I think we should delay the formal introductions for the moment in order to fetch Bram. After that, we can make a hasty exit."

"Bram?" I asked.

"Yes, Bram. Tall, dark, and irritating. He is currently bleeding out at the end of this very hallway. I assume you already know him?" The vampire sighed, clasping his hands together like a businessman on the verge of being late to a dreary meeting. "We should hurry—Bram has perhaps three minutes and thirteen seconds left to live, by my count." He sounded almost bored.

I frowned at him. Then I stared, no, I gawked, narrowing my eyes warily. "Why aren't you trying to kill me?"

He cracked his fingers and craned his neck to the left, answering like he hadn't heard me. "Come, we can talk more once we are free of this wretched place."

"Why are you pretending to help me?"

The vampire stopped and looked over his shoulder, sighing again. "I am helping you, boy, and that should be the only important factor at this moment. Let me remind you that you are in a house filled with your enemies. And you are also naked and unarmed. The odds are stacked against you at present, my friend."

"You're right—I am in a house filled with my enemies. So why should I trust you?"

He huffed impatiently, but I held steadfast so he quickly explained. "Suffice to say, I have my own reasons to prevent Meg from achieving her plans for the Netherworld. And I have reason to believe that you are at least *slightly* capable of helping me stop her. Now can we please save your colleague and leave?" He motioned to the party going on downstairs. "If I have to listen to another draconian explain the nuances of inter-species coitus, I might hurt something."

I didn't answer.

"Will you at least follow me to your friend?" he asked, gesturing to the door at the end of the hall. "If my plan were so nefarious, don't you think I would have done something by now? I could have picked you up by your hair and thrown you back into your room, perhaps?"

I grimaced uncertainly, suspicion radiating from every pore in my body. He *hadn't* done anything yet … That was the word that bothered me: yet. Every instinct inside me was on high alert, but he was right: I was surrounded by enemies and naked and unarmed.

"Fine, do what you will." He turned around and stalked down the hall, a skeletal shadow with a stilted walk.

I followed. Maybe it was stupid, but I did anyway.

At the end of the hall, he took a key out of his pocket—a small, bronze item, conspicuously belonging to the whole establishment and matching the lanterns to the tee. The importance of which Meg would definitely have noticed as soon as it went missing. Maybe he was banking on the party as a distraction—I could hear the voices from it now, hundreds of them, or at least fifty very loud individuals. The kind of voices that echoed with the stolen magic of their ancestors; not quite a hive mind, and not quite possessed either, but ever so slightly fishy. I could hear the sinister hisses of draconians, along with voices that had shortened tongues, which made their words come out all muddy and flat, and voices full of song, and voices that could only scream wordlessly. They were all conveyed to translators that, in turn, told their hostess how very pleased they all were to be there.

Basically, there was a fuck-ton of ridiculously powerful creatures downstairs, all of whom were probably just as keen to kill me as they were Meg, if not more so. If they were keeping Meg company, it was a fair bet that I'd probably helped put more than half of their kind in jail.

The vampire put the key into the lock—and at that moment, we heard someone with a swift gait and loud heels coming up the stairs.

He sighed as he opened the door. "Inside, then," he said to me wearily. "I'll take care of this."

I blinked. "Inside?" I repeated. "What? With a blood-starved vampire?"

The man raised an eyebrow. "You could stay out here if you prefer." He looked me up and down with obvious distaste. "However, you'll have to explain to our guest why you are naked and smeared with the blood of a security thrall ... or two."

He had me there—the last thing we needed was more questions, or worse, an argument. A scream, or anything else that might have drawn Meg back upstairs, or any of her equally unpleasant friends, presented too much of a risk. I nodded as I slipped inside, letting the man close the red door with a soft *click*—followed by the *ca-chunk* of a bolt sliding into place. I was immediately on high alert. Had I just foolishly allowed myself to get imprisoned again? Well, if I did, it was nothing Hades couldn't bust me out of ... whenever he chose to revisit me. We hadn't exactly parted on the best terms.

Outside, I heard the man start a conversation with a draconian woman. She was already clearly drunk and twenty yards past horny. The woman wasn't Dulcie, thankfully, and not Meg, and, therefore, nobody that might give a damn about what lay behind the conspicuous red door.

Inside? Inside was Bram. And he didn't look so hot.

CHAPTER THIRTEEN
Knight

Bram was lying on the ground, propped up against the wall, staring blearily out a window through which the sunlight must have been beating throughout the day. His face was covered in blisters, swathed in the crepe-papery red burns of overexposure. Thin, black cords were poking out of his arms and neck, and they coiled around his body. They all terminated in a heavy, white box the size of a filing cabinet, which was whirring and spitting in the corner. His eyes were wide open, but glazed, and as far as I could tell, he was breathing—which was a really bad sign. A quirky side effect of vampirism is the ultimate calcification of the internal organs, meaning that Bram's lungs had become no more than solid paperweights. If he were pretending to breathe, he was pretty far gone, enough to think he was human again, and that was more than troubling. It put him *past* the point of being blood-starved and closer to death.

Ah, shit, Bram ... I knew better than to feel pity, but damn ...

I knelt in front of him, taking the first cord between my fingers and thumb before slowly pulling it out. I pressed hard on the skin with my thumb once the needle was free. Bram's mouth popped open and he uttered a small moan, but I really doubted he knew I was there.

"*Oui, monsssieur ... ma ... ma cher poisssont ...*" said the draconian woman. The vampire chuckled, but the noise sounded like it took a lot of effort.

"'My cherished fish'? My darling, I do believe you are drunk."

The woman hissed and gagged—a draconian laugh, guttural and unpleasant. "*Dassshan'o!*"

"Yes, you are," he said, "exceedingly."

I pulled out the second needle, and the third before Bram twitched to the left, like he was trying to get away from me. Maybe he thought I was a bug or something disturbing his sleep.

"Stop moving," I whispered, grabbing Bram's arm and holding him against the wall. He was starting to thrash more now, not hard enough to throw me off, but enough to make me worry he could become conscious long enough to feed—and not stop before it was too late. "Fucking *fuck*, Bram, I'm trying to help you!"

"What'sss in there?" said the woman, and something—presumably she—slammed against the door, sliding to the ground with a vague, scratching sound.

"Nothing, my pet," the vampire responded with audible boredom. "Why don't you go back downstairs and lie down, hmm? Or get another drink and throw yourself out the nearest window?"

The woman giggled and said something unintelligible in the throaty language of the drakes—I wondered where on earth I could get a drink while I was locked in here. Maybe he expected me to drink the last of Bram's blood before throwing myself out the barred window he was staring at, which was much too thick and too high to reach. I dropped Bram's arm, letting him twitch weakly against the wall before falling over like a sack of potatoes. I was thirsty suddenly, parched, and my tongue felt as dry as sandpaper. I *needed* a drink, something very thick and soothing, something that would blur the whole world from my consciousness. And make the pain go away once I'd thrown myself out the window …

I snapped myself back to the present, gasping. *A drink? I don't need a fucking drink! I need to get out of here.* But the thirstiness remained, sharp and dusty, making my throat feel as rough as scorching gravel. I swallowed, my tongue against the roof of my mouth, which seemed like sandpaper.

The door opened, and the tall vampire walked in, blinking away his own influence and shaking his head. My urge to drink instantly evaporated, and I stared at him open-mouthed.

Oh.

"How old *are* you?" I asked quietly. He'd glamoured me by *accident* through a closed door; and I'd never met a vampire capable of that. Even Bram, one of the oldest living creatures on record, didn't have the kind of power required to *accidentally* convince someone to jump out a window. Not with conventional magic, anyway. Sometimes just talking to Bram was enough to make me consider defenestrating myself. As well as him.

The man chuckled. "*Very*," he said. "How fares our friend?"

"Not great," I said, turning back to Bram. The needles were out of him, and the little red dots where they'd been were starting to dry up, but he was nearly empty of blood. I looked down at my wrist and grimaced, wondering if Bram had enough life left in him to even *try* to drink …

"Don't bother," the man said, shedding his jacket and kneeling beside me. "Your blood is not strong enough." He rolled up his sleeve and sighed. "This is going to be … remarkedly unpleasant."

He bit into his wrist, drawing two fine points of blood, and stuck it in front of Bram's mouth. Bram's nose twitched, but he didn't move.

"Open his mouth," the vampire said. I pushed Bram's cheeks together, popping his lips apart, and pulling his jaw down. The man grimaced and wedged his wrist between Bram's teeth, pushing upward into his canines until they drew blood on their own. We stared at him for a long moment.

"I don't think," I said before Bram's eyes suddenly snapped open.

His jaw instantly clamped down hard on the vampire's wrist and he began to drink, almost violently, his throat convulsing with each swallow. Bram's eyes were very black, swirling with a haphazard color between darkness and sunlight, like a shadow with a cataract. His hands latched onto the vampire's wrist and he leaned forward, sucking in the air through his nose, dragging his teeth across the man's bones—I could hear the sharp scraping, which sounded almost metallic.

"Easy," said the man, perfectly calm, and growing more annoyed than anything else. He grabbed Bram by the throat and squeezed hard enough to break his skin, and Bram's mouth popped open. Bram slumped back against the wall, his mouth agape, blood trailing down his chin like drool. His chest heaved with breaths he didn't need—and the blackness gradually drained from his eyes.

The vampire dried his hand on his shirt, leaving a bright smear of red across his stomach. "You're welcome."

Bram blinked. His pupils dilated and contracted. He was trying to figure out the light situation in the tiny room. Eventually, he focused on me.

"Knightley," he murmured.

"Yeah," I said, lacking anything else to say. Bram and I were the furthest thing in the universe from being friends, but as of many days ago, we no longer considered each other archenemies. Reluctant allies, I guess, since we were both bound by Dulcie and our dual need to keep her safe—although nothing else. The urge to comfort him in his pain or punch him in the face, just on principle, tugged at me with equal strength.

"You …" Bram squinted. "You are naked."

The vampire sighed. "Well done! Yes, he is."

"Long story," I said before Bram could ask where my clothes were.

He smacked his lips thoughtfully. "Where … where is Dulcie?" he asked, reaching up and touching his lip before he examined the little, red speck on his finger.

"Downstairs," the vampire answered, "along with seventy-six temperamental house heads from across the Netherworld."

Bram's face twisted into a scowl. "Oh." He looked at me—specifically, at the sheen of black goop on my stomach and face. "What …" He smacked his lips, suddenly lost.

"Thralls," I answered. "Big ones."

"Ah." At last, he turned to the vampire, and his face drooped into something less friendly than a scowl. "You."

"Me," the vampire agreed.

"You know him?" I asked. Bram made a point to avoid most other vampires—he always said it was because he disliked their company, and for the same reasons most of us disliked *his* company. Now I wondered if he'd been avoiding one in particular. Not Meg, since he thought she was dead, but someone he might have known in another lifetime. Someone like this guy.

Bram didn't answer me. "Why ..." Bram lurched forward, gritting his teeth, suddenly seized by a bout of pain in his stomach. "Why ... are you ... here?"

"I was invited to the party," the vampire said dismissively. "Most of them are drunken out of their skins, so we shouldn't have a hard time escaping."

"Who are you?" I demanded from the stranger.

"Ah, yes, our introductions," he answered with a strange smile. "Ezra Grant, at your service."

His name was unfamiliar to me, but that didn't mean anything.

Bram tried to roll forward, maybe in his attempt to get onto his feet, but he collapsed sideways almost immediately. I caught him and propped him back up, but he frowned at me. "We need to get away from him at once," Bram gargled out.

"In case you both hadn't noticed, I'm helping you *escape*," Ezra replied with annoyance. "And in our behest for timeliness, it would be wiser for you both to stop doubting my intentions at once and simply accept me as your loyal ally."

I blinked at him but didn't say anything. Bram did the same.

"You do not trust me," Ezra said to me.

"No," I said, "I don't."

"Nor should you," added Bram.

"I appreciate your confidence," Ezra announced. "You *are* more than welcome to try and escape on your own. You'll never make it, but it might be fun for me to watch you try."

"I'm not leaving without Dulcie," I announced. "So unless she is part of your plan, I'm not budging."

Ezra nodded and sighed. "She is part of my plan, but, unfortunately, I cannot abscond with her just yet."

"And why is that?" I demanded, but I already knew the answer.

"She is under the influence of Meg and, therefore, she doesn't know her own self. She is currently one of Meg's minions and following her orders," Ezra explained. "It is my absolute intention to release the beautiful lady, but that must wait. For the time being, I must first release the two of you."

Bram and I looked at each other, both of us clearly loath to trust him. He was just as likely to lead us into another nightmarish trap as deliver us out outside, but … hell, he could have done that by now. I was *inside* Meg's house, with nowhere to run or hide, and no reason to be lured anywhere. He might be waiting to trick us—maybe to satisfy some sadistic urge, but I couldn't think of why.

And as far as Dulcie went, he was right. And so was Hades. Dulcie lacked her own mind, and if we tried to release her, she *would* certainly fight us tooth and nail. That much I knew.

"Fine," I said. "But if you try anything funny—"

"Yes, yes, I know ... you'll kill me," Ezra said, waving me off. "I would expect nothing less."

I hooked Bram's arm over my neck and stood up. He was surprisingly light when he wasn't full of blood.

"No, no," said Ezra. "Put him down."

"What?" I asked with Bram still hanging off my shoulders.

"I can't just *waltz* out of here with the pair of you on my tail," Ezra answered dryly. "Bram is no more capable than a vegetable right now, and *you*, sir, are still naked and covered in the blood of two substantial security thralls. Besides, there is something else in the house that both of you must see in order to fully understand just what is going on here."

I let Bram slide to the ground and looked at the window and then at Ezra, crossing my arms. "Something else in the house?" I asked warily.

"Easier to explain once we're there."

"Where exactly is *there*?" I demanded.

"A room Meg locks herself in when she's feeling particularly ... nostalgic."

"Nostalgic?" I repeated flatly.

"Nostalgic," said Ezra. "Mr. Vander, I assure you, if I wanted to kill you, or maim you, or drop you into a room filled with very hungry werewolves, I would have been strong and fast enough to accomplish any of that without you ever having seen my *face*. And contrary to what you insist on believing about me, purely based on my progeny, I have better things to do than to scare you for kicks."

I didn't respond. Ezra's smile curled into an impish grin. He opened his coat and retrieved a small folded square, which he tossed up in the air and caught. However, it was no longer a small square, but a sizeable, black briefcase with an open zipper.

Bram squinted at it. "A ..." he coughed, "a briefcase?"

"A briefcase," Ezra confirmed.

I blinked at it. "Um," I said. "Okay. And ... what's it for?"

"You," said Ezra.

"Me?"

"Yes," said Ezra. "And him," he motioned to Bram.

Bram and I exchanged a look.

I blinked at Ezra. "You want to put us in a briefcase?" I asked lamely, bemoaning my accompanying concern that Ezra was not the ally I originally thought he might be. Unfortunately for us, he was clearly insane.

Ezra nodded. "A *magic* briefcase, my dear sirs."

"Magic? How?" Bram asked.

"It is larger on the inside, actually much more so than it appears." He smirked—the smug look of a man with a very small, and definitely non-magical, briefcase into which he intended to hide two fully grown men.

Bram grimaced. "And there is … no chance … that once we are inside your … magical briefcase … that you might just … drop us out … a window?"

Ezra shook his head. "The entire house is warded except for the main entrance and several of the back doors, all of which still require us to walk past some portion of Meg's little get-together. And I'm sure Mr. Vander can tell you exactly how unpleasant these wards can be."

"Fiery," I said when Bram looked at me for an explanation. "Really hot fire."

Bram nodded and turned back to Ezra. "So … you propose …"

"To put you and your friend inside this briefcase," Ezra finished, holding it out again, just in case we'd forgotten which briefcase he was referring to. "Then I shall formally dismiss myself from the party and abscond with my pilfered captives into the night."

I twitched a little at the phrase, "pilfered captives," but saw no better way out. Actually, scratch that, I didn't see any other way out period.

I looked at Ezra and sighed deeply. "Okay, so … what's the plan, exactly?"

"To walk out of here with the pair of you under my arm like a stack of stolen books," said Ezra, placing the case on the ground. "Get in."

###

There's no comfortable way to ride in a briefcase beside a vampire.

Bram and I were squished together in all the worst ways. His knee was against my face, and his hands pressed into my stomach, while my foot was on his throat, and my dick somewhere I really didn't want to think about ... We kept getting jostled as Ezra walked, swinging the outside of the magical briefcase.

"Vander?" Bram muttered.

"What?" I hissed back.

"What ... in the *hell* ... is that putrid smell?"

It was probably a combination of sweat, fear, and liquid irritation draining from my ears, but I decided not to respond.

"Quiet," Ezra whispered. "We're about to walk through the party."

Ezra walked down the stairs with us underneath his shoulder, and the sounds of a party rocking on its heels swept in from the den. I heard lots of talking and laughing, punctuated by ringing of glasses as they clinked together in arbitrary toasts to Meg and the Netherworld or whatever else they thought was important. The sounds included hisses, growls, and sneers of wolves, drakes, and vampires. I also identified the slither and creaking of the wooden skin of Mother Dryads, along with the muttering of promises and deals. There was lots of talk about something called the "Resurrected Order," which was definitely a bad thing.

But as soon as the sounds became audible, they were gone again, disappearing as we rounded a corner or traversed a long hallway. The cheers and conversations became an unidentifiable burble of words that faded to a hush no stronger than a soft wind. Then the sound vanished entirely, and Ezra chuckled.

"Checkmate, my darling," he said, although there was no one but us he could have been talking to.

A door opened, and a door closed. The house was silent here, the only noise being the quiet hum of the ventilation. I heard a hiss like someone inhaling, and a pop; then the soft squeak of a door swinging open. Ezra took two steps forward and stopped.

"Ah," he said quietly.

I felt him placing the briefcase on the ground, and dull, greyish light flooded the inside when he unzipped it. He gave us a grim look. "Here we are."

We unfolded our contorted selves from the briefcase and stood up.

"Prepare yourself," said Ezra. "It is rather unpleasant."

We looked around.

"Oh, my," Bram said. We almost said it as one, but I couldn't find my voice.

The room was small, barely larger than a closet, and lit by a series of desk lamps. A table was pushed up against the far wall, laden with scrapbooks, binders, photo albums, glue, glitter, and decoupage hearts.

Notebooks full of chicken scratches, smeared black ink, smiley faces, and words and names, which were circled over and over again cluttered the tables. Calligraphic *Ds* were sewn into their covers, carved into the plastic, burned into wood, or woven into leather, they were all labeled beneath to identify the years and years and years. Ledgers of a lifetime, singular accounts from a singular person. I could see some of the sentences beneath the covers, words too sweet for the monster writing them, and too close, and much too *personal.* None of them were complete, however, trailing off into hearts and squiggles and dots.

And pictures. Floor-to-ceiling, wall-to-wall, in an endless collage. Nothing but Dulcie, Dulcie, Dulcie. Dulcie in uniform, Dulcie on her motorcycle, Dulcie posing with her gun and her badge at her Academy graduation, Dulcie on her couch as seen through a window, Dulcie more than half-naked in *bed* …

Dulcie with me. Her hair a tangled, blond mess of sweat and wind, staring at me, lying underneath me, and on a blanket above a cliff. Naked, both of us. My face, however, was scratched out.

"What?" I swallowed to conceal the tremor in my voice and said again, "*What* … the *hell* … is this?"

"I am not entirely certain," Ezra answered, drawing his finger along the edge of the table. "But it *appears* to be a sort of … living diary, I suppose? Like you might see with a conspiracy theorist or someone caught deep inside a delusion."

"Delusion?" I repeated, but Ezra didn't elaborate. Not right away, at least—he was looking keenly at the wall, examining the less scandalous pictures of Dulcie. And admiring them, it seemed, with sad eyes and a strange smile.

Bram, clutching his stomach and squinting at everything with the almond-grey eyes that characterized the vampire's near-death experience, stumbled forward to examine everything. He picked up a different journal, a black leather cover with a golden *D* stitched into it. It was less worn than the others, still slightly shiny, and the spine was not yet bent from a hundred thousand openings. He touched it and recoiled, like it was an open flame.

"What?" I said.

"That ..." Bram shook his head, uncertainty playing tricks with the color of his eyes—but before he could explain himself, he found something else. His eyes suddenly widened, darkening to an angry red. "Oh," he murmured.

"Oh?" I took a few steps forward toward Bram and followed his gaze to a picture frame standing at an angle on the desk. "Oh."

The frame was gilded wood, hand-carved, and intricate as all hell—but that wasn't the important bit. The part that caught both of our attentions was the picture it surrounded, the yellowed Polaroid of three people. Meg was smiling, standing next to an elf with disturbingly familiar summer-green eyes. And between them was a child. Young, too young to know what was happening, much less to remember the picture being taken.

"Dulcie?" I said. Bram pursed his lips. I turned to Ezra. "Why are you showing us this?"

"Because you deserve to know," said Ezra, "what Meg has done, and why Dulcie did all that she has done. I have spent too many years with unanswerable questions about the intentions of people who were once close to me. Constantly wondering if it were something I did, or said, or *didn't* do. I would not condemn that agony on my worst enemy—let alone, a slightly irritating officer of the law and his friend."

"Friend is a strong word," I said, unsure if I should have demanded a less convoluted answer or just thanked him.

"And what exactly ..." Bram said slowly, leaning heavily against a blank expanse of wall by the door. "What, may I ask, exactly has Dulcie become?"

Ezra stared at the photographs. He remained silent, as lifeless as marble.

"Ezra," Bram said. "I realize ..." He lurched forward and began gasping—his body clinging to the human instinct to breathe. "We are short on time ... but if you know ... *something* ... about this, I suggest ... that you begin explaining. Now." His voice was flat and empty of ire.

"You said it was a delusion," I replied. "A living diary."

Ezra nodded stiffly as he looked between Bram and me, deciding how much to tell us.

"Obsession," he said, after a long, unnecessary pause. He crossed his arms as he surveyed the room, biting his lip.

"Obsession?" I repeated blankly, but Bram's posture shifted—like he knew what it meant.

Ezra touched the wall, running his hand along the edge of another picture of me with my face scratched into oblivion. With a slow nod, he picked up a leather journal, flinching at its touch before flipping idly through it. "It's rare, but not unheard of for a vampire to become overly attached to their offspring." He frowned at the book and sighed.

I felt like I'd been sucker-punched. "What? Offspring?"

Ezra turned to me, also looking surprised. He closed the book and set it down. For a long time, he said absolutely nothing.

My hand curled into a fist at my side. "What do you mean *offspring*?" I asked, seething.

Ezra looked from me to the pictures, and back to me again, then to the portrait of Meg and Melchior and little Dulcie. "I mean that Dulcie …" He frowned, unsure of how to continue. "Meg has *altered* her. For lack of a better word."

"Altered?" I repeated blankly. "What do you mean?"

"He means Dulcie has somehow become a vampire," said Bram, sounding wholly unamused.

"Dulcie," I said through my gritted teeth, "is *not* a vampire!"

Ezra shrugged. "No," he said, "she isn't. At least, not like any vampire I have ever seen. She ages, she walks in sunlight without burning, and her eyes maintain their color … or at least they do right now. But um …" He looked down. His affected air disappeared, sloughing onto the floor like an old coat, and he seemed almost visibly uncomfortable. "Mr. Vander, Meg has done something to Dulcie. It began, as you can see, a long while ago. A vile project she began with Melchior when Dulcie was very young and, judging by Dulcie's latest progression, Meg must have resumed it very recently. I'm not certain what it is, or was."

"Progression?" I asked.

Ezra inhaled and exhaled slowly, clasping his hands together. "Dulcie has certain qualities now. The qualities of vampirism … and other races as well. I don't know how Meg has—"

"What is she capable of? Exactly?" I asked. I had to know if she was vampiric, lycanthropic, draconian, or dryadic, and Hades only knew how many other kinds of creatures were involved, or how many bloody fatal characteristics she currently carried in her. I had to know what she had to defend her now, if it came down to it.

If you have to fight her, I thought. Which was true.

But Ezra didn't elaborate on that. "I'm afraid I wasn't present for that portion of her life. So I can't say what she's done, or how she accomplished it. And I do apologize for that. I should have *watched* her, I should have known she would become something unsavory if I left ..." He trailed off. His regret sounded genuine. It showed in his face, which was twisting slowly into a grimace.

"*Unsavory*? That's what you call this?" Bram asked.

But I wasn't listening to him. No, I was thinking about why in the world Ezra would feel obligated to babysit Meg. "Are you ...?" I started to say as I glanced up at him.

Ezra chuckled bitterly and nodded, folding his hands together, examining the creases in his porcelain skin. "Yes," he said. "I am Meg's maker."

Bram scowled. "And the fool who brought her back, no doubt. Making all of *this* possible?"

Ezra's face fell a touch further and he nodded. "I am."

"Back?" I asked, looking between them.

Ezra sighed. "An unfortunate incident occurred," he replied, "a little over a hundred years ago. There was a fire. Meg was badly injured and it was too far beyond her own capabilities to heal, despite how old she was. I discovered her and helped her, and … well, now here we are. And to be *fair*," he added, looking pointedly at Bram, "she did *ask* to die."

"You blame *me*?" Bram seethed.

"No, of course not," Ezra said, holding up his hands. "Meg is her own master in all of this."

"What do you mean, she asked to die?" I demanded.

Bram groaned. "I had the opportunity to kill her after the fire," he said. "Permanently. But after she betrayed me, I had no intention of gifting her with any such release." He shook his head, obviously angry with himself. "I left her there to suffer throughout the rest of eternity. And *this* idiot—"

"Did not know how far she had fallen," Ezra finished for him. "And I am still trying to remedy the situation."

"You want to kill her now?" I asked, my tone sounding dubious. "Your own progeny, your *daughter*? You want her to die, even after you saved her?"

"Yes," Ezra said but the word seemed to pain him. "I do. I must." He sighed—a genuine sound this time, and full of anguish and regret.

"Why?"

"Because it is the duty of a father to care for his daughter," he said slowly. "And to clean up the messes he allowed her … or taught her how to make. I am responsible for her, and, therefore, I am responsible for the destruction she has visited upon the world. She has become much too powerful," he continued tersely. "She hungers for more power and she is too dangerous."

"How dangerous?" I asked.

Ezra shrugged. "She longs for an overturn of power—she wouldn't have summoned every ruling house from here to the Silver Marsh if she didn't. It would be most prudent for us to assume she intends to inflict the worst damage she can until she attains it."

"Hold up," I said, "Ruling houses? I thought Meg sought control of the ANC for the sake of the potion rings, in order to control all the portals."

Ezra looked at the little, brown door isolating us from the rest of the party and sighed.

"The ANC is just an obstacle to whatever her ultimate plan is—perhaps it involves the portals, perhaps not, but Meg already has access to more portals than any of us could count. She doesn't *need* them, but perhaps she has reason for controlling them. Or at least, to prevent anyone *else* from controlling them."

"And the potion rings?" I asked. "Where are they in all of this?"

Ezra scoffed. "Just another dog to tie up in the yard. The potion kings and their employees are minor organizations with substantial power in the Netherworld—Meg recruited them, lied to them, and set them to perform some menial tasks in the back of nowhere to keep them out of her way. If they knew what she *really* wanted, she'd have an outright war on her hands."

"And what does she really want?" I asked.

"I'm not entirely certain, but it is likely something with long-term consequences that would put a significant damper on life as we know it," Ezra said. "She is the matriarch of the House of Vogahn. I don't expect you know that name?"

I did, actually. It was an old, Netherworldian name, and rather important too, part of the original hierarchies that existed before Earthly influence and the ANC came into being. It didn't take me long to parse out what that name meant in context. "Oh, shit!"

"Oh, shit, indeed." Ezra sighed mournfully as he crossed his arms, casting his eyes almost absently at the blank wall. He shook his head. "Whatever she is up to has everything to do with the order that came before the human democracy. It's centuries old by now, but Meg would surely remember those days well. And apparently," he added, gesturing to the party we could no longer hear, "they remember her too. Fondly enough to kneel to whatever cause she's stirred up in their richly conservative minds." His expression curdled. "But I digress," he interjected, "we should be on our way."

I moved forward—grabbing the black journal almost as an afterthought. Ezra grimaced at me.

"What?" I said. "Meg will notice we're gone before she notices this is." I held the journal up—and a vague tingling sensation filled my fingertips where they touched the leather. "That's weird."

Ezra didn't hear me. He had Bram's arm over his shoulder and was helping him climb back into the briefcase. Bram's pallor hadn't changed, but he looked nauseous.

Ezra cocked his head, listening for something. "Someone is coming," he said. "A very drunken someone, so you'd best hurry."

"Um, sorry about this," I said as I squished myself around Bram. Ezra closed the zipper above us, and everything went dark. Our arms were tangled together, our thighs pressed against each other, and our hands and fingers bent around themselves. Our extremities were closer than either of us could have ever dreamed they'd be.

"Move your knee, Vander," Bram hissed when Ezra lifted the briefcase.

I felt the part of my body pressing against him the most and stiffened. "That's, um … not my knee."

There was a long silence.

"We will never speak of this," said Bram.

I gulped. "Agreed."

CHAPTER FOURTEEN
Sam

I sat in the backseat of the SUV, my hand on my throat, grimacing. We were driving out of Splendor to the illustrious City of Angels, where Casey's mother apparently worked as the Head of the Preternatural Division. That meant she stood guard over the largest and most versatile of all the government regulated portals.

Marcus was driving—Kent had begged for the wheel, but Judy produced a small, reddish something from her pocket and told Kent to sit in the back and play with that instead. He complied rather happily, lighting and gutting the flame on a small, metallic wick poking out of the object's side. A bomb, probably, and not as friendly as it looked, but he refused to let it go off. Rowena sat beside him, staring out into the dark, the magic under her skin prickling. Maybe she was getting itchy for a good clean kill. The skeleton-god creature that scratched her soul and gave her the magic was an unfriendly something-or-other with a fondness for death. It flowed through Rowena's veins, making her ever so slightly more bloodthirsty than the average person.

Casey—his soft eyes staring out of a face made infinitely more angular by shadowed stripes—was sitting beside me. He was half-lit by the streetlamps and the light of Judy's phone as she skimmed through news articles on some website while grimacing. I couldn't imagine the world view could have been very pretty at the moment.

My throat prickled—not so much with bad magic as the remnants of Dagan's touch. He had a magic all his own, the liquid malice and parched sunlight of creatures not meant for any particular world, monsters whose very nature dictated their wants for unsavory things. His soul, or whatever mass of congealed essence comprised what should have been his soul, was twisted, dark, and broken, a grasping thing that you dared to touch at your own peril. If it touched *you*, brushing against you physically, or delved into your mind to show you something just as dark, it was like inhaling sand. Something that stayed with you, choking you, and making every breath rattle like you were sick with something. It corrupted whatever it touched from the inside.

It sounds a little melodramatic, I know, but it's true. It's a feeling of violation regardless of the demon in question … But when that demon happens to be *Dagan*, suffice to say, it's way worse. So much worse.

So I was jittery and jumpy, relegated to a place far back in my brain, puzzling over Dagan's vague notion of Dulcie's location. I was still accepting the knowledge that he'd been close enough to *touch* me, and was totally unprepared for anyone or anything to get within five feet of me.

"You, um … you doing okay?" Casey asked, and I almost leapt out of my skin. "Sorry," he said.

"No, you're fine," I said, sighing. I ran my hand over my face, rubbing my temple and suppressing a sudden burning urge to scream. *Hades, just breathe, Sam. It's not like Dagan actually did anything to you.*

Yeah, but what I saw is traumatic all on its own. I didn't imagine those visuals would leave my head anytime soon.

"Are you sure you're okay?" Casey asked again, only softer this time. His mouth was a firm, grim line, and his eyes were staring, but I couldn't tell at what.

"Yeah," I said, not looking up. "Totally." *Liar, liar, ANC on fire.* I gestured vaguely to my rib, knowing damn well that wasn't what he was talking about. "Doesn't hurt too much at all."

"No, I mean …" He sighed, clearly unsure how to phrase his next question. "I mean, with … did anything … *happen* in there? Anything that made you uncomfortable?"

"Um …" I said, frowning at him and cringing into myself. The orgy was the least of my problems, but thinking about it was still extremely unpleasant. "Nothing happened. I just … watched." *Yes, perfectly eloquent, Sam. Tell the nice, young man that you just* **watched** *an orgy while you interrogated a demon about your homicidal best friend. He'll find it endearing.*

"So you're okay then?" He eyed me narrowly.

I inhaled and I exhaled. I developed an excruciating awareness of my heart and its sudden desire to explode from my chest. "I," I faltered. *Use words, Sam. Full sentences. Come on, you can do it.* "It wasn't … fun." *Okay, that's true enough.*

Casey took a deep breath and seemed to gather his thoughts. "Well, I think it's important to say that you're uh," he started, "you're safe now." He was staring at me and blinking slowly, his eyes rock-steady. I lost myself in them for a moment, swimming in their color and their cosmic immovability.

"Thanks," I said, my bones melting under his gaze like beeswax. He seemed so … not exactly fragile, but vulnerable, like he was as unfamiliar with emotional stuff as I was. I couldn't help but wonder about the last time Casey James had a girlfriend. As it was, neither one of us knew how to act around the other. It was fairly obvious that we were attracted to one another—at least, that's what I thought. As far as Casey was concerned, it seemed like he was trying to play doctor and the handsome, not-exactly-a-stranger all at once, uncertain where the line was drawn.

He squeezed my hand and smiled.

I blinked. Siphons aren't capable of glamour. This was just me looking at a massively attractive doctor and deciding it was too much trouble to look away. I managed a weak, "Thanks," but it came out as more of a whisper than a word.

He lowered his hand to the seat—still wrapped around mine—and sighed, making a visible effort to relax. "Hell of a day." There was a vague sense of the moment breaking into little, bite-sized pieces, but I couldn't decide what I wanted to happen next, if anything. Did I expect him to kiss me right in front of his team?

Yes. Yes, I absolutely did.

"Has it only been a day?" I asked.

"Technically, it's been two," he answered.

"So, your mom …" I started.

"Is the acting Head of the Preternatural Division," Casey said. "Yes."

"And she …" *is your mom,* I thought stupidly.

"Has access to a government regulation emergency portal generator? Yes."

I nodded, trying to think of something else to say. There was a strained tension hanging between our words—not an angry feeling, just afraid. The very human urge to shatter a necessary silence. To talk while there was nothing we could do but drive and stare at the road, or at each other. Finding something to say, anything, and saying it before the silence got too deep to swim out of.

I lived inside silences like that. Usually, I just let them pass. However, tension is a lot easier to brush off when you're all alone.

"What's it like?" said Casey. "Having competent magic at hand?"

"You're …" I nearly corrected him with *you're competent, you just need practice*, or something equally contrived. But he wasn't. Siphon magic, contrary to public knowledge, was designed to be exactly as lackluster as it was. I let the sentence die on my tongue.

"I know," Casey said, and he hiked his voice up into falsetto. "At least I'm pretty."

I snorted—a deep, back-of-the-throat gargle of a laugh. Casey laughed too.

"It's, uh," I said, pushing my hair out of my face in an almost hysterically cliché movement, but I had hair in my face, so sue me. "It's nice, I guess? And useful. Kind of irritating, sometimes."

"Irritating like how?"

"Like in the office." I shook my head. "Printer gets jammed or something, or somebody gets blood on their clothes. Like maintenance stuff that everybody thinks I can easily fix by just snapping my fingers. Little stuff, and it's easy, like, *really* easy, but sometimes, it's irritating to be the … I don't know, the—"

"Office mom?" he asked.

"Yeah."

Casey chuckled. "I get that. Try being the only certified doctor in a room full of creature-techs. Everybody asking if lycanthropy is contagious or airborne, or if getting scratched by a vampire is going to make them *immediately* bloodthirsty, asking if dryads can get the clap ..." He shook his head. "Not a whole lot of fun."

"*Can* dryads get the clap?" I asked.

"They can carry it, but in practice, they're immune."

"Huh." The more you know. "What's it like being a ..." Hmm. *Doctor or siphon?* "A doctor?"

"In general? Good," he said. "It's ... I don't know, reassuring, I guess. Being the person in the room that always gets called when something goes wrong."

We both sighed at once and looked at each other, grateful for this ... understanding. The shared realization that this was awkward, and we were both desperately trying to fill the silence with anything that didn't matter, anything we could quickly brush off and forget. Anything that had nothing to do with the world blowing itself to high hell all around us, or blithely accepting its demise. Trying to talk about ourselves and each other without reaching for the deeper stuff, like the reality of our own existence, because it would inevitably lead us back here, to the SUV and Casey's elite team of crazy people. I was tired of the catastrophic nonsense that dragged all of us here.

Casey smiled. I smiled, too. Maybe it was my imagination, but the tension seemed to dissolve then. Taking a backseat, I agreed to exist quietly in the absence of a proper distraction. I wanted to say something, an outward acknowledgment of this moment, the one I was certain we were having.

Something like, "We're so lame," or "The job be killing me, right?" But nothing I could think of seemed appropriate.

Then Casey just said, "Yeah. Me too."

And that was enough.

He squeezed my hand. "It's quite a drive to LA," he said. "You should get some sleep. You … uh …" He laughed. "You look like you need it.

"You don't look so hot yourself."

Casey opened his arm, gesturing for me to lean against him, and smiling gently, placidly, like it was the most normal thing in the world for a person to do. "I would *never* accuse you of not being hot."

I blinked, and we both laughed.

"That sounded smoother in my head, I swear," he said.

I leaned into him, laughing softly, and nestled myself into the crook of his arm, resting my head on his chest. Listening to his heartbeat, I was soothed by the steady thump-thumping of a man walking the razor's edge of excitement. I let my hand fall to his stomach, and it beat faster. So did mine.

Casey kissed me. Just on the top of the head, fiddling with my hair, but it was enough to jolt me with a shock that went straight through me. "We can do this," he whispered.

I closed my eyes. *We*. Nice word.

Really nice word.

And then. An explosion.

The SUV jerked and sputtered, tipping halfway onto its side, and slamming into something hard. A fizzing flash flew past my ear and Kent cursed, clamoring past me to grab it as it soared through the air. *The bomb.*

Gravity was pulling me in the wrong direction, sideways and up, while my seatbelt dug into my shoulder. The sour, acrid smell of gas hung heavy in the air, swimming up my nose and making me gag. For a moment, all I could hear was white noise, a high-pitched ringing, the whine of a siren screaming between my ears.

Once I was no longer moving, I looked around, my head throbbing, while my vision swayed in and out of focus like a pendulum. We were nearly upside-down, with two of our tires the wrong side up. A parking lot, or a street, and stumpy, city trees leaning over concrete basins, hoisted way up into the air by the grey slabs emerging from the ground. Fountains of water spewed from the wrecked fire hydrants, and shards of metal and busted tires from the unlucky cars lay everywhere. Lights kept flickering and spitting sparks, while the buildings halfway caved in on themselves, and some pockets of people emerged from their ruined vehicles and structures, wondering what the hell kind of earthquake this was. Roads encased in ice reflected their angry faces and the slippery spots of red … Something was dancing in orange and wreathed in blue.

Something was on fire.

Beside me, someone moved—Judy was cutting through her seat belt. Her mouth was moving too, vibrating, her lips shaping words I couldn't understand. I stared at her blankly, trying to shape my mouth into words of my own, something along the lines of "I don't understand! I can't hear you! I can't understand!"

Then the glass shattered inwards, and a shadow with a cigar held out his hand. Judy took it, climbing out, turning back to say something, only louder this time.

I don't understand, I thought, but my tongue was throbbing, I could taste rust, the metallic flavor of my own blood. I tried to spit it out, but nothing could move.

I closed my eyes and inhaled until my lungs nearly burst. *Breathe,* I thought as I exhaled, trying to force myself to focus, to will the agony and throbbing away. The ringing grew louder, louder, louder—

A hand landed on my shoulder, giving me a gentle shake, and a voice. "Sam?"

I opened my eyes, fumbling for my seat belt. Casey was hanging from the open door, one hand on me, the other wrapped around the car's half-exposed metal frame.

"Come on," Casey said, sounding eerily calm. "We need to hurry."

"Right," I said. "Right, um …" My seat belt clicked open and I hopped to my feet, crouching, standing up slowly on the tilted seats. Casey hauled himself out and turned back to me, anchoring me with his hand as I pulled myself onto the concrete slab lying on top of the car.

Casey hopped off the concrete slab to join the others on the only marginally less fractured ground below. "Let's go."

I hopped down on my own, landing, rolling, standing, and trying to ignore the incessant ringing in my ears. "Where are we going?" I asked, suppressing a wave of dizziness.

"There," said Casey, pointing to a skyscraper of translucent grey glass across the road—remarkably unaffected by … Was it an earthquake? No, whatever it was was too strong, and too loud, to be an earthquake. A bomb? No, Kent still had his bomb.

"What happened?" I asked, but as I looked up, I saw it myself—a cloud of smoke and lightning, spider's-eye blue and dark and imposing, was flattening itself beneath the sheet of clouds above. "Oh, shit."

It didn't take long to figure out what it was. The multicolored mushroom cloud hung like a chandelier against the sky—the smoldering remains of the Los Angeles ANC twitching and sizzling somewhere far beneath it. We could hear sirens and screaming when we got out of the car, stepping onto the streets now frozen solid with shivering rains that never happened. It made the strangest sounds under our feet, the *tink-tink-tink* like someone tapping a crystal glass with a tuning fork.

That was a really bad sign. It meant that it wasn't ice, but ether glass, slick as oil and nearly impossible to scrape away. It also meant that sometime before the ultimate destruction of this ANC, someone must have spilled something that combined with something else and congealed, creating the cocktail necessary for ether-glass manufacture. The only conclusion I could draw from that was before the ANC went up, there must have been a fight.

And it ended poorly.

We rushed into the glass building, ducking through a revolving door, two of us at a time. I looked over my shoulder at the blistering inferno, the cloud far above, bubbling with all the bad magic an ANC might have kept locked away. News helicopters circled around it almost blithely, pointing cameras at it, leaving long trails of steam behind them when they got too close to the glacier-cold, smoking spout. I once created something similar in college, mostly by accident, while trying to brew something that would … (*ahem*) heighten the beauty of a friend of mine in the eyes of her beloved.

What I ended up creating, however, was a storm-heart: a glacier-cold epicenter that preceded one of the worst blizzards Brooklyn had ever seen. It was big and loud and damn near impossible to stop—taking twenty of the college's premier warlocks and witches to end my little project, and even then, the cold lingered on for what must have been months, lasting close to a year. It made for a very unpleasant winter.

The earth trembled, and the lights in the cloud sparked like frayed plugs. Every now and then, the ground shook, causing something else to crumble, and the ether glass would crack. In a matter of seconds, a wave of silvery-white shine would pass over it, and the glass would be twice as thick as before, mending itself to conceal any fractures. If it kept up like that, all of LA—or however far the glass could spread—would be completely encased in transparent blue.

"Sam?" said Casey, and I realized I'd stopped moving.

"Sorry. Let's go," I said, and in we went.

Inside the glassy, untouched building stood a woman behind a glossy, black desk, wearing spectacles and casually picking up the clutter from the explosion. She was humming absently and seemed totally oblivious to the carnage worming its way through her city just outside. She was in the middle of a vast, otherwise completely empty, lobby of white faux-wood floors and sheer, black walls. The room lacked any chairs, tables, or a waiting area of any kind—and as far as I could tell, even an elevator. There were no stairs, no doors, no offices, no other desks, not so much as a potted plant. Just a vast, endless expanse of white and black, perfectly quiet, unapologetically chic.

Rowena walked up beside me and crossed her arms. "You feel that?"

I did—a vague pulsing between dimensions. The dull hum of magical activity that I couldn't quite pin down.

"Yeah," I said. "Know what it is?"

Rowena's eyes flashed green, the skeleton's fire burning in the back of her skull. "Some artifact," she said, "maybe whatever's sustaining the illusion." She gestured to the conspicuous absence of a ceiling—the walls rising upwards into a deep, dark nothing, disappearing into its own shadows. Going up and up forever. Kind of gaudy for an office illusion—a wildly complicated visual hex maintained for the express purpose of fooling anybody that came through the door.

Our tax dollars at work, I thought, staring up at it.

The woman behind the desk—a stocky, dark-haired human with round spectacles, no more than twenty—smiled when she saw us before putting the large stack of papers she held into the first drawer she touched.

"Good morning," she said cheerily, folding her hands together on the desk. Bubbly, bright, and looking us over with her iron-grey eyes, she had the same default suspicion Dulcie always wore on the job. "How can I help you?"

We all looked at each other, confused. Kent spun in circles, staring at the impossibly high ceiling, presumably deliberately trying to make himself dizzy.

Casey sighed and said tiredly, "Casey James to see Margaret James, please. It's an emergency."

"Of course." The woman reached for her phone, a bulky-bodied, black thing with a coil cord and the thickly set number buttons of the first model to replace the rotary phone.

"Nina?" said the woman, hopefully talking to someone on Casey's mother's floor. "Yes, he's here. Okay. All right, thank you, darling." She hung up and beamed at us. "Ms. James has been expecting you.

"Of *course* she has," Casey muttered.

The woman pressed a spot on her desk—a flat space identical to the rest of it, but when she touched it, it lit up with a small square of blue, and a soft *ding-dong* echoed through the open lobby. The floor to the left of the desk folded open, revealing a black abyss beneath, and a large rectangular box rose out of it. Its front slid sideways and down, compressing its doors into nothing before it exposed the plush white interior of an elevator.

"Off you go," said the woman, waving at us. It seemed so unprofessional, but I couldn't think of anything more to say, so I just waved back as we all stepped in.

Judy had the sense to add, "By the way, the world's on fire," before the doors closed behind us.

CHAPTER FIFTEEN
Sam

We were in an elevator and hoisting ourselves to some ungodly floor far above the cloud bank. At first, there was nothing but a thin carpet of white and equally white walls, completely opaque—until we passed the threshold of the ceiling's illusion and the walls fell away like a house of cards, exposing clear glass windows and the elevator shaft. The higher we climbed, the more I could see. Glass stretched to the horizon in every direction, ice-blue flames warring with their angry orange counterparts on the foundations of the ANC, twining around each other at the base of the cloud. Firefighters surrounded the scene, spraying the fire with half a dozen hoses, carrying the limp, smoking bodies away from the blaze. Most of them weren't moving.

"Shit," Casey muttered. He was staring through the glass, but only half-seeing the smoke, fire, and crystalline brimstone. Kent whistled behind him.

"That …" he said softly, "was one hell oove an explosion!"

"Yeah." I barely heard myself reply before I lay a hand against the glass, unable to look away, or even *blink.* Staring intently, it seemed that if I squinted hard enough, and held my breath, I could reach out and strangle the cloud, tamping out the flames with a harsh glare, snapping my fingers and raising all the charcoal-boned bodies from wherever they lay to rest. Like I could turn back time, if only I wanted to badly enough.

"The crystal isn't active magic," Rowena said, her eyes still vaguely green. I wondered if anyone else could see it, and if it were an effect she had to consciously mask. "It's just spillover from a potion leak at the ANC."

Leak, I thought. Nothing was leaking anywhere. Whatever once contained the offending potion had been blown to smithereens by some idiot with a grenade launcher and a pocket full of *fuck-yous* in the evidence locker. But there had to be more—the potion had to have mixed with something else that made it a hundred times more volatile and unpredictable than it would have been on its own.

In the corner of the elevator, Judy said, "Oh, shit."

"No kiddin'," said Kent, and the rest of us understood her tone and stiffened.

"What?" I asked when no one else moved.

Judy scratched her neck and sighed. For a minute, she couldn't say anything although she was clearly trying to, but none of the right muscles were working. "ANCs are going up in flames all over the place," she said at last. "This is one of ..." She squinted at her phone before finishing with, "Shit. Fifty!"

My heart froze and nearly stopped beating completely. I was holding my breath. "Fifty," I echoed, realizing that it was more than two-thirds of the collective.

"How many does that leave?" Casey said.

I shook my head. "I don't know. Not too many." My ballpark figure would have been around six or seven, and that was being generous. But I dared not say that out loud.

Judy's face turned grim, an expression she didn't wear well. Her muscles seemed unsure of what to do with a frown, and her body didn't know how to process the emotions that accompanied it. Or maybe it was just the first time in two days I'd seen her look anything but happy, and it caught me off guard.

"I'm sorry," she said to me, her face sagging, like she knew how worthless the sentiment was. I appreciated it anyway.

"I …" *Thanks* seemed totally inappropriate to say. "Um," I sighed, when nothing else sprang to mind.

No one else said anything either. We had no means of springing into action, no more than we already were. The haunting repertoire of your-place-of-work-and-thousands-of-your-coworkers-have-just-been-blown-to-cinders only received a quick "sorry." That was it, the end of the rope of empathy.

We sat in cold silence for a long time, listening to the bell-and-whistle jingle playing through tiny speakers in the ceiling.

I cleared my throat. "I didn't know elevator music was still a thing."

Casey nodded. "Yep."

"You, uh … talk to your mom much?"

"No."

Silence. Silence. And more silence. It hung in the air like lead curtains, drawing everything, including us, steadily toward the floor and the broken, stony ground. Ten, fifteen, twenty stories below, they were dancing with all kinds of bad light ...

"She's going to get us killed," Casey said at last.

"Your mom?" I asked. Casey's grimace deepened, but he didn't reply.

Silence, silence, silence.

"Did you have a better idea?" Judy asked absently.

Casey huffed and looked away.

"Relax," Judy replied, punching him lightly in the shoulder. "This is gonna be great." Her grin was back in full force, gleaming white teeth, brimming with the kind of deliberate mischief usually reserved for younger siblings. Only her eyes betrayed the weight of the quiet emptiness, cold as snow. Casey didn't spare her a glance.

Silence, silence, silence. Kent and I looked at each other. Marcus peered at everyone from over his cigar, which remained unlit, rolling it back and forth between his fingers. Judy stared at her phone, pretending to scroll—but the screen was black. I didn't know what Rowena was looking at.

Casey sighed. "I'm sorry," he said, turning to me. He tried to smile, and even made a valiant effort. "Um ... I don't talk to my mom often."

Fill the silence, I thought as I strained to smile back.

"She's our best shot, Casey," said Judy, trying to look sorry. "She's just ... eccentric."

Kent chuckled, tossing his bomb from hand to hand, flinching occasionally to make the rest of us think it was about to go off. He chuckled as he held up the bomb to his eyes, staring at it with wonder. He could have been holding a star in his palm instead of a petty grenade, and one that probably didn't even work properly.

"*I'm* eccentric, darling," he said, his accent curling around his words. "Mrs. Margaret James, howevah, is a fuckin' sociopath."

Judy flinched, but Casey stared straight ahead, looking stiff as a board, the tension literally radiating out of him. I touched his arm, and he looked down, almost startled.

"Um ..." I didn't know what to say. Perhaps I wanted to tell him that his mother couldn't be that bad? And every good family needs a sociopath if only to balance it out? Maybe I was going to talk about my own mom and the hundred thousand cats and spirit hounds that roamed through her apartment complex. "We won't be here long," I said at last.

Casey nodded and took my hand, squeezing it. My heart pounded—which was stupid. Only teenagers get all aflutter when someone holds their hand—but when he didn't let go, I almost exploded into an effusive spray of confetti hearts. How utterly unprofessional of me!

Not that my profession mattered anymore.

"Nobody say anything unless you absolutely have to," said Casey. "And try not to make any eye contact."

"Why? Is she gonna try to glamour me or something?" I asked. Probably not, if Casey were human by default—even if he had a singularly magical parent, it would have manifested itself *somehow*. I could have been able to read it in his phantom stitches. Margaret had to be human, even if she were crazy.

"No," Casey replied. "She'll just try and talk to you if you initiate any small talk with her, and then we'll be trapped here forever."

"Ah. Got it." I pursed my lips. "How is she going to get us killed?"

Casey groaned. "She'll start talking," he said, "and she won't stop until it's way too late to save the world."

It seemed like an exaggeration—it *had* to be.

When we got to the top, however, we found out it wasn't any exaggeration.

###

The elevator *dinged* and Casey jumped. The doors slid open. Casey sucked in a breath—I didn't hear him let it out though. The room before us was just as large and unwelcoming as the lobby—white floor, black walls, a conspicuous lack of windows. I saw a flat metal disk of beaten silver set into the floor, twice as wide across as any of us were tall. Around this were curving desks, featuring an array of buttons and dials. The irritable-looking attendants were dressed in black suits and lab coats, tip-tapping away at their computer modules, ostensibly regulating the flow of energy to and from the disk. None of them looked up as we entered.

The elevator doors slid shut quietly behind us and vanished into the shaft, like an unobtrusive family member at a reunion trying to duck out of the dining room before his divorced parents noticed each other.

I stared at the techs and their equipment: state of the art arcana—phantasma, crystalline computers built for the maintenance of extremely powerful magic. All were man-made, along with stagnant, magical artifacts like portals and enchanted mirrors. In the ghost of a whisper, I uttered, "Whoa!"

All the tip-tapping stopped at once, and the attendants looked up. One pushed her square glasses higher up on her nose. Another sniffed the air. The rest stared at us blankly, blinking like dumb animals, unsure whether to classify us as proper organisms or intrusive nuisances.

"It's stronger in here," Rowena muttered, appearing at my side from nowhere. She was right, the hum was like a swarm of bumblebees buzzing now. Loud and irritating to anyone who could sense it, the vibration started in the center of my stomach and was almost enough to make me nauseous.

"Probably the portal generator," I said, which was definitely big enough to create all the ephemeral fuss.

Casey made a visible effort to suppress the groan that seized his body and called out, "Mom?"

Nothing happened. The attendants continued to sniffle and glare, peering at us over their desks and casting furtive, protective glances at the metal disk in the floor. It seemed as though they were expecting us to whip out jackhammers and demolish their beloved project. Casey rolled his eyes at them and strode forward.

"We need to get to parallel three," Casey said to the nearest person. "Fast."

The technician adjusted his glasses and glowered at Casey. "I'm sorry, sir, but first, you will need proper clearance and permission ..." *blah, blah, blah*, and bring out the red tape.

"Hold up," I whispered. "Are there other parallels?" It was common knowledge, at least in the collegiate arcana community, that an infinite number of habitable dimensions, as well as several massively unfriendly and uninhabitable ones, existed—but to claim that the government, *any* government, had ready access to them was ... well, unnerving. Planet Earth isn't great at drawing borderlines as a rule. If they could prance into the astral plane whenever they fancied, it was only a matter of time before a slew of ghosts with unfinished business came pouring back into our dimension.

I blinked myself back to the present and saw Casey had moved. He was standing in the center of the metal disk, looking at someone. A woman.

"Oh, boy," said Kent, pocketing his little bomb and facing Casey and … his mom? Kent was clearly interested.

"Hi, Mom," Casey said sulkily.

"Casey," she answered, leaning forward to pinch his cheeks. He recoiled from the touch, but not far enough that she was forced to let go. The woman was short—shorter than Casey by a full head, despite the health-hazardous heels she was wearing. She was also pudgy with frazzled auburn hair and gold eyes. The color in her eyes was more urgent, like boiling magma, and much closer to a volcanic catastrophe than the soft chocolate in Casey's gaze.

Short, bright, and terrifying, she was wearing a skirt suit and a massive red rock on a gold chain, which, I guessed, must have been an amulet of some kind. The amulet's magic was muffled by the overwhelming aura the metal plate was giving off. I'd have to get closer if I wanted to know what it did, if anything at all, but that would have been rude.

"It's so *good* to see you," Margaret said, beaming at her handsome son. Casey sighed. "How *are* you?" she continued, looking up and noticing us for the first time. Her cookie dough-sweet smile got even bigger.

"And who are these people? Your *friends*?" She clapped her hands together excitedly.

"Not important," Casey said, answering both questions flatly. "Mom, we need to get to parallel three. Now."

His mother tutted and shook her head, clasping her hands onto her waist. "Well, now, that's not a very nice way to ask a favor, is it? And you've barely said hello, and I do *so* want to meet your friends, it's been *ages* since you brought anyone home …"

"We're not at home," Casey said. "We're at work. I have *work* to do, understand? Really important work in parallel three."

His mother sighed. "Sweetheart, if I didn't know any better, I'd say—"

"Mom, we don't have *time* for this! We really, really don't."

"What kind of son doesn't have time for his *mother*?" she asked, sashaying over to a slightly larger desk that must have been the primary terminal. She sighed dramatically, batting her eyes at Casey, and addressing the technician, "Do whatever you must to open the doors."

"Huh." Marcus grunted, immediately frowning as he turned to face Kent who merely shrugged.

"What?" I whispered to Judy, who also seemed surprised by Margaret's choice of words. "What's going on?" I continued in a hushed tone, making sure Margaret couldn't hear me too.

"She … it's probably nothing, but Margaret *knows* how to open these doors. She can do it with her eyes closed," Judy answered from the side of her mouth, her tone hushed.

"Interesting," I answered as I replayed Margaret's words. *Do whatever you must to open the doors.* Yes, very interesting. I focused on Casey and noticed he had the same suspicious expression as the others did toward his mother. But no one seemed overly concerned because no one did or said anything more about it. I figured if they were letting it go, then I should too. Maybe Margaret didn't drink enough coffee this morning.

Margaret, meanwhile, hovered over the terminal.

The technician didn't look up. "Parallel three?"

She nodded and looked up, but not at Casey—she looked at me and I felt my stomach plummet all the way to my toes. "Hello," she said. Her smile trembled.

She started walking towards me, and I heard Casey groan.

"What's *your* name?" she asked, taking my hand. She felt warm, her face was friendly, and maybe not so terrifying. *Famous last words*, I thought, but I smiled too, making sure I only looked at her nose and ears instead of her eyes. Just in case.

"Sam," I answered. It took me a moment to remember it!

"*Sam*." She laughed, like it was the most beautiful name she'd ever had the pleasure to utter. "Sam, Sam,

Sam, it's so lovely to meet you! How, may I ask, do you know my Casey, hmm?" She patted my hand, looking at me expectantly.

I looked at Casey. His eyes were wide, and he was starting to walk forward, maybe intending to break up our conversation. I smiled at him and replied to his mother. "We work together," I said, feeling sure I could handle an over-affectionate mother.

"*Work* together?" She looked between us, appearing shocked but in a dramatic, theatrical way. "Casey, darling, you've never *mentioned* her before! And such a pretty thing too ... Shame on you, boy! What became of your manners? Have you no thought for your dear mother?"

"We've only worked together for a few days," I answered.

Margaret stopped in her tracks. Hades, she looked like the Pillsbury dough-boy, just a ball of sugar and sweetness and hugs. "Oh, I see, I see," she said, tapping her chin, one hand still firmly clasped around mine. Her necklace, that peculiar amulet thunking against her sizeable chest, was pulsating now. The dimensional planes were things I could only *just* comprehend, and all at once, in a strange pattern, they came at me fast, quick as a rabbit in a firestorm, changing the beat every second or two ...

"Mother," Casey said irritably. "*Please.* We don't have time for this."

"Sir, please remove yourself from the generator," said a technician, his nose buried in his console. Casey hurriedly abandoned the disk, walking towards me and his mother.

"Sam, Sam," she said, "Sam, Sam, *Sam* ... Tell me, is that short for something? Samantha, maybe?"

"Yeah," I said slowly. My tongue felt heavy, almost numb. "I, um ... yeah, it is."

"Sam," said Rowena. She was quiet, but very urgent. I barely heard her.

"Ah, good, good." Margaret patted my hand again, running her thumb across my knuckles. "Such soft skin, darling, do you moisturize? Sam, Sam ... Samantha, dearest ... do you cook, perhaps? Are you an avid reader?"

"Yes ..." *Hades!* The pulsing of the amulet was all I could comprehend now. Like a clock, a metronome set on fast-forward, the unsteady thumping of a flat tire shredding on asphalt ...

"What kind of work do you do?"

I could barely think of an answer for her. The words came out of my mouth clumsily. "I ... um ... I'm in ANC ..."

From the corner of my eye, I could see Rowena looking at Casey, jerking her head towards me.

"Ah, yes, of course! You look human enough. What is your arcane alignment, hmm? What do you *do*?"

"I'm a ... witch ..." The room briefly spun before it melted, falling on its side, like the whole building were drunk.

"A *witch*," Margaret said, gasping. "Samantha the *witch*, how lovely. Do you like dogs? You *must* like dogs, Casey *adores* dogs ..."

Casey reached us a split second after I realized what she was doing.

I closed my eyes for a fraction of a second. The pulsating hum changed, the vibrations sounding like a distant song, which became a tendril, a fluttering ribbon in the blackness—something I could interact with. Something I could touch and strangle.

So I grabbed it. I severed it with a burst of ephemeral fire—the spiritual equivalent of safety scissors. The humming, singing, and the droning stopped all at once.

Margaret had been trying to weave a spell with no magic of her own, and no connection to the holy or the arcane, nothing that would give her sway over anything. The only thing she had was the amulet, the focus of her will, and desire, a wish-granter, a hypnotic aid. But whatever magic the amulet offered, it sputtered and died like a bad bulb. Margaret, however, didn't seem to notice.

I opened my eyes and found Margaret looking back at me. She seemed very concerned. The rock around her neck had lost much of its color—the brilliant amber was closer to the faded orange of an old car now. I'd only intended to block her will, snapping the web she was trying to catch me in, but I guess I broke the whole thing. She wouldn't appreciate that, assuming she found out …

"Are you all right, love? You look a bit faint," she said.

"I'm fine," I said through my gnashing teeth. I looked at Casey. "You didn't tell me your mom was a hypnotist."

Casey glared at his mom. Margaret paled.

Kent started laughing. Hysterically.

"Busted!" he cackled while Marcus rolled his eyes.

Judy crossed her arms and sighed at Kent. "What are you, twelve years old?"

"Oh," Margaret said, flushing pink, looking down at the amulet like she'd never seen it before. "I, um. Oh. Oh, dear …"

"*Mom*, you cannot just go around and *hypnotize* people!" Casey shouted at her. "What the hell were you thinking?"

I was more interested in the reason she tried to hypnotize me. What information was she seeking from me?

Margaret put her hands on her hips. "Oh? Says who?" She sighed. "You never can be too careful, especially with the world blowing up around us!" she added. "Sorry, dear, but we can't trust the strangers around here," she told me with a little shrug and a giggle. "I was just trying to get a read on you."

I didn't say anything but nodded quickly as Margaret turned back to Casey. She continued pleading her case although he was clearly angry. I stepped back and leaned in to Judy. "Has she done this sort of thing before?"

Judy waved her hand. "Eh … Sorta. She's unpredictable, at best."

I frowned. "Do you know how long she's had that necklace?"

Judy shook her head. "No. I've never seen her wear it before, but I don't see her very often."

Rowena was scowling now, biting her lip and staring with her stone eye at nothing in particular.

"Just please get us to parallel three and we'll talk about this later," Casey insisted as Margaret plopped her hands on her fleshy hips and frowned at him. He pointed to the metal disk in the floor. "Now, can we *please* get back to work?"

Margaret sighed. "Oh, all right. But it's going to be a minute or so."

Casey groaned, fists clenching. Margaret gave him what might have been an admonishing look.

"It takes time to *warm up*," she explained—which was probably true, given its size and the number of other parallels it likely had access to. Ripping holes in the natural barriers between worlds and dimensions is a heavy task.

Casey waved her off, visibly trying to contain himself. "Just fucking ..." He exhaled slowly through his teeth, his eyes closed. He seemed to be struggling to breathe.

Margaret turned to the technicians and started ordering them around. Kent kept laughing, and Judy glared daggers at him for it. Marcus watched it all with a troubled look on his face, fiddling with his cigar. He brought it to his lips every now and then, pretending it was lit, or maybe just forgetting that it wasn't. Rowena watched silently.

I walked over to Casey. "Well, then," I said.

Casey balked. "Well, then," he responded, tightening his lips into a straight line.

"It's okay," I said, taking his hand. "Breathe. We're almost out of here."

"I'm sorry for what my mother did to you," he started.

"What she *nearly* did to me," I corrected him. "I caught her before she did any permanent damage." At Casey's questioning glance, I continued. "Hypnosis is an art. The amulet was just a focus of mortality, something humans without magic can use to channel what little they've got. She was more intent on hypnotizing me than learning what I might have revealed under hypnosis."

"Ah," he started before a secretive smile crept up along his lips. "You're a special kind of girl, Sam," he finished, his grin broadening.

Then something else blew up, and I forgot what I meant to say.

CHAPTER SIXTEEN
Sam

The explosion was distant, muffled—a noise that sounded halfway like an earthquake, or a giant rock landing unceremoniously on something extremely fragile. Following the noise came a series of pops and bangs, soft enough to resemble little more than bursting bubbles, and loud enough to shake the floor.

All the irritable, motherly affection instantly drained from Margaret's face, and her eyes turned steely. "Oh, dear," she said darkly as she pulled a small tablet from the pocket of her coat. She tapped away at it for a few seconds, then sucked in a breath. "Oh, *dear*."

"Mom?" Casey asked, but she didn't look up. Something powerful sounded with a mechanical exhale, and the light above the elevator went out. Margaret sighed.

"I'm terribly sorry about this," she said, smiling, "but it appears we are under attack."

"By whom?" said the technician beside her, but all of us knew. Or at least, we had a pretty good guess.

"Think they're here for us?" Judy asked.

"No," I said. "Definitely not! Anybody working for the Darkness probably thinks I'm dead, unless ..." *Oh shit.* "Unless they've already toppled the

Preternatural Division from the inside out, they have no idea your team is even a thing."

That wasn't a fun thought. We all looked at Margaret, but she wasn't looking at any of us. Her eyes were fastened on her tablet, which she squinted at with iron concentration.

"They could be here for the portal. It's the only other thing in the building," Casey said.

"Except …" I started, thinking of the dozens of floors we must have passed on our way up here.

I was cut off by a horrific, groaning noise coming from the elevator shaft. We all turned toward it at once. Margaret sighed, pocketing her tablet, and walked behind the largest console, where she knelt down and opened a large drawer with a casual rumble.

"Four minutes, ma'am," said a technician, fiddling with more buttons and sliders, trying desperately to ignore the groaning.

"Four minutes," Margaret muttered, tapping and plugging at something hidden behind the console. "Four minutes …" she repeated as she looked at us and beamed. "You've got four minutes to spare, don't you, darling?"

Casey frowned at her—like something she said didn't sit right in his head—but he did not reply to her question. "Can you see who's in the elevator, Mom?"

Margaret shook her head, rifling through her drawer with lots of shuffling and clattering. "I turned it off, darling," she said. "Couldn't tell you who it is, or how on earth they're making the elevator *move*."

The groaning continued, a belly-deep, tearing sound, like metal being ripped in half, or mountains being shorn in two by giants with axes, fueled by suppressed rage. It swelled to a roar, growing even louder. *Bump, bump, bump!* went the doors, ready to receive whatever was about to enter, confused despite their robotics as to how it was possible after the whole system had been shut down.

"Brace yourself, darlings!" Margaret called out from behind us, and I heard a click and someone shuffling, like they were cocking a gun and aiming it.

The doors opened, and a man came stumbling out, panting and sweating—the silver-blue glow of his magic dancing around his hand. He was straining to keep the elevator from plummeting back into the shaft. Tall and lanky, with the monochrome-grey skin of a drow. They were the nocturnal, reclusive, and far less friendly cousins of the more common high elves. Drows were native to the expansive caves and mines that tunneled underground through most of the Netherworld.

"Casey!" he shouted, releasing the magic the second he was free of the elevator. The doors remained open, and the carrier box fell away, thundering down the long, dark tunnel from whence it had come.

"Silas!" Casey answered, aghast. "What are you doing here?"

"Tabetha's been compromised," Silas answered breathlessly, looking over Casey's shoulder at Margaret—now glaring vehemently at him and holding the black body of a weapon just behind the terminal.

"Yes," she said darkly. "It has."

Silas's eyes widened as he dropped his voice and said, "Casey, listen to me! That's not your mother!"

Casey's brow furrowed. "What are you talking about?"

"Margaret's still in Brokenview," Silas answered quickly, "She—"

Then he stopped abruptly, his mouth hanging open, his next words stayed lodged in the back of his throat. His eyes glazed over before he gagged. His magic flared in his stomach, shrinking into itself, desperately pushing outward. Like he was trying to fend something dangerous off.

Shit.

"Silas?" Casey asked with obvious concern as he took a few steps closer to him.

Silas didn't move. His soul was at war now, thrashing wildly, and rendered blind. Slowly, the color of the offender took shape, the outside magic pressing down on him—an orange haze, grey, yellow and gold, a cloud of sour influence. More power than he could contend with alone.

"Sam?" Casey asked as he turned to face me, presumably to see if there was anything I could do to help the poor man. I just shrugged and shook my head, being just as helpless as they were. This wasn't any magic I'd ever seen before so I didn't have the first clue as to how to neutralize it.

"Careful," said Rowena. "he's radioactive." Silas was bleeding strong magic into the air.

He's possessed is what he is, I thought, but there was no connecting cord. Nothing I could comprehend, at least, no connection to the spellcaster responsible. There should have been a string of the same color, stretching from Silas to whoever was controlling him, unless this was a glamour. But it couldn't be; glamours are up close and personal, and he'd been fine twenty seconds ago.

"I," he said and the word wobbled in his mouth. It spun and compressed, dancing on a swollen tongue, bouncing off his straining vocal cords. "Am. Here."

The orange energy flared, spun, and sank into him, overtaking his blue completely. He went rigid.

"Casey," I hissed. "Someone's speaking through him!"

Silas opened his mouth and his jaw hung there for a moment, moving up and down slowly. Blue wisps curled up like smoke around the orange, pushing, burning, and fighting for control. "You. Will. Sur … sur … en …" Silas swallowed the word, choking on it, and gagging up a less cumbersome replacement: "Die."

No change of inflection, no volume shift. Just the word, perfectly vocalized, but no more important than anything else. And in the harsh fluorescent light, Silas should have been blinking up a storm—he hadn't blinked once in the ten seconds I'd been watching him.

"He's possessed," I whispered, but by now, I think Casey had parsed that out for himself.

"Hail," Silas groaned, "to the Darkness."

Casey squinted at Silas, reaching out with his own modest power to blearily see what Rowena and I saw. He watched it a moment, then slowly turned, like he was following a line, a string we couldn't see. The connection eluded me.

He looked at his mom, his expression turning grim.

"I am *so* sorry about this, darling, but I'm afraid you've just committed treason," she said in her lilting, singsong voice.

I looked back. Margaret had what looked like a bazooka over her shoulder. She was grimacing as she squinted through the sight mounted on its side.

Her amulet was glowing again. Violently.

"Duck," she said.

We flattened ourselves on the ground, staring at each other, wondering where in the holy hell she'd been hiding a bazooka—and I kept watching Silas, who was staring blankly ahead, straight through Margaret into the night-black wall beyond her. He had no reaction to anything, not to us or our guns, or Margaret, or her bazooka, or her warning to duck. He was barely breathing, as far as I could tell, and standing at a weird angle, like he was hanging on wire strings. Glowing orange …

I threw up a shield at the last second—not around us, but in front of Silas, who still hadn't moved to dodge the rocket. A thin, shimmering wall of sheer will and stardust materialized between us a split second before it made contact, exploding into a burst of red and yellow light, along with desert black smoke, and the clap of a drunken thundercloud. The fire stayed where it was, but the force was enough to break the shield into little, bite-sized pieces. It blew Silas back against the elevator wall, where he slumped without a sound, the charcoal-grey fog leaking out of his skin.

"There we are," Margaret said brightly, hefting the empty bazooka off her shoulder to the ground with a clatter. "So sorry, darlings, I thought I had more competent security, I don't know *why* Deanna didn't call me."

Casey whirled on her. "Mom, what the hell?"

Margaret looked wounded. "I just saved your life."

"From *what?*" Casey holstered his gun and went to Silas, kneeling beside him. "Christ, man, are you all right?"

"Two minutes, ma'am," said the technician beside her. He cast a furtive glance at the smoking bodies, and blinked at them, then looked away hurriedly before typing something into his computer.

Margaret looked over his shoulder and nodded approvingly.

"Casey, leave him be," she said. "I'll deal with him later."

Casey looked at her. His expression was pained, and his lips were pressed together in a solid line. "I'm …" he swallowed, "just making sure he's out, Mom. It's fine."

"Casey?" I said quietly. Everything became tense suddenly, burning from the inside out with something marginally more urgent than our dread. Silas was orange from his head to his toes, drowning in a sulphurous cloud of somebody else's influence—*Margaret's influence*, it had to be. And she intended to kill Silas so he couldn't provide us with any more information. But the only problem was that Margaret, Casey's mother, didn't have the magic necessary for possessing someone. "*Casey.*"

Casey looked at me from the corner of his eye and mouthed *I know*.

"Oh, *please* leave him alone, dear. I'll take care of him after we've gotten you on your way," Margaret said, waving off the notion like an annoying fly. Her amulet pulsated around her neck at longer intervals, the heartbeat of a sleeping dragon. *Pump … pump … pump …*

Silas stirred with a flatlined, monotone, "Uh …" and suddenly, he was sitting upright, scratching his neck. Lumbering like a stiff mannequin to his feet, he seemed off balance and awkward, like a marionette caught up in a ceiling fan. He was clinging to Casey as he helped him up.

"I ..." Silas said, visibly straining. A speck of blue glowed in his core, pulsing, but dim as a flickering star. "Can ..."

"Sit *down* and *stay* there," Margaret said irritably. "I *have* more rockets, you know, and I don't think you want another one of *those* in the face."

"*Mom*," said Casey. "He's fine. I've got it."

Silas frowned. "Um ... I ..."

Pump ... pump ... pump ... went the orange rock. Faster now, throbbing in time with a panicked heartbeat. Silas's blue glow ballooned outward, pushing back Margaret's orange cloud. Margaret's expression suddenly stretched thin.

"Sam," said Rowena, her tone just a whisper but with plenty of strength behind it.

"I know," I whispered back.

"It's coming from her necklace."

"I *know*."

Silas turned his head to Casey. Slowly, jerkily, like his bones were catching on themselves, he said, "C ... Ca ... sey ..."

Margaret sighed theatrically from across the room, opening another drawer and lifting the bazooka base to her shoulder again. "I'm warning you," she sang gaily. Although she sounded slightly tremulous.

"Silas?" Casey said warily, his voice hushed. "Where is my mom?"

Silas blinked for the first time in two minutes. "Get out ... now!"

"Oh, that is *it,* young man," Margaret scolded, her voice taut as she fumbled with another small rocket, trying to fit it into the launcher.

Casey looked from her to me. "Get her necklace," he whispered.

Margaret froze and looked up. Her mouth curled into an ugly mockery of a smile. "Now, now," she said, hefting the bazooka to her shoulder. "Why would you want to do *that?*"

Casey already had his gun trained on her, his finger perilously close to the trigger. "Give the necklace to Sam."

Margaret chuckled warmly. "Oh, *darlings*," she said, drawing a line up in the air. Silas stumbled to his feet behind us, fighting her wildly.

"Silas," I said, holding out a hand. Feeling the air for the invisible strings that bound him to the amulet.

It was almost dormant, hiding in the folds of its own power, masking itself so I couldn't tell what it was. Now, it had become a screaming fire, bright as burning magnesium. I couldn't say why Margaret or whoever the hell she was would have bothered trying to hypnotize me and risk exposing the amulet's power. Maybe that was plan A, to convince me to attack my team or fall flat on my face, staying unconscious long enough for somebody else to deal with me.

Last surviving member of Dulcie's ANC, I thought, and for a second, I wondered what the Darkness believed I would do, and why it considered me so dangerous. Then I decided the Darkness was probably after Casey and his team, not specifically me. They were the last people in the world who had any chance of stopping him.

But back to the amulet. It was older than stone, a fossilized relic of a bygone age, a half-dormant, old-world artifact that Margaret *really* shouldn't have had any access to, let alone been able to *touch* it without bursting into angry flames. Artifacts as old as that are very particular about whom they allow to use them and for what purposes. They possess a kind of consciousness in their pickiness. A Wisconsin mother with no magical prowess at all wasn't on their list.

Somebody else, though, was on their list. Something that could defeat the rock's power with its own. Something that definitely *wasn't* human.

The amulet's cords recoiled from me, hissing and spitting, sending physical sparks flying through the air. Silas doubled over like he'd been sucker-punched.

Margaret's eyes shifted as I came closer, their color bleeding away into her skull—leaving them the dull iron grey of a shapeshifter.

"What is that?" Judy whispered, nodding to the amulet. Everyone had a gun trained on her now, and the technicians were cowering like good, little bystanders, peering over their consoles to gawk at their boss.

"It's a ..." *Fuck!* I didn't even know what to call it. "It's a really ancient magical doo-dad with an angry spirit stuck inside of it." Or it could have been a stockpile of magical energy from a group of powerful warlocks that *definitely* died while making it. Or possibly even dragon's blood and unicorn tears. It could have been any number of things that could turn rocks into arcane killing machines.

"It's an arcane focus," said Rowena, glowering at it.

"That sounds bad," said Marcus.

Margaret smiled. "It is."

She lifted her hand and I felt the invisible strings turn to jelly, slopping to the floor. They lay immobile for several seconds.

I had time to think, *What the hell ...*

Then the strings drove themselves right through our skin, and I stopped breathing.

CHAPTER SEVENTEEN
Sam

There was a moment of darkness. A long minute of slack lungs and stilled hearts, when nothing was working, like all of our organs were on strike. I felt like I was being sucked into myself, my bones collapsing inward, like all the blood in my body was being compressed into a black hole. The muffled sound of laughter reached my ears, manic and chaotic. Then the shrivel and pop of an opening portal …

We slammed to the ground, falling backwards and forwards from wherever we'd been standing. We hit the floor *hard*. My muscles jittered and pricked from the inside, feeling asleep. I blinked, looked left, and saw Casey's mother—or whatever had pretended to be his mother—lying on the ground with smoke pouring out of both her ears. Even as I watched, her form shifted and changed. The shapeshifter returned to her original form—a smallish woman with sharp ears and skin darker than night. The amulet was in pieces all around her, drained of its glow.

Standing above her was a rather irksome shadow.
Oh, you've got to be fucking kidding me, I thought.

I expected some snide comment, or at least a leery grin, but Dagan was all I saw glaring at me. Blood stained his face, his hands, and around his mouth. A line of red connected him to the shifter. Black leather jacket, black pants, brilliant red shirt beneath—as close to dressing casual as he'd ever been. "And I thought *my* mother had issues." He tutted softly, nudging the unconscious woman with his foot. "We should go."

I dragged myself upwards, groaning, my bones prickling with an uncomfortable heat. Casey, who was next to me, did the same, grunting and holding his ribs.

"Who's he?" Casey asked, gesturing vaguely at Dagan. Dagan scowled at him, as though everybody in the world should have known his name.

"Dagan," I said, confused even as I answered. "The demon I talked to in Splendor about Dulcie's whereabouts." I took a deep breath. "As to why he just saved us? I have no clue." And on that question, I demanded an answer. "What the hell are you doing here?" I asked Dagan.

"Saving your life, apparently," he said. "And you're welcome, by the way, all of you."

"Thanks," I started uncomfortably because I was well aware that everything Dagan did had to benefit him in some way. How this situation benefited him wasn't exactly clear yet, but I figured it would reveal itself in time. "So how in the hell are you here right now?"

Dagan sighed. "I was *following* you. I had … let's call it a *bad feeling*. So, despite my better judgment, here I am." He shrugged. "And it's a damn good thing to! Guess it's true what they say about trusting your guts and intuition."

"So who's that?" Casey asked, pointing to the woman on the floor. Rowena knelt beside her and gave the air a cursory sniff, her stone eye gleaming in a silver light that wasn't there.

"Shapeshifter," she said after a moment. "She hasn't been in this form for long."

I barely heard her. "Let me get this straight," I said, squinting at Dagan. "You had a *bad feeling* and you *followed* me. Just because you had nothing better to do, or what?" As I've said before, Dagan made Bram look like the paragon of innocence. Dagan was chaos incarnate, the living manifestation of every sour thought the world could conceive—the kind of creature that spent warm summer evenings roasting marshmallows over house fires. He would have been delighted to watch me burn, just for the hell of it.

He had absolutely *no* reason to save my life.

Dagan sighed. "I admit, it sounds a bit … *contrived*, but I assure you, I have every reason to be here."

I crossed my arms and stared at him. "Name one."

"I do not want the world, as I know it, to go up in *smoke* for one, Madam White," Dagan said stiffly. "But we can talk about this when we we're far away from here. Your shapeshifter here, as I'm sure you've gathered, is no friend to you, and there are many other unfriendly creatures making their way to this building as we speak. They intend to … *deal* with you as they see fit."

"What are you talking about?" Casey demanded. "Unfriendly creatures?"

Dagan rolled his eyes. "I mean, a very bad someone has sent some very bad people to make sure you never reach your destination."

"Who specifically?" I asked.

Dagan shrugged. "I don't know."

"And how do you know that?" Casey asked suspiciously.

Dagan shrugged again. "Aftershocks. I was touching your girlfriend's scars," he said, "and sometimes, I continue to see things."

Casey looked at me, tacitly asking, *can we trust him?* I nodded although I wasn't really sure if we could trust Dagan. But it looked like we were also out of options.

The metal disk trembled beneath us—and a moment later, it started to fold in from the outside, melting away to reveal the deep, inky blackness of a two-dimensional portal.

"Um," said a technician. "It is. Um. Ready. Sir."

Dagan sighed, storming over to a technician and picking him up by his lab coat before hoisting him a foot off the ground. "Where does it lead?" he shouted in a voice dripping with angst.

The technician swallowed. Poor guy, just trying to do his job. Probably had no idea he nearly got us killed. "Um ... the Archaic, sir," he stammered. It was an ocean, big, angry, and dark. Full of hungry fishies with very sharp teeth.

Okay, he *probably* knew we wouldn't survive that. Nice to know we escaped that horrible fate within a matter of seconds.

Dagan brought the technician closer to his face, and his irises blazed. He opened his mouth, fire crackling in the back of his throat, backlighting his white teeth. "How'd you like to go for a swim?"

"That's not ..." I started to protest, but Dipshit Scientist III interrupted me.

"The Darkness will f-find you," he said. "And k-kill you all. It's j-just a m-matter of t-t-time."

I sighed. "Never mind; fuck him."

Dagan chucked him through the portal headfirst, screaming, and we heard a muffled *splash* on the other side. Sound doesn't travel particularly well through portals. Casey opened his mouth, probably to say something about proper ethics. Good thing he shut it again.

One bad guy down, twenty thousand to go. Slow progress.

"Anybody else feeling bold?" Dagan asked. He puffed out his chest, licked his lips, and seemed to revel in the room's discomfort. Scientists looked at each other and shook their heads. None of them could tell what he was, surely, but no one dared risk making him angry, even if he were just a very aggressive human.

"We need to move," he said to me. "*Now*." More intense than I'd ever seen him, he was urgent, minutes from full-blown panic—not an emotion demons ever displayed. I bounced to my feet—swaying for a moment, and let the grey drain out of my vision. Then I nodded, pulling Casey's arm to get him standing.

"Um. What's the plan?" I asked.

We could have asked the technicians really nicely to change where the portal let out, but that would have taken time, time that we didn't have. And if we could trust them not to dump us in some godforsaken desert or poisonous bog or something even worse. Yeah, we couldn't trust them at all—not when they were probably mind-whipped by the Darkness or maybe they were the Darkness's own people ...

Dagan said nothing but held out his arm and drew a large circle in the air. His hand trailed red sparks—carving a hole in space. The magic he was calling on was unclean. Its source was a deep, dark, desolate abyss, full of moans and whispers and bellowing like a half-broken fever, an impenetrable wall of self-imposed silence, stitched together from all the worst sounds into a steady, unbroken hum ...

"Get Silas," I said to Casey.

But Casey was way ahead of me, hefting the elf over his shoulder fireman-style. Silas was unconscious and moaning, but alive. He'd have a monstrous headache when he came to, but hopefully, that would be all. Mind-control is tricky magic even when you know *exactly* what you're doing. Never mind when it's at the hands of a slack-jawed amateur! Somebody keener on making an impression than *actually* hijacking your brain. If he were massively unlucky, he'd get away with only a blood clot or brain damage as a result.

Dagan dropped his hands. There was a red spark-spitting circle hanging in the air now, a fiery ring with a flat, glossy, black center. It had to be a portal, a door that opened into the unpleasant hallway that led to the Underworld. Dagan looked at us.

"After you," he said, gesturing to it.

"What's that?" Casey asked.

"A portal," said Dagan. "What the hell does it look like?"

"A *portal*?" I said. "You can just … *make* …" I turned on Dagan. I amplified my voice to thunder, roaring, my words echoing through every hollow place in the world. "*You've been able to do this the whole time?*" I screamed at him.

Dagan shrugged, clapping the invisible dirt off his hands. "You didn't ask me for passage," he said. "You asked me for a location, which I gave you."

I grabbed him by the back of his neck, digging my nails into his skin. He melted under me, moaning and groaning, but I didn't stop or care.

"*You useless,*" I hissed, "*pathetic, selfish,* ***motherfucking***—"

"Sam," Casey said, getting between us. "We should really go."

I looked back at him through a haze of red, and he shrugged.

The flames went out. I dropped Dagan—seeing blood on my fingers.

"Oops," I said. "Um. Sorry."

"Remind me to raise your hackles more often," Dagan crooned. He touched the blood I left on his neck, bringing it to his lips, *licking* it, and sucking on his thumb—

"Where does the portal go?" Casey demanded from Dagan, clearly irked by the demon's interest in my blood.

"Same spot we're in right now," he said. "Nether side. Empty lot."

"Empty?" said Casey, frowning. "It shouldn't be empty."

"Well, it is. And you have about ten seconds before one of these fools works up the courage to raise a proper alarm, and thirty more seconds before that motley group of heavily armed non-friends I mentioned before arrives. So … if you're keen on getting the fuck out of here, I'd hurry it up," Dagan said.

Casey glowered at him, adjusting Silas on his shoulder. He eyed Judy, who looked between Marcus and Kent. They both shrugged as they looked at me. I stared at all of them and turned to Dagan.

"If you're lying, I'm going to cut off your dick and feed it to Kent," I said.

Kent choked on his own spit and stared at me, wide-eyed. "You can do that?"

"Yes. She can," Dagan said. I couldn't tell if he sounded apprehensive or eager. But this was Dagan, so maybe it was a little of both.

Kent giggled. "That's feckin' brilliant."

Dagan rolled his eyes, noticeably more tense than before. "Come on, then."

The lights went out, replaced by a blinding. red and white strobe accompanied by a screaming alarm. The technicians ducked behind their consoles, cowering. Dagan sighed.

"I warned you," he said.

I turned to Casey, sighing and stammering wordlessly for a moment. Scrambling for a different way out that just wasn't there, I sighed. "Anybody got a better plan?"

Silence. Well, not silence, but nobody suggested another plan.

"Eh. Moost be worse ways ta die," said Kent.

Running at the portal, he catapulted himself through. The black sheen rippled and spun around him until we heard a faint *Wheeeee!* echoing from the other side. We waited. Listened. And then came a muffled Scottish accent. "Joost joomp, ye feckin' pansies!"

Casey and I exchanged a look. Behind us, the elevator door slid open.

"Ah," said Dagan. "Right on time. Shall we?"

Somebody cocked a gun behind us. Lots of them. We jumped—and the room exploded into a shower of bullets behind us. Seconds later, we tumbled out on the other side, and I felt like I'd just been spat out of a pinball machine. Rolling in the dirt, gasping, grunting, I could only hope we didn't land on anything sharp.

Dirt, I thought. Not hard veneer floors or glossy tile. Just open dirt.

I sat up slowly and looked around. A vast, greenish sky spread out above us, halfway to being starry—a Netherworldian twilight, and the sun scalded the horizon. Buildings were all around us: tall, old, angry concrete and tempered glass. And everywhere else? Just dirt, dirt, dirt. Grey and red and brown and black dirt. Soil and ash and brick dust.

Empty. Just like Dagan said it'd be.

Shit.

"Does this mean 'e gits ta keep 'is dick?" inquired Kent, almost sounding disappointed.

"Yes," I answered absently, standing up. A massive square of dirt that was pockmarked with slabs of grey stone was all that was left of the broken foundation. Surrounded by scorched buildings, the delicate hum of a city on the edge was punctuated with screams and pops and car alarms. Everything had black streaks, red spots, orange shadows, and the signature hallmarks of offensive arcana. Not to mention a unique smell that tainted the air—charcoal, gas, and the incessant haze of a burnt-out fire.

"Rowena?" I said. She didn't have to reply. The look on her face was tight and painful, like she could feel every scratch in every building on her skin.

"Something happened here. Something beyond what we can see," she said quietly, wheeling to look around. Concrete monsters towered around us, scorched, grey-red towers with holes in their sides, eaten away by acid and magma, dematerialized by warlocks, and crumpled like paper by giants or necromancers with uncanny, powerful friends. We were sitting in the middle of a magicked warzone.

And there, at the base of the wall, spray-painted on the stone by someone obviously in a hurry, was their message: *Humans go home!* Civilian humans did not live in the Netherworld, so it could only mean the ANC.

Shit on a stick. So they knew about the explosions—or, more likely, the explosions must have been mirrored on this side. The general population of the Netherworld was probably making some really unhealthy assumptions.

Kent was sitting on the ground, his legs splayed out in front of him. He sniffed and stuck out his tongue, tasting the air. "Smells like soomebody ruptured a propane tank."

"Casey," I said, staring at everything.

"I know, I know." He was standing now, spinning in circles with Silas at his feet. Staring agape at the Netherworld's Los Angeles equivalent, so clearly out of sorts, it was just burnt enough, and loud enough, and silent enough to prove something was wrong. Smoke, so much of it, and deep gouges in the earth from massive claws, along with humanoid silhouettes plastered against the walls and black shadows were all the remnants of vaporization. Distant sirens, and still, *so* much screaming and shouting.

The ongoing chaos of a riot.

Or not, I thought. *Maybe it's a party. Or a city council meeting. Maybe it's a peaceful protest.*

Jitter-smack-pop! went an automatic rifle. Then another and another. Distant, but too close for comfort. Coming from somewhere north—close to the ANC.

"You hear that?" Casey asked. Stupid question, but I almost asked it, too. *I'm not dreaming, am I? Somebody's got a gun. A big one. And they're using it in a place where there's lots and lots of people screaming. You heard it too, right?*

"Yeah, I heard it," I answered.

I didn't know why I was surprised. The Darkness wanted all the ANC offices *obliterated*. Off the map, eradicated, Netherworld branches included. Corporate genocide—it's the only thing that explained how all fifty different bases could go up at once. That's fifty portal hubs, gone! He *couldn't* want the ANC for their portals, not if he were wrecking them to shit. Portals are hellishly sophisticated things, but even magical rips in space and time aren't immune to flat-out explosions.

And if his murderous party existed in the underside, that would mean he'd have entire cities of supernatural citizens to contend with, most of whom were passively supportive of the ANC. It allowed them and their children a chance to escape the drab, seventies-locked Netherworld and visit more interesting places like Fresno. Most of the Netherworld civilians wouldn't allow their sole anchor to a moderately less destructive world go up in flames, especially if the explosion seemed so premeditated and deliberate.

If this ANC were still intact, there'd be people: protesters, vigilantes, and protectors, defending one of the last links to a slightly better world.

A riot. A protest. And a gun. Probably more than just one.

"Do we check it out?" asked Judy, a gun in her hand, she was already slumped into a halfhearted but low and ready stance.

Casey looked toward the noise, scowling. We all glanced between each other uncertainly. Our primary goal: find the Darkness and put a bullet in his skull—assuming he had a skull to put a bullet through. We didn't have the time or the resources to try and diffuse an angry mob. We'd do more harm than help.

Not far to my left, Dagan stood up from the dirt, making a show of dusting himself off and adjusting the cufflinks he didn't wear. He was different here, like every magical creature was in the Netherworld. His skin was paler, and his cheekbones more pronounced. Lankier, skinnier, and all at once, more muscular—he seemed stretched thin before ballooning out into something excessively tall and angry-looking. He seemed mostly Dagan, except for his eyes—that were now black vials filled with red, merciless fire.

"That sounds unpleasant," he said, nodding towards the shouting. "Shall we have a look-see?"

Judy shook her head. "We don't have enough time. And we can't do anything anyhow."

"We should drop by it," Rowena announced, "if only to read the climate. Something's happened here, city-wide. We should know what it is before we attempt anything else."

We looked between each other and swallowed collectively. Rowena was right, but that didn't mean we had to like it.

"Fine," said Casey. "But we stay on the periphery. And we get in and out, got it?"

"We should send some someone ahead," Judy announced. "Separate the group. Seven people on the edge of an angry crowd will surely stand out to *somebody*."

Casey nodded. "Okay. Rowena, Judy—"

"And me," I said, stepping forward.

"No," Casey said immediately. "Absolutely *not*."

"Rowena and I can perceive magic and auras in ways the rest of you can't," I said, placing my hands on my hips defiantly. "If the crowd's been magically coerced into screaming, or somebody's carrying a dragon's-eye cluster bomb, we'll be able to tell. You can't." And beyond that, I also knew the Netherworld and its social expectations far better than they did. If a draconian female stumbled up to them and asked how the sky's color suited them today, none of them would know the correct reply, (*fuck off, Janice, that's how*). No one would have known that it was an old joke from their folklore. Not being aware of that could result in significantly less skin on their bodies.

But I could tell Casey still didn't like the idea at all. His face compressed itself into an expression I couldn't quite read—something between unadulterated rage, outright denial, and fear. His voice sounded *way* deeper than I'd ever heard him use.

"No!" he said, before his arms started glowing.

No, not his arms—the *runes* on his arms. The glyphs and designs of shining blue that were carved into his skin. The only cosmetic manifestation of his magic. Weird. Hot, but weird. I wondered if those glyphs meant something to him, and if branding his skin with invisible ink was an integral part of becoming a Siphon.

"I can help," I started.

Casey shook his head, and every part of him was as solid as steel. "No! *Rowena* can see enough for both of you."

Rowena screwed up her mouth to one side. She was thinking maybe that we *couldn't*, since every creature perceived the magical planes in different ways. Although I might be able to detect the calculated heat of a dragon bomb, she could point out who was actually carrying it, and where they intended to drop it.

"She should come," Rowena said. "Or *you* should. You can see a bit too." However, *a bit* couldn't help us if things got hairy. "Or Captain Leather over there," she added, waving her hand at Dagan.

"I could go with both of them," Dagan said. "They can *keep me in check*, as you say."

"And you want to help? Why? Out of the goodness of your heart, or what?" I asked, eyeing him with visible doubt. "I'm still trying to figure out what's in it for you."

Dagan grinned. "Maybe I just want to watch people shoot each other."

Everyone ignored him.

Rowena sighed. "We'll be quick."

"We're running low on time, ya'll," said Judy.

"I promise I won't let your girlfriend get trampled," Dagan said to Casey.

"Fine. You've got five minutes. If you do *anything to Sam,*" Casey started.

"I know, I know, you'll cut off my dick and feed it to Kent," Dagan said with practiced ennui. "You have my word as a businessman with precious assets he'd like to keep intact."

"Uh-huh," Casey said. He looked at Rowena, setting his jaw. "Go. And hurry."

And then, before any of us could move, something barreled around a corner. It was bloody and smothered in grey and running like she had the Megalodon on her heels.

Christina. A fairy, and part of the ANC. Also a friend of mine.

She was screaming.

"Duck!"

But none of us did in time.

CHAPTER EIGHTEEN
Dulcie

I lay in bed, slick with sweat, but still freezing. *Sebastian*. He was breathing heavily, splayed across my stomach, smiling stupidly, lost in something between sleep and drunken stupor. At least he had the presence of mind to pay me a compliment every ten seconds or so, but not quite enough acuity to turn the sounds he made into actual words.

I just lay expressionless, absently staring at the ceiling. I'd already cried myself dry, and now I just felt … numb. Empty. Like all my insides had painfully dissolved, leaving me with only a hollow shell of a person. I started drifting off while listening to the thunder of my own breath.

I'd burst into the room screaming and wailing, telling the stupid voice to shut up, shut up, *shut up!* but it wouldn't go away. Sebastian, ever the gentleman-in-training, decided the best way to soothe me would be by paper-blank sex. He tried to be slow, sensuous, perhaps his version of gentle, but he didn't have it in him, certainly not in the capacity he was aiming for. Awkward, clumsy, and painful to see but much worse to experience, he had the gall to think he was doing well, and I failed to correct him. I tried to lose myself in it—if only to bury the persistent voice in his pathetically ill-timed strokes and caresses—but the voice never faltered.

Or maybe it did. When it seemed to have gone quiet, I could only torture myself with everything it made me see.

My reverie was interrupted briefly when the sounds of an enormous explosion rocked the entire house. Another strong earthquake? Moments later, the rumbling settled and I imagined the streets would soon be rife with chaos. It's not everyday a dryad meets her doom—just another warning to the Netherworldians that they had better comply with Mother or else. Fall in line or fall flat. It was as simple as that.

"Lovely," Sebastian murmured as he looped a tendril of my hair around one finger. He seemed absolutely impervious to what had just happened. Like he hadn't even felt the house shifting abruptly with the intense, magical explosion.

Sebastian was drunk long before I entered the room. He was boozing himself up in preparation for the angry Dulcie. She always emerged after prolonged exposure to Mother's damned dignitaries: all those self-important, dogmatic, heaps of skin, bone, and scale, tenaciously clinging to their romantic, pre-Earth ideals. Nothing they could think of could function any better than the system they'd just torn down. They must have known I'd be spitting bloody murder through my teeth by the time they stopped gawking at me.

My eyes roved across the ceiling, following the shallow sheen of recent paint until they landed on a mirror hung in the center of the far wall. In the reflection, I saw the burning scarlet bedsheets and their shadows, the gold tassels hanging from the bedframe, Sebastian's limp smile and his effeminate physique …

Then I saw my face. Catatonic. Placid. Aloof. Resigned. The face of death.

I blinked at myself, trying to smile, frown, sneer, or do anything. But the muscles wouldn't respond. I stayed stuck exactly where I was, the weary expression of a sleepy schoolteacher who abandoned her students and her responsibilities. Like shock or rigor mortis, my reflection revealed the emptiness of someone who couldn't quite comprehend what was happening around her.

You can't, she said. *You're missing something.*

I turned away from the mirror in a huff and looked back at the ceiling.

"Quiet," I whispered. All at once, the false cracks and aesthetic imperfections in the molding began to morph, and I saw a face. Blue eyes, a shock of black hair. Smiling. Perfectly content just to look at me.

I sat up suddenly, tossing Sebastian off me like a throw blanket. He clattered to the floor with a groan, then a grumble, and a loud thunk when his head took most of the impact, and I pushed myself sideways. Grabbing a fluttery, white silk robe, I tied it on hastily, walking to the French doors and throwing them open. I found myself inhaling deeply, and breathing fast like a drowning victim. The vision stayed in the back of my head, the blue eyes boring holes through my brain, looking down on the dark woods and chuckling softly. We were wondering what kind of beasts lived in there ... and I began remembering one time when he and I were almost devoured by a river monster—

Enough! I thought, *Of what?!* I couldn't say exactly what I'd had enough of. The voice? The memories? Sebastian's feeble attempts at lovemaking? I didn't know. *Everything*. This ragtag string of days and incessant hours, so full of confusion and pain accompanied by the vague sense that something was very wrong. And that stupid man Mother brought home! Now her prisoner, was he also a plaything? A toy? An *instructive aid?* No. He was too particular, too handsome, and too strong for sex to be the only reason Mother wanted him. He was my enemy. A traitor. A murderer. A usurper.

You killed Melchior.

I didn't, I said, a pathetic denial.

Yes, you did. You killed him because you had to. Because he deserved it. Because it was you or him. Monotone and indifferent, it didn't sound like her normal voice—it was too quiet and docile. Too grey. Too much like me.

Shut up, I thought, addressing myself.

I should have gone back downstairs and buried myself in the niceties of conclave talk, letting the drakes, the werewolves, and the vampires fuss over me like fond grandparents, and pointing out all the parts of themselves they saw reflected in me. So what if it pinched and burned and tweaked, being massively uncomfortable? I could do it, and I probably should have. If only so I could pretend nothing happened. Nothing was different, and there was nothing I'd overlooked. No bright red flags waving madly in a high wind and practically slapping me in the face.

Because there weren't any. We'd proceed and follow through to the finish line like nothing changed, because nothing *had* changed. We were monsters full of magic, driven with great purpose, and the hell if Mother's latest plaything would undermine that.

Relax, I thought. Inhale, exhale. *Feel the cold, and let it wash over you.* Smell the woods, the leaves, the mud, the distant blood. Think about something else, anything else. Anything but those diamond blue eyes and a long, white scar that spanned a vast expanse of sculpted muscles …

I sighed, leaning on the stone railing. I shouldn't have watched. Mother's glamour must have lost its potency on me. Her magic did that sometimes, spreading through the room and trapping anything semi-sentient within range, just because it could—especially when she worked herself into a tizzy. Now I was all hot-and-bothered for some floozy Loki I'd never met, and desperate to get my hands on him, while stupidly insisting he was innocent.

***Innocent** is not the right word,* she said. *But he didn't kill Melchior, if that's what you're talking about.*

I laughed hoarsely. I was too tired to tell her to fuck off. *You know what? Sure. Maybe he didn't.*

What if Mother was lying? It wouldn't be far out of character, even if the lie were intended only for my benefit—but if she were, she must've had her reasons, and I wasn't about to question her. Not when we were so close to the end.

Maybe I could go downstairs and find her. I could hide in the kitchen and send Antoine into the crowd after her. He could lure her back with a Bloody Mary or something, and convince her to officially release her stupid spell ... I believed the effects of it were probably the only reason I allowed Sebastian to fuck me.

Fuck, I thought. Weird word. Short, and to the point. Not the kind of word I used often.

Yeah, it is, she said, only softer now. *All the fucking time.*

I blinked slowly, suddenly feeling sleepy, of all things. I shook my head and widened my eyes. Mother would be here any minute now to pull me downstairs for the final call. The last moment to drink before we went out to set the world on fire. I had to be awake for that, or at least ready to fake it. The more observant vampires and dryads might notice something was off, but most of them would be slobbering drunk by then, if they weren't already. Anything I did had to be pitch-perfect-professional. I could slit a throat in the middle of the room and the rest of the party would consider it a charming anomaly, a queer side effect from all the changes their poor, little darling had to endure.

Like going through puberty, I thought. But this time, it was some sacred ordeal, a ritual, and the realization of something that everyone in that room had *built* me up to be. Here, the watery blood of the old nymphs combined with the sap-thick sludge from the dryads, the blue vinegar from the draconian kings, and the shadowy scarlet from every vampiric House in the world. Blood on blood on blood on blood on blood, always more being added, homogenized inside a cauldron in a dark room. Spoon feeding a three-year-old who had no idea what she would become or what kind of gift she was receiving. And no clue what would be expected of her later because of it.

Not that I cared much. Destroying things for me was easy, and it seemed that's all I wanted to do anyway. Mother was the politician. The drake who wanted to marry me was of the military viewpoint, and some other fool dealt with optics and propaganda. Me? I was a big, scary gun, a magic bomb bristling with clashing energies. Ready to burst on command. It would be fun for a while, before I was regulated to something far less …

Regulated. Why did that word strike a nerve? I'd meant to say relegated.

My mental tirade came to a standstill. It all stopped so I could examine that peculiar word. Regulated, regulated, regulated … something made me feel strange, cold and blue, something from the distant past, like a half-remembered smell.

Regulator, I thought suddenly. Not an action, but a person. But what was a Regulator? A person, a person, but what did they *do*?

They catch things. Evil, angry things and confine them forever. A darker voice thought *enemy,* and all the familiarity I clung to suddenly sank into nothing. The word was just a word again, absent any memory, if I still possessed one to speak of.

Memory. And that led to another thought. An odd one, one I hadn't enough time to consider before, and never occurred to me until this very moment.

What did I remember?

Not just about Regulators or how often Mother lied, but about … *anything.* How old was I? Who were my friends? Where did I go to school? What did I look like when I was little? What books did I read? What magic did I know and possess?

All of it, the darker voice crooned. *Everything and much more.*

"More than what?" I whispered. More than nothing? Two weeks? Three weeks was more than nothing. All at once, with a terrible shock, I realized that's all I had in my brain. That's as far as my archive regressed—***three weeks***. Waking up in this room with

Mother beside me, she was telling me to shoot some troublesome burglars, and I recalled watching them bleed out on my floor. But before that? Before that ... there was nothing! Just a persistent darkness, an emptiness with a burdensome weight imbuing it, an absence with a bitter presence that refused to leave me. A deliberate awareness of *nothing*.

Maybe it was Mother's doing. I'd been lost for quite some time, or so she told me, and the change could only resume very recently—three weeks ago, or just before that. Perhaps this was another known side effect of the material shift: losing the memories of everything that came before. Or maybe it was an unforeseen side effect, something that would doom my present self, preventing me from forging any new long-term memories. Maybe I had a tumor, or hit my head, or I was allergic to one or more of the blood samples Mother kept pumping through me. Maybe my brain was sick, like a computer with a virus that suddenly erases all of its files. I was left with a single program that was barely operable. I found myself constantly reaching back for relevant information, but finding nothing. I could only fail to complete the code.

I shook my head, feeling silly. *Must be the glamour talking.* I'd never known a glamour to do that before, but I'd also never been personally glamoured either, certainly not by someone as strong as Mother. I believed it was more hormone-based than mental. Glamouring affected the primal lizard brain and all of its baser instincts. It had almost nothing to do with higher mental functions—but brain chemistry still meant *brain*, and it wasn't totally unfeasible for Mother to have temporarily wiped out my memory.

The glamour brought my thoughts back to that man, the prisoner, Knightley. Tall, dark, handsome, and so wonderfully mobile … Maybe I would go to him after all. Just to sample him, and see if sex with him drove the feeling away. Maybe I could satisfy the glamour's obsession with him and finally silence it. The way he fought Mother looked painful, but far more stimulating than anything Sebastian could provide. The prisoner wouldn't be hard to glamour again, especially not after what he just endured. And he seemed to know me, even if I didn't know him. Hell, he might even want it … I wondered if that would make it any easier.

I looked down at my hands, turned slightly green in the light of my wings, which were flapping languidly behind me. I remembered something a vampire said to me once, but now it seemed like worlds ago. He was describing the behavior of glamours. He said they removed the subject's inhibitions, giving them a green-light for whatever base urges lay beneath the surface.

He also said something about choices, and how even under a glamour, you still had them. No matter how powerful the caster was. Suddenly I felt sick to my stomach. The idea that Knightley could have engaged Mother willingly, even slightly … Ugh!

I didn't understand why that thought bothered me as much as it did. There was no explanation, just a jumble of feelings. They twisted my stomach and made my eyes burn and my heart race. They also brought back the panicked choking from before.

I squeezed my eyes shut, bit my tongue, and inhaled the frozen air. *You have to want it,* I thought, but the voice sounded different, like a whisper from a memory I couldn't completely recall. *Some part of you, however small, has to **want** it.*

So what could I have wanted so badly?

That struck me. *I'm not being glamoured.* The thought came slowly, like I was emerging through molasses with helpless arms. *That's ridiculous.* Mother's glamour, sure, but that was a wave of horniness, and nothing more. *Absolute nonsense.*

For a moment, there was silence. Not thinking anything, my mind came to a halt. Hesitating long enough to breathe. A cold wind tugged at my robe, picking up my hair, and making my wings shudder. Everything was shrouded in abysmal, desolate dark.

But if I were being glamoured, I started to say. The words crept into place, forming quiet sentences as though I were hiding from something. *If I **were** being glamoured, which I'm not, and my thoughts **weren't** really mine, what would I want more than anything?*

I thought about it. Knightley, maybe. He was stunningly attractive, and maybe I knew him somewhere in my black past. Hmm. What else could I want?

Power? Fortune? Maybe, but I hadn't done anything with the money Mother still possessed, and I didn't particularly want to. Sex? I had Sebastian, but he was nothing to write home about. Hades! What else?

Maybe Mother, herself, her constant presence, or her tutelage. Yes, there was a hole there, a vague, a misty silhouette where a person could be standing in the back of my head—and a soft, warm voice to go with it. Yes, it was the mother that I wanted! It had to be! Because I missed her. Yes, I missed her! I could feel it now in my being, all the way down to the marrow inside my bones. I missed the way she sang to me when I couldn't sleep ... and her smile whenever I got off the bus ... and all the fairy tales she told me that weren't real, and how she braided my hair ... and she always told me I could do anything I wanted, and be anything I wanted to be ... her ice water eyes, blue as diamonds, were always smiling—

Wait.

Mother's eyes weren't blue. They were grey and red and orange! Sometimes, they were black. But never blue.

Mother's eyes, no, I thought. *But ...* **Mom** *...*

And then it all came crashing down.

CHAPTER NINETEEN
Sam

The air went red and mercury-white, hot enough to blister our skin. There were lights and shouting, the distant angry crowd going up in smoke, spitting debris, hocking bricks and bits of foundation, concrete and calcified bones, along with vaporized blood. A wave, like a gust of wind, flattened us all to the ground, and we lay on top of the dirt. With the air forced out of our lungs, I didn't have the ability to even scream properly.

It was all over an instant later, leaving behind a blind expanse of heat. And then silence. Brooding, invisible, airless. Shadows moved across the edges of my vision. People, standing if they could, were complaining if they couldn't. A voice, Marcus's, asked Christina if she were all right—Christina, however, failed to reply.

Kent grunted. "Shite." He coughed and hauled himself onto his feet with a lot of stumbling. "Whut the hell was that?"

I stared at the sky, the normal green was all awash with the wrong colors—the glittering aftermath of a very specific kind of explosion.

"That's what happens when a really old spirit dies," I croaked. It could have been anything, from the world's first fairy to the mother of all dryads—although I couldn't imagine who would have taken it upon themselves to abandon their hideouts in the mountains and forests just to go off and riot in the streets. Especially if there were guns involved! Dryads openly detested modern machinery, particularly anything with the capacity to kill.

Unless it was a demon. Drawn to the chaos, demons were the first to begin feeding on it.

Or maybe someone trying to help, I thought. Some godlike, old-world entity trying to do some good, standing in the wrong spot at exactly the wrong moment. Old things are powerful, but not impervious to harm. And something old and powerful would be the first on the Darkness's hit list. I figured this carnage had to be from that—the Darkness killing something that should never have been killed.

I sat up slowly and looked at Dagan, who was still standing. The explosion hadn't ruffled his feathers at all. He stood there stroking his chin, observing the smoky shadow hanging in the air.

Eventually, he said, "Well. So much for the riot."

I felt myself explode—literally. My clothes and hair suddenly leapt to life with long tongues of violently orange fire. I wasn't ready for it, and unfortunately, neither was anyone else. "Are you insane?" I screamed at him. "People are *dead*! Is this some kind of game to you? Did you just tag along so you could have a front row seat to watch the world burn?" Doing a crazed, odd dance at this point, my arms were flailing, and I was almost laughing. "What is wrong with you?"

Dagan's grin evaporated. He looked grim, almost professional. "I'm sorry," he said, but I wondered if he meant it. He probably didn't. But I was surprised by his peace offering.

"Wait, what?" I asked, just to make sure I heard him correctly.

Dagan inhaled deeply and sighed. "I said, I'm sorry. Now is not the time for digs, I'm fully aware." He looked around at the general carnage and took a few steps towards me—I didn't step back.

"You and I have always been adversaries," he started, looking over at Christina—she was slumped in Marcus's arms, breathing and muttering to herself. She kept saying her boyfriend's name over and over again: *Quillan, Quillan, Quillan* ... "But now we have something much bigger than angry potion lords to worry about. And I'd very much like to preserve the tenuous diplomacy between the Netherworld and the American government. As much trouble as you and your coworkers have caused me, I am not ready to see you die, not just yet."

"Not just yet?" I repeated.

Dagan shrugged and smiled, but for the first time, it wasn't entirely shady. "I must allow for the shifting of my own morality."

I scoffed—I couldn't help myself. "You have morality?"

"Immorality is its own kind of morality," Dagan said with a shrug. "If nothing else, it occupies one end of the spectrum. And so ..." He offered me his hand. "In the interest of maintaining that spectrum, I would like to offer you my help. I don't know what you might request of me now, but I'd prefer not to have to live in the Netherworld forever, if it's all the same to you."

I looked back at Casey, and he gave me a confused shrug. "You know him better than I do."

I turned back to Dagan. "I'm not sure I do." This was a side of Dagan, if it were real, that I never thought I'd see.

Dagan sighed. "I'm not asking you to *trust* me," he said, "I'd never go that far. But I ask you to allow me to assist you, however marginally, in the service of continued prosperity and relative peace of the supernatural population on Earth. Whatever's happening doesn't look good for the ANC, and what's bad for the ANC is eventually bad for everybody. Especially in the eyes of the human government, right?"

"Right." I spent another minute staring at him. Then I took his hand and gave it one firm shake. I half expected him to pull me in for an uncomfortable, groping hug or an unwanted kiss, but he did neither. He simply shook my hand and let it go, standing up straight and looking as grim and professional as I'd ever seen anyone appear.

"Right, then," he said. "Where do you suggest we start?"

It took me a moment to find my voice. There was a smell in the air now: hot, acrid—bodies had to be burning somewhere upwind. "By finding the Darkness," I said at last, "we kill him, and this ends."

Dagan scoffed. "And you think you can just mosey on into the home of a creature that's powerful enough to endow Dulcie with the magic to do *that?*" He pointed to the silver scars at my throat. "And what do you expect to do? Just kill them? Squish them like bugs, no harm, no pain?"

"No *pain?*" I spat. "Dagan, we have *no* resources, no backup, *nothing*. We're grasping at straws here, *we* are the last resort, so I'm sorry if it seems a little crazy, but we're running out of time, and—"

I felt hands on my shoulders—*Casey.* He leaned down and whispered in my ear, "Breathe. It's going to be all right."

His hands crept down and he wrapped his arms around me, giving me a squeeze. I leaned back into him, almost reflexively, drawn in by his smell: sweat, dirt, and whatever remained of his cologne. His glasses poked my ear as he pressed his head against mine. I held his wrist and closed my eyes for a moment, inhaling and exhaling slowly. I was also trying to ignore the powerful stench of smoke and spray paint hanging in the air.

"Apologies," said Dagan. "Are you, then, in need of a plan?"

I opened my eyes and nodded. Casey didn't move away, but stood up, keeping his arms draped over me. I clung to one of them like a child. I almost felt like if I let go of it, the shaking ground would swallow me whole. "Yes," I said. "Yes, we are."

Dagan nodded. "We are in the Netherworld now," he said. "Much closer to Dulcie, wherever she is. If you'd permit me, I can," and he casually reached for my throat.

Casey left my side and grabbed Dagan by the front of his shirt, the lines of silvery-blue glyphs steaming along his arms and around his eyes. Dagan's magic strained against his own skin, resisting the magnetic pull of an angry Siphon. I took an involuntary step back.

"*Don't. Touch. Her,*" Casey warned. His voice was different, deeper, and echoing itself. Dagan looked over Casey's shoulder at me and gave me what he might have been considered a demure smile.

"Wouldn't dream of it," he said with an affected air. His aura was close to visible, pulsating in yellow around his bones. Fear shown tautly around his eyes, as well as his teeth. He stepped away from Casey and fussed with his collar. Casey stepped back slowly.

Dagan sighed. "I can pinpoint *exactly* where she is," he said wearily. "I am *well* past the point of lechery." He omitted "for now" at the end of his sentence, and it seemed like that was all Casey wanted to hear.

"It's okay," I said, laying a hand on Casey's glowing, bulging shoulder ... *Focus, Sam.* "If he tries something—"

Dagan's smile twitched. "May I?"

I imagined this would be a lot less pleasant in the Netherworld—but we lacked any backup plans. I pulled back my hair, squeezed my eyes shut, and let him touch the burns.

Then I promptly blacked out.

###

When I opened my eyes, I saw Casey hovering over me. He was holding me and asking me if I were okay. I blinked and sat up. Dagan was standing about three paces away from me, looking strangely bashful. I supposed he was trying not to appear threatening, so nobody would suspect he made me pass out deliberately. He eyed Casey when he finally noticed I was awake. Maybe he was afraid to look at me, in case I chose to make good on my promise to castrate him.

Casey twitched. Like he could tell Dagan was looking at him expectantly so he deliberately avoided looking back at *him*. I couldn't have been out for long, but I got the sense they'd been like that for quite a while.

"I'm okay," I said, sitting up slowly. Nothing hurt, and my head was fine. The scars on my throat pulsed and sang, the residual magic lingering in the tissue, and bright as a beacon. "I should have warned you. Everything's worse in the Netherworld." *Worse* in this case meant fire, brimstone, and the foreboding sense that a very powerful something wanted you dead—in contrast to the vague stinging I felt when Dagan touched me Earthside.

I strongly hoped that I didn't make a face when the pain hit me since Dagan would have *loved* that.

"I'm fine," I said when Casey gave me a dubious look. "Really. Come on, help me up."

Casey stood first, giving me his hand. "Do you know where Dulcie is?" he asked me.

I nodded. Most otherworldly creatures with magic find that it doesn't apply in the Netherworld—fairies trade their dust for wings, and witches get sparkly skin and an almost painful sensitivity to magic. Demons, however, are technically from somewhere else. Darker, more dangerous, and more vacuous. Less inherently "magical," so they only kept whatever tricks they had up their sleeves. Lucky for Dagan.

But because we were in the Netherworld, where the atmosphere is three parts breathable oxygen to four parts raw, ethereal energy, *everything* was stronger—Dagan's tracking magic *as well as* my sensitivity to it. I got a pixel-perfect view of the mansion Dulcie was currently in, and a foolproof map of how to get there without running into anything especially unpleasant. Like those gigantic, flying monsters with a propensity for eating tourists.

"Big mansion north of here," I said. "Ten miles outside Splendor."

"Ten miles?" Kent asked. "That's … that's it?"

"Yeah," I said with a shrug. I thought it was weird, too—and never expected the Darkness to be camped out so close to home. "Maybe it's just a coincidence?"

A coincidence that he lived within driving distance of the fairy he was so obsessed with? And her ANC? Hers had been the first one to get blown up. Somehow, all the coincidences ceased to seem so accidental anymore …

Dagan raised his eyebrows. "You believe in coincidences, Madam White?"

"No, but after all this, the universe owes me a damn favor," I said, sighing.

"And you know how to get there?" Casey asked.

I nodded. "But we're gonna need a car."

"On it," said Judy, pushing herself onto her feet. She'd been sitting in the dirt next to Kent, drawing circles and dicks with her finger. Kent was having a devil of a good time sweeping them away, while cackling under his breath. "Be right back."

"Don't break anything, sweetheart," Marcus said, adding, "or any*one*."

Judy flipped him off over her shoulder as she walked away. "Fuck you, Marcus."

"I chide because I care," he called after her.

I turned to Casey—red-skinned and smoky from the blast. "How's Christina?" I asked.

"Fine," he said, gesturing to where she sat in the dirt behind him. She was chatting idly with the now conscious drow. "Shaken up, obviously, but she's still in one piece."

Which is more than we can say for everybody at the ANC, I thought. It popped into my head from nowhere, a big, ugly thought drank by a half-empty bottle of pessimism. *Somebody might have made it out alive. Christina obviously had. Maybe, hopefully, she wasn't the only one.*

Or maybe she was, and that's why she was unaccompanied. Alone and shaky, she was trying to have a normal conversation with Silas, who, as far as I could tell, was happy to oblige her. He leaned forward, smiling softly, and nodding and laughing sometimes, even when what she said wasn't funny. They both had rusty iron in their eyes, indicating that they had seen too much in a very short time.

"Do we know why Silas was in the generator building?" I asked. I wondered if the building had an official name, or if everyone referred to it as "that place with the generator."

Casey crossed his arms, shaking his head. "I haven't talked to him yet."

"Should we?" I didn't want to make Silas uncomfortable by asking him what he'd been doing there. He'd spent the better part of five minutes under the influence of an incredibly powerful relic, and no matter who you are or what you're made to do, it's never a comfortable experience. Depending on the severity of the spell, it can be downright violating.

"Probably," Casey said, sounding just as reluctant as I felt. "He said my mom was in Brokenview. I think he knew the shapeshifter was there and came to warn us. Which ..." he whistled softly, "is bad. He didn't have any reason to be monitoring us, or the generator room. And Silas isn't the type to *stumble* onto things like this; he's always very deliberate."

"So we *should* talk to him," I said.

"Yes. We should."

We both nodded. But neither of us moved toward Silas. Even though it was necessary, the timing just seemed wrong. Questioning someone was something you did after your morning cup of coffee, when they were waiting for you in the interrogation room, and you had plenty of time to get to the nitty-gritty. It didn't seem like something you did when the world was blowing up around you and you were next in line.

We stood there in dusty-red silence. A slight wind was blowing, and the sound of the distant crackle of flames while every now and then, a loud rumble indicated another building falling away. Christina and Silas, bloody, burnt, and tired, were whispering to each other. Kent was giggling to himself, while singing under his breath and bouncing on his heels.

"Do you think we're gonna die down here?" I asked Casey as I looked up at him, shelving the task of questioning Silas for the time being. There were bigger fires to tend to.

Casey blinked at me. The question caught me off guard too. It was a stupid thing to ask—either we would, or we wouldn't, regardless of what any of us thought. There was really no use in discussing it.

He looked at me for a moment, studying my face. Thinking. Then his features relaxed and he said, "I don't know. Maybe. Hopefully, not."

I nodded slowly, exhaling, and puffing out my cheeks. "Yeah. Hopefully, not."

He wrapped his arm around me and squeezed. "We *are* going to be okay. I can feel it."

The only thing I could say was, "Siphons aren't precognitive."

Casey laughed. "Says who?"

"Me?"

He laughed again, and I laughed too. Hades only knew why.

"We might die saving the world," he said softly. "And we might not. But we're going to do everything in our power to make sure everybody comes through this."

I nodded, sighed, and stood up a little straighter. "Yeah. Okay. Come on. We should talk to Silas—and get that whole thing out of the way so we can find out what he knows and if it will help us." I was probably just putting off the inevitable—our confrontation with the Darkness—but Casey didn't call me on it.

"Right," said Casey, giving me another squeeze before letting go. I took a step forward, trying to think of the most considerate way to talk to Silas about his possession …

Casey grabbed my arm, spinning me back towards him, and slammed his lips into mine. Harder than he meant to, like he had to get it done before he lost his nerve—but a second later, it became softer and much slower. The restrained urgency of somebody on the cusp of a very dangerous adventure, and the possibility of not returning in one piece. Casey dared not miss the chance to kiss me, not because he waited too long, or hesitated, or found himself dying.

He'd already kissed me before. Little pecks on the head and cheek, comforting little nothings. This, however, was different. This was *intended* to be different. He asked me a question before I lost the chance to answer him and make sure this was what we both thought it could be.

I lifted my hands to his head, running them through his hair, and wrapping my arms around his shoulders. He pressed himself against me, his tongue snaking in and out of my mouth, his lips opening and closing around mine, without parting for more than a fraction of a second. Heat wove itself through me in a wave, building quietly at first, before fanning into a raging inferno. A rush of blood warmed my face, my shoulders, my stomach … everywhere.

Absolutely everywhere, I was on fire.

Then he pulled back. Too soon, *way* too soon. We were both breathing hard by then. Breathing hard and staring, that's all. Not sure what to say, or *needing* to say anything. We just kept staring each other in the eye, flicking back and forth, searching. And finding all kinds of things.

We smiled at each other, refusing to blink, in case we missed something. Out of the corner of my eye, I saw Kent scowling when he handed Judy a bill. Judy, smirking, took the money without looking back at him. She was staring at us with her arms crossed, and looking smug.

"Um. I think Kent just lost a bet," I whispered.

"Good," Casey said, and he kissed me again—a light peck this time, and much too short, but sweet. It sent a bright flash through me, so strong it was almost painful.

"Okay," he said softly. Our noses were almost touching, and our foreheads pressed together. "Now we can talk to Silas."

"Yeah," I said, flustered. "Um, yes. Silas."

For another second, we didn't move. Then Casey sighed, straightened up, and started walking. It took me a minute to remind my legs how to walk again.

"Casey," said Silas. Silas looked up, but he didn't stand. Christina narrowed her eyes at Casey—she could tell what he was, one of the many benefits of being fae. And she didn't like what she saw. She looked at me curiously, wondering what I was doing cavorting with a creature designed (in theory) to kill us if we ever got out of hand.

I gathered myself together and said, "Hi, Christina. This is Casey James. He's here to help."

Christina looked between the two of us, her eyebrows hiking themselves up to her hairline.

"Honest," I said. Christina screwed her mouth to one side, but said nothing.

"Um ..." I swallowed. *Where's Quillan*, I wanted to ask. Presumably, he was in the ANC *with* her. She'd taken him officially off Dulcie's hands once Melchior was dead. He was registered as an informant, but he functioned as a partner, a mini Regulator without the badge, although he was working to get it back. He should have been with her.

But Christina was always good at reading people. She patiently sought all the microscopic words hiding in the folds of people's worst expressions. "Quillan's gone," she said. "Not dead or anything, just ... I don't know where he is. In the city, I guess, we both saw the dryad die at the same time, so he probably ran ..." She sniffed and shook her head. "I'm sure he's fine." She closed her eyes as if she were repeating the mantra to herself to make it so.

"Yeah," I said. "I'm sure. He's pretty resourceful."

She smiled at me, attractive as ever and glowing. Somewhere behind me, Dagan began panting, moaning, and purring.

"What's the matter with him?" Kent asked, staring at Dagan—who was doing his best to contain himself but, predictably, failing.

"Fairies are ..." I swallowed my thought. Another quirky side effect of being a fairy in the Netherworld. Dulcie often described the phenomenon as *sexual crack*. It was an absurd moment to be prudish, but somehow, I couldn't get myself to say that with Casey standing so close. "Particularly ... *intoxicating* ... when in the Netherworld. Side effect of ... something or other," I said at last, gesturing to Dagan. "Ignore him."

"Aha. Got it." Kent continued to stare at Dagan, unabashedly fascinated.

"How you feeling, man?" Casey asked, turning to Silas. He extended his hand and Silas shook it.

Silas looked grim. "Been better. Rowena, good to see you, though."

Rowena nodded to him silently, grinning. "You too."

"What were you doing in LA?" said Casey. "You're stationed in DC now, right?"

"I am. I mean I was." Silas ran a hand over his face, visibly exhausted. "Case, we got a problem."

Just what you don't want to hear.

"What kind of problem?" Casey asked.

"Your mom," said Silas.

Kent chuckled. Judy glared at him and raised her hand, threatening to hit him. He flinched and laughed more quietly.

"Right. You said she was in Brokenview?" Casey pressed.

Silas nodded. "She sent me a message," he said, ignoring Kent, or perhaps he didn't hear him. "Said she was working the Brokenview ANC site. She wanted …" He winced and took a deep breath. "She wanted me to send down an empath. Hana somebody. See if she could confirm something."

"Confirm what?"

"That the explosion was deliberate. That it came from the inside."

"Oh, shit," said Casey, and he looked at me. I didn't know what *he* was thinking, but this had to look *really* bad for the ANC. If it appeared to anyone that we sabotaged ourselves …

Not a fun thought.

"So Mom was in Brokenview—" Casey started.

"And something else was with you guys in the gen room," Silas said. "Probably trying to prevent government brass from going someplace they shouldn't. Like, you know, the Netherworld. Easier to keep people from using your equipment if you look like the person in charge."

"A shapeshifter," said Rowena.

"Yeah," said Silas. "But not just that. I tried calling in Hana myself. Went down to her office. She wasn't there."

"So?" said Casey. "There's got to be a dozen other places she could have gone to."

"She wasn't the only one gone," Silas said. "Half the building was empty. More than a dozen offices, totally unmanned. And it looked like they left in a big hurry."

"They? Meaning …?" Rowena asked.

"Meaning senators and congressmen and all of their personal staff."

"And nobody left a memo?" Rowena said.

Silas shook his head. "Nothing. I thought it was a government shutdown, but the budget thing's been over for a week, and the other half of the building still had people inside it." He sighed. "Some of them told coworkers they were taking an extended holiday, but none of them would say where they went."

We blinked and sat on that for a moment, thinking. Half of Rowena's face fell—the other side, the ivory mask with its ocean-black eye, was gleaming, and lit from within by a sharp, green light. If anyone else could see it, no one said anything.

"And you were in LA," said Casey. "Because you found out the shapeshifter was there."

"Yeah. You radioed in to say where you were heading, but by then, your mom had already left for

Brokenview and gone radio-silent. She was worried somebody would be listening in, which I thought was crazy, her line was secure, but when I went to Rickson about changing the keys, I got shot down. Hard."

"What do you mean?" I asked.

"I mean Rickson wouldn't take my call. And there were some schmucks I'd never seen before standing outside his door, telling people *the boss could not be disturbed*. Nobody else would take my call either, which was weird, and all I was trying to do was make sure a replacement primary technician was stationed at the portal. The key to that thing is enormous and it's not something everybody in the agency gets to carry around. That generator changing hands is, like, a *huge* deal."

"Shit," said Casey, grimacing like he suddenly understood. "Rickson wouldn't take your call. And Mom thought she was being spied on."

"Yeah," said Silas. "That's what I was thinking too."

"Um … what?" I asked, not following.

"Rickson is one of two other people that has a legitimate backup key for emergencies," Silas said. "And the only person besides Margaret that can give somebody else permission to run the show. Margaret didn't think she was safe on a division-only phone line, and she kept saying she was being followed. She's anything but paranoid." Silas almost laughed. "It means the agency's gone bad. Real bad. Totally lost control, and somebody upstairs isn't letting anybody out in the field. Our best bet is to lie low, and wait it out."

"Wait *what* out?" said Marcus. "This isn't a blown black op! This is a hostage situation turned into a massacre. That's not something you *wait out*."

"I know," said Silas, "that's why I ducked out and found you. By the time I got somebody to answer a damn question, someone discovered what I was looking for. A bunch of guys in suits I'd never met before came swarming in from nowhere, insisting that the generator was in good hands and telling me to stay the hell out of your operation. That was obviously suspicious. I kept asking where you were and why we weren't offering ground support, saying we *had* the clearance to know about this, but they shut me down every time. Said you were on your own and anything we might try to do to help would just blow your cover."

Casey groaned while walking in an ever tightening circle. "And we're not even *under*cover."

"Yeah," Silas said ruefully. "So, uh … I don't know if it's just the support team, but we've been compromised. At least, all the way to Rickson. This Darkness character has an in, or he paid somebody to pay someone else to stay out of it, or somebody's trying to cover up something *else*, and I don't know how the hell the congressmen are involved, but their timing can't be another coincidence …" He shrugged.

"I don't know. But something's up. Something really bad."

"Did you call Johnson?" Casey asked Silas, adding, "Rickson's boss? Last guy below my mom?"

"Yep," Silas answered with a clipped nod. "And his wife, and also his brother. They haven't seen him in days, and his secretary said he called in sick last Monday and she hasn't heard from him since. And Casey? I called Odyssey."

"And?" Casey asked.

"She didn't answer. Hana did."

"What did Hana say?" Casey asked warily.

"That Odyssey was not to be disturbed," Silas said. "That she was busy. I told her it was about your op, but Hana wouldn't budge."

"*Fuuuuck*," said Casey, turning, pulling on his hair. "Fuck fuck fuck fucking *fuck!*"

"Me too, man," Silas said bleakly, resting an arm on his knee. He looked at me, not for the first time, and tried to smile. "Sorry. Who are you?"

"Samantha White," I said. "Um." *Lone survivor of ANC Splendor.* That was probably what he was asking. He wanted to know where I came from and why I was now part of Casey's merry band of psychopaths. But I couldn't say that out loud.

"Silas, do you think you could get back in? Give us eyes topside?" Casey asked.

"Probably," Silas answered. "I could find a computer and a back door, and hack into the cameras.

They *definitely* know I was in LA, so I can't just walk in, but I'll figure something out. But you know ... I'd have to get back to the office first ... and out of the Netherworld."

"Right—the office which is in a different dimension," Casey muttered. "*Fuck!*"

"Maybe the portal at the ANC here is still intact?" Christina asked, sounding hopeful. "I mean, I doubt it is, but it's worth looking into, isn't it?"

"Portal generators are really fragile," I said with a sigh, shaking my head. "If we're *really* lucky, it's in a million pieces."

"Pieces we could put back together?" Casey asked.

I cocked my head to the side. "Not beyond the realm of possibility."

"And what if it's not in pieces?" Marcus asked.

"Then it's been reduced to a pile of dust beneath a bigger pile of dust," I answered bitterly. "But ... I don't know, we're kind of low on options. Maybe we'll get lucky."

Casey sighed. "We don't have time to try and sift out a broken generator. And we sure as hell aren't splitting up—luck hasn't exactly been on our side lately."

"Then what's your plan?" Marcus asked Casey.

"Find and kill the Darkness," Casey answered, his chin jutting out in a stubborn hold. He pulled his gun from its holster, dropping the magazine to check his bullet count before popping it back in and glowering. "We can figure the rest out when we don't have a massive, powerful Netherworld monster blowing up my fucking country."

I had a horrible thought. "And … what about Dulcie?"

Casey grimaced—then his expression softened, and he sighed. "Sam," he started slowly. "She's powerful. We're going to do everything in our control to get her out of this in one piece, but if … if she *tries* something, we might not have any choice."

My blood froze—but before I could reply, we heard tires squealing and the low hum and jitter of a muscle-car engine. Damn near everything in the Netherworld was on a three-decade cultural lag. Then a long, green station wagon rolled up to the empty lot, kicking up plenty of dust.

Judy rolled down her window and probably would have honked if she didn't think something nasty could hear us. "Get in, losers, we're going to save the world!"

CHAPTER TWENTY
Dulcie

I leaned over the railing and vomited. There was barely anything in my stomach, just acid, bile and lots of wine. But it kept coming up.

"What the *fuck?*" was all I could think to say. The word came out as a sob; no, a muted scream. A panicked declaration to no one in the room, not Sebastian's unconscious body, or my reflection in the mirror, so ideally perfect I wanted to scream. No blemishes, no pimples, no moles, and I *knew* I had one or two before all this began ... I felt violated, like I'd been fast asleep during something that was down-and-out dirty.

I wanted to collapse or cry, sob, and scream until I broke the windows. I began wondering if I were really back in control of myself again. I couldn't stop thinking about everything I'd done under *her* influence: shooting Knight, *sleeping* with Sebastian, watching *her* rape Knight, standing idly by, screaming at myself to move, wondering why the fuck I didn't *move* ...

I gagged, but there was nothing left to eject. Just dry heaves that hurt my ribs.

No, I thought. I didn't have enough time to panic. *No, no, calm down and breathe. Stay in control of yourself! Whatever you do, you can't let Meg have the reins over you again.*

I took a shaky breath in. My arms and legs were jelly, barely holding me up. The sober part of my brain said, *Stay calm. Play the part. Whatever's happening, you have to stop her.*

"What's the matter?"

Her voice was coming from directly behind me. I stiffened and swallowed hard. *Shit.*

"Nothing, Mother," I said, dissolving back into character. "Just admiring the woods."

I turned to face her and found her standing in the doorway. She was wearing a long, black dress, her hair all in curls, and her face done up to the nines and beyond. Blisteringly beautiful. The sight of her set my blood boiling.

Meg, I thought, clenching my teeth. Bram's stupid maker who turned my brain to putty and stretched it thin. The bitch who had me kidnapped, before she shrink-wrapped my soul, drained Bram, and raped my boyfriend.

I'm gonna kill you, I thought, *and very slowly.*

I smiled at her, feeling as cold as marble.

She smiled in turn and held out her hand. "Get dressed, my darling. It is time."

Time. The word clanged between my ears like a gong. "All right."

Meg nodded and started out of the room but stopped when she saw Sebastian, apparently for the first time, and smiled. "How did he do this time?" she asked over her shoulder.

Pitifully, I thought. But that's not what I said. "Passably well," I replied, trying my best not to speak through my clenched teeth. "You were right. He learns quickly."

Meg inclined her head, smiling. "Good to hear."

"He has a long way to go, of course. Would there be time for me to visit the Loki?" I asked, trying to sound innocent. "Strictly for the purposes of note-taking? He seemed to please you well enough." *Good, keep your voice level, look her in the eye, and smile, smile, smile ...*

Meg chuckled. "Later, princess. We've just a short meeting to attend to, and you can play with your new toy as long as you like."

New toy, I thought bitterly. Still thinking I was under her influence, she encouraged me to prance back and forth between the incapable Sebastian and Knight, *taking notes* so I could teach my new lover how sex was *supposed* to be performed.

"All right," I said. "I'll be down in a moment."

Meg nodded, her eyes flashing—and I felt it, the crimson pull of an impossibly old creature trying to wrangle my spirit.

Well, that's not very nice, I thought inanely. Lasting only a brief moment, just a cursory reassertion of her control, but already I was having trouble keeping my thoughts in order. They clustered, crumbled, and fell apart before they could become full sentences. I felt my anger draining away too, replaced by flat complacency and a dull hum like distant thunder.

No, I thought furiously, *no, no, think about Knight. Think about Knight, focus on the blue of his eyes, his eyes that you know so well ...* My words came out in a jumble, falling through my teeth like sand.

Then, out of the din, a voice like satin and shadow: *Think about Knight and think ... about Sam.*

Sam. The absent party in all of this. Totally removed from Meg's house of horrors. I could see her face so clearly in my head ... Sam, my best friend, my sister, my beloved witch ... so wildly intelligent, so beautiful ...

I heard footsteps descending the stairs. Meg left, and I hadn't even noticed. *Thank Hades ...*

I sighed, slumping back against the bed, feeling suddenly exhausted. My head was pounding ... but it was still my head, my mind, and my asinine thoughts. *Okay,* I thought. *Okay. Sam. I can do this.* ***We*** *can do this.*

I dressed in a red, flouncy ball gown, something I vaguely recalled Meg requesting *specifically* for this event. She mentioned something about universal colors, so the more visually impaired creatures would be able to see me. She wanted me sticking out like a star in the abyss, glowing, a sweet, little something capable of devouring entire planets. The dress was more glittery than even Lady Gaga would find prudent, and shining brilliantly, like I was supposed to be a fairy princess.

Fuck, I guess that's *exactly* what I was. Gross!

The rest of my ensemble? White gloves, black heels, and rosy lipstick. More blush than I'd like to admit, but it appealed to the Brainwashed Dulcie and reflected *her* taste. I put it all on against my better judgment—wishing to high hell I had a gun I could stash somewhere. When I looked in the mirror at my dollish face, I had to restrain a scowl.

Smile, smile, smile. Just a little bit longer.

I saw Sebastian on the way out and even toyed with the idea of waking him, but decided I couldn't pretend I liked having his hands all over me in front of a crowd. Or even alone, for that matter, but that had to be shelved for another time. I could be with Knight, pretending it was for Sebastian's benefit, and never come back, claiming Knight was the superior lover, which was absolutely true.

I couldn't wait to see the look on Sebastian's face. I wondered how Meg would take it—and if she'd commandeer my "toy" because she thought I was becoming too overly fond of him.

I sneered at Sebastian. "Showtime," I said underneath my breath, and I went downstairs.

###

The party came to a screeching halt. Everyone held their drinks in their still hands, waiting, watching eagerly as I made my way to the front of the room. Heading to the vast marble expanse of a fireplace where Meg stood with a glass in her hand, I wondered what was inside the glass. It was filled with a suspiciously viscous fluid that stuck to the sides. People nodded deferentially to me as I passed, and I nodded back, wondering if that were the correct protocol, or more forward than the glamoured Dulcie would have allowed herself to be. I tried to look shy, concealing my insane urge to rip off their heads and start laughing like I'd gone completely mad. Bulky werewolves, vampires in pinstripe suits, draconians in colorful robes, and a hundred or more mixed-race creatures with physical features I couldn't pin down. Many creatures that were a million times more powerful than the average fairy.

And yet, I felt like I could win, if I really wanted to. I could take it upon myself to wreck their shit, burn their stupid clothes, set their alcohol on fire, and watch Meg's precious mansion burn down to a pile of cinders and ash just like what she'd done to the ANC, my home.

I almost stopped. The memory slapped me in the face, gold and glowing, blue and green and silver, all the signature colors of a really bad, and definitely magical, explosion. Ruined offices, a busted Mr. Coffee lying in a corner, and Blue! Sweet, little Blue barking up a storm as I wrapped my fingers around a pearly white throat. Burning her, I began melting her skin.

Then somebody swooped in to save the day, ripping me away from Sam and throwing me sideways before I could do any real damage. Hades bless him, whoever he was. I made a mental note to find him and buy him a drink—once I finished chopping Meg into tiny, little pieces.

"Dulcie, my princess," said Meg, extending a hand. I took it, smiling as widely as I could manage, and stepped up onto the stone base of the hearth. She looked at me, her eyes rippling with pride, and the vicious gloat of success. "Dulcie. *My* Dulcie."

To everyone else, it sounded like an endearing sentiment. In my ears, however, it rang like a battle cry, the shriek of a hideous, ancient beast.

I could kill you, I thought. Now that I was looking for it, the awful powers she'd endowed on me—a chaotic coalescence of power and magic beyond magic flowed through me. The fire of the drakes, the speed and shadow of vampires, the raw strength of werewolves. The liquid sense of purpose of the dryads, creatures that could call on the water or the wind or the trees to do anything they wanted. *I could summon the chimera in here right now and have him rip out your throat.*

But Meg wasn't stupid. She had plans heaped upon other plans, plenty of backups and contingencies, last resorts, and enough replacements for every person in the room. People were already in place, ready to blow the whole world to smithereens if something happened to her and her coalition. This wasn't just a power grab anymore, it was a *sacred* rite to her. It wouldn't matter if she were dead, she'd find some way to get what she wanted. If she went up in smoke, Hades only knew what her people in the ANC would do.

Maybe they'd scatter and give up whatever they were set there to do once they had no one to obey, I thought and hoped.

But it was far more likely they'd all take matters into their own hands, presenting a slew of unrelated crises for us to deal with, most of which would, no doubt, escalate immediately into hostage situations. Better to stick around, read the room and play to win. Follow Meg to the end of the rainbow and strike only when it was far too late for her to call for help.

I didn't have a plan to go with the sentiment, but an out-and-out massacre seemed, while *extremely* attractive, a rather poor choice.

So I didn't kill her. Just in case.

"Greetings, friends," she said, speaking in a language I knew but couldn't identify—one of a thousand that were now embedded in my brain. "Allies and *partners*," she continued.

It was an odd moment to critique Meg's talent for public speaking, but I was cringing all the same. Her emphasis made every word sound passive-aggressive, a veiled insult she didn't think anyone was smart enough to catch. She looked at me, smirking—which indicated she was doing it on purpose.

"It has been a long, hard road. But here we are. Only mere moments from our restoration."

Restoration. Old world, old Houses. Drakes who wanted to marry me to solidify an alliance. *Oh, Hades!*

She didn't have to say much more—all of her guests knew why they were there, and the goal they were so perilously close to accomplishing. I looked across at them, studying their faces, watching their eager eyes and their fingers drumming against their glasses. Standing with their chins up, all half-smiling. Most of all, they seemed so *hungry*.

"It's a long time coming. A very *long* time."

The crowd laughed and elbowed each other, like it was some secret joke they all shared. *Remember the night we decided to take over the world? Good times!*

"But we've made it. It's done."

Count your successful coups after they hatch, I thought. Unless she'd already done something excessively nasty and this was the celebration of victory. I assumed it was the sendoff for the final patch of fireworks that would incinerate whatever she wanted so badly.

"Tonight, we suffocate the thieves in their own smoke. We make them regret the moment they defied us. Tonight, we reclaim what is rightfully *ours!*" Meg raised her glass higher. Everyone raised their glasses with an approving roar, then tipped the strange fluid back into their mouths. Nothing like a stiff drink to temper the end of the world.

"To Vogahn!" someone shouted before the rest of the room took up the cry.

"What do you say, darling?" Meg asked me, placing a frozen hand on my shoulder. "Shall we pay President Odyssey a visit?"

Odyssey? I thought, all at once confused. *Who's Odyssey?*

A second later, I understood.

Of course. Odyssey, *President* Odyssey. The deciding senate vote happened ten years prior after the case of *The People v. Ala.* She was the first magical creature to make herself known, and she established the precedent that allowed Netherworldians to live Earthside. She also heralded the rise of human influence in the Netherworld. The call for open travel between the worlds went up before a modest disagreement in trading policy spiraled into an all-out war. When it was finally over—and all the old government branches and their people had retreated, hidden, surrendered, or died—only one functioning government body was left in the whole damn plane.

The Association of Netherworld Creatures.

Regret the moment they defied us. That was the moment we swooped in after the dust settled, assuming the mantle of leadership as if it were a shiny penny we picked up in the street.

Smile, smile, smile. "Yes, Mother."

CHAPTER TWENTY-ONE
Sam

We drove for a really long time in stony silence. Everybody was patiently waiting for Dagan or me to tell Judy when to turn. The car was cramped, and the general air of *oh fuck, we're almost out of time* hung over us like a black cloud, ominous and smothering.

"What's the plan?" I asked after a while—but before Casey could answer, I added, "'Kill the Darkness' is more of a goal than a true plan."

Casey smiled weakly and looked at Rowena. She was staring out the window, resting her chin in her hand.

"Rowena can do things," he said quietly, "if she needs to. Hopefully, we'll be able to sneak in, eliminate the Darkness, and sneak out again without any problem. But if we can't ... or if it's too heavily guarded, or too many civilians, or we just straight up can't find a way in ... then we'll send for her." He grimaced. "God willing, it won't come to that. It's ..."

"Painful," I said. I could only imagine. Whatever lived in Rowena must have given her its sight, and most likely by accident. Whether she were connected to an entity in a far-off parallel or it was physically bound to her body, calling on it wouldn't be pleasant. Especially if she asked it to do something particularly taxing—like turning her invisible so she could sneak into a heavily guarded enemy compound without being detected. The kind of unpleasant that having your skin sheared off your muscles might be compared to.

I'd seen somebody do it once, a long time ago. He called on an old god he was once connected to, asking it to manipulate something outside his body, something in the physical plane, although it didn't have a direct connection with it. It tried and failed. There were lots of screams, and lots of blood. Way too much blood.

"Okay," I said. "So we get there."

"We see how well the place is guarded," Casey said. "Judy and Rowena can look for a way in. You can help us detect any unfriendly magic, wards, traps, or other things. If we can find an easy way in, Marcus will enter first, quiet as a mouse. He'll stay in contact and locate the Darkness. If Marcus has an opportunity, he'll have to take it. If he doesn't, he'll tell us where he is and one of us will go after him, probably Judy or me. If we can't find a way in, and not too many people are onsite, Kent can make us an entrance. And if all else fails, Rowena can summon her demon friend from wherever he is and tell him to raze the whole place to the ground. Or something."

Rowena sighed. "He's not a demon," she said. "And he doesn't raze things to the ground unless you ask him very nicely."

Casey grimaced. "Well, hopefully, it won't come to that."

"Hopefully," I said, thinking of every time Dulcie and I got thrown into the fray with no plan, no resources, no time, and no real training. That time Dulcie managed to deal with a dreamstalker in his own domain with *literally* no ephemeral backup. Another was when we had to go to war with no concept of how to maneuver a thousand-man army. And once, lacking even three-tenths of a plan, Dulcie broke into Melchior's house anyway, going through a window and almost getting herself killed. Trey got killed instead ... Yes, I was fairly convinced that a simple "just follow my lead" is the token recipe for *miscommunication catastrophe a la death.*

So, based on my professional track record, I didn't have a lot of faith in the strategy of *just getting there and seeing how it goes*. It didn't sound like that's what Casey intended to do, but I didn't know, since he seemed so *calm* about it. And so certain that everything would work itself out for the better that he didn't need to worry.

He sounded like Dulcie. The voice she used when she knew she made a really stupid decision to save somebody's ass and even though she knew how stupid it was, she insisted on sticking to it with everything she had.

"Sam, I know it sounds contrived," Casey began, "but we're not just a bunch of gun-hauling dumbasses with badges! We're trained professionals. We were sent here for a reason. I promise."

"I know," I said. "I'm just ... I'm sorry, it's a *huge* house. And it wasn't heavily guarded on the outside, from what I could see, but acres and acres of forest lie behind it, and there could be *anything* lurking in there." *And I fear you might try to do something heroic and stupid.*

"We're almost there," said Dagan. "Ten minutes, tops."

"Great," I said. "Okay. Okay. We'll be fine." I sighed. "But."

Casey nodded. "Dulcie."

"Yeah. I know," I said, before he could stop me, "I know it might … get bad. I know that." I didn't want to *think* about it though, knowing it was a very real possibility. "You'll do what you can, but if you can't…"

"I'm sorry," he said. "I promise we'll try."

I wanted to protest and scream something in Dulcie's defense, but I couldn't figure out what to say. Beg for us to hesitate long enough for Dulcie to miraculously pull herself out of it? Offer her cookies and ice cream and a trauma blanket in the hopes that they would be enough to stop her from blasting us into oblivion? My mouth hung open, full of words, but I was unable to sort through any of them.

They would try. *He* would try. But it might not be enough. I couldn't think any other thoughts beyond that. Before Casey could say anything, Judy slammed hard on the brakes and swung the car off the road into a tight mesh of trees, jarring everyone forward.

"What the *fuck*, Judy?" Casey yelled.

"Everybody keep low," she whispered, sliding her gun from its holster.

"Why?" I asked, ducking down.

"Big, scary, government-type vehicle at twelve o'clock." She pointed with one finger, keeping her hands on the wheel. "Hang tight, it … huh … They aren't going very fast." She peered forward curiously, squinting in the dark.

The dreaded thought that we were too late crossed my mind—and I worried that this car was just the beginning of a long, evil convoy, the parade of monsters marching blindly towards the end of the world. What if this were the long drive leading us to wherever the Darkness intended us to go next? Perhaps we were ignorantly following his grand scheme without ever intending to.

At the very least, it was most likely a patrol vehicle filled with some random werewolves and trolls. They were packed tightly into a big, black something-or-other, watching for intruders like us. Their semiautomatic weapons probably filled to bursting with dragon's blood bullets.

I peeked up. The SUV was meandering down the gravel path, slowly, patiently—or maybe at the mercy of a paranoid driver. No other cars were crawling along behind them—so we were alone, as far as I could tell. The SUV curled into the edge of the road, and stopped. The driver door opened slowly, along with the back passenger door. Three shadows tumbled out—one of them twitching his nose like he'd caught a scent.

"Oh, shit," I whispered. If they were human, there was a good chance they couldn't see us—but when I saw the one doing the sniffing, I had to think that wasn't the case. Whatever he thought he smelled was dim enough that he had to search for it, and get out of the car to hunt it down. Muffled voices drifted towards us, arguing, and someone was growing irritated, insisting that there was *something* there, just give him a second.

"Three outside," Judy whispered. "No more than two in the car. We can take 'em."

I ducked back down. There was a soft rustling as everyone in the car went for their weapons. We sat silent, taut, still, and waited.

"Um. You don't … know them, do you?" Judy asked me, pointing to the shadows.

"I doubt it, probably not," I answered with a shrug. Everyone I knew in the Netherworld worked for the ANC, and none of them had any reason to ever be this far out into the country. "Why?"

"Because the shirtless guy is waving at us."

"What?! Does he have a gun?" I asked as I peered into the dark, trying to see what Judy was seeing.

"Nope. Just … a shirtless guy," she answered.

"What's he doing?" Casey asked. "I can't see him."

"He's off to the right of the road, cloaked in the dark," Judy answered. "He's walking this way. Just ... waving."

"At *what*?" I asked. "Us?" If we'd been seen, why weren't we being shot at? Unless maybe this wasn't one of the Darkness's people?

"I guess not?" Judy asked more than said. "He's not attacking, if that's what you're asking."

I strained harder to see whatever Judy could see. Two shadows stood beside their own vehicle, aiming at the third, and their postures suggesting confusion. The one who kept waving at us wandered closer, until I could see dark hair, tannish skin ... but I couldn't make out much more ... He was just waving, like he was desperately trying to get our attention ... I reached over Casey and opened his door, popping my head out, and hoping to see better.

The man in front of us stopped short and brought his hands to his mouth, calling, "Sam?"

I froze, and my stomach felt like it was impaled by a glacier. "Knight?" I whispered. I couldn't say it any louder.

"No fucking way," Casey said with a laugh of disbelief.

"Get out of the car," I said. Nobody moved. "Get out of the *car*! Come on, move!"

Casey pushed the door open all the way and I barreled out, practically crawling over him, before I tackled Knight in the most grasping hug I could manage, squeezing him so tightly that I worried I might break his ribs—I couldn't, of course, since he was built like a Sherman tank, but I continued squeezing him as hard as my little bird arms could manage. I tackled him too, and he stumbled.

"Knight!" I started crying.

"Fuck! It's good to see you," he said, hugging me back, just as hard.

I paused. "We thought ... *I* thought ..." And then I started blubbering like an idiot. Knight hugged me again, and I cried into his shoulder, remembering somewhere in the back of my head that Knight was my boss and this was wildly unprofessional ...

"I'm okay," he said. "It's okay. I'm okay, Sam."

"Told you I could smell her," one of the shadows said. *Bram*.

"Yes, and we're all *so* proud of you," said the other. A voice I didn't recognize that was deep, old, and dusty.

"What are you doing here?" Knight asked. "How did you even *get* here?"

"We, um." I stepped away abruptly, wiping my eyes on my sleeve. "I was ..." I stopped. "Knight, you're ... um." I blinked at him, my eyes finally adjusting to the dark. *Naked*, I thought. And I couldn't look away. *Dulcie always said he was well hung but ... hot damn!*

"Oh, yeah," he answered, blushing furiously. He looked around for a minute, no doubt seeking a way to cover himself. Eventually, he dove back into the SUV and retrieved a black briefcase, which he modestly held over his substantial friend. "Forgot. Sorry, Sam."

"You're, uh ... fine, I guess?" It couldn't be angry at him for being naked ... It probably wasn't his *choice*, but it felt weird. "I'm just glad you're okay."

"Knight," Casey said behind me, "I'll be damned. Thought you were dead."

Knight stiffened. "Ah, hell. Casey James?"

Casey came forward, waving and smiling. "Nice to see you too?"

Knight hesitated, sighed, and relaxed, but with visible effort. "Do I want to know what you're doing here?"

"Not really," said Casey. "Dude, are you ..." he chuckled. "Are you ... naked?"

Knight just nodded. "Yeah. Long story."

"Where were you?" I asked. "What happened?"

"Meg," Knight answered. "Meg is the Darkness. She's a vampire."

"The Darkness is a woman?" Casey asked, shocked.

"If you want to call Meg a woman," Bram responded icily.

"Bram tracked Dulcie to her base and we ... well, obviously, it didn't go well," Knight finished as he looked back at Bram, as if he were waiting for him to add something. Bram sighed and looked away.

"The Darkness, apparently, is also my maker," Bram said.

"Your maker?" I repeated—but I wasn't as concerned with the Darkness's connection to Bram so much as how substantially that increased her age. Bram was centuries old, a Master Vampire, and his abilities had advanced to insane degrees by the final change in his body. The part of his human self that hadn't quite begun calcifying became even more powerful.

The older a vampire got, the further from his humanity he was separated, and consequently, the more magic he could contain. I guessed that Meg, Bram's maker, had to be a hundred or more years older than he was. Why? Because vampires cannot create any offspring in their first immortal century. Thus, Meg had to be even *older,* putting her leagues ahead of Bram, lightyears even … I supposed that would explain how she'd managed to keep herself hidden all this time, even from her own people.

"Ah," I said at last, looking to the left of Bram. A tall, dark, strangely calm person was standing with his hands in the pockets of a black suit coat. His skin was as pale as fogged glass, and he stooped and slouched, a man hundreds of years past caring about his sloping posture. "And this is?" I was almost afraid to ask.

"*Meg's* maker, Ezra Grant," Knight answered. "He's with us."

"Meg's maker …" I repeated. That made Ezra the grand-sire of Bram—and, at a guess, close to a thousand years old. "Oh. Um. Hi?"

Ezra smiled sadly at me. "Greetings, Ms. White. I am sorry for this," he said. "Truly."

Dagan stepped forward, scowling. "Madam White, you saw this as well, so correct me if I'm wrong, but the household of the Darkness was *extremely* well guarded inside," he ground out, throwing his arms across his chest. Then he glared at Knight. "How did you manage to escape with your conspicuously naked friend?"

"Knight's on our side, Dagan," I said underneath my breath, dismissing Dagan's accusatory tone.

"*Dagan?*" Knight asked, baffled as he turned to face me. "*What* the hell is *he* doing here?"

"Pleasure to see you too," Dagan managed. "Bram, I trust you are well?"

"Dagan? If you would kindly … do me an *enormous* favor …" Bram started, "and throw yourself into … the nearest active volcano …"

"Sam, what the hell is he doing here?" Knight demanded again, his eyes aflame.

"I am *helping*," Dagan responded, rolling his eyes in exasperation. "For your information, this jolly party would have gotten nowhere without me."

"That's true," I admitted to Knight with a frown. His frown drooped even deeper.

"And the question still stands," Dagan continued. "How *did* you get out?"

"Yeah, I'd kind of like to know that myself," I added.

Knight and Bram eyed each other. Knight coughed and looked away. Bram crossed his arms, and his eyes turned darkish brown.

"We managed," Bram said at last. Behind him, Ezra chuckled.

"That's it?" I asked, clearly unimpressed. "That's not it."

"Yes, I'd *love* to hear the story," said Dagan. Knight's hands curled into fists.

I suppressed a groan. "Dagan. *Please.*"

Dagan held up his hands and took a step back. "Apologies all around. Proceed."

Knight shot Dagan a glare before turning to me. "We were looking for Dulcie. Bram tracked her blood to the place down the road and we broke into the house …" He grimaced. "It was too easy, and we should have known. We went upstairs and found Dulcie with Meg, but she was … *different*. Wrong, she was in some kind of trance … She didn't recognize Bram, *or* me. Then at point-blank, Sam, she shot me! And she didn't even blink!"

"Shit!" I said. *Sounds about right.* "Yeah, um … I ran into her too. She …"

How do I even say this? How do you tell your boss his girlfriend was possessed by a homicidal maniac? And she not only killed his employees, but also *tried* to kill you? She left a whole city in shambles, with burnt-out buildings that folded in on themselves like waterlogged origami cranes.

"Sorry if we thwarted your rescue," Bram started before Knight could ask me to finish my sentence. "But it was getting rather stuffy in there." He sounded out of breath.

Then I noticed for the first time how weird he looked. How slowly he was speaking. Vampire faces are frozen forever, and totally incapable of the physical changes that occur when you haven't gotten enough sleep. But Bram was swaying on his feet, with his eyes half closed. And staggering whenever he moved, like he was half-drunk. That was impossible, and even if he *did* drink something, he lacked the metabolic process that pumps the alcohol into his system. Hell, he didn't have a system to pump it into. He could not be out of breath either, for that matter.

"Are you okay, Bram?" I asked, taking a step forward. Not that I *cared,* but if he was about to pass out, we needed to know.

"I have had an interesting week," he said simply.

"Interesting?" I asked. Interesting didn't even *begin* to cover my week, and I could only assume it didn't accurately describe his either.

"Meg tried to drain him again," Knight answered. Bram shot him a look—probably not a point of pride for the illustrious Master Vampire. "And she damn near succeeded," Knight added, probably to rub it in.

"Again?" I asked—I didn't know she'd tried it already. "Shit, Bram. Maybe you should ... I don't know, sit down?"

Bram snorted. "I will be fine. We have ... more important things to do ... than to fuss over me."

"So, let me guess," Knight started. "You all were on your way over here to save us?" He probably guessed correctly that we were taking the backroad to the mansion.

"The plan was to kill the Darkness and, hopefully, free Dulcie from whatever spell she was under," Casey answered. "But I'm sure your name would have come up eventually."

He said it as a joke, but Knight didn't laugh. "How did you know where Dulcie was?"

"Um," I answered, my heart swimming with liquid dread. *Time for the really bad news.* "I ... Dagan ..." *Just breathe, Sam.* I released a quick breath and pushed my hair to the side, exposing the sinewy, grey burns on my neck.

"Dagan did that?" Knight asked, his eyes flashing with pure heat.

"No!" I nearly yelled before taking another deep breath. "Dulcie did." I let my hair fall. "She attacked Splendor. I ..." *was the only survivor.* I shook my head. "The ANC is gone. Not just ours, but all of them, almost every base we've got."

"Gone? What do you mean, *gone*?" Knight's voice was quiet, tense. He sounded like he knew, or at least could guess what I meant.

"She means, they went *boom*," Kent said sadly.

"Boom," Knight echoed, shaking his head, but still not understanding.

"The Darkness, or Meg, made Dulcie blow it up," I said. "She's ... I don't know, glamoured or possessed or something. I thought it was to prove that Meg had control, convincing her to wreck her own building ... but Knight, it's *all* of them. The LA offices went up within *minutes* of each other, Earthside and here. It's a coordinated attack, Meg has control of all the bases, and she's *deliberately* ..." I stopped. "You're not listening to me!"

Knight was scowling, standing with his arms crossed, his face as stony as a pallbearer at a funeral. After a moment, he looked up. "Sorry, hang on. Bram. Where's that book?"

"What book?" I asked. Bram pulled a small, black journal from his pants pocket, wincing as though it hurt him to touch it. Knight took it from him with his free hand that wasn't holding the briefcase to cover his nudity. He flipped the book over and opened it, reading something. He scowled even deeper, if that were possible.

"Here," he said as he handed it to me. "Take a look."

I immediately noticed the golden D stitched into the cover. My fingers tingled wherever I touched it so I guessed it was probably a spell to render the paper inflammable, or to keep any offensive magic being used in the room from leaking into its pages. A basic, double-sided ward, the kind of spell you cast when you don't want something to light up like a Christmas tree if an intruder who can *see* looks for magic in your evil lair.

"This is ..." It had a physical weight to it, actually metaphysical, and the haunted aura of an abandoned church. It echoed of fixation, obsession, love gone sour ... and a very particular emotion, something Meg had to have poured into it almost certainly by accident. Rowena was giving it a look, leaning in, and her onyx eye was glinting—she could feel it too, even from a distance. "Heavy," I finished.

"It's Meg's," said Knight. "It's a log of Dulcie's life, the progression of her change, letters—"

"Her change?" I said. "What change?"

"Ah, yes," said Ezra, stepping forward. He was homely for a vampire, a little more square than the other ones I'd met. It made him look more human. "When Dulcie was quite young, Melchior and Meg began to inject her with various things. Blood, ground scales, and the liquid essence of other creatures. The reason they did it is still a mystery, and we do not know why, but it managed to make her exceedingly powerful."

"The *result*," Bram said, "is the new Dulcie. A living, walking weapon of mass destruction."

"Which could explain this …" I touched the burns on my neck almost subconsciously.

"There's a lot of not so great stuff in there," Knight said, gesturing to the journal. "Sam, whatever they've done to her, it's turned her into an impenetrable, magic tank."

"That doesn't sound good at all," I said. But it sounded right, and it matched up with all the destruction she'd wrought in Splendor. It *really* sounded like Meg was headed for war, but she already had what she wanted, didn't she? Control of all the portals, and a litany of explosions that would keep anyone else from interfering. What more could she ask for?

"Impenetrable? Damn!" said Kent. "This is gonna be a foon fight."

"There isn't going to *be* any fight," I said. "Dulcie's still my friend!"

"A friend who's already tried ta kill you twice, darlin'," Kent answered, unimpressed. "Ah'm sure she's nice as anybody else, boot if she's becoom a magic *tank*, I dunno what you expect us ta doo."

"I expect you to *try*," I said, my voice rising. Casey laid a hand on my shoulder, trying to smile.

"And we will," he said. "I promise."

"But if we can't get through to her," Marcus started.

"Then we'll do whatever we have to do," Casey answered with tight lips.

"*Do what you have to do?*" Knight demanded. "What the hell does that mean?"

Casey sighed. "Knight, I don't know if you've seen Dulcie attack anything lately, but she's insanely powerful now. Such as none of us have ever seen before! She's that formidable. If we have a shot at her, we might have to take it, you *know* how this works. It's a last resort, but if we're not ready to make that decision when we get there, we'll hesitate. However, we can't *afford* to hesitate, not with Dulcie being whatever she has become now." Knight took a deep breath and his knuckles went white from the fists he was making. Casey noticed it too. "I know, it's awful, but it's something we have to think about, and plan for."

Knight was silent. We looked at each other, hunting for the right words. I was trying not to think about if we had to pull the trigger on Dulcie. Knight would be killing the only woman he loved, and I'd be killing my best friend.

"Just keep reading," Knight said at last—clearly refusing to think about it any longer.

I looked at him a brief moment, but there was nothing else for me to say.

I kept reading.

I flipped through the book, scanning the lines in confusion. Lists of Dulcie's powers were enumerated as they manifested: the fire of the drakes, which she so clumsily used to burn me, the speed of the vampires, and line after line after line of Meg extolling Dulcie's virtues. She sounded like a doting parent, or an adoring fan—the first hints of chronic obsession, something vampires occasionally experienced with their offspring.

And then, the last entry. Black ink, and splatters of red. One line, no date.

"It is time to end their Odyssey, and begin ours," I read aloud before I clapped the book shut. "Well, then."

"That's a bit—" said Judy.

"Dramatic?" Kent supplied.

"Yeah," Judy answered.

"Hardly," Bram interrupted. "If anyone dares to wax poetic about someone's impending demise, it absolutely has to be Meg."

Oh, shit. "Guys. *Odyssey* is capitalized."

Casey's face fell. "Oh, shit."

"President Odyssey," Judy said the words softly.

"*End their Odyssey,*" I repeated as I shook my head, my shock raging through me. "Meg wants to assassinate her!"

CHAPTER TWENTY-TWO
Sam

"Maybe Meg wants to assassinate Odyssey," Knight started. "Or maybe she just thought it sounded poetic enough to write it in her diary?"

"Or it's a planted statement, something to throw us off. Something she planned," Marcus added.

"Meg is more ambitious than she is intelligent," Ezra replied, shaking his head. "Even on a good day, there is absolutely no way she thought that far ahead. Besides, she doesn't even think that highly enough of any of you to guess you'd ever find it."

Bram twitched at hearing that, but he didn't comment.

"But why kill Odyssey?" Casey asked. "If it's portal control, she's already had that for ages. Why blow up the ANCs and wreck her ports? And why kill the president? That act, alone, won't gain her any favors. Nobody will take her side."

I blinked. "Unless …" I started.

"Unless?" Casey repeated blankly.

Shit, shit, shit. "Unless that's just something she told the kingpins to get them on her side."

"What? That she'd kill the president?" Kent asked.

"No, that she would take control of the portals," I reasoned. "That's what Jax kept insisting was happening, and we still don't have any reason to believe that wasn't the case—or at least, that he didn't *think* that was the case. But maybe Meg lied to the uppity-ups just to get their help."

"What kind of help would she need from the rings?" Ezra asked.

"Manpower, for one," Casey and Knight said at the same time.

"Maybe she asked to keep the ring leaders off her back. The potion lords have maybe five working brains between them," Marcus said. "If they found out Meg intended to monopolize the portals they use to transport their product, they'd start causing plenty of trouble. So, how do you solve that? By bringing them in on the deal, if only to get them off your back, right?"

"And she probably also wanted access to the drugs, themselves," Judy added, throwing a sidelong look at Kent. "Lots of things go *boom* if you know what you're doing. She might have been looking for things like that mandrake-Adderall juice, you know, stuff to give her soldiers to get them all hot and bothered before a fight."

"Soldiers," said Marcus. "Great. That's a fun word to associate with an ego-maniacal vampire overlord."

"Over*lady*," Judy corrected him. But somehow, overlady failed to have the same ring.

"Okay, so let's say for the sake of argument that Meg lied," Casey started. "Just to get manpower and drugs. Fine. But the question still remains: where does assassinating the president come in to play?"

I frowned. Casey was right. Anyway you looked at it, Meg had *nothing* to gain from Odyssey's death. Killing the president certainly wouldn't secure portal control, and would probably expunge every portal in the United States. Put them on total lockdown. She wouldn't have access to the plane anymore, or the human customer base Jax was so revved up about. She had the whole circus of potion masters at her disposal, as well as that nameless mystery drug Jax mentioned, addictive as hell without any pleasantly fatal side effects—no side effects at all, actually. If Meg *killed* Odyssey, she would be cutting them off indefinitely from their primary demographic—those idiotic human teens, of which there was a small population in the Netherworld.

Maybe killing the president was just some petty wish, a pipe dream that had nothing to do with Meg's overall plan … If it *were* part of the plan, the world would go into a frenzy. Everyone would start bitching about the ineptitude of the Association of Netherworld Creatures and its potential involvement. After all the explosions, we were *bound* to get some of the blame. Whatever happened, the aftermath would be a PR nightmare …

Wait.

Meg had nothing to gain, and everything to lose by killing the president. So what would she lose? What did she dare to sacrifice?

What would disappear if Odyssey died?

Why did she take the ANCs? Why did she blow them up from the inside? Why did she try to make it look like it was *our idea* from the beginning? If the ANCs went down, so did the portals. Along with all access, regulated or otherwise, to the Earthly plane from the Netherworld.

*Shit, shit, shit, **shit**!*

Unless that's exactly what Meg wanted.

"Maybe she wants the ANC totally gone," I said. "Just … gone. Obliterated."

Marcus shook his head. "Wouldn't do her any good. Odyssey, or whoever replaces her, will have to put up an ephemeral blockade if the ANC goes down completely. Nobody could go in or out. If there's no regulation, there's no *anything*."

"Which is why it's so weird that she keeps blowing up all the ANCs," Casey muttered, drawing his hand over his mouth. "Meg *had* control, complete and total, and nobody knew it. *Nobody*. If she'd put more competent people in her offices, we'd never have noticed a damn thing. She removed all portal access and has complete and total legislative control over every aspect of Earthly preternatural existence, and what does she do? She blew it up!"

"Oh," Bram started with a frown. "Actually, Meg has my portal ripper."

I almost punched him square in the face, giving him a knuckle blast that would have shattered somebody else's nose—but it couldn't do a damn thing to Bram's plastic skin. I took a deep breath, exhaled, and said in a voice shaking with rage, "*What?*"

"We used it to get here in the first place," Bram explained. "And Meg took it when Vander and I were … accosted by Dulcie."

And that matched perfectly with every horrifying thought I was having right then. "Then it never mattered?"

Casey looked up. "What do you mean?"

"I mean Meg doesn't care about the portals," I said. "She doesn't care about keeping them open or closed. And Odyssey …" *Oh, Hades, this is gonna be so bad.*

"Odyssey?" Casey prompted, but by that point, Knight already caught on.

"If Odyssey dies at the hands of the ANC itself, it goes under for good," Knight said, nodding. "Catastrophic failure, no recovery, no rehabilitation. Shit, this has *nothing* to do with getting access to anything."

"And everything to do with cutting it off," I finished.

"Ezra, you said that Meg—" Casey started.

"Was the matriarch of an old house," Bram finished for him. "Who now has a spiritual daughter carrying the essence of all the oldest races ever to walk the dark. She is more than ready to put the hammer down on the human scourge. Someone everybody in the underground will be *salivating* over, picking out the pieces of her that reflect themselves. Creating their version of the perfect Nether queen."

"That's why the shapeshifter pretending to be your mom could handle the amulet," I said. "That shapeshifter was probably part of the house that *made* it."

"Which means Meg has more than one of the old houses already at her disposal," Ezra added. "Meg's probably restoring the old order."

"And she has my portal ripper," Bram repeated with another frown. "The portals in the ANC offices were rendered unnecessary from the moment they started exploding."

"And she's got a way to get back once they're all gone," Knight added. "Blockades won't go up immediately. She'll have enough time to cross over to the Nether-side."

I scoffed in disbelief—not only at the crazy genius of Meg's plan, but at how little time we probably had now to stop her. "So she can blow it all to hell and not have to stick around for the consequences. And Hades knows how many government plants are ready to corroborate any story she wants them to tell."

"That's where all the congressmen have gone," Casey said, in a voice thin with dread. "They *know* Odyssey's directly in the line of fire."

I nodded. "Meg needs the government out of the Netherworld completely. We're the ruling body right now, and the only infrastructure the Netherworld *has*.

Without us, there's nothing—an empty place Meg can fill with herself and the old ruling houses. Maybe she'll come back for the potion rings, I don't know, but right now, that isn't the *point.* She's taking down our order and restoring hers, the only way to keep us out for *good* is to convince the world it's too dangerous for the supernatural community to have a presence on Earth at all, or for *them* to have a human presence in the Netherworld. She's trying to scare the planet into isolating the Netherworld again—and she's doing it by turning our regulators into terrorists."

"So this has now become a question of priority," Knight started. "Whether we go after the Darkness or we go after Odyssey."

"The president's safety is always the number one concern," Casey answered immediately. "Meg will have to wait. We secure the president's safety first and worry about Meg and Dulcie afterwards."

"That is, if Meg hasn't already gotten to Odyssey," I interjected.

Casey faced me and nodded his agreement solemnly. "Yes, if Meg hasn't gotten to her already."

"And there's only one way we have to find that out," I continued with a deep breath. "So we're going after Odyssey no matter what?"

"Yes," Casey answered as he faced Knight. "Are you on board?"

Knight swallowed hard. I could see that he wanted to go after Meg and, of course, Dulcie. "Knight, we will need all the help we can get—first with Odyssey and then with Meg and Dulcie afterwards. If we split up, we'll be that much weaker."

He nodded. "I'm on board."

"First things first," Bram nearly interrupted. "We need to get Vander some clothes."

"That's true," Knight said as he glanced down at the briefcase. "I'm getting sick of carrying this thing everywhere."

"Yeah, you should probably be dressed if we're going to see the president," I added with a nervous laugh. If we were lucky, this would amount to nothing more than a whirlwind meeting and quick crackdown on personal security, giving Odyssey enough time to do whatever she had to do to clean up this mess.

"Hades, *fine*. Christina, could you get me some clothes?" Knight asked as he turned to face her. "I'm not sure why no one thought of that before," he finished, eyeing everyone with irritation.

"Including you?" I asked with a broad smile.

"Including me, I guess," he responded before his eyes fell on Christina again. "Ahem! I haven't got all day and it's cold out here, in case you hadn't noticed."

"What do you want me to do about it?" Christina answered with a frown.

"Oh, I don't know, maybe magick me up some clothes!" Knight responded with a "duh" tone.

Christina scoffed. "From where, exactly?"

Knight shrugged. "What do you mean from where? From your magic."

"From my magic," she repeated incredulously.

"Yeah. Dulcie did it all the time."

"Did *what* all the time?"

"I don't know, she manifested all kinds of shit out of the air. I thought it was a fairy dust perk," Knight shrugged.

Now Christina looked *really* confused. "No, it isn't. Fairies can't *do* that and, besides, even if I could do that, my magic doesn't work in the Netherworld, remember?"

Knight stared at her blankly. "What do you mean *fairies can't do that*?"

Christina groaned. "We can't just make something out of nothing! Fairies can make plants grow and heal wounds, but that's about it. Fairy dust is just positive, celestial energy that fairies pull out of the air to amplify their own willpower, for things like stitching skin or knitting bones back together. That's why we have such an intensely sexual pull in the Netherworld—fairy dust becomes the most potent there, almost like a conscious morphine high. But we can't just *make* shit. That's not how it works."

"Christina, I've *seen* Dulcie do it," I said slowly. "She can make or summon things with fairy dust. Just by imagining them."

"First time we worked together, she manifested leather pants and a red, flouncy shirt from *nothing*," Knight added, nodding at me.

"I do recall that," Dagan said wistfully. "Good times."

We ignored him.

"Then she's not a fairy," said Christina, sighing. "Which I *know* isn't true because I've *met* her, but guys, I don't know what to tell you, except that fairies *can't* do that. Do you have any idea how many laws of physics and arcana would be broken? Alchemists can transmute one thing into another, but you can only use up the matter you *have*, and it has to be the same mass and basic chemical makeup …" She trailed off, biting her lip. "What the hell? How could you even *do* that?"

Knight and I looked at each other. We'd both seen Dulcie do it a hundred times. And we never met another fairy until Christina—since they were so very rare—so we never had any reason to think Dulcie was different. Hell, now that I thought about it, I'd never even seen Christina *use* her own dust.

"I don't know what creature they could have pulled it from," said Ezra, "but this is undoubtedly another side effect of Melchior's experimentation."

Yeah, thanks, Sherlock, we already got that far, I thought, but the word "experimentation" sent shivers up my spine. I didn't want to think of Dulcie as the lab rat of a mad scientist and his manic vampire friend— that spelled trouble in a lot of ways. Enhancement was one thing, but they were trying to turn Dulcie into a fusion of the races, somebody to rule the old world when Meg was done with it. Experimentation implied a more fervent degree of uncertainty—not only the attributes of other races, but *new* powers we didn't even have categories for. Like spontaneous materialization.

"I was under the impression we had a president to save," Bram said. "Perhaps we can discuss this later?"

"Um. Yeah," I said. "Right. Everybody just keep that in mind. Dulcie will have a lot of unknowns in her arsenal, so be ready for anything." I offered Knight an apologetic smile. "We'll just buy you something to wear or maybe we can find a curtain somewhere or a pillow case or something."

"A curtain or a pillowcase?" Knight repeated.

"Just trying to be helpful," I said.

"Well, please stop," Knight replied.

"I mean, that's if we even find the time. There's a really good chance when we get to Odyssey, something catastrophic will happen and you'll have to save the world … naked or not," I finished with a laugh. Everyone else, minus Knight, also laughed at it.

"If we're lucky, we can get there before Meg does something inflammatory," Casey started. "And put Odyssey somewhere safe, play an ally card, and get an unbiased body of people to sort through Meg's agents."

Shouldn't be too hard, I thought. The vast majority of Meg's personnel had the cumulative intelligence of a Fabergé egg.

"Sounds like fun," said Judy. "How we gonna get there?"

Silence. Crickets chirping, cold night wind blowing. Everybody looked between each other, waiting for somebody else to solve the dilemma with a brilliant idea.

"Dagan," I finally said, groaning.

He smiled innocently at me, knowing what I was about to ask and thinking about what *he* would ask for in return. "Yeeeesss?"

"Could you make a portal that can transport us to DC?"

"Where in DC, madam?" Dagan batted his eyelashes, clasping his hands together. I almost slapped him.

"Pennsylvania Avenue," I answered, resisting the urge to be equally glib.

"Ask me nicely," he said.

"*Please*."

"There, was that so hard?" Dagan flourished a bow, his shirt billowing in a nonexistent wind. "Of course. It would be my pleasure."

Not something you want to hear from someone who thrives on other people's pain. But, you know, we suffered from a distinct lack of more attractive options.

"Relax, Knightley," Dagan said. "As I've already explained to your colleagues—I would really prefer not to be confined to the Netherworld forever."

"Just do it," said Knight, crossing his arms.

Dagan spun his hands through the air, his eyes shut tight, muttering to himself. First came the address, then a slew of words in a demonic tongue I didn't recognize, and a modified dematerialization spell I *did* recognize. More complicated this time, probably because the portal generator topside was so *big*, we had to rip a hole in the dimension barriers. That was one thing. Traveling through the in-between places to get somewhere other than the exact mirror-reflection spot of where you are *now,* is another. And the District of Columbia and its beloved leader were very, very far off.

Or maybe he was just killing time to irritate me.

Dagan went quiet before he snapped his fingers, and sparking, orange lines materialized in the air. This time, the portal appeared as a tornado, a swirling mass of fire and wind, spun from the vacuum created between here and there. It was the kind of entry you can only get when you're asking the universe to bend in really uncomfortable ways.

"After you," said Dagan, waving his hands at it. I eyed the portal dubiously, and he sighed.

"Darling, if I wanted to kill you, I simply wouldn't have saved your life the first time around," he said. "Go on. Time's a-wasting, as they say."

Not wrong. Not reassuring either, but not wrong. "Whatever," I said before taking a flying leap into the little, red storm.

###

The experience was only slightly more miserable than I thought it would be.

We swam through a vast swathe of oppressive emptiness for the better part of three-and-a-half seconds, invisible hands twisting our skin and pulling our organs, before becoming liquid in the airless, deep space. We sought the half-world of the under-places where the bigger, badder creatures lived and worked, weaving their chaos through the material world.

And then with a hop, a skip, and some muffled shrieking of the damned, we landed on blackened grass. We found ourselves behind the brick and steel of a crushed gate, surrounded by smoke. Everything was lit up red in the dark, and shadows were writhing on the walls. I could hear lots and lots of screaming.

"Oh shit," I said.

I stood, jumping sideways when Casey and the rest started coming through the portal one-by-one, stumbling and cursing as they recovered from the shadow plane. The city was wreathed in fire, choking on smog that was black and blue and green, while rippling with magic. Lightning spun across the metal rails and exposed the cording, winding up the walls like ivy.

And everywhere I saw hordes of blind-furious supernatural creatures—werewolves in full form, vampires tearing through civilians with a red-eyed blood frenzy, dryads and naiads and nymphs, all ripping through the concrete and glass with their massive roots, tearing the covers off manholes and fire hydrants, directing the water with shaking hands into cars and windows, burrowing into the ground with the force of a crashing plane, and making everything shake violently. The National Guard, shouting in their heavy gear and carrying big guns, were on every corner, doing battle with the various monsters. Every ten seconds or more, one would fall, shrieking, its skin fizzing as dragon's acidic blood spread throughout its system. Every fifth soldier was glowing. The Siphons were drawing on their mediocre power to electrocute, burn, and shatter the creatures too weak to resist them.

In front of us stood the White House, its noble face reflecting fire and shadow and smoke. The gate was smashed in. Armored cars peppered the lawn, smoking and burning. Soldiers in full fatigue and security officers in suits and Kevlar vests were sprawled out on the fire-scarred grass. None of them were moving.

The ANC wasn't anywhere near here, and there was too much smoke in the sky, not to mention all the congealed magical energy everywhere, to know if it had been destroyed as well—but it was probably fair to assume it had. Meg's people were fighting out in the open, so, clearly, whatever hostage situation they'd been maintaining before was now no longer the case.

We landed in the middle of a war zone. Probably one of many since I couldn't imagine this was the only venue for an uprising.

"Jesus," Casey said, standing up with his gun in his hand. I could barely hear him over the din. "What's happening?"

"Meg's already here," I answered. It was too noisy to be another distraction. Odyssey would have been taken to a bunker the *second* the noise began—if this riot stood for anything, it was for making a statement. A formal declaration of how badly the supernatural community detested humans, capped off with Odyssey's death. This was Meg's final game, flooding every possible street with what anyone on the ground would have assumed were certified ANC employees. "We need to move. Now."

The White House, itself, seemed in modest condition, but if Meg had *planned* a nationwide riot, she probably would have cut the power, too, jamming all the signals, turning the whole city dark ... Then again, Meg wasn't operating under human standards. All her offense was magical, any jamming would prevent the ANC survivors and Siphons from casting spells—which she clearly hadn't done. In fact, we seemed to be at exactly the same point where all her concise planning came to a screaming halt.

Nobody had seen us yet, and I didn't suspect they would for a while unless one of them blundered over to the front of the building on their own. They were smashing, burning, electrocuting, ripping, and eating their way through the street, but every creature seemed disconnected from the rest—as though their only orders had been to *wreak havoc.* Were they allowed to roam? Perhaps, since not a commanding officer could be spotted among them. I wondered if that were deliberate—if Meg intended to leave her people to rot after she'd done the deed—or if this were an example of her grip slipping. A herald of the steady decline of a leader's control.

Maybe this is where we get lucky, I thought.

Or trampled by that draconian alchemist who was riding a giant, orange, armadillo-looking beast and currently taking a large bite out of a downed mannequin from some poor boutique.

"Dulcie will be in there," Bram said. "I can't imagine Meg would leave her behind for something like this."

Dulcie, I thought, my heart panging, and feeling more than hollowed out. Glacier cold, tight as a collapsing star. *Dulcie's in there.*

What if she's turned permanently? I heard the words echoing through my head. *What if she's beyond the point of saving? What if the real Dulcie is already dead and gone?*

The questions slammed into a wall, turning into static, and refusing to develop any further. The answer was: we might not be able to stop her—and she might have to die.

"I'm going back to the DC office," Silas said. "See if I can get you some eyes on the inside."

"Do you see this?" Casey said, gesturing to the *everything*. "You'll never make it."

"Would you rather I go blundering in there with you?" Silas pointed to the White House, scowling. "I'm not a field agent, man. I can do you more good from the console. I have access to every camera in the building."

Casey drew a hand over his face, sighing, as if he were about to protest again.

"I can accommodate him," Dagan said, sparks dancing at his fingertips. Becoming all grim and quiet, a dark look shadowed his face. He was suddenly down and devoted to the business of saving our little corner of the world. "The Preternatural Division, I assume?"

Casey hesitated another moment, then nodded. "Fine. Marcus, go with him. And don't let him touch anything."

"So much for not separating," Knight said with a frown at Casey.

"I will return as soon as I deliver Silas," Dagan announced.

"Just go," said Casey.

"Any address, my friend?" said Dagan.

"Seven blocks south of here," said Silas.

Dagan nodded, spinning his hands before he ripped a portal open in the air—and a second later, they were gone.

"Uh. Guys," said Judy.

"What?" I said.

"I, um." She swallowed, staring out into the city. "I think I know what happened to the Netherworld's LA."

We followed her gaze. There, digging its claws into the crystal walls of a skyscraper, its wings casting mountain shadows and tail lashing back and forth in the air, something was dragging itself through the torn steel beams and electric wires. Wreathed in fire and lightning, it was screaming thunder. Scales glinting green, bright as glass.

"Dragon," I whispered.

"Kin I blow it up?" Kent asked, glancing down at his grenade.

"You're welcome to try," I said.

CHAPTER TWENTY-THREE
Dulcie

"Go," Meg said to her people at the party. "You will know when it is over."

They all nodded and departed at once. Those who could dematerialized immediately, letting their wine glasses drop and shatter on the floor. Most of them formed a line to pay their respects to Meg personally before they departed for private portals and anchored wormholes. The werewolves bowed, and the vampires who stayed behind kissed my hand. The drakes had a very particular way of showing deference that involved using their tongues and the tip of the other person's nose. Meg leaned into it readily, fully expecting it. I smiled and tried not to flinch because it was, in a word, gross.

When they all left, Meg sighed contentedly, staring into her empty glass. Antoine swept up the glass debris and the bones of several small animals that sadly wandered in from the forest and became midnight snacks.

"Finally," she said. "After all this time ..." She smiled widely, hideously, nodding with sweltering pride. Then she turned to face me. "But now is not the time for a monologue, wouldn't you agree?"

"Yes, Mother," I said.

Meg grinned. "We are so *close*," she said, appearing on the verge of tears—tears she couldn't shed. Her tear ducts had calcified centuries ago, along with every other organic part of her body. But her face still remembered how to receive a hard-won triumph. So she smiled and laughed, setting her eyes someplace far away. "When it is over ... when we are *done* ..." She clenched her fist, breaking her glass.

"Done with Odyssey?" I asked innocently.

Meg looked up and patted my head. "Yes, darling. With Odyssey."

"What are we going to do?"

She smiled at the *we*. "We," she said, "are going to kill her and take back everything she stole from us."

"Don't we have everything already?"

"Almost, my princess," she said. "But ... not quite."

She got down on her knees, tossed away the glass, and took my hands. "Are you ready, my dear? My darling Dulcie?" She was talking to me like I was a teenager, getting ready for my first big dance. As if I were nervous, and she thought it was cute.

Her eyes pulsated and glowed, dragging me under a sea of liquid steel, cold, alive ... hungry ...

Fight it, Dulcie! I told myself. *Resist her power!*

"Yes, Mother," I said, pulling myself back, away from the precipice of Meg's authority, and her power. "Yes. Of course." My head was swimming, throbbing. Hopefully, it didn't show.

"Good," Meg said, and her smile was genuine. Excited, she displayed the eagerness of a child at a theme park. "*Good*, Dulcie. Come, then."

I thought I would get a moment alone to change clothes, and ask for a gun, and say goodbye to Sebastian (and sneak in to see Knight), but Meg grabbed my hand. She whispered a single word, and the room around us disappeared.

The air contorted, turning grey and black and blue, blurring, sputtering cold wind—the essence of dematerialization, the kind that spins you through the shadowy dimensions where the really nasty things hibernate between the apocalypses. It lasted for a fraction of a nanosecond, and then I was on the ground again, but dizzy as a top.

Standing in a smallish room with curving walls and powder-white couches, the shelves were full of books, and I saw side tables with black lamps. Flowers, a boorishly official, brown coffee table, and doors concealed in the walls. The legislative seal was stamped into the beige and blue carpet.

Meg stuck something in her pocket—a smallish, red thing about the size and shape of a can opener. Bram's portal ripper!

"Where's the party?" someone inquired.

I turned and found a woman sitting at the desk. Hands folded in front of her, she was flanked by flags and two bodies, bleeding from their throats. Dark hair pulled tightly in a bun at the nape of her neck, she was staring at us. And absurdly calm.

"President Odyssey," Meg said with a sneer. Odyssey only adjusted her posture slightly. Meg noticed and smirked. "It is a pleasure," Meg continued, flourishing a bow. Blood stained her fingers and her mouth. It was from the officers she'd just killed, slitting their throats in less than a nanosecond. Faster than light. "My name is Meg Vogahn. This is my daughter, Dulcie."

I curtsied and felt clumsy.

"Dulcie," said Odyssey, putting no inflection into the word. She turned to look from the security officers to me with a blank expression. "Pleased to meet you. Lovely dress," she said, her words slightly tighter now. Did she recognize me? At least, she knew my name.

Meg wasn't looking at me, so I took the moment to mouth *help*—not that I didn't think I could take Meg on my own. It was probably a good idea to sound an alarm for whatever errand she'd sent her lords and ladies on.

Odyssey looked from me to Meg without any acknowledgment, and sat back in her chair, feigning nonchalance. Or maybe she was giving herself an opportunity to trigger the silent alarm she hopefully planted on the underside of her desk.

"To what do I owe this unexpected visit, Meg Vogahn?" Odyssey asked. Behind her, the world was red and flickering. There was too much noise and too much light, but none of it was coming from the sky—everything capable of combustion was exploding: gas tanks in cars, generators in buildings, even the batteries in phones being discarded by the fleeing civilians. Everything that could went *poof* on the whim of one or another of Meg's warlocks, snapping their fingers and throwing glass bottles against the walls—Molotov cocktails, with a little extra something to make them burn and burn and burn.

A city at war. Creatures descending upon humanity with oppressive force, demanding the return of something they didn't even know was missing. I didn't want to think what kind of hell would rain on the supernatural community when this was all over. *If* it ever was over.

"Nothing in particular," said Meg, disappearing into a blossoming cloud of black smoke and reappearing behind Odyssey's chair. She put her nails at Odyssey's throat, drumming her fingers against her skin. My heart started to pound. "Just a social call."

Odyssey didn't flinch. "I see. Tell me, is this a hostage situation, or an assassination?"

Meg put her face right next to Odyssey's, drawing her tongue up to Odyssey's jaw, all the way into her ear. Pushing her nails into Odyssey's skin until she drew blood, the pinpricks of red trailed down, staining the president's blouse. Meg inhaled sharply, savoring the smell of it, and letting it paralyze her. She was waiting for something. Listening to the thunder, the rough-and-tumble shutter of sounds beyond the window in some street we couldn't see.

In a threadlike whisper, Meg said, "What do you think?"

Here it was. The last moment, all of Meg's people coming into play. Whatever backups she had planned, if any, they were too far off now to do her any good. She had nobody on hand to take up her mantle if she dropped the ball.

Or if, for some reason, her beloved daughter shot her in the face with a dead man's gun.

A glimpse of movement was all it took for me to dart forward, snatching a gun from the hands of the security officer—dragon's blood on principal. Flying backwards, I was aiming and firing …

Bang!

I was fast, but Meg was just a hair faster. She dodged to the side, pulling Odyssey with her, maybe hoping to catch the bullet with the president's head. But I adjusted as she moved, becoming no more than a black blur with a broken smile. It scared me for the two seconds I spent thinking about it. *I shouldn't have been as fast as a vampire, I shouldn't have been able to see her move.*

I moved with her and pulled the trigger. Just a tad slower than her. I was aiming for her head, and the bullet struck her hard in the shoulder, leaking out the green dragon's blood.

She didn't even flinch.

"Fuck, how old are you?" I screamed at her.

The dragon's blood should have taken her down, or at least given her a run for her money. It was a contact-lethal substance, so she shouldn't have been able to *touch* it without going down, never mind cantering through her bloodstream like an overeager tourist.

Meg stared at me. For a moment, she looked genuinely shocked. Devastated, even, or something *just* at the edge of a human emotion. Then the expression fell away, replaced with snarling teeth, and a gnashing, guttural, animal sound that began rumbling in the back of her throat.

"I love you," she said, her words splintering and breaking. "I *loved* you!"

"Sure you did," I said. My words slurred together, but they were mine, and sounded mostly unhindered.

Don't look her in the eye, Dulcie!

I fired again. Another bullet sank into the skin below her collarbone. She howled, with rage or pain, I didn't know. It was a hideous sound, like the moaning of a wolf in the middle of the night, or the chittering cries of the chimera in the woods, wailing for something that got away.

She sprang back to Odyssey's side, grabbing her by the back of her shirt, holding the knife to her throat. Odyssey looked at me, calm as a morning lake. Her eyes flicked to the window—maybe listening for the sound of her city being destroyed, or perhaps she was indicating to me that help was on the way.

Not that we could afford to wait for it.

"This is the culmination of everything *we* have worked so hard for!" Meg seethed at me.

"No, it's everything *you've* worked so hard for," I replied stonily.

Then she just looked at me, her eyes swimming with a glamour on a hook, sharp and glinting; she was *calling* me. "This is what you want, Dulcie, this is your mission!" The words clawed their way out of her throat, and she began sobbing and pleading.

"This is never what I wanted," I protested.

"This is your destiny!" she screamed at me. "With me at your side, your mother, the one person who loves you above everyone else!"

"You are not my fucking mother," I ground out.

She didn't like that at all.

But instead of slitting Odyssey's throat, Meg screamed. Eyes shut, she was wailing at the top of her lungs.

I shot again. This one hit her squarely in the mouth, punching through the back of her throat and landing in the wall behind her with a violent, red splattering. She slumped back against the wall, letting the force of the shot carry her backwards—dropping mostly from shock than anything else. Her knife slid across Odyssey's throat and she nicked it, drawing some blood before it fell away and clattered to the floor.

I darted forward. Odyssey's face was mostly expressionless, but her eyes reflected her jangled nerves. I lifted her up in my arms—and she weighed no more than a child's doll.

"Madam President," I said, nodding inanely before I threw open a door and started to run.

I immediately stopped at the end of the hallway half a second later, startled by the sudden white-on-black blur that surrounded me. I looked at the door twenty yards away. Meg's screams became lung-stretching sobs, coughing, gasping, shrieking, banshee kinds of sounds.

Speed, I thought. One concise word, another instance of something I shouldn't have possessed.

Fuck if I wouldn't use it, though.

I turned a corner and ran down a flight of stairs, the world going crystal-white around me the faster I went. I became no more than a shadowy blur—but I could make out every detail and see every chair I might bump into, as well as every discarded book I might trip over—but not seeing them so much as knowing they were there. My awareness was far more disturbing than my new speed, mostly because it wasn't something that came from vampires.

Something to brood about later, I thought. I'd been drinking potion after potion after potion at Meg's behest, cocktails of vampire blood and honey and

Hades knew what else. With no clue how much of it affected me, I'd have quite an arsenal to sort through.

The sound of wood splintering and metal tearing alerted me that Meg was ripping a door off the wall.

"Where's a way out of here?" I asked—searching for any door: front, back, maintenance access, I didn't care. Odyssey was shaking, her face still blank, her body rebelling against both options: a non-human speedy escape; or the prospect of being murdered by a lunatic vampire.

After a moment, she pointed somewhere without looking up.

I ran and I kept running, ignoring Meg's doomsday screaming, and not giving the time of day to the hundreds of scattered corpses I found throughout the building. They were stippled with bleeding green bullet holes, and I began leaping over banisters to floors two stories below, landing hard enough to put cracks in the shining floor ... Keep moving, and don't look back! *Move!*

I was fast—but Meg was faster.

She plowed into me from behind, sinking her nails into my back. I stumbled forward, pulling myself out of the monochrome glitz long enough to drop Odyssey and turn on Meg. I grabbed her by the shoulder, pulling her the rest of the way down the stairs and onto the ground. We made it as far as the entry hall, a vast expanse of beige and brown checkerboard floors, pillars, and red carpeted stairs. Littered with bodies, the men in suits still lay with their guns at their sides, steel shells scattered around them like confetti.

Blood was everywhere.

I feared the blood might send Meg into a frenzy. But perhaps it would distract her long enough for me to grab Odyssey and get away, burying myself in the chaos outside. Her people had no reason to believe I was anything but a loyal daughter. If they saw me running off with a ragdoll president, they'd surely assume she was already dead, and I was looking for someplace to display the cadaver.

But Meg didn't seem to notice the blood surrounding her. She was on all fours now, with blood on her palms, her face, and her back. Mine, too We rolled a short distance before coming to a stop. Now we were barely inches from each other, staring, glaring, and waiting for something.

Meg started crying. Soft little sobs, she tried to keep quiet, but they echoed in the room.

"I don't understand," she said as she shook her head. "Why ... why are you doing this? You are supposed to love me as much as I love you!"

She looked so pitiful then. And breakable. So impossibly fragile. If I touched her, or pushed her a little too hard, I feared her skin would fold in on itself, and she would disappear.

So I hesitated. I looked at her for half a second longer than I should have, feeling sorry for her. Until she lunged forward. Snarling like a rabid animal, she sank her teeth into my neck.

I didn't know what she thought she would do. Kill me? Maybe. Drain me until I couldn't move? Or just stay there, her fangs in my skin, and not do anything? Was she forcing me to be close to her again, if only to allow her broken mind to pretend everything was okay?

Whatever she wanted to do, she didn't get the chance. I froze underneath her, staring at the ceiling and shook my fist behind her back. The golden dust was gathering between my fingers, absorbing my thoughts. Shaping itself into a long, curving blade of pure silver.

It glinted above her, catching the distant firelight. I saw my reflection in it, my eyes narrowing hard, my mouth clenching. I plunged it into her back, dragging it down as hard as I could.

She screamed and pushed me away. I let go and the blade stuck in her back, halfway down her spine, wedged between the marble bones. Blood, deep scarlet, gushed from the jagged, red line. She reached back, wrenching the knife free, and tossing it aside.

"You ungrateful *bitch*," she hissed, the blood staining her teeth. Maybe it was mine, or hers, or maybe it belonged to one of the dead men lying all around us.

"You're fucking crazy," I said—making a very astute observation, but not much in the way of a taunt.

She charged—slipping in blood, and stumbling rather than running. She was also blurring every third second like she couldn't control her own speed. Drunken with grief, she was three seconds slower than she ought to have been. Giving me three seconds longer to wonder what vampires were afraid of.

The first word that came to mind was *fire* … Then there it was! Glimmering in the palms of my hands, the flickering bulbs of orange flame began reaching and twisting. Blinking like static, it was barely fluid enough to control. I lifted my hands up, my palms forward like a shield, resisting the ward, and I imagined them growing, coiling around Meg, *daring* her to get close enough to burn.

She stopped. But she didn't just *stop*—she stumbled, and slipped on a slick of blood, her eyes going wide. Staring in wonder, fear, and awe, she began suddenly gasping for air she didn't need. Clawing her way backwards, and never blinking, she never took her eyes off the fire as it winked in and out of existence. Power surged through me, too much to control, too much for me to try to contain. The flames grew and spread, rearing back their heads like dragons roaring, lurching towards her, their mouths open, hungry …

They sank into her, like teeth of burning amber, and she screamed.

Bloodcurdling screams, a high whine of pure terror as the gleaming, orange bodies wrapped themselves around her, blistering her skin. I watched, my face growing hard, my eyes even harder. Staring, my hand curling shut, I drew deeper heat and brighter light from the fire.

Something shifted. Meg blinked, and her breathing slowed, then stopped. Her eyes changed too—from brown to black to blistering red, and to black again. Swimming with all the magic she had inside her, every ounce of her control.

And then she was right in front of me, and faster than I could follow. Trailing orange and white smoke. She was grabbing my face, *forcing* me to look at her.

"You are *nothing*," she hissed, her voice sounding thin, her eyes wild, "without *me*."

My mind went blank. The dark pulled me in, swaddling me, in warmth and quiet. The flames died. A glamour entered my soul, turning all my nerves to stone.

"What do you say?" she demanded. Her hair smoking and clothes scorched, half her face burned pink and white, webbed with layers of skin that didn't remember how to scar.

"Y … es. M … Mo … ther …" I said, incapable of thinking anything else.

The anguish melted off her, and she smiled. She let me go, and I sank to the ground. My dress billowed out around me, soaking up the blood, turning black at the edges.

"There, there," she said, leaning down to pat my cheek. "It's all right. Everything is going to be okay. I forgive you." She kissed the top of my head and spun around, pulling a sharp, needlelike knife from her belt, before sauntering towards Odyssey where she lay on the stairs. Blood was gushing from her nose—maybe it was broken from when I dropped her, *maybe*. Dropped her? Why was I carrying her? Where were we going?

Away, away from here, away from her. Focus, Dulcie, focus. Fight Meg's power! a distant voice railed inside me.

Mother—no, *Meg,* not Mother, *Meg, Meg, Meg*— Meg put her knees on either side of Odyssey's stomach and leaned over her, waving the knife above the president's face like a stick of incense.

"Time to meet your doom," she said, tapping Odyssey's nose with the flat blade. Odyssey's eyes snapped open and she blinked, staring blearily up at Meg.

I looked at a gun on the floor. The magazine was half open with three bullets still inside.

Move, I thought. *Move.* My words could have been spoken underwater, the soundwaves trapped in amber.

My fingers twitched. Prickling and numb. My arm moved. Spastic, uncontrolled.

Meg began carving a thin, red line into Odyssey's cheek. Even from here I could smell it, rusty iron and the dull tinge of pheromones—anger and stoic resignation. Fear. I moved my hands to the floor. Shaking and forcing myself to breathe.

"This is the end of everything," Meg whispered to Odyssey.

Stand. Up. I did. Slowly. Agonizingly. Fighting every muscle in my body.

Walk.

Meg drove the blade into Odyssey's shoulder, deep enough to pin her to the stairs.

Keep walking. Pick it up. Close the magazine. Carefully. Slowly. Don't make a sound.

"The Houses of the Nether appreciate your valiant sacrifice," Meg said. She took three precious seconds to laugh and that was all I needed.

I lifted the gun. Higher, higher. Fighting for control. I pressed the barrel firmly against my temple.

"Mother," I called to her.

Meg turned to me. Her eyes went wide, yellow swallowing their hungry red—fear. Pure, unadulterated fear.

"Step away from Odyssey," I said.

She did.

CHAPTER TWENTY-FOUR
Sam

The dragon reeled toward us, spinning through the sky in a wild, uncontrolled dive. Its eyes were flashing furious red.

"Go!" said Casey. For a fraction of a second, nobody moved. We just stared at the massive, lurching body of the wyrm, careening down …

"Go!" he shouted again, and we took off across the lawn.

As though we thought we could outrun it! *Sure.*

Its shadow fell over us, eclipsing the splintered glow of the city. A wash of orange fire split the earth beside us, drawing a fine, black line through the grass. I lifted my hands, shielding my face, my skin searing while the fire licked the air, remaining just out of reach. Then, with a violent *thud*, the beast landed in front of us, its sharp teeth glinting and wings outstretched.

Casey fired at it. Everybody did on reflex, but the bullets didn't make a dent in its scales—some disappeared into the soft spot just beneath its jaw, which wasn't much more than a small thorn to a dragon. The Preternatural Division carried dragon's blood-tinged weapons—which were absolutely useless against the very dragons they came from.

The dragon reared its huge head back, roaring, and sounding more irritated than anything else. It opened its mouth, the embers coiling in the back of its throat, preparing to spit fire again.

"Duck!" I screamed as I dove to the side, seeking shelter behind the burnt-out skeleton of an armored car. I saw people's shadows also diving for similar cover, behind slabs of stone from the busted fountain, or mounds of bricks and dust and mortar, or the pillars, now fallen on their sides. The dragon followed us with molten eyes, twitching, squealing, and dragging itself backwards and forwards and sideways—it seemed to be at war with itself, and scrabbling for control, or running scared, like in a bad dream.

It opened its mouth, and the smoky red and orange and white it exhaled singed a half-circle inferno onto the lawn. The heat blasted right past me, burning the air, scalding my lungs before it was gone, rotating, trying to find us all. Running its hot, iron claws over the bodies already fallen on the lawn, it seemed to be turning calm at seeing the bloody faces of pink and brown and black.

The downed soldiers looked a lot worse up close. Most of their bodies were mauled into nothing, scratched and bitten into bloody pulp by the werewolves and draconians, both races too old fashioned or bloodthirsty to use more efficient magic. The SUVs weren't faring well either—an armored car is a fortress, but even steelplast and automatic rifles can only do so much when facing a battle-mad dragon with an agenda. The car windows were busted in, the doors ripped off their hinges, and deep gouges ran the length of the exteriors, the painted metal curling up around the deep impressions. Melting, now, the rubber tires sloughed to the ground like jelly, too hot to touch, even on the car's far side, where I was hiding.

I peered around the corner. The dragon was on all fours, crouching, its neck pulsing like it was choking on something. Smoke curled up from its nostrils, its latest round of fire spent and dead. Its breathing sounded thin, ragged, like a razor on a piano wire— and it kept digging its claws into the earth, clenching them like fists, its eyes squeezing shut and popping open, wild, frantic, searching …

Those eyes.

Its eyes were red and burning. I spotted the starry, black swirls of a glamour. One that was just barely keeping hold of its host. And could be commandeered by a more powerful vampire.

"Ezra!" I screamed, and he popped out from his hiding place on the far side of the lawn—the only vampire in the world who was older than Meg. And the only one potentially capable of slipping an established glamour out from under her.

"Glamour!" I said, pointing at the dragon.

I didn't have to say anything more. Ezra followed my hand, locating the dragon's eyes, and his expression went dark. Not just grim, but physically darker, his eyes twisting to match the dragon's corrupted colors. He mouthed "Bram," too quietly for me to hear, but a moment later, I saw Bram emerging from a mass of ruined cars. His eyes had the same blistering darkness. Staring comets into the dragon, he was muttering under his breath.

The dragon's head twisted left until it hit the ground and started digging its horns into the grass, turning up divots of turf and crimson flowers. Its rear claws buried themselves, clawing, churning, howling, before its entire body began writhing—the eyes going from black to red to yellow to black again. Bram and Ezra were playing tug-of-war with its mind.

Now was as good a time as any to get inside the White House. Bram and Ezra were standing out in the open now, their magic rippling the air around them. Behind Bram was Casey, who was slowly standing, watching in wide-eyed wonder as the dragon slowly pressed itself into the soft earth and closed its eyes—twitching, still struggling for control, but losing the fight.

Casey turned to me, Judy, Rowena, Christina, and Kent, in turn, pointing us towards the front door. He began drawing a long circle in the air with his finger, mouthing "go around it." We nodded and ran off, skirting the dragon, venturing only as close as we dared. Its tail rose up in the air and thrashed, slamming down hard enough to make the ground shake. I stumbled, fell, rolled, and popped back up. I began running, my heart pounding and ears ringing—and beneath the ring, I heard a subterranean roar, the metallic hum of magic weaving itself through a powerful mind.

I slammed against the front wall of the building, panting, with only the pillars and a hundred feet separating me from the monster. Casey and the rest were with me half a second later, appearing from nowhere as I watched the dragon struggle. Bram and Ezra continued chanting soundlessly, flanking the beast now, staring unblinkingly into its soul, pulling, pulling, pulling—

"Talk to me, Silas, what are we looking at?" Casey said into his phone from where he stood right next to me. His back was against the wall, and he was breathing hard. He was dusty black with smoke and dirt.

Silas's voice rumbled through Casey's phone, just loud enough for the rest of us to hear. "Besides the dragon?"

"Yes, besides the dragon!" Casey spat. "What's inside?"

"Well, nobody's going to stop you."

Casey looked at me—I couldn't say why. "What do you mean?"

"I mean, there's basically nobody in the building. Nobody alive, anyway. It looks like a lot of people cleared out of there in a hurry. A lot more than before. There's *nobody* here."

"That doesn't sound good," Casey muttered. It sounded like a hell of a lot of somebodies had known

Meg was coming and scurried out instead of warning anybody. Which didn't bode well for any help we thought we might receive.

"Where's Odyssey?" Judy asked, leaning forward. She was standing still against the wall—a gun in her hand, I guessed it was probably missing more than half of its magazine.

"Hang on, I'm looking, I'm looking …" said Silas. We heard the click and clack of scuttling keys, the clicking of a mouse, and Silas murmuring to himself. "Holy shit."

"What?" we all said together, looking at each other.

"Entry hall," said Silas. "Like, right inside the front door. Meg's on top of her! You need to move!"

"We're moving," said Casey.

We ran in a straight line for the door, and Judy and Kent leapt across it to the other side, plastering themselves against the wall. I snapped my fingers, and a wick of fire sprang to life in my palm. It fluttered there meekly, making Casey's gun shimmer.

Casey and Judy locked eyes and nodded. They counted down under their breaths. *Three … two … one …*

Kicking the door open, the air exploded with a hideous scream.

CHAPTER TWENTY-FIVE
Knight

I was still outside, crouched behind a mountain of rubble, watching Bram and Ezra mentally wrestling with a fucking dragon. I couldn't deny that I was impressed.

Casey motioned for the others to move, and I started to follow.

Before I could take another step, I heard a voice.

I see you survived, said Hades, appearing in a rush of black smoke. He was steaming and calmly appraising the situation at hand. *Or have I spoken too soon?*

"I don't suppose you're here to help?" I grumbled, knowing damn well he wasn't. No, he wanted to send me to Magic Mountain where all the Lokis could get together and have a fucking party.

Hades's eyes flashed, sparking silver. *I am here to remind you of your purpose.*

"Isn't my purpose to kill Meg?"

Your purpose is to claim your army from the depths and destroy everything she is from the inside out. That means more than just her death.

"I don't have *time* for that," I spat back at him. "There's a dragon on the White House lawn and a crazy vampire somewhere inside that wants to kill the president. Not to mention, I have no idea where Dulcie is."

And there is an army waiting for its general, Hades said impatiently. *This is not where Meg meets her end.*

"I'm not gonna walk away," I said, starting for the front door—which was open now. The high whine of a distant scream suddenly spilled out from within.

*You **are**,* Hades said, manifesting in front of me a moment later. *If you value your life and the continuation of the world, you **will** depart at once.*

"For the mountain?"

For the mountain.

"Where I can get all the Lokis together and have a tea party before the world ends?"

You mock me at your own peril.

"If you're this all-knowing god, why the hell haven't you realized that Meg is *here*! If you want me to kill her, I can do that right now!"

As I've already told you, Meg does not meet her end here, not on this day. This is not the way it will unfold.

"Then change the fucking story!" I railed back at him. "What sense does it make to run away from an enemy who's lying in wait for me?"

*I am warning you. If you value your life and the lives of every creature on this **planet**, you **will** depart this place at once.*

"Get out of my way."

But he refused to move. *No. She does not die here.*

"That's not the *point!*" I said, screaming. I was steaming, and fire could have been leaping from my eyes—Hades's spirit gift was boiling in the back of my heart, bubbling over, spitting acid, and my temper broke and flared. "Dulcie is in there! And I *damn well* intend to get her out. Fuck you and *fuck* your stupid fucking army! *I* have people to worry about, do you get that? Do you *see* that there is an *entire fucking **city*** on fire behind me? Do you *realize* that if we let Odyssey die today, the whole fucking community of supernatural creatures is going to get *booted off the planet forever?* We'll never recover from an attack of this scale, which you *know* we'll be blamed for, and if you're not here to prevent the whole fucking world from going apeshit on *your people,* then I have *no idea* what you want with me."

I want you to go to the mountain.

"You know what? *I don't care.*" I shook my head, more than furious. "What kind of worthless, piece-of-shit god can stand in the middle of *all of **this*** and say that he's got better things to worry about?"

Hades was silent. His expression suggested he was thinking.

You will not defeat her here, he said at last. *You have no chance. The powers she draws on are too effective. This is not where it ends.*

I shook my head in disbelief. "Fuck you!" And I made to storm off.

A cold, ethereal hand grabbed me by the arm. *Wait.*

I scoffed. "For what?"

If I help you now, will you go to the mountain and claim your birthright?

"Birthright?" I asked. "What do you mean *birthright?*"

Will you, or won't you?

I sighed. "If you actually do something useful? *Sure.* I'll go to Magic Mountain to get your army and do whatever the hell else you want me to, but that's only if you help me now."

Hades let me go, straightened up, and sighed, his teeth clacking together. He turned to look at the dragon again, as well as Bram and Ezra who tried to take it over. The dragon was back on its feet, now, standing at half its height, choking out roars and rumbles and whimpers—steadily gaining ground. Whether its strength came from within or from the original glamour, I couldn't say.

Hades clicked his tongue and said, *A valiant effort. But Ezra should really know better.*

"What do you mean?"

Meg has augmented her powers, he said. *Inflated them with magic from the Abyss, and siphoned power from creatures like Leviathan and Geress Mountain-breather. They are monsters of ancient repute, much older than their own names. And friends of mine. She drinks their chaotic energies, too many for her to control—which may have driven her quite mad by now, but her power will not wane with her insanity. Ezra was there when she underwent the change, calling on them the first time. He should know they don't have the power to overtake her glamour.*

"Okay," I said, wondering what that kind of power and insanity would translate into in a final confrontation. *Abyss* sounded really bad. "So what's your plan?"

He spent another moment looking at the dragon. *I have an idea. But first, a question.*

"What?" I asked warily.

Hades turned to me. His face didn't change, but I got the distinct impression that he was smiling. *You aren't afraid of heights, are you?*

CHAPTER TWENTY-SIX
Dulcie

Meg's scream echoed through the room and she looked at me with wide, horrified eyes. I saw more panic than I'd ever seen on anyone.

Good.

The door crashed open across the room, splintering with orange light and loud thunder. Some shadows glided across the floor, long and dark, peeking in from either side of the entrance. I could smell them, six of them in all—humans and a fairy, each one radiating magic of varying strength and potency. One of them was laughing quietly.

Meg didn't notice.

"Dulcie ..." she said slowly, standing away from Odyssey. Swallowing and shaking, she didn't have the muscles to get jittery, so that was all for show as well.

"Keep moving," I said. "Get away from her. Go."

Meg scuttled away, holding up her hands. "Dulcie," she said, verging on tears, "*please.* Please don't do this. I love you, I *love* you!"

"No. You don't," I said. "If you loved me, we wouldn't be here. Nobody would be dead. Nothing would be burning either."

Meg looked out the front door—but failed to see the four silhouettes hovering there. The fire beyond, along with the thunderous roaring of her dragon, and the background shatter-and-scream of a shambling DC were all she noticed.

"But, but I did this *for* you!" she said, lurching forward. I adjusted my grip on the gun, and she stopped.

"Call them off," I said. "All of them. Now!"

"Dulcie, I can't. You know I can't."

"You can," I said. "You will. Or this is where I die."

Meg stiffened. "No!" she said. Eyes wide and yellow, she was panic stricken. "No. *No*. Dulcie. Princess," she said, her voice lilting, trembling, "put down the gun, sweetie. Put it down. It's all right now, Mother's here." Meg held out her hand and started walking towards me again. "Mother's right here, my darling."

I took a single step backwards. "Call. Them. *Off*."

Meg's face twisted with anguish. "I can't, I *can't*, it's not that simple …"

She kept talking, and the silhouettes crept farther inside—quietly whispering to each other, carrying guns in their hands that reeked of rust and steel and dragon's blood. Meg either didn't hear them, or she was doing a spectacular job of ignoring them.

"Fine," I said to Meg as I cocked the gun—or rather, I pretended to cock it. My weapon was already set to shoot, so I tried to emulate the *click-pop*. I opened my mouth and the sound poured forth perfectly. It sounded very realistic and believable.

Meg stopped cold. "No," she said in a hoarse whisper. "*No!*"

"Yes," I said. "Call off your people. Send them home. *Now.*"

The shadows crept around the edge of the room, keeping to the walls, but now they had faces. Dark, angry, and worried, they were all faces I didn't recognize, with laser-blue eyes and scraggly beards and an ivory half-mask and … and *Christina,* of all people!

My blood froze. *Sam.*

Standing a hundred paces behind Meg, she held fire in her hands. She was staring at me with terror in her eyes and standing next to a tall, handsome man I'd never seen her with before … somebody with spirit strings that linked the pair of them, heart-to-heart and soul-to-soul. Glittering blue, it was an accident of amateur magic and something else I shouldn't have been able to see.

I had to wonder who he was. And why he was here. Was this the man who saved her from me in Splendor? The ghost with a blue heart? The Siphon?

Maybe. I hoped it was.

Then I heard something—actually, I felt it more than heard it. The distant rumble of a beast in the air, and the rippling thud! of it landing on the roof, but light as a feather. Then the stippled-lightning rhythm of stored energy. It must have been getting ready to breathe a blaze strong enough to bust through two floors of solid stone and steel.

I looked at Sam. Fire rose in her hands. *Fire* ...

"You ... you wouldn't," said Meg. "You couldn't. You *can't*. I won't *let you*."

Meg's eyes went dark with a glamour—weak, thin as spring ice, nine-tenths panic and one-tenth desperation. Too much of her own desire blocked it, but she had enough, *just barely* enough, to tweak my mind.

But not enough to make me do anything more than smile.

"Mother," I said, in a level tone. The word was mine, and a huge improvement from Glamoured Dulcie's devotion.

Meg sighed, visibly relaxed. "Dulcie," she said. "My ... my *darling* Dulcie ... my daughter ... come to me." She held out her hand.

The building shook and the ceiling cracked, dust and rubble falling everywhere, echoing with a fantastic roar. The metallic stench of something with blood and scales, scorched lightning in its throat, and the glacial tugging in the pit of my stomach that could only mean it was a dragon. My fairy's awareness overcame me all at once. I was stretching upwards through stone, snatching the beast's identity right out from under it.

Meg looked up, then back at the sound—then she saw Sam and the others for the first time.

Her fingers twitched, forming shadows in the palm of her hand—dark magic, cursed energy. Deep and dangerous, it was something I'd never seen her use before, and she seemed fully ready to drive it like a spear through their beating hearts.

Rumble-thump-shake went the building. Three seconds later, the roof came down. I had only one more second before Meg would start her killing rampage.

Even as that thought crossed my mind, Meg raised her hand. Shadows fell on her body like lightning bolts.

"*You*," she hissed, and Sam took a step closer. Fire was spitting and flickering in her hand as the void of a vacuum occupied the space, drawing magic from a place no physical creature should have been able to call on. The roof collapsed above us, caving in and splintering—one floor to go, and two more seconds. Not enough time! Ribbons of inky black danced across Meg's fingers, as she kept rearing back, ready to lurch, but only managing to choke and swallow.

Above us, the dragon on the roof—now the second floor—took a deep breath. The air burned in preparation, igniting the kerosene at the back of its throat. Ready to bust through the final floor to reach us, and fully intent on burning us to cinders.

But something else was there. Not just the dragon, but something smaller and bolder, straddling its back. Coaxing it downwards with softly whispered words, its heart was pounding. It wasn't quite human, which, on any other day, would have been concealed by the dragon's own essence—however, today my own strange sight and this person's peculiar, volcanic strength combined to shine as brightly as a beacon in the dark.

I thought I recognized him, but he was so much stronger than he should have been—bolder, a firestorm of emotion and magic. A burning silhouette of what he used to be. Just slightly *more* than he was.

But if I were right ...

It was time to risk a gamble.

"You," I said, "were *never* my mother."

Meg turned just in time to see me pull the trigger.

CHAPTER TWENTY-SEVEN
Sam

"No!" I screamed, lurching forward until Casey caught me by the arms.

Dulcie crumpled where she was, collapsing backward and landing in a pool of blood and dust. Meg forgot about the rest of us at once and lost herself in a scream, an abyssal lament, loud and heartbreaking, a pitiful sound of fury combined with every grief in the world.

Half a second later, the ceiling fell inward, and the dragon landed on the floor with a loud crash.

Floor tiles began splintering and shattering, forming a deep crater around its feet. The wretched beast cast its eyes around the room, no longer black and red, but a deep, iridescent blue. Its wings, now neatly folded at its sides, previously managed to collapse the wall pillars and snap the stair rail right down the middle, showering the unconscious Odyssey with bits of stone and wood.

The dragon turned slightly, its shoulders shifting, its head thrashing. Then I saw the person on its back, buck naked! Eyes glowing an icy blue, and rippling with magic that didn't belong to him.

"Knight, what the hell?" I shouted, but he didn't hear me. Nobody could for all the cacophonous cracking and rumbling the dragon created.

Knight had his hands on the dragon's neck, and he was whispering to it. It leaned back and seemed to listen before taking three steps backwards into the building. It stepped over Odyssey carefully, driving its hind legs through the walls in the conference rooms and the hallways beyond.

Meg didn't pay the dragon any mind. She was on the floor beside Dulcie, hefting Dulcie into her arms and wailing, her eyes shut tightly. Knight turned and spotted Meg, then Dulcie, and the blood on her face and her throat, along with the gun in her hand …

But Dulcie was breathing. Albeit slowly. Meanwhile, Meg, who was drowning in her own panic, didn't notice.

I couldn't tell if Knight saw it, but he leaned forward and whispered a command to the dragon, which opened its mouth, blowing out a flame at Meg. Then it wrapped its teeth around her and bit down hard.

It lifted her into the air, letting her head thrash back and forth, snapping her limp body hard enough to break all of her bones. The beast's throat stretched and convulsed—gathering fresh fire, ready to incinerate her to ash. Its teeth were lit from within, a pulsating red and orange light that gleamed on its tongue. Meg thrashed and screamed, her puny arms helpless and as useless as a bag of bones.

The fire roared, rumbled, and blasted through the dragon's teeth, enveloping her. Her scream vanished in the thunder and she disappeared in an orange flash.

The world went still. Frozen solid for a miniscule fraction of a second. Long enough and slow enough, however, to see Meg's fingers curl up, and an arc of razor-sharp shadows form in her hand. As the fire faded around her, she drove her shadow straight into the dragon's snout.

The dragon opened its mouth, screaming, and spewing what remained of its fire skyward. Meg dropped and fell hard, splashing down in a crimson puddle of blood. Ankle deep, she was burning up, a shrieking pillar of fire, spinning like a top. She fell, rolling in red, and drowning the blaze with her blood.

The dragon's head reared back, dropping its mouth open and ready to strike her again. Demolishing the building behind it, the poor beast struggled to gain purchase on the slick floor.

Meg sprang to her feet, whirling on the beast, her eyes yellow and wild. Her skin was all red and blistered, melting like wax. "No!" she protested, her voice breaking. "*No!*"

It sprang forward with teeth and claws before collapsing to the floor, rolling sideways, and pitching Knight into the wall. The impact was hard enough that we all heard something crack. The dragon twitched and screamed, steaming, and dissolving from within—its green scales turning black as ink before evaporating.

The muscles began to peel away, drifting up like blackened ash in the wind. Blood streamed from a wide gash in its throat, *black* blood. Shadows were coiling up from the edges of its wound like smoke, floating through the air into Meg's open hand. Glinting like steel, and sharp as cold wind, she was drawing the whole room into itself, using the shadows for concrete weapons, powered by an unholy presence.

The manifestation of the Abyss. Empty, cold, dark. The icy wrath of the void.

Five seconds later, the dragon vanished. No bones, no blood. Just a dark spot on the ground where a single shadow now lingered, waiting.

Meg stood there a moment, panting and smoking. Her hair was burned half off, and her clothes hung in greyish-black tatters. She stared at the huge crater the dragon made when it landed, seeing something that wasn't there. Her eyes had a vacant expression.

"No," she whispered. "No. No, no, no, no-no-no. No. *No.*" Her hand curled into a fist. "***No.** Never again.*"

"Well, she's not very nice." Kent blinked at Meg. He appeared rather entranced, either by Meg's bloodstained appearance or the awful ruckus she was making. If Meg heard him, she didn't look up. Kent's eyes flashed as he lit the fuse of his grenade, cackling with joy to finally set it off. He wound up his arm, preparing to throw the device. Meg suddenly snapped back to reality, her eyes going wide—then narrowing and turning a violent red when she saw us.

Before he could throw it, she dematerialized in a rush of black shadows. Kent waited.

"Where'd she go?" Casey asked, turning around the room and pointing his gun at anything that moved. Judy mirrored him, guarding his back.

"*Shh!*" said Kent. Grinning, he turned around and threw the grenade straight at the open front door.

A split second before Meg rematerialized.

Hades only knows how Kent timed his action so well.

Her plan was to catch us off guard, and flank us, so she never expected to encounter the little ball of fire and fury. She realized what was happening a split second too late—and by reflex, reached up to catch it.

"*Boom!*" said Kent.

The grenade happily obliged.

Meg was consumed in a burst of white-hot flames. We dove out of the way, our ears ringing. Those of us who were armed pointed our weapons at Meg, firing over and over and over again into the cloud of dust. The doorway collapsed around her, the walls buckled, and everything began to cave into the swampy foundation far below. The roof above us trembled and shook, raining debris outside as the façade continued breaking off in chunks. I briefly wondered if I could sue an organization that didn't exist anymore for property damage.

The powder-grey cloud vanished, and Meg was definitely gone—but she reappeared a second later on the other side of the room. She was babbling frantically, rolling around in pools of blood to put out flames that clung to her coat.

"No," she muttered, "No, no, no, no!"

The fires were finally extinguished, and she pushed herself to her feet, panting! Since that was a human reflex, I had to assume it was a sign of her desperate fear. She looked at us and laughed, sounding like the frenzied pizzicato of a lonely coyote. She was bleeding from everywhere, green and red and black, signifying her own bad magic. But she refused to die.

She continued to twitch like a malfunctioning android, turning her back to us. She gave us a crooked smile and choked on a laugh as she cocked her head.

"I tire so quickly of your games," she said as she opened her arms, as if she were stretching. Her voice changed, turning deeper and more abrasive, echoing too. Then her eyes rolled back into her head, and she dragged the room into the Abyss.

A wave of force shot us backward before pinning us all to the walls. Ribbons were swirling and dancing in the air, their tips dagger-sharp, their spears aimed toward us. They cocooned us, like spiders spinning webs around flies. The air evaporated, turning to dry ice that burned when I tried to breathe it in. It stuck to my lungs like wet sand, clogging the air ducts, and leaving me choking. My skin tightened around my bones and began squeezing, then I was burning, stretching, tearing … The lights dimmed until we could hardly see our hands in front of our faces. The only light came from the fires beyond the collapsed door, a shivering, red flicker that cast long shadows on the floor.

The will of the shadow plane seemed to be caught in the emptiness of space. The vacuum became oppressive, crushing us into specks of dust. Meg remained standing in the middle of it like the self-proclaimed goddess of chaos, screaming, laughing, but making no sounds.

I snapped my fingers and concentrated on fire, lightning, ice, the cosmic pull of gravity, anything but what I saw. My mind went blank. I had no magic, no light. And no air. Nothing for a fire to consume, or lightning to travel through, no moisture in the air to freeze so I could sharpen the droplets into tiny daggers that I could throw. I had nothing I could call on.

My lungs shriveled and shrank. They dried up, empty and vacuous because there was nothing for me to inhale. For two seconds, nothing changed. Everything came to a standstill. A hush of sound that seemed without end, everyone waiting to see who would be the first to drop.

I looked around when there was enough light to see. The barest remnants of the real world indicated where everyone was. Meg was spitting toxic shadows, aiming them at us, suffocating us by vacuuming our oxygen. Kent, Judy, Casey, and Christina were plastered to the wall like decorative dolls, their arms splayed, staring at the cold, empty darkness or just waiting for it to swallow them whole. Everyone's limbs were straining, reaching for guns, or throats, or anything they could grasp.

Rowena had her arms out and her eyes closed. She seemed totally removed from the blackness, standing in a spotlight, an untouched circle of tile. Her shadow stretched on the wall beside her, morphing into something tall and thin, almost skeletal. She was ringed in suspicious light, which probably wasn't light at all. Glowing with a power that shouldn't have existed, it was older than alchemical magic.

Rowena's skin stretched, ripped, and bled, turning from talcum white to grave-dirt black. Her eyes glowed, and light poured from her mouth. It was shining in the depths of her being, swelling inside her, filling her body with an ancient power, the parting gift of the creature that burned her so long ago.

Changing. An iridescent green glow, like the prismatic rainbow shine of a bubble—seemed only seconds from bursting. Casey's eyes went wide as he realized what she was doing. He mouthed, *No!* But if he made any sound, it was swallowed up by the ether. Not that it mattered. Rowena was already past hesitation. The light pulsed and shrank before it exploded from her in a rush of burning, emerald fire.

It wasn't like any other fire. It could burn where there was no air. The shadow plane dissolved, and we dropped to the floor, all of us sucking in breath, or trying to. The light returned, orange and grey, the colors of sunrise and fire.

Meg screamed and fell before she scrambled backwards, shrieking and wailing. When she hit a wall and the persistent fire reached her, her skin was the first to regret it. Her clothes were green and glowing, feeling hot even from a distance. Sulphur and brimstone, Greek fire, something that could not be put out. It fed on the blood of others, spreading, devouring, and filling the room with towers of contorting color.

"No, no, no, no!" Meg screamed before she started tearing off her clothes. Ripping the fabric, shredding it with her nails, she bit all the latches and buttons that stubbornly refused to come off on their own. Her eyes were alive with panic, and the fire itself left her trembling. The human part of her still remembered how it felt to fear death.

She began to stammer, screaming wordlessly, slamming herself against the wall and rolling on the floor, but the fire clung tenaciously to her. Blistering her skin before slowly melting it, she was turning to charcoal despite her dire attempts to frantically push it away. She lost the battle and all of the homicidal impulses drained out of her. There was nothing left but raw fear.

Until she simply vanished. Wrapping herself in dark shadows, she began screaming at the top of her calcified lungs. Then she popped, fizzled, and strangled herself on her own dark chords. She just disappeared, leaving behind a smoky silhouette and no more than a whisper of white fire.

Gone!

The light gradually diffused in Rowena, contracting into her core. The skeleton shadow vanished in a rush, his purpose fulfilled. The flames that remained snuffed themselves out. Rowena collapsed beneath a lingering shadow, a darkness with no tangible form. It caught her and set her gently down—staying only long enough to kiss her forehead and stroke her hair.

Then it faded, washed away like sidewalk chalk in the rain. Rowena lay motionless on the cold, broken floor. Still breathing, yes, but out cold, and the steam radiated off her skin. For ten blissful seconds, we all just sat there. Breathing. Observing. Listening.

Dulcie got to her feet slowly. She tossed the gun aside and looked down at herself, scowling at her dress and the pervasive bloodstains.

"Dulcie!" I shouted.

She looked at us. Then, specifically, at me. "She's gone," she said. I got up and walked over to her, wanting to run but I was hardly able to stand. Dulcie met me halfway, tackling me in a bear hug. We gripped each other and I started crying, listening to

Dulcie shush me, loving her smile, laughing all the tension away. My legs buckled, but she held me up—without a flinch, she supported me, like I weighed no more than a paper doll.

"Dulcie, what ... what the *hell* ..." I said through my blurry tears. "You ... you shot ... you shot yourself—"

"No," she said, sounding sleepy. "I didn't. I just pretended to. I'll, um, explain later." She smacked her lips and looked around. "She's gone?"

I nodded. "She's definitely gone."

Dulcie nodded slowly, squeezing her eyes shut like her head hurt. "Ow," she said, pressing her hand on her temple.

"Dulcie?" I said. A thousand questions filled my head, cramming themselves into my mouth, and I started stammering. "I can't believe ... what happened ... Meg and you, and ... Knight ..."

"Dulcie?"

Landing on my feet, I was ready to support my own weight again, and I graciously stepped aside. Knight was not far behind me, and blood crusted one side of his face. Still naked and gleaming with sweat, the blue glow was gone from his eyes. It was replaced by the molten copper glow of a Loki's claim when he sees his love, the greatest source of his terror, and his chosen mate, Dulcie.

"Dulcie," he said again, his voice sounding heavy. His eyes began watering.

"Knight," Dulcie said quietly as she turned to face him. Then they both just stood there, staring at each other. For a moment, neither of them moved until they began embracing. They remained totally silent, just breathing each other's scent in and holding on tightly, as if by letting go, they risked losing each other again.

"Dulcie," Knight whispered. "I ... I'm so sorry."

She squeezed him tighter. "Not now. Please don't say anything now."

Knight nodded, resting his chin on her head. He didn't say anything else, but he kissed the top of her head and closed his eyes, clinging to her like he'd never release her.

The room became very quiet and the rest of us stood up. My shoes were sticky with blood, and the distant fires made grey shadows dance across the broken walls, spilling in from the busted ceiling.

I felt warm hands on my shoulder as Casey turned me to face him. He was smiling, despite being covered in dust and dirt and blood. His glasses were crooked on his nose, and one lens was shattered beyond repair.

"Hey," he said, placing a hand on my cheek. "Are you okay?"

I nodded and met his hand with mine before I squeezed it. I just wanted to soak up his warmth. "Yeah. I've been better, but I'm all right."

He nodded and kissed me. Slow, cozy, and still recovering from the sudden calm.

I pulled away first—we had work to do. "Odyssey," I said, suddenly remembering why we were here.

"Right."

We ran to the stairs where the president was still pinned to the floor, a knife buried in her shoulder two inches deep. A fine, red line was scored on her cheek, and she had scratches damn near everywhere. Blood was oozing from around the knife in pulsating, scarlet waves.

"This is going to hurt," Casey said.

Odyssey was barely conscious or breathing, like a heavy weight was crushing her lungs. "Just ... do it."

Casey nodded, grabbing the blade by the handle.

"Hang on," Christina said as she pushed herself to her feet. She walked over to the stairs on quivering legs, sitting down hard next to Odyssey, and shook her fist, conjuring a mound of fairy dust.

"Dulcie," Knight whispered behind us. "There's something I have to tell you ..."

"Okay," Christina said. "Go."

Casey nodded and slid the blade free. No serrations, thank Hades—just a flat, sharp blade. Christina let the dust fall over the wound before she closed her eyes and began humming softly. Slowly, the skin stitched itself back together. Odyssey sighed and sat up. She looked around at the brave, dead bodies, and her expression was grim.

She sized up all of us. Turning her eyes to the door and the city that was being torn to pieces, she said, "I need to make a call."

CHAPTER TWENTY-EIGHT
Sam

Justin Trudeau is a remarkably accommodating man.

President Odyssey returned to the Oval Office with us—the same one which Meg had ripped and shredded and torn to shit, but that didn't really matter. The phone was still intact and, thankfully, secure. Odyssey sat on the desk and dialed the number. Within hours, we had the entire Canadian militia helping what was left of our home-base military sweep the streets of more than a dozen cities, arresting all the creatures who surrendered and killing the ones who refused to surrender.

Nobody called it a loss.

The officials who weren't onsite when Meg launched the attack arrived quickly, moving into a large tent on the front lawn—a temporary office until the building could be cleared, the photos taken, and all of the bodies carted away. The rubble from the walls and ceilings and busted mirrors also had to be removed. Everybody was talking with Canadian officials, trying to decide how to repay their kindness—but maybe not in so many words. A whole cupboard of diplomatic implications and consequences could result from this impromptu aid, and we had to be prepared for anything.

A man named Simon Richmond was particularly miffed about the whole thing.

"How did this happen?" he railed, pacing the length of the tent. Kent uncovered a bottle of something, which might have been rubbing alcohol from a paramedic kit—and he kept taking shots every time Richmond repeated himself.

"Somebody helped Meg get her people inside," Casey insisted with a shrug, like that much should have already been apparent.

"You can't just replace senators and reps with shapeshifters," Richmond balked.

"True," Casey replied. "Meg already tried to, but the shapeshifters she employed didn't know enough about anything to be convincing. When she learned that lesson, she resorted to less extreme measures."

"Really? Those measures being?" Richmond asked.

"Bribery, blackmail, and threatening to slander every government official until they agreed to look the other way while Meg blazed her murderous path through every agency in the country. Those officials who didn't join her, died for their cause."

"*Our people* would never take bribes or allow themselves to be blackmailed," Richmond protested huffily.

Judy snorted. "Have you met, like, *any* of your coworkers?"

Judy, Casey, Kent, and I were the only ones still here! Bram and Ezra had vanished almost immediately after Meg disappeared, and Dulcie was in the hospital, along with President Odyssey. Rowena was lying on the lawn, being treated by paramedics for what amounted to a moderate stroke.

I had no idea where Knight was. At the hospital, maybe, getting his head examined. He hit it pretty hard when Meg's dragon threw him against the wall. Hopefully, he'd found some pants too.

After giving our statements to every agency that requested them, and running through our stories, we were asked to describe the dethroning of Melchior O'Neil. Apparently, we hadn't done nearly as good a job at covering up as we assumed. Even if the ANC proved innocent of corruption and conspiracy to commit treason, we expected some kind of legal trouble.

"Who's missing?" I asked. "Excluding the White House employees. What people who would have had the pull to call for replacements?"

Richmond shrugged. "We don't know yet. Half a dozen secretaries, some speech writers, who might have been persuaded not to go to the media … Senator McCarthy, a big, federal reform guy, the secretary of state … and we won't know the identities of the dead or missing until the building's been emptied."

A man in a black jacket with FBI stamped on the back in bright yellow letters stepped into the tent—

Agent Thompson. He was only one of many people taking notes about all the trouble we'd caused.

"If you've given your statements to everybody, then you are free to go," he said, eyeing me in particular—the only one without a scrap of government clearance. I really shouldn't have been inside the tent at all, but Casey insisted. Keeping me close to his side, he was trying to guard me from any jumping shadows or angry teeth that might have barreled out of the ether.

Casey looked at me now with gentle concern. I smiled at him.

"I really should go see Dulcie anyway," I said. "I'll be fine."

"We can escort you to the hospital," said Agent Thompson.

"That'd be great," I said. Casey reached over and squeezed my hand, smiling.

"I'll be done in a bit," he said. "Wait at the hospital, and I'll come find you."

He'd probably be here for hours, I guessed, since he was directly overseeing the whole mess.

"Okay," I said, wondering what his reports would say about me.

CHAPTER TWENTY-NINE
Knight

"Dulcie?"

She looked up. Sitting in her hospital bed, she slowly dressed herself in her normal clothes. Her honey-blond hair was pulled into a ponytail and her eyes were as green as summer, but I noticed a heaviness in them now that I hadn't seen there before. The weary expression of someone who's seen too much tragedy, or witnessed too much pain. The expression of someone haunted by unpleasant memories and images that never abandoned her.

She froze when she saw me, turning still as stone. A vampiric paralysis she'd never displayed before.

"Hi," she said with a timid smile as she glanced down at her small hands.

For a long time, we just stared at each other. Watching. Trying to come up with any kind of issue to discuss. Some words to describe what happened. It wasn't just her being possessed or the crimes she committed under Meg's direction or because the ANC was in very deep shit; we all were mired in very deep shit. The conversation at the top of both of our minds was what could have happened between Meg and me and Sebastian and her.

There didn't seem to be any good way to introduce it.

"Dulcie," I said, fighting the urge to move onto the bed, grab her in my arms and kiss and hold her, but I couldn't. Dulcie kept staring at me with broken-spirited, doe eyes, looking more than fragile, almost skittish—as if I came any closer, she could start screaming.

"I'm ... I'm so sorry."

"I know," she said shakily. "Knight ..."

"I don't ..." I pursed my lips, my heart pounding before folding in on me like a house of cards in the wind. "I don't know why I didn't ... *stop* ... her. I tried, and you must believe that I tried. I tried with all of my power and strength, but it was no good."

"Meg's power exceeded everyone's imagination," she answered softly. "I, of all people, should know." She took a deep breath. "There was no way you could have defeated her. She was basically invincible."

"Just so you know," I started as I tried to clear my throat. "I don't blame you for anything that happened while you were ... you know, under her influence."

She took a deep breath and expelled it slowly. "I can't believe the death and destruction," she said as she shook her head. "All in my name. At my hands."

"That wasn't really you," I nearly interrupted her.

"Me," she said with a rough snort. "I don't know who *me* is anymore. I don't know what *I* am."

"I do, you're Dulcie," I said simply with a shrug and a little smile.

But she shook her head and looked up at me with wide, sad eyes. "No, I'm not," she started. "I'm not the me I used to be, and that's for sure. Everything about me is different." She flexed her fingers and focused on them for a few seconds. "I have powers and abilities I never had before, and I discover a new one almost every time I turn around."

"Then consider it a wonderful gift," I said.

"A wonderful gift?" she asked me, her eyes narrowing. "How can you call this curse a gift?"

"Because what else can you do?" I asked as I breathed in deeply. "You are different, just as you said you were. But that doesn't have to mean it's bad to be different. You can realize all your newfound abilities and use them however you choose to. It's up to you to embrace the new you or despise it. But one thing I can tell you is this: your life will be a hell of a lot easier if you simply accept what you are. You can only be stronger for it."

"You sound like a sappy after-school special," she said with a smile, but I could tell she didn't feel it.

"I know we need to talk about what happened between Meg and me," I started, dreading the conversation but recognizing its necessity, all the same.

"I've really tried not to think about it," she started.

"But you can't stop thinking about it, I'm sure," I interrupted. "Just like I can't stop thinking about it. Or seeing you with that vampire."

"Sebastian."

"Right. At least, for me, I didn't have to see it."

She nodded and exhaled heavily. "And I did."

"Can you forgive me?" I asked hollowly, afraid of her response.

She faced me with tears in her eyes and smiled. "I want to, Knight, I really fucking want to."

"But you can't?" I asked, and my stomach dropped all the way to my toes.

"I don't know," she answered as her gaze settled on her fingers again. "My head is such a mess right now, I don't even know what's up and what's down."

"You'll need time to make sense of it all, and process everything that happened. That's natural."

She nodded. "I just keep asking myself how we come back from this," she said as she glanced up at me again. "How do we forgive each other, and more importantly, ourselves for what we did?"

"Because we both have to realize we weren't in our right frames of mind."

"I tell myself that until I look at the facts and then I … I just want to throw up." She was quiet for a few seconds and focused on the scenes outside the window along with all the devastation beyond it. "Do you know how glamours work?" she asked quietly.

I had to admit I did. *You have to truly want whatever you're being glamoured into doing,* I thought. *At least a little.* I said nothing for a long time. And then replied, "Yes."

Dulcie pressed her lips together, shutting her eyes, like she was fighting back the urge to scream. Then the words came spilling out of her, released before she could think better of it or try to retrieve them.

"Knight, that means you *let* Meg have sex with you," she said quickly.

"No," I started, shaking my head.

"There is no way she could have glamoured you into doing that, not unless there was a small part of you that wanted it."

"Did you want to kill all those people and destroy everything you did?" I demanded, throwing my arms across my chest.

She laughed and shook her head. "I've thought about that too. Of course I didn't want to, but I did it all the same, and Meg managed to glamour me into doing whatever the hell she chose. That thought keeps haunting me and won't let me go. I keep asking myself if it means I really wanted to do those things."

"No, it doesn't mean that," I countered. "All it means is that Meg was one sadistic fuck who happened to be incredibly powerful. She forced us both into doing her bidding, not ours."

She started sobbing and I reached up instinctively, stopping myself before I could touch her. I sat there, staring at her, trying to think of what I could do, something useful that wouldn't feel wrong. I didn't know why but I felt dirty, tainted. Like my tryst with Meg was tattooed on my forehead. If Dulcie didn't feel like the same person she was before all of this, I was right there with her.

After a moment, she looked up. Not at me but the wall, staring with red, puffy eyes at a watercolor painting of a purple flower. Her voice was rough as sand and coarse as iron.

"I can't be around you right now," she said. "I *can't*. I can't even look at you, and I know, I *know* that's not fair, but … I *can't*." She shook her head and sighed. "I feel like I'm caving in on myself and drowning in all of this and I can't take it anymore. I just need some space to think, and breathe."

Silence. A tangible mass of it wedged between us, stifling us. For a while, I didn't say anything but just looked at her. Dulcie, my beautiful Dulcie, who couldn't even look at me anymore. I understood what she meant, because I couldn't look at me either.

CHAPTER THIRTY
Sam

The hospital was crowded. Full to bursting with people and creatures, burnt and blistered, electrocuted, half-drowned, some who were thrown off buildings, or through glass, or pounded by slabs of concrete. Conversations, along with screams and yelps and crying and laughing all blended together, refusing to let one travesty overshadow another. The smell of antiseptic was everywhere, only slightly more powerful than the smoke drifting in from the outside and clinging to the skin of every patient that was brought in. The waiting rooms were crammed with people, patients with shards of glass in their hands or cuts on their arms. The ones who could afford to wait slightly longer were standing next to the parents and friends of the ones who couldn't. Every fourth step, I heard a doctor say, "I'm sorry," and the crying in the room would grow louder.

Our fault, I thought. This was entirely our fault. This should have been a contained conflict, a blip on the ANC's radar. No more than a "we had some trouble, but it's fine" scribbled hastily at the bottom of someone's final report.

Instead, we had this. A massive blunder on the scale of a natural disaster. A supernatural disaster. A small part of my battered brain almost found that funny.

When I got to Dulcie's room, I started to walk in, until I caught Knight's voice. He was almost whispering, his voice breaking like small waves against a ship.

"I'm ... so sorry, Dulce."

"Madame White?"

I squeaked my surprise, whirling around and almost punching Dagan in the face. He caught my fist and lowered it slowly, grinning.

"Apologies," he said. "I didn't mean to startle you."

"Oh, sure, is that why you snuck up on me rather than announcing your arrival like any normal person?" I asked, pulling my hand back.

He shrugged, turning his ear to the room with a grimace. "Oh, that doesn't sound good," he said.

"It's none of your business," I said sharply.

Dagan held up his hands. "Forgive me, I only wanted to see that everyone managed to make it out all right."

I narrowed my eyes, crossing my arms. Doctors bustled around us, jostling Dagan and me when one of us strayed too far from the wall.

"Honest," he said. "I haven't quite returned to the totally immoral, decadent soul you're so fond of and familiar with."

Fond wasn't the word I would use. "Why are you *actually* here?" I asked.

"Checking on my *friends*," Dagan responded. "As I said."

"You don't have any friends."

Dagan grinned, leaning against the wall with his arms crossed. "Says who?"

"Says me and literally everyone who's ever met you … *ever*."

"Sam, I'm hurt," he said, placing a hand over his heart. "I'm a changed man. Need I remind you that I saved your life—and, by extension, the entire world?"

I hesitated and sighed. *Point taken*. Trying to relax, I ignored my temporary irritation and sleepiness, reaching in my heart for the undying gratitude it required to thank a demon, even if I weren't convinced by his explanation. The day that Dagan became a good, law-abiding citizen was the day I bought a bridge in the desert.

"Thank you, Dagan," I said. "Really. You're a very peculiar kind of guy and I don't know *why* you helped us, but we really appreciate it." I cleared my throat. "And I'm sure it's only a matter of time before you tell me exactly why you did help us and exactly how much it's going to cost the ANC."

Dagan grinned lasciviously at me. "Of course I will wait until the ANC is back on its feet before sending you my bill," he said, in a voice as slick as oil.

"Say, but if you ever find yourself wanting to *really* thank me …"

"I'll put you on my Christmas card list," I said, rolling my eyes. And for a second, Dagan's smile looked halfway genuine again, almost playful. Bordering on innocence, or whatever he thought innocence could encompass.

"I will—" he started.

"Not send me a damn thing," I said, thinking immediately of a long list of unsavory toys Dagan might have taken it upon himself to give me. I had no intention of waking up anytime in December to find an X-rated Christmas card contaminating my other correspondence.

"Very well. *Adieu,* Madame White. I pray we meet again."

After he vanished in a puff of red smoke, I could only wonder to whom a demon might pray.

Knight walked out of the room a minute later. He didn't acknowledge me as he passed. I turned to watch him wiping his eyes and figured he didn't want an audience. After waiting ten seconds, I walked in.

Dulcie was … okay. Mostly. Sitting on her hospital bed in street clothes provided by the FBI, she was getting ready to leave and vacate the room for somebody else. Patched up by stitches and staples as well as pinches of Christina's fairy dust, only a couple of persistent bruises and a general sense of dread were left to show for her ordeal.

"Hey," I said, knocking lightly.

Dulcie looked up and smiled weakly, wiping tears from her eyes. "Hey."

I sat down on the bed, looking at the door. I waited another moment before I said anything. "How are you?"

"Great. Except I feel like I got roundhouse-kicked by a fucking elephant."

I laughed. "That's better than bad?"

"Yeah. Sure." Dulcie sniffed. "Sam, I am so sorry."

"For what?"

"Trying to kill you," she answered. "And blowing up the ANC—and for all the other horrible things I did."

"Dulcie, *no*," I said, "no, don't you *dare* apologize." I hugged her head and began rubbing her back. "You were glamoured; you didn't know what you were doing."

She sniffled, holding back tears. "Sam, I ... I called her *Mother*. She wanted me to believe she *made* me ..." She trailed off, taking a deep, shaky breath. "Sam, glamours only work if you *want* them to work. Even just a little ... and I must have wanted ... Well, I mostly wanted my mom back. So badly that I almost *killed* you." Tears streamed silently down her cheeks, her lips trembling—and she tried not to make any noise.

"It's okay," I said, squeezing her hand. "Really. Meg was at least a hundred years older than Bram, and she was drawing on abyssal magic like I've never seen before. We're shocked you could break away from her control long enough to *think*, let alone shoot yourself in the head."

Dulcie nodded, drying her eyes on her sleeve. She smiled at me and looked at the floor.

"Um. About shooting yourself in the head," I started.

Dulcie laughed. "Right. I didn't really. I just needed to scare Meg. I magicked myself into making the noise." She opened her mouth and a soft *bang* rang through the room—a perfect mimicry of a gunshot. Sound replication was something draconians could do. "I heard the dragon and I thought I could sense Knight nearby or something. And I knew she was going to kill you …" Dulcie shrugged. "I gambled. I made a *bang* noise and fell and I hoped that would be enough."

"Wow," I said—more concerned with the sound she made than anything else. "That's …"

"Scary," she said. "Yeah. I've, uh … probably got a lot more skills now."

A lot more power too. And a lot scarier things she shouldn't have been able to do. "Don't worry. We'll figure it out." I grinned. "Maybe you can test some of them out on Dagan."

"I thought he was helping you?"

"It's *Dagan*," I said. "By helping, he just means he wasn't actively trying to kill us. I'm fully expecting a bill from him. In some form or another."

Dulcie nodded and laughed. There was a long silence.

And then.

"He, uh. He had sex with her," she said.

My heart stopped. "What? Who?"

"Knight," she said. "He slept with Meg. She glamoured him, and I had to … *watch* … and now, I *can't* …"

Oh, Hades, I thought. Not for the first time, I wondered why Knight was naked when he left Meg's house. Now it all made sense—but a horrible, terrible, awful sense. Dulcie started to cry. I pulled her against me, hugging her, letting her tears soak my smoke-stained shoulder. Stroking her hair, I kept telling her it was all right to cry, and let it all out.

We stayed there a long time.

CHAPTER THIRTY-ONE
Knight

I sat on the curb around the corner, listening. Not quite ready to face Odyssey again, or explain to her why I lost contact. I had no excuse for chasing after my girlfriend, or leaving my post totally unattended. My single, stupid decision nearly toppled an entire country.

Instead, I just listened to the sounds of the city around me. Cold gusts of wind, car horns, sirens, the spiral and splash of fire hoses. The hissing and pops of bending spacetime.

Hades materialized beside me. Sitting on the curb, resting his wrists on his knees, he was staring out at DC and watching the last of the smoke drift away.

That went well, he said.

I scoffed.

Problem?

I scoffed again, louder this time—if only to convey my disbelief, shock, and wonder. *That went well.* Like the dragon was his backup plan, or a lucky contingency, like we'd had the power inside us all along! Easiest thing in the world. "You almost got everybody killed."

Really? How so?

"Your stupid dragon died," said Knight. "Meg popped up with her shadows and it was just …" I snapped. "Gone like that."

Yet here you are. Alive, if not slightly unscathed. I wonder how on Earth that happened?

His voice was laced with sarcasm. I frowned at him. "You knew about Rowena."

Hades nodded. *I did. The entity she carries is an old friend of mine.*

"Old *friend*?" I asked incredulously as I shook my head.

Is it so hard to believe I have friends?

"Yes," I said. "Yes, it is."

Hades sighed. *I knew about Rowena's abilities … and that she would not summon her spirit unless all other avenues had been exhausted.*

Unless we could scare the Darkness into playing her power card by setting her on fire ourselves, and proving once and for all there was nothing anybody else could do. We had to cash in as a last resort.

By killing a *dragon*.

"Seems excessive."

Hades shrugged, his bones clicking. *Her passenger is vast and immovable—painful and dangerous to call on. Anything less spectacular, and Rowena would have hesitated long enough for all of you to die.*

I nodded slowly. For a minute, we were silent, listening to the white noise of a slow recovery.

If you're finished here, Hades said at last, *you have a contract yet to honor.*

"An army I must collect?"

Yes. And an absolute Darkness to vanquish. You saw what Meg is capable of. The powers she calls on are darkness beyond the darkness, and evil of the worst caliber. The Darkness of the Abyss lives inside her—and it must be undone.

Darkness? *Abyss?* I thought he wanted me to kill Meg, not to send me gallivanting off into the ether to look for ancient monsters …

Oh.

I scoffed. "You're here because Meg's tapped into something big, bad, and off limits," I said.

She has opened a gate to the Abyss, yes, said Hades. *That gate needs to be closed, or it will swallow this world and all of the rest.*

Not because the lives of Odyssey or Dulcie were in danger, I thought, *not because Meg was going to take over the world. Just because she left a fucking **door** open!*

Yes, he said. *In a sense.* I forgot that he could read my mind.

"So you never gave a damn about the fate of the nation or all the people that died today," I said through my clenched teeth.

As I've said. Those were not conflicts that concerned me.

I turned away. Glaring at nothing and hoping if I looked at something else for long enough, he would just disappear. For a while, he didn't say anything.

"And I'll need the Lokis in order to do this," I said. "To close the gate to the Abyss?"

Yes.

I sighed. A long, heavy sigh. I was dreading what came next.

But it wasn't like I had anything keeping me here—not as long as Dulcie needed space away from me.

"So how do I locate this mountain?"

To Be Continued….

H. P. Mallory is a New York Times and USA Today Bestselling author who started as a self-published author.

She lives in Southern California with her son and her enormous dog, where she is at work on her next book.

Made in the USA
San Bernardino, CA
09 March 2018